A
HAUNTING
COLLECTION

For information about permission to reproduce selections
from this book, write to trade.permissions@hmhco.com or
to Permissions, Houghton Mifflin Harcourt Publishing Company,
3 Park Avenue, 19th Floor, New York, New York 10016.

www.hmhco.com

Library of Congress Cataloging-in-Publication Data
for individual titles is on file.
ISBN: 978-0-544-85452-9

Printed in the United States of America
DOC 10 9 8 7 6 5
4500700143

A HAUNTING COLLECTION

Deep and Dark and Dangerous
Wait Till Helen Comes
All the Lovely Bad Ones

WRITTEN BY
MARY DOWNING HAHN

Houghton Mifflin Harcourt

CONTENTS

DEEP AND DARK AND DANGEROUS

One rainy Sunday in March, I opened a box of books Mom had brought home from Grandmother's house. Although Grandmother had been dead for five years, no one had unpacked any of the boxes. They'd been sitting in the attic collecting dust, their contents a mystery.

Hoping to find something to read, I started pulling out books—*Charlie and the Chocolate Factory, Misty of Chincoteague,* and at least a dozen Nancy Drew mysteries. At thirteen, I'd long since outgrown Carolyn Keene's plots, but I opened one at random, *The Bungalow Mystery,* and began flipping the pages, laughing at the corny descriptions: "Nancy, blue eyed, and with reddish glints in her blonde hair," "Helen Corning, dark-haired and petite." The two girls were in a small motorboat on a lake, a storm was coming, and soon they were in big trouble. Just as I was actually getting interested in the plot, I turned a page and found a real-life mystery: a torn photograph.

In faded shades of yellow and green, Mom's older sister, Dulcie, grinned into the camera, her teeth big in her narrow face, her hair a tangled mop of tawny curls. Next to her, Mom looked off to the side, her long straight hair drawn back in a ponytail, eyes downcast, unsmiling, clearly unhappy. Dulcie was about eleven, I guessed, and Mom nine or ten. Behind the girls was water—a lake, I assumed.

Pressed against Dulcie's other side, I could make out an arm, a shoulder, and a few strands of long hair, just enough for me to know it was a girl. The rest of her had been torn away.

I turned the photo over, hoping to find the girl's name written on the back. There was Grandmother's neat, schoolteacherly handwriting: "Gull Cottage, 1977. Dulcie, Claire, and T—."

Like her face, the rest of the girl's name was missing.

Alone in the attic, I stared at the arm and shoulder. *T* . . . Tanya, Tonia, Traci, Terri. So many *T* names to choose from. Which was hers?

Putting the photo back in the book, I ran downstairs to ask Mom about Gull Cottage, the lake, and the girl. I found her in the kitchen chopping onions for the vegetable casserole she was fixing for dinner. Standing there, head down, she wore the same expression caught in the photograph. Not surprising. She always looked sad, even when she wasn't.

I waved the photograph. "Look what I found—a picture of you and Dulcie at a lake somewhere. And another girl—"

Mom snatched the photograph, her face suddenly flushed. "Where did you get this?" She acted as if I'd been rummaging through her purse, her bureau drawers, the medicine cabinet, looking for secrets.

I backed away, startled by her reaction. "It fell out of your old book." I held up *The Bungalow Mystery.* "It was in one of those boxes you brought back from Grandmother's house. Look, here's your name." I pointed to "Claire Thornton, 1977," written in a childish scrawl on the inside cover.

Mom stared at the photograph as if I hadn't spoken. "I was sure I'd thrown this away."

"Who's the girl sitting beside Dulcie?" I asked, unable to restrain my curiosity.

"Me," Mom said without raising her eyes.

"No, I mean on the other side, where it's ripped." I pointed. "See her arm and her shoulder? On the back Grandmother wrote *T*, but the rest of her name was on the torn part."

"I don't remember another girl." Mom gripped the photo and shook her head. "At the lake, it was always Dulcie and me, just Dulcie and me. Nobody else."

At that moment, Dad came through the kitchen door and set a grocery bag on the counter. "Salad stuff," he said. "They didn't have field greens, so I got baby spinach."

"Fine," Mom said.

"What are you looking at?" Reaching over Mom's shoulder, he took the photo. "Little Claire and little Dulcie," he said with a smile. "What a cute pair you were. Too bad the picture's torn— and the color's so awful."

Mom reached for the photo, but Dad wasn't finished with it.

"This must have been taken in Maine," he said.

"Yes." She reached for the picture again.

"Hey, look at this." Dad handed her the photo. "There's another girl sitting next to Dulcie. See her arm? Who was she?"

"This picture was taken thirty years ago," she said sharply. "I have no idea who that girl was."

Slipping the photo into her pocket, Mom went to the kitchen window and gazed at the backyard, which was just beginning to show green after the winter. With her back to us, she said, "Soon it'll be time to mulch the garden."

It was her way of ending the conversation, but Dad chose to ignore the hint. "Your mom and aunt spent their vacations at Sycamore Lake when they were little," he told me. "They still own Gull Cottage, but neither one of them has gone there since they were kids."

"Why not?" I asked. "A cottage on a lake . . . I'd love to see it."

"Don't be ridiculous," Mom said, her back still turned. "The place has probably fallen to pieces by now."

"Why not drive up and take a look this summer?" Dad asked her. "Ali would love Maine—great hiking, swimming, canoeing, and fishing. Lobster, clams, blueberries. We haven't had a real vacation for years."

Mom spun around to face us, her body tense, her voice shrill. "I hated going there when I was little. The lake was cold and deep and scary, and the shore was so stony, it hurt my feet. It rained for weeks straight. Thunder, lightning, wind, fog. The gnats and mosquitoes were vicious. Dulcie and I fought all the time. I never want to see Gull Cottage again. And neither does Dulcie."

"Oh, come on, Claire," Dad said, laughing. "It couldn't have been *that* bad."

"You don't know anything about it." Pressing her fingers to her temples, a sure sign of a headache, she left the room and ran upstairs. A second later, the bedroom door slammed shut.

I turned to Dad, frustrated. "What's the matter with Mom now?"

"Go easy on her, Ali. You know how easily she gets upset." He sighed and headed toward the stairs. "Don't you have a math test tomorrow?"

Alone in the kitchen, I opened my textbook and stared at a page of algebra problems. *Go easy on your mother, don't upset her, she can't handle it.* How often had I heard that? My mother was fragile. She worried, she cried easily, sometimes she stayed in bed for days with migraine headaches.

From the room overhead I could hear the drone of my parents' voices. Mom's voice rose sharp and tearful. "I've told you before, I don't want to talk about it."

Dad mumbled something. I closed my algebra book and retreated to the family room. With the TV on, I couldn't hear them arguing, but even a rerun of *Law and Order* couldn't keep me from thinking about the photo. I certainly hadn't meant to start a scene—I just wanted to know who "T" was.

I never saw the photo again. No one mentioned Sycamore Lake or Gull Cottage. But the more we didn't talk about it, the more I thought about it. Who was "T"? Why didn't Mom remember her? If Grandmother had still been alive, I swear I would've called her and asked who "T" was.

I thought about calling Dulcie and asking her, but if Mom saw the number on the phone bill, she'd want to know why I'd called my aunt and what we'd talked about. Mom had "issues with Dulcie"—her words. They couldn't be together for more than a few hours without arguing. Politics, child raising, marriage— they didn't agree on anything.

Maybe because I couldn't talk to anyone about the photo, I began dreaming about "T" and the lake. Week after week, the same dream, over and over and over again.

I'm walking along the shore of Sycamore Lake in a thick fog. I see a girl coming toward me. I can't make out her face, but somehow I know it's "T." She seems to know me, too. She says, "You'd better do something about this." She points at three girls in a canoe, paddling out onto the lake. One is my mother, one is Dulcie, and I think the third girl is "T." But how can that be? Isn't she standing a few feet away? No, she's gone. The canoe vanishes into the fog.

That's when I always woke up. Scared, shivering—the way people feel when they say, "Someone's walking on my grave."

I wanted to tell Mom about the dream, but I knew it would

upset her. Although Dad didn't agree, it seemed to me she'd been more nervous and anxious since I'd shown her the photograph. She started seeing her therapist again, not once but twice a week. Her headaches came more frequently, and she spent days lying on the couch reading poetry, mainly Emily Dickinson—not a good choice in my opinion for a depressed person. Dickinson's poems were full of things I didn't quite understand but that frightened me. Her mind was haunted, I thought, by death and sorrow and uncertainty. Sometimes I suspected that's why Mom liked Dickinson—they were kindred spirits.

Except for my dream and Mom's days on the couch, life went on pretty much as usual. Dad taught his math classes at the university, graded exams, gave lectures, and complained about lazy students and boring faculty meetings—standard stuff. I got involved in painting scenery for the school play and doing things with my friends. As the weather warmed, Mom cheered up a bit and went to work in her flower garden, mulching, transplanting, choosing new plants at the nursery—the best therapy, she claimed.

And then Dulcie paid us an unexpected visit and threw everything off track.

2

One afternoon in May, I came home from school and found Dulcie and Emma in the living room with Mom. My heart gave a little dance at the sight of my aunt's tall, skinny figure, her fashionably baggy linen overalls, the familiar mop of long tawny curls, the rings on her fingers. Right down to her chunky sandals and crimson toenails, she looked like what she was—an artist.

"Ali!" Dulcie jumped to her feet and crossed the room to hug me. "It's great to see you."

"You, too." I hugged her tightly and breathed in the musky scent of her perfume.

Holding me at arm's length, she gave me a quick once-over. Her silver bracelets jingled. "Look at you—a teenager already." She turned to Mom with a smile. "They grow up so fast!"

"She's only thirteen," Mom murmured. "Don't rush things."

Dulcie frowned as if she might start arguing about how grown up I was. Before she could say anything, though, Emma flung herself at me. "Ali, Ali, Ali!"

"Whoa," I laughed. "You're getting so big, you'll knock me down! Look at your hair—it's almost as long as mine."

Emma giggled and hugged me. "That's 'cause I'm almost five. Soon I'll be as big as you."

Keeping an arm around my cousin's shoulders, I turned back to Dulcie. "Are you in town for a show or—"

"I had to see the owner of a gallery in D.C. She wants to exhibit my work in a group show next fall, and I need peace and quiet to paint, so . . ." Dulcie glanced at Mom who sighed and shook her head, obviously worried about something.

"Your mother thinks this is the worst idea I've ever had," Dulcie went on with a laugh. "But I'm going to fix up the old cottage at the lake and spend the summer there."

I stared at her, hardly daring to believe she was serious. Sycamore Lake, the place that had obsessed me for two months now. Before I could bombard her with questions, Mom said, "Dulcie, I really think—"

"No arguments. My mind's made up." Dulcie smiled at Mom and turned to me. "I need a babysitter to entertain Emma while I paint. I'm trying to talk your mom into letting me borrow you for the summer."

"Me?" My face flushed. "I'd love to baby-sit Emma at the lake! I've wanted to see it for ages. I found a—"

"Ali," Mom interrupted. "I *told* you what it's like there. Rain and mosquitoes and cold, gloomy days. Nothing to do. Nowhere to go. You'll hate it."

"Don't believe a word of it," Dulcie told me. "Sure, it's cold and rainy sometimes. It's Maine—what do you expect? But there's plenty of sunshine. The mosquitoes aren't worse than anyplace else. The lake's—"

"The lake's deep . . . and dark . . . and dangerous," Mom cut in, choosing her words slowly and deliberately. "People drown there every summer."

Dulcie frowned at Mom. "Do you have to be so negative about *everything?*"

To keep Mom from starting a scene, I jumped into the conversation.

"I've taken swimming lessons since I was six years old. I know all about water safety. I'd never do anything stupid."

"Please, Aunt Claire, please, please, please!" Emma begged. "I want Ali to be my babysitter." She hopped back and forth from one foot to the other, staring hopefully at Mom.

Say yes, I begged silently, *say yes*. My best friend, Staci, was going away, and a boring summer stretched ahead. I loved Emma, and I loved my aunt. A few months at the lake would be perfect.

Ignoring my pleading look, Mom shook her head. "I can't possibly make a decision until Pete comes home from work. Ali's his daughter, too. We have to agree on what's best for her."

Dulcie dropped onto the sofa beside Mom. "Sorry. I'm used to making my own decisions about Emma." Tossing her hair to the side, she grinned at me. "It's one of the many advantages of being divorced."

"I didn't mean——" Mom said.

"How about some coffee?" Dulcie asked, quickly diverting Mom. "And some fruit juice for Emma?"

"Of course." Mom got up and headed for the kitchen with Dulcie behind her. I trailed after them, but at the doorway, my aunt turned and smiled at me. "Why don't you read to Emma, sweetie? She put some of her favorite books in my bag."

Secrets, I thought. *Things they don't want me to know about.* I was tempted to follow them into the kitchen anyway, but it occurred to me that Dulcie might have better luck talking to Mom without my being there listening to every word.

Emma rummaged through her mother's big straw bag and pulled out *The Lonely Doll*, a book I'd enjoyed when I was little.

"I like when Edith meets the bears, and she isn't lonely anymore." Emma climbed into my lap and rested her head against my shoulder.

"I like that part, too."

Emma opened the book to a photo of Edith looking sad and lonely. "Someday I'll have a friend," she said. "And then I won't be lonely anymore."

"Silly," I said. "You must have friends. Everyone has friends."

She shook her head. "Not in New York. Everybody I know there is grown up. And grownups can't be your friends."

"Can I be your friend? Or am I too old?"

Emma gave me a solemn, considering look. "It would be better if you were five or six or even seven," she said, "but I guess you can be sort of a friend."

"Thank you, Princess Emma." I gave her a little tickle in the side. "I'm greatly honored by your majesty's decision."

She giggled. "Will you read now?"

When we were about halfway through the story, we were distracted by rising voices in the kitchen.

"We're adults now," Mom was saying. "I don't have to do everything you say. Ali's my daughter. I'll raise her the way I see fit!"

"It must be nice to own a child," Dulcie replied.

"'Own a child'? What's that supposed to mean?"

"You're so overprotective, you might as well keep her on a leash. Sit, Ali. Heel, Ali. Roll over, Ali."

"How can you say that?" Mom's voice rose. "I love Ali and I want her to be safe. She's not going to spend the summer running wild, swimming, going out in boats—"

"Don't hold on so tight," Dulcie interrupted. "Ali's growing up. She has to start making her own decisions. It might be good for her to get away from you. She—"

"You always took everything away from me when I was little!"

Mom shouted. "And now you want my own daughter! Can't I have anything?" She started sobbing.

"Oh, that's right," Dulcie said. "Cry when you can't think of anything else to do." There was an edge of cruelty in her voice I'd never heard before. "Grow up, Claire. You're not a little kid anymore."

Emma put her arms around my neck and pressed her face against my chest. "Make them stop, Ali."

The voices in the kitchen dropped so low that I couldn't hear what Mom or Dulcie was saying.

"I think they stopped all by themselves, Emma." I patted her back, but my mind was racing. Dulcie was right. Mom *did* overprotect me; even Staci thought so. She never let me do *anything*—not even spend a night at Staci's house or go the mall with my friends. I really did need to get away from her for a while.

But at the same time I was agreeing with Dulcie, I was feeling bad because she'd upset Mom. I was confused, as well. Why did Mom think Dulcie wanted to take me away from her? What else had she taken? It was enough to give *me* a headache.

Emma nudged me. "Read, Ali. I want to hear the part where Little Bear and Edith play dress-up, and Edith writes, 'Mr. Bear is just a silly old thing!' on the mirror with lipstick and Mr. Bear gets cross." She giggled. "And then Edith calls him a silly and he spanks her and she's scared Mr. Bear will take Little Bear and go away and she'll be lonely again."

"You sure know this story well."

"Edith is lonely like me, and she has blond hair like me, and she lives in an apartment in New York like me. And she wishes so hard for a friend that Mr. Bear and Little Bear come to her house just to be her friends. And that's what I wish for, too. A friend. Somebody who likes me best of all."

I started reading again, and Emma pressed against me, mouthing the words silently as if she knew the story by heart.

While I read, I kept one ear tuned to the kitchen, but I couldn't hear what Mom and Dulcie were saying. If Emma hadn't been sitting on my lap, I would have tiptoed to the door and listened.

3

At the end of the story, Mr. Bear promised Edith he'd stay with her forever.

"'Forever and ever!'" Emma shouted along with Little Bear.

We said the book's last three words together: "'And they did!'"

"When I was little, I wanted a doll just like Edith," I told Emma.

"I want one, too," Emma said, "but Mommy says they're very, very expensive."

I sighed, thinking about things that cost too much to own—a horse, a mountain bike like Staci's, a swimming pool in the backyard, even a doll. . . .

The front door opened, and Dad stopped at the threshold to grin at Emma, who ran to him.

"What a nice surprise!" Dropping his briefcase, he scooped Emma up and gave her a hug. "Look at you—just as beautiful as your mommy!"

Emma laughed and kissed Dad's nose.

The kitchen door swung open. Mom and Dulcie seemed to have made up after their quarrel, but Mom still looked tense, worried, uneasy.

"It's good to see you, stranger." Dad put Emma down and gave Dulcie a hug and a kiss. It was a long hug, I thought. I glanced at Mom. She was watching the two of them, but I couldn't read her expression—except that I could tell she wasn't happy.

"What brings you here?" Dad asked Dulcie.

"I'm in a group show at a D.C. gallery next fall," Dulcie said. "Emma and I took the train down so I could talk to the owner. Since we were so close, I called Claire, and she picked us up at the station. We're going back to New York tomorrow morning."

Emma grabbed Dad's hand. "Mommy wants Ali to baby-sit me at the lake, but Aunt Claire says she can't."

Dad turned to Dulcie and raised his eyebrows. "Sycamore Lake?"

"I drove to the cottage a couple of weeks ago," Dulcie said. "Considering how long it's been empty, it's in pretty good shape. A couple of broken windows, a few leaks in the roof, and a dozen or more mice nesting in the cupboards."

Dulcie glanced at Mom. "A trap will take care of the mice, and I've hired a contractor to fix everything else. By the time he's done, Gull Cottage will have electricity, indoor plumbing, fresh paint inside and out, a new roof—and the old boathouse will be my studio."

"In other words, it'll be better than new." Dad turned to Mom. "So why can't Ali baby-sit Emma?"

"You know I hate the lake." Mom's voice rose a few notches, tense, anxious. "Ali could drown, she could get Lyme disease from a deer tick, she could get bitten by a snake, she—"

"Oh, for heaven's sake." Ignoring Mom's whimper of protest, Dad looked at me. "How do you feel about the idea, Ali?"

"I want to go," I said. "Staci will be away all summer. I'm sick of the swimming pool and the softball team." *And of Mom watching me all the time*, I wanted to add, *keeping me on a leash, owning me.* Instead, I said, "The lake would be fun—an adventure, something different."

"Please, please, *pretty* please?" Emma begged. "I'll be so lonely without Ali."

"Let her go, Claire," Dad said. "She loves Dulcie and Emma. And they love her."

"I'll take good care of Ali," Dulcie put in. "I won't let her or Emma run wild. I promise."

"You'll get absorbed in your painting and forget all about them," Mom muttered.

Dulcie exhaled sharply, clearly exasperated. "I've had sole responsibility for Emma since she was a baby. Does she look neglected?"

The argument went on during dinner, which made it hard to enjoy the pasta topped with Dulcie's special marinara sauce, concocted from her ex-husband's Italian grandmother's recipe.

"It's the only good thing I ever got from that man," Dulcie said. "Besides Emma, of course."

Dad laughed and Mom allowed herself to smile, and then they returned to the argument. Round and round they went, saying the same things over and over again. Mom refused to give in: I was too young to leave home for a whole summer, too young to be responsible for Emma.

At the end of the meal, Dad laid his fork and knife on his plate and said, "I've heard enough. Ali's a sensible, responsible girl. There's absolutely no reason why she shouldn't spend the summer at the lake."

Mom put her coffee cup down and stared at him, obviously shocked. "Pete, please——"

Whatever she was about to say was drowned out by Emma's shout of joy. "Hooray! Hooray!" She jumped up from the table and ran to hug Dad. "Thank you, Uncle Pete, thank you!"

I looked at Mom uneasily, taking in the defeated slump of her shoulders. "Say it's okay," I begged. "Say I can go and you won't be mad." *Or hurt. Or betrayed. Or worried.*

She wiped her mouth carefully with her napkin. "If it means so much to you, go." Without looking at anyone, she rose from the table and began gathering the dinner plates. The set of her jaw and her jerky movements clearly showed her anger.

"Give me a break, Claire. Don't get in one of your moods." Dulcie picked up a few glasses and followed Mom into the kitchen.

Carrying the serving bowls, I trailed after them, with Emma close behind clasping a fistful of spoons and forks. She handed them to Mom, then ran off to the living room.

Without speaking to anyone, Mom began loading the dishwasher.

"It's the silent treatment," Dulcie whispered to me. "She inherited it from our mother—and perfected it."

I turned away, unwilling to criticize Mom. Dulcie was right, of course—silence and tears were Mom's weapons. But it made me uncomfortable to agree with my aunt. After all, I had no reason to complain. I'd won. I was going to Sycamore Lake.

Leaving Mom to clean up, I followed Dulcie into the living room. Dad was reading *The Lonely Doll* to Emma in a sweet bumbling bear voice.

I perched on the arm of Dulcie's chair. "Can I ask you something?"

"Sure, sweetie." Dulcie pushed her hair back from her face. Her long dangly silver earrings swayed and her bracelets jingled. She smiled, waiting for me to speak.

"Well, a couple of months ago I found an old Nancy Drew book in a box in the attic. While I was leafing through it, a photograph fell out. It was of you and Mom at Sycamore Lake—I could see the water behind you."

Dulcie smiled. "Your grandfather loved taking pictures. Every time you turned around, there he was, pointing a camera at you.

They were usually awful. We thought he had a special ugly lens he used for our pictures."

"There was another girl with you," I said, "but all that shows is her shoulder and arm. The rest is torn off."

"Another girl?" Dulcie shook her head, and her soft hair brushed my cheek. "We didn't have any friends at the lake. Gull Cottage sits out on a point, all by itself. There were no other kids around—just your mother and me."

"Grandmother wrote your name and Mom's name on the back," I went on, trying to make her remember. "She wrote the girl's name, too, but only the first letter is still there—'T.'"

"'T'?" An odd look crossed Dulcie's face. "Did you ask your mother about the girl?"

"I told her I didn't remember." Mom stood in the doorway, her hands clasped, staring solemnly at her sister.

"I don't remember, either," Dulcie said quickly.

"What did you do with the picture, Mom? Maybe if Dulcie saw it—"

"I threw it away," she said. "It was old, torn, faded." Without another word, she picked up a gardening book and began to read, her way of saying she was still in a bad mood.

Before I could ask another question, Dulcie scooped up Emma. "Time for bed."

"But Uncle Pete is still reading about Edith and the bears," she said.

"You know that story by heart, sweetheart." Ignoring Emma's further protests, Dulcie carted her off to the guest room.

Dad turned on the TV to watch one of his favorite crime shows. It looked as if no more would be said about "T" that night.

~ 4 ~

After Dulcie and Emma went back to New York, Mom nursed her bad mood for weeks. She refused to take me shopping for summer clothes, so I tagged along with Staci and her mother. She wouldn't talk about the lake or give me any baby-sitting tips. She spent almost all her time working in the garden, down on her hands and knees, weeding till her knuckles bled, watering and fertilizing, rearranging plants, adding new ones. *Just to avoid me*, I thought.

Even Dad found it hard to be patient with her, especially after she changed her mind about driving me to the lake.

"If Dulcie wants Ali to baby-sit, she can pick her up and drive her to Maine herself," she told him.

He stared at her. "But, Claire, what about our plans to spend a few days on the coast?"

"I can't leave the flowers. They'll dry up. The weeds will take over." Mom folded her arms tightly across her chest, her face taut with anxiety.

Dad's frown deepened. "You realize that coming all the way down here to get Ali will add hours to Dulcie's trip."

Mom shrugged. "It was Dulcie's idea to take Ali to the lake. Let her figure it out. She can always find another babysitter."

Close to tears, I glared at Mom. "You're still trying to keep me from going, aren't you? Why don't you just put me on a leash and tie me to a tree in the backyard?"

My outburst surprised Dad, but Mom nodded her head angrily. "You should've been Dulcie's daughter—you're more like her every day."

"Good. Maybe I won't grow up scared of everything, afraid to have fun, ruining everybody else's fun."

Too upset to reply, Mom ended the conversation by leaving the room.

Dad grabbed my shoulders and gave me a little shake, more to get my attention than anything else. "Don't talk to your mother like that. Can't you see you're hurting her?"

I wanted to say Mom was hurting *me*, but Dad had already followed her out of the room. *She's not having a nervous breakdown*, I shouted silently. *She's just crying because she can't think of anything else to do.*

I sighed and grabbed an apple from the bowl on the counter. Living in this house was good practice for crossing a minefield. If you weren't careful, you could set off explosions with every step you took.

While I ate my apple, I stared out the kitchen window at the neighbor's dog, tied to his tree. He lay in the dirt, his nose on his paws—totally bored, I was sure, but safe.

The day I left, Mom refused to get out of bed, claiming she had a migraine, the worst she'd had in over a year. Dad pulled the blinds to darken the room and sat with her for a while, reading a book as she dozed, another way to avoid talking.

When Dulcie arrived, Mom didn't feel well enough to see her, so we said our goodbyes in her bedroom. "You don't have to stay at the lake if you're unhappy or homesick," she whispered. "If anything scares you or worries you, call us. Your father will come get you."

"Don't worry. Everything will be fine," I assured her.

Mom squeezed my hand. "I know you think I'm too protective," she said, "but I want to keep you safe. You're so young. You don't know the terrible things that can happen, how quickly one's life can change."

"What do you mean?"

She closed her eyes. "My head hurts. I can't talk anymore."

I leaned over and kissed her gently. "I'll be careful in the water," I promised, "and I'll take good care of Emma. Please don't worry. I love you and I'll miss you."

Keeping her eyes closed, Mom said, "I love you, too."

On the way downstairs, I asked Dad if the migraine was my fault.

"Of course not," he said. "It's tension, anxiety . . ."

Then it is my fault. I caused the tension and anxiety, didn't I? I pushed the guilty thought away. Mom often had migraines. I couldn't be blamed for all of them. *Maybe this one, though.*

Moments later, Emma was hugging me, squealing with delight, and Dulcie was assuring Dad she'd drive carefully and keep a close eye on me all summer.

Dad wedged my suitcase and bag of books into the van. I belted myself in the front seat, and Dulcie secured Emma in the back seat.

As I waved goodbye to Dad, I thought I saw a hand raise the blind in my parents' bedroom. Mom must have felt well enough to watch her sister take me away for the summer.

The ride to Maine seemed to last forever—one boring interstate after another, dodging trucks, passing cars and motorcycles, stopping a couple of times at fast-food places for hamburgers and fries. Not what she usually ate, Dulcie assured me, but the quickest way to fill our stomachs.

Late in the afternoon, we left the last interstate and followed a network of roads, each narrower and more winding than the one before.

Emma leaned over the seat. "Are we almost there?"

Dulcie nodded. "See that tree? The one with the long limb like a trunk sticking out over the road? Claire and I called it the elephant tree. We'll be at the cottage soon."

A few minutes later, Dulcie slowed down and pointed out a little white store by the side of the road. Its windows were boarded up and a weather-beaten sign over the door said, OLSON'S. Weeds grew in the parking lot, and a row of seagulls perched on the roof.

"Claire and I used to ride our bikes all this way for home-made ice cream—the best chocolate I ever tasted." Dulcie sighed. "Too bad it's closed."

Soon after, she said, "It's the next left, just past that patch in the asphalt that looks like a bear. See? There's the sign for Gull Cottage." She pointed at a neatly lettered arrow-shaped board nailed to a tree. Below it was a mailbox, its door down, empty.

Dulcie turned onto a one-lane dirt road and we headed into the woods. The setting sun shot golden beams through the trees, but the light was dim and greenish, almost as if we were underwater.

We rounded a curve, and there it was, a small cottage sheltered by tall trees. The clapboards had a fresh coat of blue paint, and the steep roof was newly shingled. The lake itself was down a flight of wooden steps. I could see a dock and a small building beside it. Beyond a curve of sandy beach was the water, dark in the early evening light, stretching out to the horizon.

"It looks almost exactly the same," Dulcie said. "Joe did a great job."

With Emma close behind, I followed Dulcie across a deck and through the back door. I don't know exactly what I'd expected—cobwebs and dust, stale air, maybe a gloomy, spooky atmosphere—but the cottage was bright and airy. Blue checked curtains hung at the kitchen windows, and the cabinets had been painted a sunny yellow, the walls pale blue, the table and chairs bright blue. The stove and refrigerator were a brand-new dazzling white.

"The old ones were antiques," Dulcie said. "Plus they didn't work."

She led us into the living room, which was furnished with a pair of soft armchairs and a matching sofa sagging beneath faded flowered slipcovers. A big stone fireplace took up one whole wall, and windows with a view of the lake took up another wall. Shelves full of books and board games covered the third wall from floor to ceiling.

"The cottage was filthy when I saw it in April," Dulcie said. "Joe hired a cleaning crew to scrub and vacuum. They got rid of spiders, squirrels, mice, and a family of raccoons living under the deck."

"But they didn't hurt them, did they?" Emma asked, her voice full of concern.

"Of course not, sweetie. They caught the mice and squirrels and raccoons in Havahart traps and let them go in a nice part of the woods, and they picked up the spiders very gently in tissue and carried them outside."

"That's good." Emma looked pleased. "If they come back, they can sleep in my room. I won't mind."

Dropping her suitcases at the foot of a narrow flight of steps, Dulcie pointed down the hall. "Two bedrooms—one for Emma and one for me. Plus a brand-new bathroom."

My room was upstairs, tucked snugly under the eaves. A faded patchwork quilt in shades of blue, yellow, and green calico covered the double bed. Its iron frame had been painted white to match an old dresser and a table and chair as well as built-in shelves, already holding books and toys. Fresh muslin curtains hung at the windows, and a rag rug covered most of the floor.

"This was your mom's and my room when we were kids," Dulcie said. "Same wallpaper, same furniture."

She picked up a conch shell lying on the bureau and turned it slowly, studying its shape and colors before putting it back. "Our mother left everything here. I guess she thought we'd come back one summer, but we never did."

Her voice had dropped so low, I barely understood what she'd said.

"Why didn't you come back?" I asked. "Did something happen?"

Dulcie stared at me. "Of course nothing happened. Whatever gave you that idea?"

"Mom, I guess. The way she talks about the lake, like it's a scary place." Suddenly embarrassed, I picked up the shell Dulcie had been looking at. "This is really pretty."

"Let me see." Emma reached for the shell, and I handed it to her. She held it as carefully as if it were made of glass and pressed it to her ear. "I hear the ocean," she whispered.

Dulcie looked at me over Emma's head. "Everything scares Claire," she said. "Deep water. High places, low places. Inside, outside. Upside, downside."

Even though I'd often thought the same thing, Dulcie's tone of voice stung. Mom was lying in bed at home, sick, in pain, while I'd traveled all this way without her. "She can't help it. She worries, that's all."

Dulcie shrugged. "To answer your question, I guess we didn't come back because we got tired of coming here. For kids, there's not a whole lot to do. We spent our summers traveling instead—Yellowstone, the Grand Canyon, Yosemite, Niagara Falls, the Canadian Rockies." She laughed. "Dad did a lot of driving in those years."

Emma picked up one of a pair of teddy bears sitting in a small rocking chair. "He looks just like Mr. Bear," she said.

"He belonged to Claire," Dulcie said. "And that's just what she called him. Mr. Bear."

"That's the bear's name in *The Lonely Doll*. Mr. Bear and Little Bear, the friends Edith wishes so hard for." Emma hugged the bear. "If I wish hard enough, will a friend come?"

Dulcie leaned down to kiss Emma's cheek. "Just wait till you start kindergarten in the fall. You'll have so many friends, you won't have to wish." She smoothed her daughter's silky hair back from her face, tucking it behind her ears.

"Does Mr. Bear belong to you now?" Emma asked me.

"You can have him," I told her. "I think he likes you best of all."

Emma grinned and hugged the bear. "And you can have the other one."

"He was mine." Dulcie picked up the bear, a sad companion to Mom's. His fur was almost worn off, stuffing leaked from one paw, and he was missing an eye.

"Poor old thing," Dulcie said. "Claire took good care of her toys, but I was rough on everything—toys, clothes, books. Even people."

She sighed and gave the bear a hug. "His name is Rufus M., after the little boy in the Moffat Family books." Dropping the bear on the foot of the bed, she stretched. "I guess it's time to start dinner."

5

When Dulcie was gone, Emma sat on the bed and watched me put my things into the bureau drawers. "Is Aunt Claire mad at Mommy?" she asked. "Is that why she didn't come down to see us before we left?"

I shook my head. "My mom gets awful headaches," I told Emma. "They're called migraines. When she has a really bad one, she stays in bed and doesn't talk to anyone."

"Poor Aunt Claire." Emma stroked Mr. Bear's fur. "I'll make her a get-well card tomorrow. It'll be from me and Mr. Bear. Would she like that?"

I grinned. "She'd *love* a card, especially from you."

Emma looked at me thoughtfully. "Aunt Claire doesn't like the lake, does she? She almost didn't let you come with me and Mommy."

I opened the casement window and leaned out to look at the water. The evening star hung low in the sky, kept company by a half-moon, but it was still light enough to make out the horizon, a dark line against the fading pink of the sunset.

"My mom's scared of water," I said. "I've never seen her go swimming. Not once. Even when she took me to the pool for lessons, she sat on the grass and watched me. All the other mothers were in the water with their kids. But not my mother."

Beside me, Emma shuddered. "Maybe she thinks she'll drown. She doesn't want her bones to come out."

I looked at her. "What are you talking about?"

"Bones are inside us, you and me and Mommy and everybody. When we die they come out, and then we're ghosts."

"Where did you get that idea?"

"I saw pictures in Mommy's drawing books. She said they're skeletons. We all have them inside—until we die, and then . . ." Emma hugged Mr. Bear. "He doesn't have bones, just stuffing. And he's not alive, so he can't die. Or be a ghost."

"There's no such thing as ghosts."

Emma turned her hands this way and that, as if observing the movement of the bones under her skin. "How do you know? Maybe you just haven't seen one."

"Don't be a Silly Billy." I forced myself to laugh. "Of course I haven't seen a ghost. And neither have you."

"I've seen one in my dreams." Emma spoke so softly I had to lean down to hear her. "The ghost is very sad and lonely. She wants to go home, but she's down deep, deep, deep in the water. She's been there so long, she's just bones. No one knows where she is."

Emma's whispery voice made my skin race with goose bumps. I pulled her small body close to mine and hugged her. Mr. Bear's fur tickled my nose. "That's very scary," I told her, "but it's just a bad dream. Everybody has them."

Emma peered into my eyes. "Do you?"

I thought about "T." I hadn't dreamt about her for weeks— until last night. I must have been worried about coming to the lake, leaving Mom, all that. I hoped I wouldn't dream about her now that I was actually here.

"Not very often," I fibbed to keep from alarming Emma.

While we'd been talking, the room had darkened. Shadows gathered in the corners, and a cool breeze fluttered the curtains.

Somewhere outside a bird cried once . . . twice . . . three times.

I took Emma's hand and led her toward the stairs. "Let's go see what your mom's doing."

In the brightly lit kitchen, Emma ran to Dulcie. "Mr. Bear wants dinner," she said, waving him at her mother. "He's hungry."

Dulcie gave her a kiss. "It's almost ready. Why don't you and Ali set the table? The forks and knives and spoons are in that drawer." She pointed to the cabinet by the sink, and Emma began counting out the utensils—four of each.

"There's only three of us," I said.

"You forgot Mr. Bear." Emma sat the teddy in the extra chair and laid a fork, knife, and spoon in front of him.

I laughed a little louder than I'd meant to, in relief, I guess, that Mr. Bear was joining us . . . not the ghost from Emma's dream.

Dulcie brought over a big yellow bowl of spaghetti and set it down in the middle of the table. "The sauce isn't as good as my ex-mother-in-law's," she said, "but it's not bad with plenty of parmesan sprinkled on top."

She tucked a napkin around Emma's neck and served us each a heaping portion.

"Don't forget Mr. Bear," Emma said. "He hasn't had anything to eat for years and years and years."

Dulcie put a small amount on a saucer and set it in front of the bear. "Eat up," she told him. "I don't like bears who waste food."

After dinner, Dulcie lit a fire. Emma and I sprawled on the rug and roasted marshmallows. I let mine turn black on the outsides and sucked the gooey white insides into my mouth. "Yum."

"Ugh," said Emma. She liked hers barely toasted, but Dulcie burned hers even blacker than mine.

We washed the marshmallows down with hot chocolate, then lay still and watched the flames devour the logs. Our faces felt warm, but our feet were cold.

On the sofa, Dulcie sighed happily and stretched her long legs toward the fire. "I'd forgotten how chilly Maine gets at night," she said. "We'll need extra blankets. And cozy flannel jammies."

Emma yawned and rubbed her eyes.

"Look like someone's ready for bed." Dulcie scooped her up and gave her a hug. "Let's go, sleepyhead."

"You come, too." Emma stretched her arms toward me. "And bring Mr. Bear. He's scared of the dark."

Carrying the bear, I followed Dulcie and Emma to the small room at the back of the cottage. As soon as Emma was ready for bed, she found *The Lonely Doll* and handed it to Dulcie. "Read this one."

"But I read that book last night and the night before and the night before that—"

"It's my favorite," Emma insisted. She climbed into bed and tucked the bear under the covers beside her. "I bet Ali wants to hear it—don't you?"

"Sure." I stretched out on the bed beside Emma and listened to Dulcie begin the story.

After she'd read a few pages, Emma interrupted her. "It's so dark outside my window. Why aren't there any lights or any people? I don't even hear any cars."

"We're out in the country now, Em, where it's peaceful and quiet."

"Will you pull down the shades so I don't have to see the dark? Ghosts could be out there, watching me."

Before Dulcie could move, I jumped up and shut out the night with a few yanks on the blinds. Emma was right. It *was* dark out there. Very dark. No lights anywhere. No sounds but the lapping of the lake against the shore and the wind in the treetops. The cottage was spooky at night, dark, full of shadows, not at all the way it was in the daytime.

"There," I said. "Is that better?"

"I guess so." Emma's voice was low, almost a whisper. She held Mr. Bear tightly. "Read, Mommy."

Dulcie read three *Lonely Doll* books, as well as *The Cat in the Hat*, *The Cat in the Hat Comes Back*, *Horton Hatches the Egg*, and *The Owl and the Pussycat*. But it was *Goodnight Moon* that finally lulled Emma to sleep.

Leaving a night-light glowing, Dulcie tiptoed out of the room, and I followed. She closed the door softly and leaned against it for a moment.

"Let's hope Emma adjusts to nights in the wilderness quickly," she said. "I could barely stay awake to read those books."

She yawned and gave me a hug. "I'm beat from all that driving, Ali. I'm going to put out the fire and get into bed."

More tired than I'd realized, I climbed the stairs to my room. Trying to ignore the darkness beyond the bedside lamp, I snuggled under Great-Grandmother's quilt and opened *To Kill a Mockingbird*, number one on my school's summer reading list. I'd seen the movie, but I'd never read the novel. Dad said the book was even better than the movie, but Mom said nothing could beat Gregory Peck as Atticus Finch.

My bed faced the casement windows, slightly open to the cool night air. Through the pine branches, I could see the moon, tipped into a crooked smile. Insects chirped, an owl hooted, the pines sighed in the breeze, and the lake washed against the shore.

With Rufus M. tucked in beside me, I tried to read, but after half an hour, I gave up. It wasn't the book. I loved the story, and I loved the way Harper Lee wrote. I simply couldn't stay awake another second.

I closed my eyes, expecting to fall asleep immediately. But the moon shone in my face. In the woods, the orchestra of insects chirped and thrummed and buzzed, louder and louder.

I found myself thinking of Mom and Dulcie, sharing this bed when they were younger than I was. Had they talked and giggled together? Or had they quarreled the way they did now?

I hugged Rufus. "If you could talk, you'd tell me," I whispered to the old bear. "You were there."

His glass eye glittered in the moonlight, giving him a slightly wicked look. But if the bear knew anything about those long-ago summers, he wasn't telling. Like Mom and Dulcie, Rufus M. knew how to keep secrets.

6

It rained during the night. In the morning it was still coming down, darkening the lake to black and blurring the trees. The air smelled like wet earth and old leaves. A squirrel perched on the deck's railing, his droopy tail wet and pitiful. A few sparrows hopped about here and there, looking almost as wretched as the squirrel.

After breakfast, Dulcie handed out umbrellas and led Emma and me down the steps to the dock. Flinging open the door of the small shingled building, she said, "My studio. Isn't it marvelous?"

Large skylights let in the gray light of the rainy day. Blank canvases leaned against the walls, primed and ready to paint. A long table ran along the back wall, holding paints and brushes, stacks of drawing paper, and books. Above it, built-in shelves bulged with more art supplies and books.

A wood stove and a couch draped with a faded paisley print bedspread occupied one corner, along with a couple of well-worn easy chairs and the potter's wheel Dulcie used to make bowls, mugs, and platters.

I breathed in the smells of paint, turpentine, and linseed oil mingled with lake water and damp, mossy woods. "It's perfect," I said. "I want one just like it!"

Dulcie smiled and pointed to an easel in the middle of the studio. "What do you think of my latest?"

I stared at the large oil, washed in shades of blues, greens, and grays, splashed with flashes of yellow and white. "It makes me think of water."

Dulcie grinned. "It's the first of a series based on the lake and its moods." She turned to the window and stared at the water, dull and gray in the rain. "I want to capture the power in water and rocks and trees—capture it as it captures me." She stood silently for a few moments, toying with a long strand of curly hair. Almost as an afterthought, she added, "Maybe I'll manage to free myself."

I wasn't sure what she meant or even if she were talking to me, so I simply nodded.

"Mommy, can I show Ali my pictures?" Emma asked.

Without looking at either of us, Dulcie said, "Of course. Your folder's on the table."

Emma carefully untied the strings holding her folder closed and began spreading pictures on the table. "I made these in New York," she explained, "and the moving truck brought them here, just like it brought Mommy's paintings."

I looked at the array of rainbows, birds, suns, and flowers, painted in bright reds, yellows, greens, and blues. In some, people with huge smiling faces and long stick arms and legs floated just above the ground. She'd printed her name in big sloppy letters across the top of every picture.

"These are great, Emma. I love the bright colors and all the happy people."

"I'm going to be an artist when I grow up," Emma said, "just like Mommy."

"Me, too. We'll all three be artists together."

Emma clapped her hands. "And this will be where we paint— all three of us. And we'll live together in the cottage. And we won't be lonely."

Dulcie had finally left the window and was now mixing paints on her palette. A new canvas faced her. As she lifted her brush to make the first splash of color, she turned to Emma and me. "Would you girls like to paint, too?"

Emma grabbed a box of tempera paints and handed it to me. "You open the jars," she said, "and I'll get the paper and the brushes."

Soon all three of us were absorbed in painting. Rain pelted the skylights, the lake slapped the shore, the wind blew. Dulcie's CD player was loaded with classical music, Bach and Mozart——or was it Haydn? Well, no matter who it was, the music was perfect, and so was the rain and the wind and the sound of the little waves.

I watched Dulcie wash her canvas with thin layers of color in grayed shades of blue and purple and green: a rainy day at the lake. I tried doing the same thing with the tempera paint, but my brush was too wet. The colors ran and pooled and wrinkled the paper.

"Look, Ali." Emma held up a painting as blotchy and runny as mine, its colors mainly dark blues and blacks with a blob of white.

"Is that the lake on a rainy day?" I asked.

Emma looked at her painting. "Yes, but it's got something else." She pointed to the white blob. "This is a skeleton ghost. See? Here's its head."

Dulcie took the picture and looked at it intently. "What gave you the idea to paint a ghost in the water?"

Emma shrugged. "It's something I dream about." Her voice sank to a whisper. "Bones in the water, bones that come out and chase me."

The studio was so quiet, I could hear raindrops splash against the skylights. A cold draft slipped under the door and wrapped around my ankles. I shivered.

Emma hugged Dulcie. "Don't be mad, Mommy."

Dulcie stared at Emma. "Why would I be mad?"

Emma stroked Dulcie's sleeve. "I don't know."

Dulcie laid the picture on a stack of paper on the table and picked Emma up. "How about painting a rainbow and a smiling sun and a flower?" she asked. "Can you do that for me?"

"I already did lots of those, Mommy." Emma picked up her pictures and sorted through them. "One rainbow, two rainbows, three rainbows," she said. "And here's you and me sitting under a rainbow, and here's one flower, two flowers, four, five, seven flowers."

Dulcie looked at them. "Very nice," she said. "Much better than bones in the lake, don't you think?"

"I guess." Emma went to the window and looked out at the lake. "I wish the rain would go away."

"Me, too." I joined her and frowned at the dark clouds over the dark water. In the glass, I saw Dulcie's reflection behind me. She was sitting at the table, staring at the ghost picture. The expression on her face made me uneasy.

That afternoon, I read to Emma until she fell asleep. While she was napping, Dulcie came in from the studio and made a pot of tea for us. We sat at the kitchen table, warm and snug and dry. Rain gurgled in the downspouts, poured from the eaves, and ran down the windowpanes in large drops.

"Emma has an amazing imagination," I said.

"Sometimes I think she spends too much time alone," Dulcie said slowly. "I wonder if it's good for her."

"I'm an only child, too," I said. "It might be nice to have a

brother or sister, but I'm perfectly happy the way things are."
Except for Mom, I thought. *If only she was like you—never depressed, no headaches, full of energy, going places, doing things.* I stopped myself, guilt stricken.

Dulcie opened a tin of fancy cookies and offered me one. They were thin and crisp, smelled lovely, and tasted even better. Given the opportunity, I could have eaten every one and not left a crumb.

"In New York, we live in a neighborhood with lots of artists but not many kids," Dulcie went on, talking to me as if I was her age, her equal, not a little kid. "I've kept her at home because I can't afford preschool."

"She'll be in kindergarten this fall, won't she?"

Dulcie nodded. "Maybe she'll make friends then."

"Of course she will." I took another cookie. "And this summer she'll have me to play with."

Dulcie smiled and patted my hand. "I'm so glad Claire decided to let you come."

"She almost didn't."

Dulcie shrugged. "Your mom worries too much."

"Has she always been like she is now?"

"Pretty much." Dulcie sighed. "Our mom overprotected her—said she was 'sensitive, delicate, sickly.'"

"Was she?"

"I don't know. I was just a kid myself." Dulcie peered into her teacup as if the answer might be there. "Every time we had a fight, it was my fault. I got blamed for everything." She looked at me. "Sometimes I think Claire played it up to get attention."

Shocked by Dulcie's unkind words, I leapt to Mom's defense. "She has horrible migraines, and she's always feeling bad. Grandmother was probably right about her."

"I know, I know. Believe me, I know." With that, Dulcie gathered the empty teacups and carried them to the sink. "I have to get back to the studio. Please fix Emma a snack when she wakes up. Cookies and juice. Not too much, though, or she won't want dinner."

I jumped up and followed Dulcie to the door. "Are you mad at me? Did I say the wrong thing?"

She gave me a quick hug. "I had no business criticizing your mom. We're just so different, you know? It's hard for us to get along. Always has been."

I watched Dulcie leave the cottage and pause at the top of the steps. She stood there for a few minutes, staring out across the lake. The rain had stopped, but the water was still dark under the gray sky. The wind tugged at her hair, pulling curly strands from her ponytail. She looked small against the churning clouds.

I went back to reading *To Kill a Mockingbird*. After a while, Emma came into the kitchen, still sleepy from her nap. I closed my book and fixed her a glass of juice and a couple of cookies. Outside the rain started falling again and the wind blew. I began to worry Mom had been right about the weather.

That night, Emma's screams woke me from my own dream about "T" and the girls in the canoe. I sat straight up in bed, clutching the covers. Downstairs, Dulcie's footsteps hurried to Emma's room. I ran to the top of the stairs just in time to see her open Emma's door.

"Emma, what's wrong?" she asked.

"The bones came out of the lake," Emma cried. "They're going to get me!"

"It's okay, sweetie, it's okay." Dulcie's voice shook as if

Emma's dream had frightened her, too. "There aren't any bones in the lake. You were dreaming."

I leaned over the railing. "Is she all right?"

In the hall below, Dulcie hugged Emma tight. "She had a bad dream. A nightmare."

Emma looked up at me, still frightened. "The bones came out," she sobbed. "The bones came out."

For a moment, I had a scary feeling that someone else was in the cottage—unseen, watching, waiting. I looked behind me, into the shadowy corners of my room. No one was there, but I couldn't get rid of the feeling or the goose bumps on my arms.

Dulcie smiled up at me. "Everything's all right, Ali. Go back to bed. You look cold."

As Dulcie carried Emma to her room, I wished I could run down the steps and squeeze into the big double bed with them. But that would have been way too babyish. After Dulcie's door closed, I went to my room and snuggled under Great-Grandmother's quilt, shivering with cold.

In my head, Emma's words repeated themselves like a song you can't get out of your mind. *"The bones came out, the bones came out, the bones came out."*

Without wanting to, I pictured skeletons wading out of the dark water and creeping toward the house, their bony arms out-stretched. Outside, trees rustled in the breeze, and sticks snapped as if crushed under bony feet. Inside, the floors and steps creaked as if those same bony feet were tiptoeing through the house, upstairs and down, searching the rooms.

Holding Rufus tight, I curled into a ball and willed myself to sleep, but Emma's little voice went on saying, *"The bones came out, the bones came out."*

7

The next morning, the lake was gray under heavy clouds. The pines were blurred by mist, but the rain had stopped, and the air smelled clean and fresh.

It was too chilly for swimming but not too cold for a walk along the shore. Emma and I each put on a sweatshirt and jeans, and strolled by the lake. The sandy beach turned to stones not long after we passed the boathouse. I was glad I'd taken Dulcie's advice and worn sandals. If I'd gone barefoot, I'd have been hobbling along like an old lady.

While Emma ran ahead, I gathered stones. They were smooth and round, in shades of pale green, pink, gray, and black. I had an idea I might do something artistic with them, put them in ceramic bowls, maybe, and add driftwood and seagull feathers. I could make the bowls myself and sell my arrangements in gift shops. I'd learn how to throw clay on Dulcie's pottery wheel, I'd mix glazes, I'd use the kiln behind the studio.

I was thinking so hard, I almost walked right past Emma. To my surprise, she was standing beside a stranger, a girl who appeared to be nine or ten years old but small for her age. Her hair was white blond, her eyes were the same gray as the lake, and her skin was a deep tan. Despite the chilly weather, she wore a faded blue bathing suit.

"This is Sissy," Emma said. "I just met her, but she wants to be friends."

Sissy looked at me slantwise, as if she were sizing me up. Would I be good to know? Was I nice? Was I bossy? I gave her the same look. There was something about her I disliked on sight—a sharpness in her eyes, a mean set to her mouth. She was the type who'd lie and get you in trouble.

"This is Ali," Emma told Sissy. "She's my cousin, and she's staying here with Mommy and me. Mommy's an artist, so Ali takes care of me while Mommy paints. She's not a babysitter because I'm not a baby."

Sissy continued to stare at me. "Where's *your* mother?" she asked. Her voice was too high pitched to be easy on the ears.

"In Maryland," I told her. "Where we live. She didn't want to come."

"Why not?" Sissy asked.

Something in her voice, a sassiness I didn't like, annoyed me. "I don't know what business it is of yours." It was a huffy thing to say. Rude, even. But somehow it was her fault I'd said it.

Sissy shrugged, and her shoulder blades jutted out like wings. "I was just wondering. Since when is that a crime?"

Emma laughed uncertainly, not sure if Sissy was joking or not. "Aunt Claire doesn't like the lake. That's why she didn't come."

"Is she scared of water or something?" A breeze from the lake blew Sissy's hair in her face, and she smoothed it behind her ears.

Emma glanced at me as if she thought I'd answer. "I think so," she said uncertainly. "But I'm not."

"I'm not, either." Sissy looked at me. "I bet *she's* scared—just like her mother."

I stopped trying to ignore her. "Back home I'm on the swim team. I've won more trophies than anybody in my class."

"Do you think I care?" Sissy turned to Emma. "Let's build castles."

Emma dropped to her knees beside Sissy, and the two of them began heaping up stones, blond heads together as if they'd been friends forever. I hated to admit it, but I felt left out. Emma was my cousin, my friend, and here she was trying to impress a bratty stranger.

"Are your parents renting a cottage around here?" I asked Sissy, hoping she'd say yes, we're leaving tomorrow, you'll never see me again.

Without looking up from her pile of stones, she said, "I live here."

"Where?" Emma asked.

Sissy pointed. "That way."

Emma peered down the shore. "I don't see a house."

"I walked a long way," Sissy said with a shrug.

"Can we come see you and play at your house sometime?"

Sissy shrugged again. "Maybe."

"We have sand at our beach," Emma went on. "We can build good castles there. Want to come home with us?"

"Not today." Sissy stood up and kicked her pile of stones. Down it tumbled.

"Why'd you do that?" Emma asked.

"It wasn't any good." Sissy scooped up a handful of stones and watched them run through her fingers, *clickety-click*. "I have to go. See you later."

She turned to leave, but Emma ran in front of her, blocking her way. "Will you be here tomorrow, Sissy?"

"Maybe." Dodging Emma, she walked away, her skinny back arrow straight, her skinny arms swinging, her skinny legs zipping along beside the water. Her silky hair floated around her head, lifted by the breeze. She didn't look back. Not once. Soon the mist swallowed her up.

When Sissy was out of sight, Emma took my hand. "Do you think she likes me?"

"Everybody likes you." I swung Emma's hand as we walked. "Do you like her?"

"Of course. Don't you?"

"Not especially."

"Why not?"

"I don't know. I guess we aren't, well, very copacetic."

"Cope-a-what?"

"Copacetic. It means getting along with somebody." I was pleased with myself for remembering one of my favorite vocabulary words.

"Well, Sissy's very copacetic with me." Emma broke away and ran along the edge of the water, singing a *Sesame Street* song.

I followed slowly, thinking about the very un-copacetic Sissy. There was something about her I didn't trust. Maybe it was her way of looking past you, not at you. Maybe it was her way of never quite answering questions. The frown on her face didn't help. It wouldn't hurt her to smile once in a while.

"Come on," Emma called. "Catch me!"

I ran after her and picked her up, pretending I was going to toss her into the lake. She shrieked and giggled and broke away from me again. I let her think she'd escaped and then caught her. It was a game Emma never tired of playing.

At lunch, Emma told Dulcie about her new friend. "Her name's Sissy."

"Where does she live?" Dulcie asked.

Emma shrugged. "Around here somewhere."

Dulcie looked puzzled. "I didn't think *anyone* lived around here."

"She said her house was that way." I pointed in what I thought was the right direction.

"She walked a long way," Emma put in. "And all she was wearing was a bathing suit."

"On a day like this? Brr." Dulcie wrapped her sweater tighter around her skinny body and sipped her coffee. "Did Sissy tell you her last name?"

Emma and I shook our heads.

"When you see her again, ask her. Maybe I knew her family from when I was a kid. She probably lives up the road in Webster's Cove."

"Can we go there and see her?" Emma asked.

"Without knowing her last name, how would you find her house?" I asked Emma, glad to think of a reason for not seeing Sissy.

"We could walk around and look for her. Maybe she'd be playing in her yard or something."

"Webster's Cove is a small place, but I doubt you'll find Sissy that way." Dulcie gathered up the dishes and carried them to the sink. "I'm going to the studio now. Be sure and take your nap, Emma. Otherwise, you'll be a crab tonight."

Emma held up her hands like little claws. "Watch out, I'll pinch you, Mommy."

Much to Emma's disappointment, we didn't see Sissy the next day or the day after or the day after that. I didn't mind a bit. The clouds had vanished, and the sun shone. It was perfect weather for swimming, but Emma said the water was too cold. While I practiced my backstroke, she sat on the sand and made castles. Like Sissy, she kicked them down before we left the beach. "No good," she said in a good imitation of her so-called friend.

At the end of the week, Emma suggested walking to Webster's Cove. "Mommy said Sissy might live there, remember? Maybe we'll see her and we can ask her to come home with us and have lunch."

"It's a long way," I said. "If you get tired, I'm not carrying you."

"I won't get tired. I'm big now."

It was about a forty-minute walk, but Emma didn't complain once. She trotted along beside me, talking about Sissy, Sissy, Sissy. What was her favorite color? Did she like chocolate or vanilla ice cream? Did she have sisters or brothers? What TV show did she like best—*Sesame Street* or *Mister Rogers' Neighborhood*? Was she afraid of the dark? Did she have bad dreams? Did she like pizza with extra cheese? Did she have a pet—a cat, a dog, a guinea pig? What did she eat for breakfast—Rice Krispies, Cheerios, Cap'n Crunch?

Emma had so many questions, I almost felt sorry for Sissy.

Webster's Cove was bigger than Dulcie remembered. Cars with out-of-state license plates jammed the narrow streets. People mobbed a little boardwalk running along the edge of the sand. Beach umbrellas tipped this way and that, almost hiding the water. The air smelled of popcorn and suntan lotion and French fries. Kids ran in and out of the lake, shouting and splashing, while their parents watched from folding chairs and blankets.

Emma tugged my arm. "I don't see Sissy."

"It would be hard to find anybody under seven feet tall in this crowd."

Taking her hand, I led her down the boardwalk and into Smoochie's Ice Cream Shop. Maybe the chocolate wouldn't be as good as Olson's, but it would be just as cold and sweet.

I pulled a five-dollar bill out of my pocket. "What would you like?" I asked Emma. "A soda? Ice cream? Candy?"

"Can I have a soda *and* ice cream?"

I checked the price board. I had enough for two small cones and two small sodas. "What flavor do you want?"

Emma pressed her nose against the glass and studied the choices. After several changes of mind, she settled for chocolate and a ginger ale. I picked mint chocolate chip and a root beer.

While we were waiting, Emma peered up at the teenage girl scooping the ice cream. A tag on her polo shirt said her name was Erin.

"Do you know a girl named Sissy?" Emma asked.

Without looking up, Erin said, "Can't say I do."

"She's ten going on eleven and she has long blond hair and she's pretty," Emma went on.

Skinny and mean-eyed, I felt like adding. *Not very nice and not really pretty.*

Erin smiled at Emma. "Sorry, but I don't know her. Maybe her family's here on vacation."

"She lives here," Emma persisted. "All year round."

"I live here all year, too, but I don't know anyone named Sissy. Are you sure she lives in the Cove?"

"No," I put in. "It was just a guess."

Erin handed us our cones and drinks. "There are loads of cottages scattered around the lake," she said. "She could live anywhere."

"I think it's near our cottage," Emma said.

Erin rang up the sale and took my money. While she made change, she asked, "Where do you live?"

"Gull Cottage, down on the Point."

She stared at me. "You're kidding! Nobody's lived there

for ages. Not since——" She frowned and handed me my change.

"Since what?" I asked.

"Huh?"

"You said nobody's lived there 'since.' And then you stopped."
I licked my ice cream. "What were you going to say?"

Erin shrugged and brushed a few stray strands of sun-
streaked hair behind her ear. Without looking at me, she said,
"Since about thirty years ago. The people who owned it came
every summer, but then one year they didn't come back. The cottage has just sat there empty all these years."

"Do you mean the Thorntons?" I asked her.

Erin nodded. "I think that was their name."

"Well, they're back now," I told her. "At least my aunt Dulcie
is."

"Really?" Erin stared at me as if she didn't believe me. "Dulcie
Thornton's here?"

"That's my mommy's name," Emma said. "She's an artist. Do
you know her?"

"Of course not. How old do you think I am?" Erin leaned over
the counter until she was face to face with Emma. "But my mom
knew Dulcie when they were kids. They used to play together all
the time. I think she had a little sister, too."

"Yes," I said. "Claire. That's my mother."

Erin studied Emma and me as if she was memorizing every
detail of our appearance—our clothes, our hair, our faces, even
how many freckles we had. Her scrutiny made me uncomfortable. Did she think we were strange? Was there something weird
about us?

"I'll tell Mom that Dulcie's back," she said at last. "She'll be
really interested."

Struck by a sudden thought, I took a deep breath. "What's

your mother's name?" I was hoping she'd say Toni or Terri or some other name that started with a *T*, but no luck.

"Jeanine," Erin said. "Jeanine Donaldson, but her maiden name was Reynolds. I know she'll want to see Dulcie. She still talks about her and Claire and what—"

Just then a man herded a couple of cross, sunburned children into the shop. "Two vanilla ice cream cones, please," he said. "Small. And one large diet Sprite."

"I want strawberry," the boy wailed.

"You said vanilla."

"No, no! Strawberry, I want strawberry!"

"Make that one vanilla and one strawberry," the man said. "And an extra-large diet Sprite for me."

"Can we go now?" Emma tugged at my T-shirt. "Maybe Sissy's waiting at home for us."

I waved goodbye to Erin, and we began the long trudge home. The further we walked, the hotter we got. The sun beat on our heads and shoulders, and our clothes stuck to us. Even wading in the lake didn't cool us off.

Before we'd gone halfway, Emma asked me to carry her.

"You promised you'd walk," I reminded her.

"I'm tired," Emma said, close to tears.

"Okay, but just a little way." I picked her up and carried her piggyback style. "Thank goodness you're a little skinny old thing," I told her.

"I'm just a bag of bones," Emma whispered into my ear. After that, she was so quiet I suspected she'd fallen asleep, worn out from the walk. I was pretty tired myself.

When we were almost home, I thought I saw Sissy watching us from a stone jetty poking out into the lake. I didn't wave. Neither did she. She just stood there as still as a heron waiting for a fish. But she was very far away, small in the distance. I could have been mistaken.

At any rate, I was glad Emma didn't see her.

8

In the end, I carried Emma as far as the studio. I lowered her to the ground and woke her up. "You'll have to climb the steps yourself."

The studio door opened, and Dulcie rushed out as if she'd been waiting for us. "Where have you been? You've been gone for ages!"

"We walked to Webster's Cove," I told her. "Emma wanted to find Sissy's house."

Emma threw her arms around Dulcie and burst into tears. "We didn't see Sissy anywhere, and I got so tired and hot."

"We stopped at Smoochie's," I told Dulcie. "The girl who works there, Erin, didn't know Sissy, but she said her mother knows you and Mom. She used to play with you when she was little."

"What was her name?"

"Jeanine something—I forget."

Most people would have paused to think about the name. Not Dulcie. Her answer was quick and sharp. "I don't remember her."

"But she remembers you."

Dulcie frowned and shook her head. "Next time you sashay off to Webster's Cove, please let me know."

I wanted to ask if she had a memory problem, but the grumpy look on her face silenced me.

"It's past time for lunch. Emma must be starved." Dulcie loped up the steps, and Emma and I followed, too tired to keep up with her long legs.

After we ate, Dulcie returned to the studio, and Emma settled down on the couch beside me.

"Will you read this to me?" Emma held up *The Moffats*. "I want to know about Rufus M."

Like most of the things in the cottage, the book was old. The cover was faded, and the pages had a soft, pulpy feel. My grandmother had scrawled her name on the title page, followed by the date June 5, 1945. Under it, Dulcie had written her name and June 2, 1977. Mom added her name the next year. It looked as if another name had been scribbled there, but someone had erased it. All that remained were a few faint pencil marks, impossible to read.

By the time I finished the first chapter, Emma was fast asleep. I lay on my side next to her, tired from our long walk. A fly buzzed against the window screen. The lake lapped the shore. After resting for a while, I went to my room and put on my bathing suit. Leaving Emma to her nap, I ran down the steps to the lake.

Before I waded into the water, I stopped by the studio. Dulcie was sitting on a stool, staring at an unfinished painting, another canvas washed with blues and grays and green. "Where's Emma?" she asked.

"Asleep. Is it okay if I go for a swim?"

Dulcie hesitated. For a moment I was afraid she'd say no. Mom would have. "Promise to stay out of deep water, and be careful." She dipped her brush into blue paint. "Be back in a half-hour or so."

I leaned against the door for a moment and watched Dulcie go to work on the painting. She was soon absorbed in adding daubs of dark blues and blacks.

Completely forgotten, I slipped outside and walked down to the lake. The water was so clear, I could see my toes and the pebbles on the bottom as if I were looking through glass. Schools of silver minnows darted in and out of clumps of grass, turning this way and that in perfect unison, tickling my legs as they swam past.

I waded through knee-deep water, watching the minnows. Every now and then I glimpsed bigger fish—trout, maybe—but they disappeared before I got a good look at them. Seagulls dipped and circled overhead, and the pine forest behind me rang with the cries of crows. The trees made the air smell like Christmas.

I was enjoying myself until I saw Sissy at the end of our stretch of sandy beach. Unaware I was near, she bent over a pile of sand, patiently shaping it into a castle with turrets. I watched her for a few moments, glad Emma was safely at home.

When Sissy began to dig a moat, I splashed out of the water. "Well, well, where have you been?"

She looked up, startled. "What's it to you?"

"Nothing," I said. "It's not like I missed you or anything."

Sissy frowned, her eyes narrowed against the sun. "Where's Emma?"

"Taking a nap." I sat down, scooped up a handful of sand, and watched it trickle slowly through my fingers.

"It's boring to sleep." Sissy went on digging her moat as if it was a lot more interesting than I was. She was wearing the same faded bathing suit. One strap slipped off her shoulder, and she pulled it back in place.

"Emma was pretty tired." I scooped up another handful of

sand. "We walked all the way to Webster's Cove and back this morning."

"Why did you go there?"

"Emma was looking for your house. She thought—"

Sissy shook her head. "I don't live in Webster's Cove."

"Where do you live, then?"

Sissy pointed in the opposite direction. "That way."

"The other day you pointed toward the Cove."

She smiled an odd little smile, more of a smirk, actually, and began to make a road to the castle with beach stones. She placed each one carefully. "Maybe I don't like unexpected company."

Maybe I don't, either, I thought. *Especially when it's you.* Out loud, I asked, "What's your last name?"

Sissy smoothed her castle's walls, stroking the sand with both hands as if it were a cat. I could see the little knobs of her spine under her skin and the sharp jut of her shoulder blades. She was definitely ignoring me—which annoyed me.

"Do you have any brothers or sisters?"

No answer.

"What's your father do?"

Still no answer.

"My dad's a math professor at the university. He—"

Sissy shrugged as if she didn't care what my father did.

I made a path with bits of broken shells and pebbles. "I'm just trying to be friendly."

"No, you're not. You're being nosy." Her face hidden by her hair, Sissy decorated her castle with bits of driftwood.

What could I say? She was right. I wasn't being friendly—I wanted to know more about her.

After a while, Sissy brushed her hair to the side and looked at me. "Emma says Dulcie's an artist. Is she good?"

I nodded. "She's getting ready for a show in Washington, D.C."

"Lucky her. I've never been there. "Sissy frowned and tossed a stone at a seagull. It missed, and the bird hopped a few feet farther away. "I've never been *anywhere*. Just here—boring Sycamore Lake, boring Webster's Cove, boring Maine."

"But Maine's beautiful. People come from all over to see the ocean and the boats and the lighthouses—"

"They must be really stupid." Sissy threw another stone, harder this time. She missed again, but the gull squawked and flew away. "I'd give anything to leave here and travel all over the world."

"Maybe when you grow up—"

"You know what? You're stupid, too."

I stared at her, but she was too busy building a little driftwood fence around her castle to look at me. "Why are you so mad all the time?" I asked her.

"What makes you think I'm mad?" She stuck a seagull's feather into the top of her castle and sat back to study the effect. "How about your mother? Is she an artist, too?"

"No."

"Why doesn't she like the lake?"

"Like Emma said, she's scared of water." I paused. Even though I didn't trust Sissy's sly eyes and mean mouth, she'd lived around here all her life. Maybe she'd heard people talk about the cottage. Unlike Erin, she wouldn't change the subject to spare my feelings.

Sissy stared at me, waiting for me to go on. Taking a deep breath, I said, "I think something happened the last summer Mom and Dulcie came to the cottage—something they don't want to talk about. Maybe something . . ." I hesitated and dropped my voice to a whisper. "Maybe something bad."

"You're right," she said. "Something bad happened, and lots of people know just what it was."

I drew in my breath and let it out slowly. "Do *you* know?"

Sissy tugged her bathing suit strap into place again and got to her feet. "That's for me to know and you to find out," she said with a smirk.

I jumped up and faced her. "You don't know anything, and neither does anyone else. You're making up stories, that's all."

"Think what you want. See if I care." Sissy turned her back on me and ran down the beach toward the Cove.

I watched her until I couldn't see her anymore. Brat. Did she really know something? Or was she lying? With one kick I demolished her castle and then splashed home through the water, sending the minnows racing for cover. The next time I saw her, I'd tell her to stay away from Emma and me.

Emma was perched on the boathouse steps, waiting for me. In the studio, Dulcie had Wagner turned up loud. I could see her through the door, painting another canvas with dark shades of purple and gray. A stormy day at the lake, I guessed.

"Where have you been?" Emma asked.

"For a walk."

"Did you see Sissy?"

I watched a gull land on one of the dock's pilings. "No," I lied.

"I wonder where she is." Emma gazed up and down the shore, as if hoping to spot Sissy.

"Oh, she'll turn up one of these days," I said, sure it was true. No matter how much I wished she'd go away, Sissy would keep coming back. She probably didn't have any other friends. Who'd want to play with someone like her?

"She'd better. Next to you, she's my best friend." Emma followed me up to the cottage, looking back every now and then, still hoping.

"Let's play a game," I said, thinking I might get her mind off Sissy. "How about Candy Land?"

"Okay." Although she didn't sound very enthusiastic, Emma watched me pull the box down from a shelf stacked with checkers, dominoes, Chinese checkers, Clue, Parcheesi, Chutes and Ladders—everything you could possibly want to play.

I laid the board on the floor between us. While Emma picked out four green playing pieces, I noticed that Mom and Dulcie had written their names in two corners of the board. The handwriting was loopy and childish, and I imagined my mom with a crayon in her hand, laboriously printing "Claire."

"What's that say?" Emma pointed to the names.

"Dulcie and Claire. I guess this was their game."

"How about this?" Emma pointed at a scribbled-over place on the third corner. "What's it say?"

Under a dark smear of black crayon, I made out the letters T-e-r-e-s-a. "Teresa," I whispered. "It says Teresa."

I stared at the board. A little prickle as sharp as a razor raced up my spine and tickled my scalp. *Teresa. T for Teresa.* The girl torn from the photograph, the girl I dreamed about—was her name Teresa?

"Why did somebody scribble on her name?" Emma asked.

"I don't know," I said. But I'd find out.

"Maybe Mommy didn't like her," Emma said.

"Maybe not." Suddenly uneasy, I picked up the dice. It was

weird how the cottage changed when evening shadows gathered in its corners. "Do you want to go first?"

We played three rounds, but it was hard for me to keep my mind on the silly game. My eyes returned again and again to Teresa's name. Who was she? Why was her name almost hidden by layers of black crayon? Why had she been ripped out of that photograph? I had to find out.

At the dinner table, Dulcie asked us what we'd done all afternoon. "We played Candy Land," Emma said. "I won two games, and Ali won one. She says I'm a champ." She held up her arms and flexed her muscles.

Dulcie laughed. "You've always been a champ."

Emma paused, her fork halfway to her mouth. "Who was Teresa, Mommy?"

"Teresa?" Dulcie stared at Emma, her body tense. "I don't know anyone named Teresa. Why?" She quickly got to her feet and began to gather the plates. The knives and forks rattled, the glasses clinked.

"She wrote her name on your Candy Land game." Emma followed Dulcie to the kitchen. "But somebody scribbled all over it with black crayon."

"I don't know what you're talking about." Dulcie scraped leftovers into the trash, her face hidden.

"I'll show you." Emma ran to the living room and came back with the Candy Land board. "See? Here's your name and Aunt Claire's name, and right there is Teresa's name."

Dulcie glanced at the board and shrugged. "Our mom used to buy stuff at church rummage sales. Some girl named Teresa probably owned the game before us, so we wrote our names and scribbled hers out."

It was a good explanation, but I didn't quite believe it. Something about that name upset Dulcie. She was tense, anxious.

"Remember that photo I told you about?" I asked her. "The one where the girl had been torn out? Well, her name started with *T*, and I was wondering—"

"Will you please stop talking about it? How often do I have to tell you? I don't know Teresa, I don't know why her name is on that stupid game board, and I don't know who the girl in the picture was! She could have been named Tillie or Trudy or Toni."

Dulcie's sharp voice startled both Emma and me. I stared at my aunt, puzzled. Why was she so angry?

"Don't be mad, Mommy," Emma begged, close to tears.

"I'm not mad." Dulcie plunged her hands into the soapy water and began washing the dishes with swift, jerky movements. If she weren't careful, she'd break everything in the sink.

I grabbed a dish towel. "Want me to dry?"

Keeping her back turned, Dulcie shook her head. "I'd rather you read to Emma."

"But, Mommy," Emma began.

"Go with Ali," Dulcie said. "I need some time to myself."

Emma followed me into the living room and sat beside me, her small face glum.

I put my arm around her and drew her so close I could smell the sweet scent of her hair. "Would you like to hear another chapter about the Moffats?" I asked.

Emma nodded and snuggled against me. While I read, I thought about my aunt's reaction to Emma's questions. She remembered Teresa, I was sure she did. Why wouldn't she admit it?

9

The next morning, I slept late, probably because I'd tossed and turned most of the night, dreaming about Teresa. When I stumbled downstairs, eager for orange juice, I found Emma sitting at the kitchen table with Sissy. Turning her face so only I could see it, she smiled her smirky smile.

"Look who's here!" Emma cried, obviously delighted. "Sissy came to play with me!"

"Whoop-di-do," I muttered. "Where's Dulcie?"

"In her studio. She's got lots to do today, so we shouldn't bother her."

I took my seat at the table. Dulcie had already filled a bowl with my favorite cereal. As I added milk, I was aware of Sissy sitting beside me, close enough to touch. I wasn't in the mood to put up with her. Not after a bad night's sleep.

Ignoring me, Sissy busied herself pushing Cheerios around her bowl with her spoon, sinking them into the milk and watching them pop up again. As far as I could see, she hadn't eaten any of them.

I tapped her shoulder to get her attention. "It's bad manners to play with food." Even to myself, I sounded like a crabby old lady.

"So?" Sissy shrugged and continued to stir the cereal into a gloppy mess.

"So, if Dulcie was nice enough to fix cereal for you, you should eat it."

"Dulcie didn't give me this. Emma did. I told her I wasn't hungry, but she fixed it anyway."

I looked at Emma, and she nodded. "Mommy wasn't here when Sissy came, so I got to be the hostess."

"I hate cereal unless it's got lots of sugar on it." With a frown, Sissy pushed her bowl away. "Let's go to the lake, Emmy."

"I still have my jammies on."

"Get dressed, then, slowpoke." Sissy followed us into the living room and flopped on the couch. "I'll wait here."

Leaving Sissy looking at a magazine, I took Emma to her room and helped her out of her pajamas and into her favorite yellow bathing suit.

Emma ran to the living room to make sure Sissy was still there, and I dashed upstairs and yanked on my bathing suit. When I came down, Sissy was looking at the names written on the Candy Land board. The minute she saw me, she shoved it aside. The board fell off the table and onto the floor with a faint thud.

"Candy Land is a baby's game," Sissy told me. "I outgrew it a long time ago."

"Emma likes it," I said.

"No, I don't." Emma stood in the doorway, frowning as if I'd betrayed her. "I'm way too big to play it."

"You weren't too big last night," I reminded her.

"Well, today I am!" Emma flounced past me and smiled at Sissy. "Do you want to swim or build castles?"

"Both." Sissy let Emma take her hand. I followed the two of them outside.

At the top of the steps, Sissy looked back at me. "You aren't invited."

"Sorry, but Emma doesn't go anywhere without me," I said.

"I don't need you to baby-sit me," Emma protested. She was

learning to scowl exactly like Sissy. The nasty expression didn't suit her sweet little face. Nor did the sly look she gave Sissy, hoping for her approval.

Sissy ran down the steps ahead of Emma and me and stopped at the bottom, almost as if she was afraid to go farther. "Is your mother in the studio?"

Emma nodded. "She's painting a big picture of the lake, all dark and scary, like a storm's coming." She reached for Sissy's hand. "Want to see it?"

"Dulcie'd love to meet you," I added.

Sissy took a quick look through the open door. Dulcie stood with her back to us, hard at work on another painting, darker than the first two. *Lake View Three,* she was calling this one.

"Hi, Mommy," Emma called. "We're going swimming!"

Sissy drew in her breath sharply and ducked away, as if she didn't want to be seen. Not that it mattered. Without turning around, Dulcie said, "Stay close to shore, Emma. Knee-deep, remember?"

Sissy ran to the end of the dock and posed in a diving position. Her tanned skin contrasted with her faded bathing suit and her pale hair. "Dare me?" she called to Emma.

"Not unless you swim really good," Emma said uncertainly.

"The water's over your head," I added.

"I'll do it, if you do it," Sissy said to Emma.

"No." I grabbed the straps of Emma's suit. "Emma can't swim."

"I can so!" Emma struggled to escape.

I held her tighter. "You're not allowed to jump off the dock unless your mother's here."

"Do you do everything Mommy says?" Sissy asked Emma. "Are you a little goody-goody girl?"

Emma looked confused.

"She has rules," I told Sissy, "like everyone."

"Not me," said Sissy. "I don't have any rules at all. I do whatever I want." With that, she jumped off the dock and hit the water with a big splash. She popped back up almost at once, laughing and spluttering. "Emma's a baby. She sucks her thumb and poops her pants and drinks from a bottle."

Emma began to cry. "I'm not a baby. I'm almost five years old. I can do whatever I want, too!"

With a sudden twist, Emma broke away from me and ran to the edge of the dock. Before I could stop her, she'd leapt into the lake. One second she was beside me, the next she was gone. I stared at the water in disbelief, too surprised to move.

In a few seconds, Emma's head emerged, eyes shut, mouth open, gasping for breath. Before she could sink again, I was in the lake beside her, holding her the way the lifeguard had taught me in swimming class.

Emma clung to me but turned her head to shout at Sissy, "See? I'm not a baby!"

Sissy paddled closer. Her hair floated on the water like pale yellow seaweed. "I bet you wouldn't jump if Ali wasn't here."

"I'll always be here," I told Sissy. To Emma I said, "If you do that again, I'll tell your mother."

"Tattletale, tattletale," Sissy taunted. "Nobody likes tattletales."

"I'll jump again if I want," Emma said, but she made no effort to break away from me. I had a feeling she'd scared herself. The water was deep, and she couldn't do much more than dog-paddle a few feet.

On the sand, the three of us built castles. Neither Emma nor

Sissy said a word to me. They sat close together, their heads almost touching, whispering and giggling.

"It's rude to whisper," I told Emma.

Sissy smirked. "So? Nobody invited you to play with us."

Emma carefully duplicated Sissy's smirk. "Why don't you go home? Sissy can be my babysitter."

"Two's company, three's a crowd," Sissy added. "Don't you know that yet?"

"If anyone should go home, you should!" I wanted to slap Sissy's nasty little face, but I knew that would only make things worse.

"Just ignore Ali," Sissy told Emma. "We don't like her, and we don't care what she says or what she does. She's mean."

"Meanie," Emma said. "Ali's a big fat meanie."

"Ali's so mean, Hell wouldn't want her." Sissy's eyes gleamed with malice.

Emma stared at her new friend, shocked, I think, by the word "Hell." Sissy smiled and bent over her castle, already bigger than the one she'd built yesterday. "It's not bad to say 'Hell,'" she told Emma. "It's in the Bible."

Emma glanced at me to see what I thought about this. I shook my head, but Sissy pulled Emma close and began whispering in her ear. Emma looked surprised. Then she giggled and whispered something in Sissy's ear that made her laugh.

I pulled Emma away. "What are you telling her?" I asked Sissy.

"Nothing." Sissy pressed her hands over her mouth and laughed.

"Nothing." Emma covered her mouth and laughed, too. She sounded just like Sissy.

I wanted to get up and leave, but I couldn't abandon Emma.

Instead, I moved a few feet away and watched the two of them. Their castles grew bigger and more elaborate. Everything Sissy did to hers, Emma copied. It was pathetic.

"It's nearly lunchtime," I told Emma. "Why don't we go back to the studio and get your mom?"

"Do you want to eat lunch with me?" Emma asked Sissy.

She shook her head. "It's almost time for me to go home."

"I thought you didn't have any rules," I said. "I thought you could do whatever you want."

Sissy gave me a long cold look. "Maybe I *want* to go home."

"But you don't have to go," Emma persisted. "My mommy's very nice. She fixes good peanut butter and jelly sandwiches."

Sissy made a face. "I hate peanut butter and jelly sandwiches."

"I hate them, too," Emma put in quickly. "Mommy can fix something else for us. Tuna salad, maybe."

I happened to know Emma despised tuna salad, but I didn't say anything. What was the use? She probably thought it sounded more grown up than peanut butter and jelly.

"I don't want to eat at your house." Sissy looked at me. "Not with Ali there."

"Maybe we could have a picnic, just you and me," Emma said. "Outside on the deck."

"Some other time." Sissy stood up and looked down at the castles. "They're pretty enough for a mermaid to live in," she said. "Do you like mermaids, Em?"

"I saw *The Little Mermaid* ten, twelve, a dozen times. It's my favorite movie."

Sissy tossed her head to get her hair out of her eyes. "Twelve is the same as a dozen, dummy."

"I'm not a dummy," Emma said. "I just—"

With a sudden jerk of her foot, Sissy kicked Emma's castle down.

"You ruined my castle," Emma wailed. "Now a mermaid can't live in it."

"Hey!" With a couple of kicks, I leveled Sissy's castle. "There! How do you like that?"

"I don't care." Sissy laughed. "I can build another one, better than that, and so can Emma. We have all summer to build castles for mermaids."

She laughed louder. After a moment's hesitation, Emma joined in. Shouting with laughter, they held hands and spun round and round in circles until they staggered and sprawled on the sand, still laughing.

I stared at them, slightly worried, maybe even scared of their behavior. "What's so funny?"

"Everything," Sissy giggled. "The whole stupid world is funny."

"Ali's funny." Emma laughed shrilly. "Mommy's funny. You're funny. I'm funny. The lake's funny, the seagulls are funny, the—"

Suddenly, Sissy stopped laughing. Her face turned mean. "Shut up!" she shouted at Emma. "*You* aren't funny. You're stupid. And you're a copycat."

"I'm not a copycat." Obviously bewildered by Sissy's mood change, Emma began to cry.

"Baby, baby copycat," Sissy chanted, "sat on a tack and ate a rat." Without looking back, she ran toward the Cove, still chanting.

Emma threw herself against me and pounded me with her fists. "Look what you did! You made Sissy mad! Why can't you leave us alone?"

I grabbed Emma's shoulders and held her away from me. Little as she was, her punches hurt. "I didn't do anything to that brat. She's a troublemaker, she's mean to you, she's——"

"Don't you talk like that. Sissy's my friend!"

"Some friend," I muttered. "Calling you a baby, daring you to jump off the dock, knocking your castle down. Why do you want to be friends with a girl like her?"

"You're just mad 'cause she likes me, not you."

"Don't be silly. I don't like *her*. Why should I care that she doesn't like *me?*"

"Sissy says you're jealous—that's why you don't like her, that's why you're not nice to her. You want me all to yourself!" Emma muttered.

I stared at her, amazed. "How can you believe that?"

"'Cause it's true!" Emma shouted. "Sissy doesn't lie!"

With that, she ran away from me. Surprised by the speed of her skinny little legs, I chased her. What would Dulcie think if Emma came home crying?

By the time I caught up with her, it was too late. She'd flung herself into her mother's arms.

"I hate Ali!" she sobbed. "Make her go home. I don't want a babysitter!"

Dulcie looked at me, perplexed by Emma's words. "What's going on?"

"I'll tell you later." Without waiting for my aunt or my cousin, I trudged up the steps toward the cottage.

If Dulcie wanted to send me home, fine. Sissy had turned Emma into a nasty little brat, just like herself, and I was sick of both of them.

10

Dulcie fixed the usual peanut butter and jelly sandwiches and chocolate milk for lunch.

Emma pushed her plate away. "I don't like peanut butter and jelly," she whined.

Dulcie looked at her in surprise. "Since when?"

"Since now." Out went Emma's lower lip in a classic pout. "They're for babies."

"What do you mean? Ali and I eat them. We're not babies."

"I want cheese," Emma said.

"I thought you liked tuna salad," I said.

Emma glared at me. "I can like whatever I like!"

Dulcie put her hands over mine and Emma's. "Would you girls please tell me what's going on?"

"It's Sissy's fault," I told her. "She's a bad influence on Emma."

"She is not!" Emma scowled at me.

"Then why was she so nasty to you?" I asked, trying to stay calm.

"She wasn't," Emma said. "*You* were!"

I stared at my cousin, truly shocked. "What did *I* do?"

Emma turned to her mother tearfully. "Ali called me stupid and said I was a baby."

"I did not!" I told Dulcie. "I'd never say anything like that. Sissy called her names, not me."

Emma climbed into her mother's lap and began to cry. "Ali's not nice to me and Sissy," she insisted. "Just 'cause she's bigger, she thinks she's the boss."

Dulcie rocked Emma, but her eyes were on me. I had a sick feeling that my aunt wasn't sure which one of us to believe. From her mother's lap, Emma watched me closely, her face almost as mean as Sissy's.

"It's not true," I said weakly. "Sissy—"

"Ali pushed me off the dock, too," Emma interrupted. "If Sissy hadn't been there, I would have drowned—"

"That's a lie and you know it, Emma!" Close to tears I turned to Dulcie. "Sissy dared Emma to jump. I tried to stop her, but she got away from me. She wants to do everything Sissy does."

Dulcie looked from Emma to me and back to Emma, her eyes worried. "I can't believe Ali would push you off the dock, Emma."

"Yes, she would," Emma insisted. "Ali's so bad, even Hell doesn't want her."

"Emma!" Dulcie stared at her daughter. "Where did you pick up that kind of talk?"

I spoke before Emma had a chance to answer. "Sissy told her cussing was fine. She could say whatever she wanted."

Dulcie stood Emma on the floor and got to her feet. "I've heard enough. Sit down and eat your sandwich."

"I don't want any stinky lunch!" Emma started to run out of the kitchen, but Dulcie grabbed her arm and stopped her. "What's gotten into you?" she asked. "You've never acted like this before. Never."

"I told you," I said. "It's Sissy's fault."

Dulcie ignored me. This was between her and Emma. "Sit down," she said. "And eat your lunch."

Emma took her place between Dulcie and me. She didn't look at either of us but ate quietly, her head down, her jaws working as she chewed. She left half the sandwich on her plate, despite Dulcie's pleas to eat it all.

"Do you want me to read a Moffat story?" I asked, hoping to resume our normal relationship.

Emma scowled. "I hate the Moffats. They're dumb. Just like you!"

"Don't talk to Ali like that," Dulcie said. "We never call anyone dumb."

"Leave me alone," Emma said. "You're dumb, too."

Dulcie frowned. "If this is how you act when Sissy comes here, I don't want you to play with her anymore."

Emma responded with a major temper tantrum. She screamed and cried. She told Dulcie she hated her. She threw herself on the floor and kicked.

Finally, Dulcie hauled Emma to her room and put her to bed. Closing the door firmly, she left her to cry herself to sleep.

She dropped back into her chair, her face puzzled. "How can this child have so much influence on Emma so quickly?"

I'd been wondering about this myself. "Maybe it's because Emma's never had a friend before. She wants Sissy to like her, so she does everything Sissy tells her to do."

Dulcie went to the stove and poured herself another cup of coffee. With her back to me, she said, "I guess I really don't know much about kids. Sometimes I wonder if I was ever actually one myself."

She laughed, not as if it was funny, more as if it was sad or odd. "I have friends who remember every detail of their childhoods, their teachers' names, what they wore to someone's birthday party when they were eight years old, what they got for

Christmas when they were ten. Me—I can't remember a thing before my teen years."

Dulcie carried her coffee outside. The way she let the screen door slam shut behind her hinted she wasn't expecting me to follow. She sat at the picnic table, her back to the window, her shoulders hunched. Even without seeing her face, I knew she was unhappy. Maybe her summer wasn't going any better than mine. Who could have imagined a kid like Sissy would turn up and spoil everything?

I stretched out on the sofa with *To Kill a Mockingbird*. I was on the seventh chapter with many more to go.

While I read, I heard a car approaching the cottage. I sat up and looked out the window. For some reason I expected to see Mom and Dad, but a big red Jeep emerged from the woods. Dulcie walked toward it hesitantly, apparently unsure who it was.

"Dulcie, it *is* you!" A plump woman with short silvery blond hair jumped out of the Jeep and stood there grinning as Dulcie approached. Her tailored shorts and pink polo shirt contrasted sharply with my aunt's black T-shirt and paint-spattered jeans.

She stopped just short of giving Dulcie a hug. "Look at you," she exclaimed, "you're just as skinny as ever!"

"I'm sorry," Dulcie said, smoothing her mop of uncombed curls back from her face, "but I don't remember—"

"Well, no wonder. I wasn't this fat when we were kids!" She laughed. "I'm Jeanine Reynolds—Donaldson now. We used to play together when you and Claire came to the lake."

"Jeanine," Dulcie repeated. "Jeanine. . . . I'm afraid I—"

"Oh, don't worry about it. Good grief, it's been what? Thirty years, I guess."

"My sister would probably remember you."

"Is Claire here, too?"

"No, but her daughter, Ali, is staying with us this summer."

Jeanine nodded and looked at the cottage. "It's just the same as I remember. I hear you had Joe Russell working on it. He's good. Not cheap, though."

"Compared to New York, he's a bargain," Dulcie said.

Jeanine sat down at the picnic table. "Is that where you live?"

Dulcie nodded. "Would you like something to drink? I've got mint tea in the fridge, if you'd like that."

"Anything, as long as it's cold," Jeanine said. "Today's a real scorcher."

Leaving the woman on the deck, Dulcie came inside. By then I was in the kitchen, ready to help with cheese and crackers if she wanted them.

Dulcie rolled her eyes. "There goes the afternoon," she whispered.

A few minutes later, I was setting down a tray with an assortment of crackers, cheese, and sliced fruit. Dulcie poured glasses of iced tea for herself and Jeanine and offered me a can of soda. The three of us settled ourselves comfortably under the patio umbrella.

"My daughter, Erin, tells me you're an artist," Jeanine said. "I'm not surprised. When we were kids, you were always drawing. You carried a sketchbook and pencils everywhere we went."

Dulcie smiled as if she were beginning to warm up to Jeanine. "Yes, I guess I did."

"You were so talented. We were always asking you to draw pictures for us. Teresa, especially. She was crazy about your mermaids—remember?"

All traces of friendliness suddenly disappeared from my aunt's face. She gripped her glass of iced tea and shook her head. "No, I don't remember Teresa. Or any mermaids I might have drawn."

I held my breath and waited to hear what Jeanine would say next.

Staring at Dulcie in disbelief, she said, "You *can't* have forgotten Teresa. What happened to her has haunted me all my life—"

"I don't know what you're talking about." Dulcie stood up so fast her chair fell over with a bang that made both Jeanine and me jump. Her hair seemed wilder than before, and her body was so tense, you could have snapped her in two.

She stood there a moment, glass in hand, avoiding our eyes. "Excuse me," she said in a lower voice. "I have work to do, paintings to finish for a show this fall."

Without looking at us, Dulcie left Jeanine and me sitting at the picnic table and ran down to her studio, her sandals flapping on the steps. The door slammed. For a few seconds after that, the only sound was the lake quietly rippling against the shore.

"Oh, dear." Jeanine's face flushed. "I guess I shouldn't have come, but I—well, I've always wondered what became of Claire and Dulcie. I thought—"

She broke off and reached for her car keys. "I'm so sorry, Ali. I never meant to upset your aunt. I hope she, you— Oh, I just don't know why I'm so thoughtless, coming here, bringing up the past." She started to rise from her chair.

I touched her hand to keep her from leaving. "Please tell me what you're talking about. Who was Teresa? What happened to her?"

Jeanine sipped her iced tea silently, her eyes on the horizon and the blue sky beyond. She wanted to finish what she'd started, I could tell.

Sure enough, the next thing she said was, "I don't see how Dulcie could have forgotten that child—or even me, for that matter. The two of us spent a lot of time at this cottage, especially

Teresa. Why, your grandmother used to call us her borrowed daughters."

She paused to watch a squirrel dart across the deck and leap onto a pine tree. A branch swayed, and he was gone. Her eyes turned back to me. "Your mother didn't tell you about Teresa?"

I toyed with my empty soda can, turning it this way and that. "Mom never talks about the lake. She hates it so much, she almost didn't let me come with Dulcie." I hesitated and rubbed the wet ring my soda can had made on the table. "You saw how Dulcie is—she claims she doesn't remember anything. But—" I stopped, not sure what to tell Jeanine. Her face was kind, her eyes understanding, and I desperately wanted to talk to someone about Teresa.

"But what?" Jeanine helped herself to another slice of cheese.

I watched her sandwich the cheese between two crackers. "Well, before Dulcie invited me here, I found an old photo of her and Mom when they were kids. Another girl had been sitting beside Dulcie, but someone had torn her out of the picture. On the back, all that was left of her name was a *T*. Mom got really upset and swore she didn't know anyone whose name started with *T*."

"And you think it was Teresa," Jeanine said.

"The lake was in the background, so it *must* have been her."

Jeanine nodded and helped herself to another piece of cheese. She seemed to be waiting for me to tell her more.

"Last night, I got out an old Candy Land game," I went on. "Mom and Dulcie had written their names on the board. Teresa's name was there, too. But someone had scribbled over it with a black crayon. Dulcie said she didn't know why 'Teresa' was written on the board. She got mad and shouted at me."

I lowered my head, almost ashamed to finish. "Dulcie remembers Teresa—I'm sure she does. Why would she lie about it?"

"Maybe it has something to do with Teresa's death." As she spoke, Jeanine looked at the lake, her face expressionless.

"Teresa *died?*" Shocked, I gripped the soda can and stared at Jeanine. I'd never imagined Teresa dead. All this time, I'd pictured her living around here somewhere, stopping by for a visit, forcing Dulcie to remember her. "How did she die?"

"It was the last summer your mother and aunt came to the lake." Jeanine sipped her tea. "For some reason, no one knows why, Teresa went out in your grandfather's canoe all by herself. It was rainy, foggy. The canoe washed up nearby, but . . ."

Shivers raced up and down my bare arms.

Jeanine looked at me, and a shadow crossed her face—worry, maybe. "I hope I haven't upset you." She patted my hand, white knuckled from its grip on the soda can. "Teresa's been gone a long time now."

She broke a cracker into pieces and tossed the crumbs to a pair of sparrows hopping around our feet. For a moment, she sat silently, watching the birds fight over the crumbs. Without looking at me, she said, "It must have been very painful for Claire and Dulcie. It certainly was for me."

She threw more crumbs to the sparrows. Several others arrived, as if word had gotten out that food was available.

"What was Teresa like?" I asked at last.

"Just an ordinary kid, I guess. Smart, kind of cute, but . . ." While Jeanine talked, her eyes drifted from the sparrows to the bumblebees droning in the hollyhocks.

"But what?"

"Oh, nothing. I'm just running my mouth, as usual." She looked at her watch. "My goodness, it's almost time for supper, and I haven't got a thing in the house. I'd better go."

Jumping to her feet, Jeanine gave me a quick hug. "Please don't worry about what I told you. It happened so long ago. Maybe your aunt and your mother really have forgotten. After all, they didn't spend the rest of their lives here, listening to people talk about poor Teresa."

After landing a kiss on my cheek, Jeanine hurried to the Jeep. "Tell Dulcie I'd love to see her again," she called, ". . . if she wants to see me."

With a smile and a wave, she put the Jeep in reverse and backed down the drive.

Long after Jeanine left, I sat on the deck, gazing out at the lake's calm water. No wonder Mom hadn't wanted me, her one and only child, to spend the summer here. No wonder she was scared of water and boats. No wonder she feared for my safety. If Teresa could drown, so could I.

But I had a feeling there was more to Teresa's death—much more. Jeanine hadn't told me all she knew. She'd been edgy, nervous, uneasy. While she'd talked, she'd looked at everything but me: the lake, the sparrows, the bumblebees in the hollyhocks. And she'd left in a hurry, before I'd had a chance to ask her any more questions.

It seemed the answer to one question always led to another question. And that answer to another question, and so on and so on. Was anything ever settled and done with?

11

I was still sitting on the deck, half asleep in the afternoon sun, when I heard Emma's bare feet patter into the kitchen. The refrigerator door opened and shut. Soon she was staring at me from the doorway. A purple Popsicle dripped down her arm and stained her mouth.

"You can't make Sissy go away," Emma said. "She'll be my friend forever, no matter what." Her face was closed off and hostile.

Grumpy and out of sorts from the heat, I frowned at Emma. "Your mother doesn't want you to play with Sissy anymore."

Emma sucked her Popsicle, leaching the purple out, something I'd enjoyed doing when I was her age. "Mommy can't make Sissy go away. No one can."

I picked up a *New Yorker* magazine and fanned myself. I was tired of the conversation, if you could call it that. "Do you want to go swimming?"

Emma studied the colorless lump of ice on the Popsicle stick. "With you?"

"I don't see anyone else. Do you?"

"Not now." Emma scowled at me. "But I bet we'll see Sissy later." With that, she stalked off to her room. I followed to see if she needed help with her bathing suit.

"I can do it myself," she said and closed the door in my face.

A few minutes later, the two us were wading in the shallow

water along the shore. To my relief—and Emma's disappointment—Sissy wasn't in sight. The ruined castles lay where we'd left them. Emma knelt beside hers and began to repair it.

Leaving my pouty little cousin to work on her castle, I began collecting interesting stones and driftwood. I hadn't talked to Dulcie about my idea yet, but I was sure she'd let me use her potter's wheel.

After a while, Emma came over and nudged my pile of stones with her toe. "Want to play in the water?"

I took her hand, and we waded into the lake. Emma seemed almost herself. She splashed and dog-paddled in the shallow water, wallowing like a puppy.

When I noticed her lips and nails turning blue, I led her to shore and dried her with a big beach towel.

"Do you want to go back to the cottage?" I asked. "You're shivering."

Emma shook her head. Droplets of water flew from her wet hair. She spread the towel on a sunny patch of sand and sat on it. I saw her glance toward the Cove as if hoping to see Sissy.

"Why did Sissy get mad at me?" Emma asked. "We were having fun and laughing, and then all of a sudden she got mad."

I wasn't sure what to say. If I criticized Sissy, Emma would get cranky again. To avoid that, I shrugged and said I didn't know why Sissy acted the way she did. "Some kids are like that."

Emma hung her head and toyed with strands of her wet hair. "Sissy mixes me up," she whispered. "Sometimes she's nice, and other times she's mean."

"Maybe we should go to the Cove tomorrow," I said, "and find some other kids for you to play with."

Emma hunched her bony shoulders. "I don't want any friend but Sissy."

I lifted her chin so I could see her face. "You just admitted she's mean. Why do you like her so much?"

Emma pulled away, pouty again. "I wished and wished for a friend, and she came."

I looked at her more closely. "Wishing didn't have anything to do with it. You were at the beach, and she was there at the same time. That's how people meet."

Emma poked at the sand with a stick. "She came because I wanted her to come."

"That's what you think." Sissy stood a few feet away, her hands on her hips, her hair a cottony tangle. "Nobody can make me do anything. I only do what *I* want to do."

"Where did *you* come from?" I was definitely not happy to see her.

Sissy pointed toward the woods behind us. "I sneaked up on you, didn't I? I'm as quiet as an Indian."

All smiles, Emma jumped to her feet and ran to grab Sissy's hand. "I was scared you were mad at me."

Pulling her hand away, Sissy flopped down beside me. "How old are you?"

"Thirteen. Why?"

"Do you have a boyfriend?"

"No."

"When my sister was thirteen, she had a boyfriend." Sissy looked me over, taking in my skinny legs and arms. "She had a really good figure, and she wore lipstick and nail polish. She was pretty, too. In fact, she won a beauty contest when she was only fifteen—Miss Webster's Cove. She got to ride in a motorboat parade and throw roses in the water." Sissy hugged her knees to her chest as if she was holding tight to the memory.

"I didn't know you had a sister." Emma squeezed in between Sissy and me. "Why doesn't she ever come here with you?"

Sissy picked up a small scallop shell and examined it. "She's grown up now. Why would she want to hang out with kids?"

"What's her name?" Emma asked. "How old is she? Is she still Miss Webster's Cove?"

"Don't you know it's rude to ask so many questions?" Tossing the shell away, Sissy jumped to her feet and pointed at the lake. "Look at those guys out there."

Not far from shore, two boys sped toward us in a motorboat, towing a suntanned girl on water skis. Over the engine's noise, we heard them laughing and shouting to each other.

"Lucky ducks," Sissy said. "I wish I had a boyfriend with a boat." Her voice was so full of longing, I almost felt sorry for her.

"You're too young to have a boyfriend," I said. "Just wait till you're a teenager. You'll have plenty of boys to take you waterskiing."

"Don't be stupid." Sissy pulled at a strand of hair, her face angry. "I'll never have a boyfriend."

"Why do you care?" Emma said. "Boys are dumb."

Sissy gave her a look intended to wither. "What do *you* know about boys?"

Emma drew in her breath and edged away from Sissy. She wasn't about to argue.

"I'm hot," Sissy said. "Let's go swimming."

Emma jumped up and splashed into the lake behind Sissy. I followed, letting the cold water creep up my legs, chilling my skin. When she was waist deep, Sissy dove in and disappeared.

A few seconds later she popped out of the water and ducked Emma. The moment Emma came up for air, Sissy ducked her again. And again. And again. Her face was angry, her eyes cruel.

By the time I pulled Emma away, she was spluttering and coughing.

"What were you doing?" I shouted at Sissy. "You could drown somebody that way!"

Sissy paddled a few feet away, her anger replaced with a sly grin. "I was just fooling around," she said. "Don't get so worked up."

"You scared Emma."

"Can't you two take a joke?"

"It wasn't funny!" I yelled.

Emma clung to me, shivering and crying. "I want to go home!" she wailed.

"That's just where we're going." I stalked back to shore, carrying Emma. "You go home, too, Sissy. And don't come back till you can be nice."

Sissy stayed where she was, knee-deep in the lake, a skinny kid in a faded bathing suit. "I was playing," she yelled after us. "That's all. It was a game."

I guessed that was the closest to an apology we'd ever hear from Sissy. But I was still mad. And Emma was still upset.

"Never do that again!" I shouted.

With a smirk, Sissy spread her hands, palms out, and sloshed to shore. Turning toward the Cove, she walked away.

For once, Emma wasn't sorry to see her go.

The next morning was bright and sunny, a perfect day—too pretty to work, Dulcie said. Instead of going to the studio, she loaded Emma and me into the car and headed for the ocean. We explored the rocky cliffs and the lighthouse at Pemaquid Point, and threw bread crumbs to the seagulls like all the other tourists. We stopped in Boothbay and browsed in art galleries and craft shops. I bought two Maine T-shirts, one for me and one for my friend Staci. Dulcie treated Emma to a fuzzy handmade bear, a notebook with a hand-tooled leather cover for me, and warm wool sweaters for all three of us. On the way home, we stuffed ourselves at a fudge factory.

The next day was just as perfect as the day before. Dulcie took us to a dairy farm, where we bought slabs of pale cheese and jars of honey and blueberry preserves. We spent the afternoon riding rented horses on wooded trails.

The sunshine came to an end with an evening thunderstorm. A heavy rain fell all night and into the next morning. At breakfast, Dulcie frowned at the gray skies. "Back to work," she said glumly.

Just as Emma and I began a game of Candy Land, we heard what sounded like a scream or a shout of some kind.

"What was that?" Emma whispered.

"I don't know." I went to the door and peered out into the rain, my heart thumping with fear. Had it been a cry for help? Someone drowning?

Dulcie came running toward me, her hair wild from the wind and the rain. Her wet, paint-smeared T-shirt clung to her skinny frame, and her faded jeans dripped water.

"It's your mother," I told Emma. "Something's wrong."

Emma knocked the board aside, scattering the playing pieces, and ran outside. I followed her, unable to imagine what had happened, and stared at my aunt fearfully. I'd never seen her cry, never seen her so upset.

"My paintings," Dulcie wailed. "Someone broke into the

studio and wrecked everything. All my work, my paints, my brushes."

Emma clung to her mother. "Mommy, Mommy," she sobbed. "Don't cry."

"I can't believe it," I whispered. "Who would do something like that?"

"Come and look." Dulcie ran back down the stairs to the studio.

Emma and I hurried after her. The rain pelted us, and we held tightly to the railing, afraid of slipping on the wet steps.

From the studio's doorway, Dulcie gestured at the wreckage. It looked as if someone had thrown bucketsful of sand and lake water on the floor. Paint tubes were scattered, tops off, colors oozing out. Brushes stiff with dried paint littered the worktable. Splattered with ugly shades of reds, yellows, and green, the paintings lay in a heap in a corner.

One painting leaned against the easel. In black paint and large clumsy letters, someone had scrawled:

I'M WATCHING YOU
TELL THE TRUTH
OR ELSE

Emma clutched her mother's hand and pointed at the painting. "Bones," she whispered. "There's bones at the bottom."

I drew in my breath. She was right. In the painting's lower right-hand corner, in the darkest part, was a small, clumsily drawn skeleton.

Hiding her face, Emma cried, "I don't want to see the bones."

I didn't want to see them, either. As scared as Emma, I looked at Dulcie. "Do you think it's—" I broke off, afraid to say Teresa's name. The damp air was full of her, she was everywhere, I could almost feel her cold hands touching my shoulders.

In a fury, Dulcie pulled away from Emma and grabbed a tube of black paint. She squeezed what was left of it on the painting, spreading it with her hands until she'd covered the words and the bones. "There—it's gone!"

"But—"

Dulcie turned on me. "I don't want to hear another word about this. It's a case of teenage vandalism—that's all." She picked up a broom. "Now, if you don't mind, I want to clean up."

I backed away, hurt by the anger in her voice. "Can't I help?"

"Take Emma to the cottage, read to her, play games, do what I hired you to do." Dulcie gripped the broom so tightly her knuckles whitened. The veins in her neck stood out like knotted cords, and she was shaking. "I'll take care of this."

I reached for Emma's hand, but she clung to Dulcie. "I want to stay with you, Mommy. Let me help you."

"You heard what I said. Go with Ali and leave me alone." Dulcie freed herself from Emma and began sweeping the sand toward the door. Underneath her mop of wild hair, her face was an odd colorless shade—ashen, I guess, like people in shock.

Emma began to cry, but Dulcie was in no mood to sympathize. "Please, Ali, take her to the cottage."

Somehow I managed to haul Emma up the steps, rain and wind and all, and get her inside.

"Mommy's mad at me," Emma sobbed. "She hates me."

"No, Em, she's not mad, just upset." Trying to comfort her, I began stripping her wet clothes off, not easy when your hands are shaking. Dulcie's anger had frightened me. I'd never seen her behave like that. But the words and the skeleton scribbled on the painting had scared me even more.

As I rubbed Emma dry with a big soft towel, I stared out the window. All I saw was rain. All I heard was the wind in the pines and the monotonous lapping of lake water. I shivered, suddenly sure something was out there, hidden in the trees, watching us.

I helped Emma into a T-shirt and fastened her overall buckles. Warm and dry, she was still shivering. After I changed my clothes, I fixed cookies and hot chocolate. Then I read all three *Lonely Doll* stories, trying to comfort myself as well as Emma.

By the time we settled down to play Candy Land, we were both feeling pretty normal. Maybe Dulcie was right. The boys we'd seen in the motorboat could have vandalized the studio.

But why had they left that message? What did they think Dulcie was lying about? Why did they draw bones on her painting? It didn't make sense.

Let Dulcie believe what she wanted, especially if it made her feel better, but those boys hadn't vandalized her studio. Someone else had.

Emma shook the dice and made her green man hop along the road to Candy Land. "Your turn, Ali."

I shook the dice and moved my blue man seven steps closer to the corner where Teresa had written her name.

What really happened the day Teresa drowned?

~3 12 3~

A sudden rattling sound at the front door startled me. I wasn't sure what I expected to see, but for once I was almost glad it was Sissy. Nose pressed against the screen, she yanked at the door, hooked tight against the wind. "Let me in!"

Emma went to the door. Without opening it, she frowned at Sissy. "You can't come in unless you promise to be nice."

"I *told* you I was just fooling around," Sissy said. "You have to learn to take a little teasing."

"But—"

"Can I come in or not?"

Emma reached up and slowly unhooked the door. "If you're mean, you have to go home."

Good for you, Emma, I thought.

"You're all wet," Emma said.

"It's raining," Sissy said. "Or didn't you notice?"

"Aren't you cold?" I asked.

Sissy shook her head. Her wet hair swung, spraying water like a dog shaking itself.

"But all you have on is a bathing suit."

"So? You wear a bathing suit to go in the water. What difference does it make if you get it wet in the rain or in the lake?" Sissy's voice dripped sarcasm, just as her hair dripped water, but her teeth chattered as she spoke, and her lips were blue with cold.

I grabbed a towel from the bathroom and handed it to her. "Dry yourself off. You're dripping all over the floor."

"Do you want a sweatshirt?" Emma asked.

Sissy shrugged. Taking that as a yes, Emma ran to her room and returned with a bright yellow Winnie the Pooh sweatshirt.

"I'm not wearing that," Sissy said. "I hate yellow, and I hate Pooh."

"I do, too," Emma said quickly, even though I knew it was her favorite sweatshirt, my birthday present to her last year.

"Then why do you think I want to wear it?" Sissy asked.

Poor Emma was in over her head, and she knew it. Shoulders drooping, she walked back to her room, dragging the sweatshirt behind her.

"That wasn't very nice," I told Sissy. "Maybe you should go home—like Emma told you."

Without answering, Sissy did a little dance around the living room. She turned and spun, hair and towel flying, then collapsed on the couch.

"I used to have this book." Sissy picked up *The Lonely Doll* and leafed through it, pausing now and then to look at an illustration. "Where do you think Edith's parents are? Does she live all by herself?"

"I don't know. It never says."

"It's kind of strange, don't you think? A little girl living alone, and then these bears come along, and Mr. Bear's like her father and Little Bear's like her brother, but there's still no mother."

Sissy waited to hear my opinion. "I never really thought about it," I admitted.

"It bothered me when I was little," Sissy said quietly. "But now it's just another silly kid story." She tossed the book aside and looked around the living room. "Where's the TV?"

"We don't have one. My aunt hates TV. She says it rots your mind."

"She sure has some stupid ideas." Sissy slid down lower on the couch, stretching her skinny legs way out in front of her. "I don't have a TV, either. I was really hoping you did."

I felt a little twinge of hope. Maybe she would stop coming around now that she knew there was no TV to watch. "I'm going to see if Emma's okay," I said.

"She's one spoiled kiddo," Sissy said.

"It takes one to know one," I muttered under my breath.

I found Emma in her room, surrounded by heaps of clothing she'd pulled out of her bureau. Holding up a faded red sweatshirt, she said, "Do you think Sissy will like this? It even has a hood."

"Oh, Emma," I sighed. "Stop trying to please her. She promised to be nice, remember? And now she's being her usual horrible self."

Ignoring me, Emma ran down the hall to the living room. "How's this, Sissy? It used to be Mommy's. It's too big for me, but I bet it's just right for you."

Sissy took the sweatshirt and slipped it over her head. "It's kind of ugly, but at least it's not yellow."

"Want to play a different game? We have Clue and checkers and Parcheesi and—"

"I'm bored by board games." Sissy laughed. "Get it? Bored and board?"

Emma laughed to please Sissy, but I don't think she understood the joke. Not that it was very funny. I didn't even bother to smile.

"Where's your mother?" Sissy asked Emma.

"She's in her studio." Emma frowned. "Some bad teenagers

wrecked it last night. They ruined all her paintings, and Mommy got mad."

Sissy glanced at me and smoothed her damp hair behind her ears. "It was probably kids from Union Mills. They're always doing stuff like that. My sister dated a boy from there, but Daddy chased him off. He was no-good white trash, Daddy said."

For a second, a look of sadness crossed Sissy's face, but it was gone so fast, I wasn't sure if I'd really seen it.

Emma nodded as if she knew all about the no-good white trash in Union Mills, but Sissy leaned toward me, her cold eyes fixed on mine. "Did Dulcie call the cops?"

I shook my head. "Not yet."

"It would be a waste of time. They'd never figure out who did it. If you want to know the truth, the cops in this town are morons."

I slid away from her, tired of her know-it-all attitude about everything. "What makes you think you know anything about the police?"

"Just listen to this." Sissy scooted toward me, closing the gap between us. "Did Dulcie ever tell you about Teresa?"

"The girl who drowned in the lake?"

Emma stared at me. "Teresa's dead?"

"That's what usually happens when you drown," Sissy said, laughing again at her own joke.

I'd forgotten Emma didn't know, but it was too late to take the words back. "It was a long time ago," I told her, "way back when your mom and my mom were little."

"Poor Teresa, poor, poor Teresa." Emma shuddered and moved closer to me.

I put an arm around her. "It's very sad," I whispered to her, "but don't cry, please don't."

Emma sniffed and wiped her eyes with her hands. With one finger, she touched Teresa's name on the game board. "She wrote this," she told Sissy. "She played here before . . . before she . . ."

"Before she *died*," Sissy finished Emma's sentence. Turning to me, she said, "You know what else? The cops never found Teresa's body. *That's* how dumb they are. Teresa's parents couldn't even bury her!"

Emma pressed her face against my side and covered her ears. Almost as shocked as Emma, I hugged my cousin and stared wordlessly at Sissy.

She sat back, enjoying the effect of her story. "Poor old Teresa. Her bones are still out there someplace, deep down in the dark, dark water. All cold and lonely."

"Is Teresa a ghost?" Emma asked in a shaky voice. "Do her bones come out?"

"Maybe." Sissy kept grinning. "Maybe not. Who knows?"

The room seemed to grow cold and damp and shadowy, and I held Emma tighter. I knew I should tell Sissy to shut up and go home, but I didn't. Jeanine hadn't said Teresa's body was still in the lake. Maybe she'd left that out because she didn't want to scare me. What else had she kept to herself?

Sissy pushed herself even nearer to me and grinned. Her face was so close I could see the cavities in her small yellow teeth. "Want to hear the best part?"

Ignoring Emma's whimper, I nodded, as eager to hear as she was eager to tell.

"Everybody thinks your mothers were with Teresa the day she drowned," Sissy said. "After all, she fell out of your grandfather's canoe. What was she doing taking it out all by herself?"

"Make her stop," Emma whispered to me. "I don't want to hear any more."

"It's okay," I told her, my eyes held fast by Sissy's. "You can go to your room if you don't want to hear."

Emma shook her head and again hid her face against my side.

"Teresa's mother told the police to talk to your mothers," Sissy went on. "But the cops were too dumb to get anything out of them."

She paused a second. "Some people say Dulcie pushed Teresa into the water, and then she and your mother left her there to drown—that the canoe washed up on some rocks, and they walked home and lied and lied and lied. They said they'd never been out of the cottage, they hadn't seen Teresa, they didn't know why she took the canoe. *That's* why they never came back here—they were scared of what they'd done."

While she'd been talking, Sissy's voice had risen higher and higher. Shaking with anger, she paused and took a deep breath, then another, and another, her chest heaving under the sweatshirt.

"Your mothers should be punished for what they did to Teresa," she said in a calm voice. "Murder—that's what they did. *Murder.*"

"How do you know all this?" I felt cold, achy, weak in the knees, as if I was coming down with the flu. Or maybe something worse—fatal, even. If Sissy meant to scare Emma and me, she'd done it.

"People still talk about Teresa," Sissy said with a shrug. "Unlike your mothers, nobody in Webster's Cove has forgotten her."

Turning to Emma, Sissy pulled her hands away from her ears and whispered, "Oh, and lots of people have seen Teresa's ghost. On foggy days, they hear her calling, '*Help, help, don't let Dulcie drown me.*'"

Emma covered her ears again and started rocking back and forth, humming loudly to keep from hearing.

I shoved Sissy away from Emma. "Shut up!" I yelled. "Shut up! It's not true, you liar." I raised my hand to slap her face, but she spun out of my reach, laughing.

"Teenagers didn't wreck Dulcie's paintings," Sissy crowed. "Teresa did. She's still here. You know it, and so does Dulcie."

"No," Emma wailed, "no!"

"Teresa could be *anywhere*," Sissy went on. "She could be in this room right this minute, hiding in the shadows, just waiting to drown you like your mom drowned her. She could come through the window and get you in the middle of the night, she could——"

"Get out of this house, Sissy!" I rushed at her again, wanting to hit her hard, to hurt her, to make her admit it was all a lie.

"I'm going, I'm going." Pulling the hood of the red sweatshirt over her hair, Sissy stuck out her tongue and ran into the rain. "Watch out for Teresa!"

Emma hurled herself into my arms. "Teresa can't get me, she can't drown me. Not unless I go to the lake where her bones are. And I'll never go there again."

I hugged her shivering body. "Sissy made it all up," I murmured into her ear. "The next time she comes over, we'll tell her to go away. We won't let her in."

Emma cried herself to sleep in my lap. Sissy had exhausted her. She'd exhausted me, too, but I was too upset to sleep. I wanted to believe what I'd told Emma. It was a lie, all a lie. Our mothers had told the truth, they hadn't been in the canoe that day. Teresa was dead and gone—she wasn't in the house, she hadn't wrecked the studio.

But no matter how hard I argued with myself, I had a feeling that at least some of what Sissy had said was true. Hadn't I dreamt about Teresa night after night? Didn't ghosts come to people in dreams and demand justice? *Tell the truth*, the note had said. *Tell the truth or else.*

Or else what?

Emma stirred and woke up. "I want Mommy," she said sleepily.

As she slid off my lap, I peered into her eyes. "I know Sissy scared you, Em, but don't tell your mother what she said."

Emma looked puzzled. "But—"

"Please promise you won't tell." I held her tightly to keep her from running down to the studio. "Dulcie doesn't want to hear anything about Teresa. You should have seen her face when Jeanine Donaldson started talking about her. She was so upset, she walked off."

"But suppose the ghost gets in our house? Suppose it's . . . already here?" Emma peered fearfully at the familiar living room. Her eyes lingered on shadowy corners.

"Teresa's not here." I tried to sound sure, but it was all too easy to picture Teresa watching us from the hall, perched on the steps, maybe, or here in the living room, hovering near the Candy Land board where she'd once written her name. As Sissy had said, she could be anywhere.

"She got in the studio," Emma whispered. "She drew the bones. Mommy should know she was there. Teresa might hurt her."

"Teresa can't hurt anyone. She's—" I stopped myself from saying "dead." Gripping Emma's shoulders so tightly she winced, I said, "Promise not to tell."

When I released her, Emma relaxed her shoulders and let her head slump. Without looking at me, she muttered, "Okay."

I pulled her hands from behind her back before she had time to uncross her fingers. "That's cheating, Em. Promise again."

In a low voice, Emma said, "Are you sure Teresa won't get us?"

"I'm positive," I lied. At this point, I had no idea what Teresa might do. Maybe she was real, maybe she wasn't. Maybe she wanted to hurt Dulcie, maybe she wanted to hurt Emma and me, maybe she was just drifting around in the rain and the mist. It was hard to look at my cousin and pretend I wasn't just as scared as she was.

Emma's eyes welled with tears, but she drew her finger back and forth across her heart. "I promise not to tell Mommy." Her voice was so low I could barely hear her.

Hoping I could trust her, I gave her a hug. Then, making an effort to speak in a normal voice, I asked, "Would you like a glass of juice? And a chocolate-chip cookie?"

Emma followed me to the kitchen and sat at the counter while I fixed our snack. She took a small bite of the cookie and a tiny sip of juice. Then she pushed both away. "Not hungry," she mumbled.

I toyed with my cookie, no hungrier than Emma. Outside the leaves rustled, and I shivered. *Go away, Teresa, go away. Leave us alone.*

13

The next morning, the rain stopped, but the mist hung on. I was beginning to think Mom hadn't exaggerated the lake's bad weather. Or the hordes of mosquitoes and gnats that seemed immune to bug sprays.

When I came downstairs, I saw Dulcie staring out the window at the water. After a while, she said, "I'd better get back to work."

She'd cleaned up most of the mess and discovered that the paintings weren't as badly damaged as she'd thought. Except for the one she'd smeared with black paint, she'd managed to clean them.

After she left, I sat at the table and enjoyed a cup of coffee with plenty of sugar and cream. Mom never let me drink it at home, but Dulcie said caffeine wouldn't hurt me. She lived on it herself. Emma was still sleeping—she'd been awake all night with bad dreams, but she wouldn't tell Dulcie what they were about. I was pretty sure Sissy's story had inspired her nightmares. I'd dreamed about Teresa myself. This time I thought the girls in the canoe were Mom and Dulcie, but I wasn't sure. I still couldn't see anyone's face clearly.

Between the sighing of the wind and the dark day, I felt lonely and sad. In an effort to escape my mood, I opened *To Kill a Mockingbird*. I was more than halfway through, but I hadn't read much before I fell asleep with my head on the open book.

The sound of the back door opening woke me up. I turned and saw Sissy standing a couple of feet away. She was still wearing Emma's red sweatshirt.

"What are *you* doing here?" I didn't bother to hide my annoyance. "Emma's asleep, but even if she was wide awake, I wouldn't let you near her."

"I didn't come to see Emma. I came to see *you*."

"Why?"

She twirled the sweatshirt hood's drawstring. "I didn't have anything else to do."

"Well, *I* have plenty to do."

"Like what?"

"Like read this book, for one thing."

Sissy craned her neck to see the title. "*To Kill a Mockingbird*. I never read that. Is it good?"

Determined to ignore her, I held the book in front of my face and tried to read.

"I guess you're mad about what I said yesterday," she mumbled.

I lowered the book. "Why did you tell Emma those stories? She had bad dreams all night. That's why she's still asleep."

"She shouldn't be such a fraidy cat," Sissy said. "I was just kidding around."

"That's what you said when you almost drowned her."

Sissy shrugged. "I guess I'm the only one around here with a sense of humor."

"If you think that kind of stuff is funny, you're sick."

She laughed. "At least I don't read books about bird killers. *That's* pretty sick, if you ask me."

"You are so ignorant," I said in a nasty voice. "*To Kill a Mockingbird* isn't about bird killers."

Sissy sat down at the table across from me. "What *is* it about, then?"

"I haven't finished reading it yet, have I?" I marked my place and laid the book down. "It's required summer reading for eighth grade. I have to pass a test and write an essay on it when school starts."

"Big deal. I hate school. I'm glad I don't have to go any-more."

"What do you mean? You're too young to quit school."

"I mean for the summer, stupid. I'm on vacation. Like every-body—including you." Sissy tilted her chair back so far I was sure she'd fall on her head any second. Not that I cared. Maybe she'd leave if she hurt herself.

"How's Dulcie this morning?" she asked. "Are her paintings ruined?"

"Why should *you* care?"

Sissy rocked back and forth on the chair's legs, as if she were trying to figure out how far she could go without tipping over. "I wish I could've seen her face when she found that mess. I would've laughed and laughed."

"It *was* you!" Sure I was right, I glared at Sissy. "*You* wrecked the studio, didn't you? And then you made up all that stuff about Teresa!"

"You're crazy," Sissy said. "Why would I do something like that?"

"Because you're a spiteful little brat!"

At that point, Sissy finally overbalanced the chair and crashed to the floor. She made such a loud noise, I jumped up, scared my wish had come true and she'd really hurt herself. "Are you okay?"

She rubbed the back of her head and threw my own words back at me. "Why should *you* care?" Without waiting for an answer, she went to the back door. "I'm going for a walk. You can come if you like."

I stared at her in disbelief. "What makes you think I'd go anywhere with you?"

"I want to show you something." Sissy gave me one of her sly smiles. "I guarantee you won't be sorry."

When I hesitated, she added, "You're always asking me questions—where do I live, what's my last name, personal stuff like that. If you really want to know, come with me. Maybe I'll tell you."

Maybe you will, I thought. *Probably you won't.* Giving in to curiosity, I glanced at the kitchen clock. Nine o'clock. Emma would sleep for at least another hour. "I can't go far," I said. "Emma will be worried if she wakes up and nobody's home."

"Plus you don't want to get in trouble with your crazy aunt," Sissy added.

With a shrug, I let her lead me outside and into the pine woods. We walked single file along a narrow path that wound around trees, roots, and mossy boulders bearded with ferns. Mosquitoes hummed in my ears, and gnats circled my head. Except for the cries of gulls and crows, it was very quiet.

"Where are we going?" I asked.

"To a place I know."

We came out of the woods on a hill above the lake. Down below, the water lay still and calm, as gray as the sky above it.

Sissy walked to the end of a rocky overhang and dropped to her knees, right on the edge. "What I want to show you is down there." She pointed at the lake.

"You'd better come back. You might fall." I spoke loudly, so she wouldn't guess I was afraid of high places.

A gust of wind swirled through her hair and lifted the hood of her sweatshirt. "Fraidy cat." She leaned farther out, crouched like a gargoyle on the rock. "I'm the only one who knows what's down there."

"Oh, sure." Sick of her grin, sick of her show-off personality, sick of everything about her, even her bathing suit, I backed away from her and the scary place she'd led me.

"I thought you wanted me to tell you my secrets," she taunted in a singsong voice. "Sissy, Sissy, where do you live? What's your mommy like, what's your daddy like? What's your last name? Oh, Sissy, Sissy, tell me your secrets."

I put more distance between us. "I'm going home. Emma's probably awake now. She'll wonder where I am."

"You're as big a baby as she is." Sissy got to her feet and walked toward me. "Are you scared I'm going to push you off the cliff?" She lunged at me as if she really meant to do it. When I jumped backward, she laughed. "Baby, baby, baby."

"Go away!" I yelled at her. "I never want to see you again."

She met my eyes dead on, giving me the full benefit of the cold stare she was so good at. The wind toyed with her hair, whipping pale strands across her tan face. "You can't get rid of me . . . even if you try."

High above our heads, the tall pines swayed and murmured. A gull cried. Waves splashed against the lake's rocky shore. Drops of rain began to fall.

With a laugh, Sissy shoved me aside and darted off into the rain. "So long," she called. "Goodbye, ta-ta, adieu."

I watched her for a few moments, and then I followed her. If she wouldn't tell me where she lived, I'd find out myself. I'd go right up to her door and tell her mother that Sissy wasn't welcome at Gull Cottage anymore.

As little and skinny as she was, Sissy was fast. I couldn't keep her in sight, try as hard as I could. Just as I was about to give up, I glimpsed her, far ahead, disappearing into a grove of tall pines. By the time I reached the shelter of the trees, the rain was pouring down and Sissy had disappeared.

I looked around, bewildered. Where had she gone? There was nothing here. Just pines and tall grass and tangles of wild roses and vines growing over outcrops of mossy stones.

When I heard a car whoosh past, I ran through the pines to a road. On the other side, I saw a small yellow house with blue shutters and a curl of smoke coming from its chimney. A rock garden and beds of flowers bloomed around the porch, their colors brightening the gloom.

I ran across and knocked on the door, sure I'd found Sissy's home. She'd be surprised to see me on *her* doorstep for a change.

Inside, a dog began barking and someone said, "Hush, Chauncy." The door opened, and a woman peered at me. "Yes?"

The dog kept barking. He was large and brown and had a plumy tail, but he didn't look especially fierce. Just noisy.

"Is Sissy home?" I asked.

"Sissy?" The woman shook her head, puzzled. "I don't know anybody by that name." Turning back to the dog, she said, "Be quiet!"

Chauncy regarded her with mournful eyes and lay down, head on his paws, as if he were ashamed of himself. His tail thumped the floor.

"That's better," the woman told him, and his tail thumped harder. "Now," she said to me, "you'd better come in and dry off. You're soaked."

I hesitated a second, but I was cold, drenched, and worn out from chasing Sissy. The woman had a friendly look, and the dog was quite sweet now that he'd stopped barking. The room beyond the open door looked warm and cozy—and dry.

"My name's Kathie Trent," the woman said. "But I don't believe I know you."

"I'm Ali O'Dwyer. I'm staying with my aunt Dulcie at Gull Cottage."

She nodded. "Jeanine Donaldson told me Dulcie was back."

"Do you know my aunt?"

"I haven't seen her since she was about your age, maybe younger." She looked at me closely. "You're shivering. Let's get you dried off before you catch pneumonia."

I followed Ms. Trent to the bathroom. Handing me a towel, she said, "There's a robe on the back of the door. Put that on, and I'll toss your clothes in the dryer. Then you can tell me all about yourself—and Dulcie and Claire, too."

Soon I was bundled up in a fluffy bathrobe, sitting near a small wood stove and sipping hot tea. Chauncy dozed near my feet, and Ms. Trent sat across from me in a rocking chair. She wore her gray hair in a long braid down her back, but her face was unlined and rosy. Her jeans were faded, and her gray sweatshirt was several sizes too big; however, I could tell she was as slim as Dulcie, even though she was older.

She regarded me over the rim of her teacup. "No one here thought Dulcie or Claire would ever come back to the lake."

Here we go again, I thought. Aloud I said, "I guess Mrs. Donaldson told you she came to see Dulcie."

Ms. Trent nodded and waited for me to go on.

"Dulcie didn't remember her, but she was friendly at first. Then Mrs. Donaldson mentioned Teresa, and Dulcie got upset.

She said she didn't remember her, either, and went off in a huff."
I tied the robe's belt tighter.

"It was really embarrassing," I went on, "but Mrs. Donaldson was very nice about it—she even apologized for upsetting Dulcie."

"Jeanine's a sweet person," Ms. Trent said.

Unlike Dulcie, I added silently. "Mrs. Donaldson knew Teresa. Did you know her, too?" I asked.

"Yes, I did." Ms. Trent took a sip of tea. "I hate to say it, but her older sister, Linda, and I spent a lot of time running away from the poor kid. Teresa wanted to tag along everywhere we went, but she was five or six years younger—a big difference when you're a teenager and your little sister is ten. If we left her out, she'd tattle on Linda just to get her in trouble."

She leaned back in the rocking chair and watched the rain run down the windowpanes. "It's an awful thing to say, but I don't think anyone liked Teresa—kids or adults. She was just too difficult. Always mad about something. From what Jeanine says, she caused so much trouble between Dulcie and Claire that your grandmother used to send her home."

She sighed. "After what happened, I've often wished I'd been nicer to her. She couldn't have been very happy."

For a while we sat quietly. I thought about Caroline Hogan—in third grade everybody hated her, I don't remember why now. Then she got hit by a car. She didn't die or anything, but when I saw her on crutches, I felt terrible. If something bad happened to Sissy, I guessed I'd feel the same way. Maybe I'd try to be nicer the next time I saw her. *Maybe.*

As I sipped my tea, I stared at the quilt hanging on the wall across from me. It was done in shades of blues and grays ranging from dark to light, and its patterns swirled like water. The quilt had a melancholy feeling, sad beyond words. It reminded me of Dulcie's lake paintings.

Ms. Trent turned to see what I was looking at. "That's my interpretation of the lake," she said, "its colors, its currents, its depth. One of my best pieces, I think, but no one has ever offered to buy it. Several people say it's too depressing. The blues and the grays . . ." With a shrug, she tilted back in the rocker and drank her tea.

"Is it true Teresa's body was never found?" I asked.

"Did Jeanine tell you that?"

"No, Sissy did—the girl I was looking for."

Ms. Trent sighed. "The lake often keeps its dead. The water's deep, you know, and dark. The bottom's rocky. Bodies get caught under ledges. . . ." Her voice trailed off. "Well, there's no sense dwelling on the morbid details. It was a sad end to an unhappy child's life."

I tucked the robe around my feet and curled up as small as I could. I wanted to let go of Teresa, but I had more questions.

"Sissy also told me Mom and Dulcie were in the canoe with Teresa the day she drowned. She said it was their fault—that they murdered Teresa."

Ms. Trent set her teacup down with a tiny clink. "There was a lot of talk at the time. Teresa's parents were sure Dulcie and Claire were involved. They even got the police to talk to your mother and aunt, but nothing came of it." She paused. "In case you're wondering, I think Teresa took the canoe out on a whim, and that Dulcie and Claire had nothing to do with it."

I reached down to pet Chauncy. Without raising my head, I asked, "Do people ever say they've seen Teresa's ghost?"

"Of course not." Ms. Trent laughed. "Did Sissy tell you that, too?"

"She scared my cousin, Emma, half to death." *And me, too.*

"I wonder who that child is," Ms. Trent mused. "Do you know her last name?"

"She won't tell me. I don't even know where she lives. That's why I followed her today." I frowned. "I want to find her house so Dulcie can talk to her mother. Sissy's a bad influence on Emma. She ought to stay away from us."

A clock struck eleven times like a miniature Big Ben, startling us both. I jumped up, stricken with guilt. I'd walked off two hours ago and left Emma sleeping. Dulcie was probably furious. "Are my clothes dry? I have to go home."

Ms. Trent disappeared into the laundry room and came back with my jeans and T-shirt and underwear, still warm from the dryer.

"It's raining too hard to walk all the way back to Gull Cottage," she said as she handed them to me. "Why don't you call Dulcie? I'd love to see her. I'd drive you myself, but my poor Volvo's in the shop having yet another overhaul."

As soon as I was dressed, I dialed Dulcie's number. Just as I'd feared, she was cross at me for leaving without a word to anyone. But she was also relieved I was safe.

"I'll come right away. Where are you?"

"At Ms. Trent's. It's a yellow house on Sycamore Road. She has flowers everywhere, more even than Mom has. You can't miss it."

"What on earth are you doing there?"

"I tried to follow Sissy home, but I couldn't keep up with her. I thought she must live in Ms. Trent's house, so I knocked on the door and she invited me in, but she doesn't know Sissy."

"Sissy, Sissy, Sissy." Dulcie sighed into the phone. "I wish you'd never met that girl."

After she hung up, I sat down on the sofa. My aunt wasn't the only one who wished I'd never met Sissy. Chauncy nudged my knee with his nose and looked at me hopefully. I petted him, and Ms. Trent laughed.

"He'll expect you to keep that up for hours," she said. "I've never had a dog who needed more love than Mr. Chauncy."

A few minutes later, Dulcie's car pulled into the driveway next to the cottage. I glimpsed Emma in the back seat, her face pressed against the window.

Despite all attempts to silence him, Chauncy ran to the door and barked loudly, just as he had when I'd arrived.

Ms. Trent greeted Dulcie. "Ignore that silly dog. He never bites."

Dulcie carried Emma inside. "Don't put me down," Emma begged. "I'm scared of dogs."

"His name's Chauncy," I told Emma. "He's an old sweetie pie. See?" I petted Chauncy and he leaned against my legs, huffing happily.

"I don't like dogs," Emma said.

In the meantime, Ms. Trent was introducing herself to Dulcie. "I'm Kathie Trent," she said, "but you'd have known me as Kathie Miller. My folks worked at Lake View Cabins, way back when the Abbotts owned the place."

Dulcie ran her fingers through her rain-dampened hair, but nothing she did could tame it. "I'm sorry but—"

"It's been a long time," Ms. Trent said.

"My memory's terrible." Dulcie looked around the cottage, her eyes caught by the quilts. "These are beautiful. Did you make them?"

"Yes, I did." Ms. Trent smiled. "Ali tells me you're a painter. I'd love to see your work someday."

Dulcie shifted Emma so she could reach into her purse for a business card. "I'm in the studio every day, a converted boathouse down on the shore. It's a lovely spot to work."

"That's the lake." Emma pointed at the blue and gray quilt. "All deep and dark and scary."

"What a perceptive child," Ms. Trent said, clearly impressed.

"What's perscective mean?" Emma asked.

"'Perceptive' means you understand stuff," I told her.

"I do understand stuff," Emma agreed. "Lots of stuff."

"We'd better go," Dulcie said. "Thanks for sheltering my errant niece. I hope she wasn't a nuisance."

"Ali's welcome anytime," Ms. Trent said, "as are you and the perceptive Emma."

As soon as we were in the car, Dulcie let me have it. "It was extremely irresponsible to go off and leave Emma alone. If you do anything like that again, I'll find someone else to take care of my daughter. Someone who's more mature than you are."

"I'm sorry," I mumbled. "But Sissy—"

"Stop blaming Sissy for everything," Dulcie cut in. "You're thirteen years old. Act like it."

Stung into silence, I slumped in the front seat and gazed out the rain-streaked window. Dulcie stared straight ahead, her face closed, her hands tight on the wheel.

Strapped in her child seat in the back, Emma was unusually quiet. The only sound was the *slappity-slap* of the windshield wipers and the hiss of rain under the tires.

─❧14❧─

Gradually, Dulcie got over being angry at me, probably because Sissy stayed away. I read to Emma, played games with her, and, when the sun finally came out, took her swimming. We painted pictures and made things with clay—lopsided pots, oddly shaped animals, dishes and cups that Dulcie fired in the kiln. I tried making my shell-and-stone displays, and Dulcie liked them. She said I was an artist, too—it obviously ran in the family.

After more than a week had passed without Sissy, I began hoping she was gone for good. Moved, found someone else to torment—I didn't care where she was or where she'd gone. Just so she didn't come back.

One afternoon, Emma and I were sitting at the picnic table, fooling around with clay. The sun was hot. Perspiration soaked the hair on the back of my neck. Bumblebees buzzed and hummed to themselves in the hollyhocks. A mosquito whined in my ear, and another bit my arm.

Just as I was about to suggest a swim, Emma turned to me, her face thoughtful. "I wonder what Sissy's doing now."

"After the way she acted last time, I don't care what she's doing. Not one bit. Not even a teeny tiny smidgen of a split atom."

I exaggerated to make Emma laugh, but she didn't even smile. Bending her head over her clay pot, she said, "Sissy promised she'd come see me today."

"How could she tell you that? We haven't seen her for over a week."

Ignoring me, Emma concentrated on rolling a coil of clay between her hands, making it long and smooth like a glistening snake.

I lifted her chin and forced her to look at me. "Has Sissy been here?"

Emma jerked away from me. Dropping the coil of clay, she flattened it with her fist. "Squish," she said. "Squash. No more snake."

With a Sissy smirk on her face, she ran into the house. The screen door slammed shut behind her. A squirrel, frightened by the sound, scurried up a tree trunk and disappeared into the leaves. From somewhere in his green hiding place, he chitter-chattered his outrage.

Emma hadn't answered my question, but she didn't have to. The way she acted told me she'd managed to see Sissy without my knowing. But how? I was with her all the time—except when she took her nap and went to bed at night. I doubted Sissy was allowed out after dark, so she must be sneaking into Emma's room in the afternoon.

If that's what was going on, I'd soon put a stop to it. The sneaky little brat wasn't welcome here—and she knew it. Leaving my clay cat baking in the sun, I went inside to talk to Emma.

She was lying on the couch, her face bored and sulky—in a Sissy mood, for sure. "Has Sissy been sneaking in here while you're supposed to be taking a nap?"

"That's for me to know and you to find out." Emma's voice sounded just like Sissy's, mocking and spiteful.

I grabbed her shoulders and gave her a little shake. "I don't want her in this house. And neither does your mother!"

Emma pulled away from me. "Sissy's right. You're jealous because I like her better than I like you."

Disgusted with Emma, I stalked off to the kitchen and poured myself a glass of iced tea. Just as I sat down to drink it, Dulcie came in. She didn't say hello. She didn't smile. In fact, she didn't even look at me. She went straight to the coffeemaker and started a pot brewing.

While she waited, she turned to me. "Where's Emma?"

Annoyed by her tone of voice, I kept my eyes on the *New Yorker* I'd been reading. "She's sulking in the living room."

Dulcie sighed in exasperation. "What's going on between you two? Why can't you get along with each other?"

Like bad weather, I sensed blame coming my way again. "It's not my fault—"

"Oh, no, it's never your fault. It's Sissy's fault or Emma's fault. Maybe it's the weather's fault—it's too hot, too cold, too rainy. But it's not *your* fault. You aren't to blame for anything."

Hurt by her sarcasm, I started to cry. At the same moment, Dulcie reached into the cupboard for a coffee mug and dropped it. It shattered on the kitchen floor.

The noise brought Emma running. "What was that?" she asked from the doorway.

Dulcie was down on her knees gathering up bits of china. "I broke a cup. That's all."

"Why's Ali crying?"

Dulcie looked at me, her face stricken. Getting to her feet, she gave me a quick hug. "I'm so sorry, sweetie. I shouldn't have snapped at you like that." She looked past me at the lake, darkening now under a parade of clouds drifting across the sky.

"Everything's wrong," she muttered as she dumped the remains of the cup in the garbage. "You and Emma quarrel constantly, I can't sleep, I . . ." Finishing the sentence with a shrug, she reached for another cup and filled it with coffee.

I felt like saying she probably drank too much coffee, but I bit my tongue. She was already on edge, jumpy and jittery. It wouldn't take much to make her angry again.

"Your mother was right," she went on. "Coming here was a mistake. My paintings are terrible, too bad to show. I do the same thing over and over again—the lake, the fog. . . . They're hideous, but I can't paint anything else, just the dark water, the dark sky, and the—"

She broke off, sat down at the kitchen table, and covered her face with her hands. Emma patted her mother's shoulder, stroked her hair, and whispered, "Mommy, Mommy, don't cry. Everything will be okay."

Emma sounded like herself again, sweet, comforting, all traces of Sissy gone.

Keeping her face in her hands, Dulcie muttered, "I'm beginning to think we should close up the cottage and go home. Maybe I'll paint better in New York, in my own studio, away from all this water and wind and rain."

Emma drew back. "We can't leave," she cried, her voice suddenly shrill in the quiet kitchen. "We can't, we can't, we can't. Sissy—"

Dulcie seized Emma's shoulders. "Do you know how sick I am of hearing that child's name? Ever since you met her, there's been nothing but trouble between you and Ali. I don't want her coming here. I don't want you playing with her. Do you understand?"

Emma shrank away from Dulcie's angry face. I thought she'd cry, but her lip jutted out and she looked at her mother, defying her. "Sissy's my friend! I won't stop playing with her! You can't make me!"

Dulcie leapt to her feet and drew back her hand. I cringed, sure that she was going to slap Emma. Emma must have thought the same thing because she raised her arm to protect her face. "Don't hit me," she cried. "Don't hit me!"

Dulcie threw herself back down in the chair and began to sob. Emma looked at me, clearly frightened by her mother's behavior. Scared myself, I took Emma's hand. I was used to my mother behaving like this, but not Dulcie.

In a moment or two, Dulcie managed to control herself. Wiping her tears away with the back of her hand, she pulled Emma into her lap. "I'm sorry," she whispered. "Sometimes I don't know what gets into me."

With a sigh, she pushed her hair back from her face. "Why don't we get dinner started? Spaghetti, maybe. How would you two like that?"

In a voice so low that Dulcie didn't hear, Emma muttered, "I'm sick of spaghetti, and I'm sick of Ali, and I'm sick of Mommy."

I looked at her, but she turned away, hiding her face.

Making cheerful noises with pots and pans, Dulcie and I began fixing the meal. I boiled water and dropped in spaghetti. Dulcie whipped up tomato sauce, and Emma got out the bread and butter. My job was tossing spaghetti noodles at the wall. If they stuck, they were ready. Mom would never have let me do something like that.

At dinner, we sat together at the table, laughing and talking as if the earlier scenes had never happened. Emma ate most of her spaghetti. No one mentioned Sissy. Instead, we planned a hike and picnic in the state park, as well as another trip to Pemaquid Point.

But when darkness came, and I lay in bed alone, I found myself thinking about Dulcie. Before we came to Gull Cottage,

I'd never seen her angry or upset, never imagined her crying over anything. She was my tough New York City aunt, my artist aunt, my sophisticated, worldly aunt, smart and talented, witty and quick and daring—everything I wanted to be someday.

But now . . . well, I didn't know what to think. The longer we stayed here, the more she reminded me of Mom.

Gradually, I drifted into the Teresa dream: rough dark water, gray sky, fog. Three girls huddled in a canoe, quarreling, rocking the canoe. The fog thickened, hiding everything. A splash. A cry—I woke, terrified, clutching the old teddy bear.

Rain blew in the open window by my bed and struck my face. Shivering with cold, I leapt up and closed the window. In the sudden silence, I heard Emma shouting as if she, too, had awakened suddenly from a bad dream.

Wrapping a quilt around my shoulders, I ran to the top of the steps.

Emma stood in the hall below me. "Where's Mommy?"

"Isn't she in her room?"

"No." Emma began to cry. "I had a bad dream and I went to get her and she wasn't there."

I hurried down the stairs and checked Dulcie's room. Emma followed me, clinging to one hand. The empty bed was a mess of kicked-back sheets and blankets, and the window was wide open. I slammed it shut and went to the front door.

"She must be in the studio," I told Emma. "You stay here, and I'll go look."

I tried to pull my hand free, but Emma held tight. "Take me with you."

"But it's dark and rainy. The steps are slippery. You might fall."

"Don't leave me here," she begged. "The bones will get me."

I tried to calm her down, but she was crying too loudly to listen.

"Okay, okay," I said. "You can come, but be careful on the steps."

Still sobbing, Emma let me help her into her slicker. After I pulled mine on, I grabbed a flashlight and led her out into the rain and dark. Above the wind, I heard waves smashing against the shore. Thunder cracked and lightning flashed.

Emma pressed her face into my side. "I hate thunder," she whimpered.

By now, we were at the top of the stairs. Slowly and cautiously, we inched downward, feeling our way from step to step like blind people.

Lights shone from the boathouse windows. Without knocking, I opened the door, and Emma and I stumbled over the threshold.

Dulcie spun around and stared at us, her eyes momentarily wide with fright. "What are you doing here?" she cried. "You scared me bursting in like that!"

"I had a bad dream." Emma began crying harder. "I couldn't find you, you weren't in your bed—you weren't anywhere."

While Dulcie comforted Emma, I studied her paintings. What she'd said about them was true. They leaned against the walls, tall, narrow canvases, maybe three feet by seven feet, stark and ugly. She'd covered all of them with streaks of blue and gray washed on in thin layers. Then she'd added clumsy daubs of black and splashes of reds and dark blues and purples.

What really scared me, though, was the pale blob at the bottom of each painting. A stone, a shell, a skull—too blurry to be sure what it was.

I certainly wouldn't have wanted one of those paintings in my house. Not if I wanted to feel good or sleep well. They looked as if they'd been vandalized again—only this time Dulcie had done the damage herself.

My aunt caught me looking at the paintings. "I couldn't sleep," she said in a flat voice. "The storm kept me awake. I thought I might get some work done, but . . ." She shrugged. "Just being here depresses me."

"They scare me." Emma hid her face against her mother's side. "Don't let me see them."

Dulcie freed herself from Emma and turned the paintings so they faced the wall. "Let's go to bed," she said in a low, toneless voice.

Silently, Emma and I followed Dulcie out into the storm. As we climbed the stairs to the cottage, I glanced over my shoulder. For a second, I thought I saw someone on the dock watching us. I blinked the rain from my eyes and looked again. No one was there. Waves pounded the shore, and the wind blew in gusts.

"Come on, Ali," Dulcie called from above. "You'll catch your death in this rain."

Catch your death. I'd never thought about it before, but suddenly the expression made no sense. *Catch your death, Catch your death,* I repeated, as I climbed the steps to the cottage. Wasn't it the other way around? Didn't death catch you?

Shivering with cold and fear, I was tempted to ask Dulcie if I could sleep with her instead of going upstairs to my lonely room. But I was thirteen—surely too old to be scared of the dark. So I went to bed alone and read *To Kill a Mockingbird* until the sky began to lighten behind the clouds.

~⟨15⟩~

The next day, the sun shone, but Dulcie's mood didn't lighten. She frittered the morning away drinking coffee and puttering around the cottage. In the afternoon, she took a long walk alone, despite Emma's plea to go with her.

"Sorry," she said. "I need time to myself."

Emma and I watched her stride away up the cliff path. When she was out of sight, Emma said, "I hope Sissy comes over today."

"You heard your mother. She doesn't want you to play with Sissy." I sighed. "Besides, we have more fun together when she's not here."

Emma pulled a rose off a bush by the door and twirled it in her fingers, wincing when a thorn pricked her. "You don't know *anything* about Sissy."

She pulled the rose apart and scattered its pink petals on the grass, where they lay like confetti. Then without another word, she ran inside, letting the screen door slam in my face. I yanked it open, and she retreated to the doorway of her room. "You better not hit me," she shouted. "I'll tell Mommy!"

"Why would I hit you?" I stared at her, perplexed.

"Because you're hateful!"

"Emma——" I began, but she closed her door.

"Don't come in here!" she cried from inside. "Go away!"

I retreated to the kitchen, a total failure as a babysitter. I couldn't do anything right. Not for Emma. And not for Dulcie, either. My aunt was in a perpetual bad mood. Irritable, jumpy, tense—all because her paintings weren't going well. As if that was *my* fault.

While I stood at the window, brooding on my miserable vacation, it started raining. Another cold, gray day in Maine. Summer-school algebra would have been more fun than Sycamore Lake.

I looked at the phone hanging on the kitchen wall. Maybe I should call Mom. She'd said I could come home if I was unhappy. I lifted the receiver and pushed 1 for long distance. Just as I was about to dial the area code, I caught sight of Emma crossing the lawn. What was she doing outside in the rain? I hung up quickly and ran to the back door just as she disappeared into the trees.

Instead of calling her to come back, I grabbed my slicker and followed her, sure she planned to meet Sissy. Ducking behind trees, I kept her bright pink jacket in sight.

She stopped in a gloomy grove of pine trees not far from me. Sissy was perched on a boulder, waiting for her. In the dim light, I could see that Sissy was holding something.

"You brought her!" Emma held out her hands, but Sissy thrust whatever she carried behind her back.

"You said I could play with her today," Emma protested.

"I didn't promise," Sissy said. "I said maybe you could. Just *maybe*."

"Please, Sissy." Emma sounded close to tears.

Sissy wrinkled her forehead as if she were thinking hard. "If I let you play with her, will you promise to do everything I say?"

"Yes," Emma said.

"Cross your heart and hope to die?" Sissy asked.

Solemnly, Emma crossed her heart with one finger.

Sissy smiled and brought a doll from behind her back. Its hair was a dull greenish gray, brittle and caked with mud. Its face was discolored, and its ragged clothes were stained. I'd never seen a more hideous thing, but I recognized it.

And so did Emma. "Edith," she crooned, "Edith." She cradled the Lonely Doll in her arms. "Can I really keep her?"

"Just for a little while." Sissy came close and whispered in Emma's ear. Emma nodded, nodded again, and kept on nodding, agreeing to everything Sissy said.

Unable to stand it anymore, I jumped out from my hiding place and startled them both. "Give that ugly doll back to her, and don't do anything she tells you to!" I yelled at Emma.

"Who's your boss, Em?" Sissy asked. "Her or me?"

"You," Emma said. "You're the boss. I do what *you* say, Sissy, not what Ali says. Not what Mommy says."

I reached for the doll, intending to throw it at Sissy, but Emma was too fast for me. Holding it tightly, she ran to Sissy's side. "Go away, Ali. Sissy and me don't want to play with you."

"I don't want to play with *you*," I yelled as if I were eight instead of thirteen.

"Ali, are you shouting at Emma?"

I whirled around and saw Dulcie standing a few yards away on the cliff top. Sissy disappeared so fast you'd think the woods had gobbled her up. Emma ran to her mother.

"Ali was mean to me," Emma wailed. "Don't let her stay here. Send her home."

"What now?" Anger edged Dulcie's voice. "Here I am, just getting my head together, and here you are, out in the rain, soaking wet, and quarreling again. Can't you two ever get along? What's wrong with you, anyway?" The rain had curled her hair so tightly, it bushed around her face, making her look like a madwoman—scary, raging with anger, her wet clothes sticking to her skinny body.

Emma held up the doll. "Ali's jealous because Sissy gave me Edith."

Dulcie stared at the doll as if it had come from some dark, secret place. "Where did you get that?" she whispered. "God in heaven, Emma, tell me!"

Emma drew back from her mother, even more scared by her tone of voice than I was. "She belongs to Sissy. She said—"

Dulcie grabbed the doll's arm and pulled so hard she yanked it off. Losing her balance, she staggered backward. For a moment, I froze, sure she was going to fall off the cliff. Instead, she spun around and hurled the doll's arm into the water far below. With her back to us, she stared down at the lake.

"You broke Sissy's doll," Emma screamed. "She'll be mad!"

Dulcie turned to face Emma. "I told you not to play with that girl!"

"And I told you Sissy's my friend and I'll play with her if I want to!" Emma's face flushed with anger.

"You'll do what I tell you!" With one quick move, Dulcie grabbed Edith. Pivoting, she threw the doll off the cliff. "Filthy, horrible thing!"

"I hate you!" Emma screamed.

"That's enough!" Dulcie picked up Emma and headed for the cottage. I ran along behind them, barely able to keep up with Dulcie's long-legged stride.

Ahead of me, Emma yelled and protested and struggled to escape. Dulcie said nothing. Nor did she look back to see where I was.

Letting them get even farther ahead, I stopped and tried to pull myself together. I was shaking, not just from the rain and the wind but from the scene I'd just witnessed. Why had the doll upset Dulcie so much? She'd acted like a crazy woman, throwing the doll off the cliff as though it were a threat, something evil, dangerous. The scene replayed itself in my mind, over and over—Dulcie grabbing the doll from Emma, screaming, her hair flying around her face, hurling it into space. Strange as it seemed, my aunt had clearly been terrified of that filthy, water-stained doll.

At that moment, standing alone in the rain and the wind, I wanted my mother more than I'd ever wanted anyone in my life. I also wanted my father, my house, my room, my friends. Emma's behavior scared me—and so did Dulcie's.

Soaked and shivering, I ran to the cottage. Emma's bedroom door was closed, but I could hear Dulcie saying, "That doll wasn't fit to touch, let alone play with."

"It was Sissy's," Emma wailed. "You threw Sissy's doll away!"

With a sigh, I trudged up to my room. Rain drummed on the roof, and thunder still rumbled in the distance. I thought again about calling Mom and asking to come home. All that stopped me was the thought that she'd say, *I told you you'd hate the lake*.

I stayed in my room for at least an hour, hoping Dulcie might come up to see if I was all right. Downstairs, all was silent. Not a sob, not a voice. The only sound was the mournful murmur of the wind in the pines outside.

I tried to read, but my room was cold. Shadows gathered in the corners. I began thinking someone was hiding in the dark place by the closet, breathing slowly in and out, in and out. Every time I looked, I was sure I'd just missed seeing who it was.

Unable to stand it anymore, I ran downstairs. Dulcie huddled under a blanket on the couch, reading an art magazine. When she saw me, she put her finger to her mouth and beckoned me to follow her to the kitchen.

The moment the door closed behind me, Dulcie said, "Why did you let Emma go out in the rain? Don't you have any sense?"

"I didn't *let* her go anywhere," I said. "She went to her room, and the next thing I knew she was running across the field toward the woods. She must have climbed out her window or something. Sissy was waiting—"

"Leave Sissy out of this," Dulcie broke in. "Emma is *your* responsibility, Ali."

Without answering, I turned my back to hide the tears in my eyes. It wasn't fair to blame me. I was trying hard to take care of my cousin—no easy task with Sissy around. Why couldn't Dulcie see that?

For a few minutes, the only sound was the endless rain and the ticking clock. The kitchen was shadowy, the yellow paint dull and cheerless. At that moment, I hated Gull Cottage and the lake and the bad weather. It was all I could do not to call my mother to come and get me.

Suddenly, my aunt broke the silence. "I'm sorry, Ali. I don't know what's wrong with me. I'm just not myself. I can't do anything right anymore. I can't sleep, can't paint, can't be a good mother—or a good aunt, either."

She sounded close to tears herself, and when I looked at her, I saw my mother in my aunt's face. "It's okay," I mumbled, even though it wasn't. Saying something mean and then claiming you're not yourself doesn't take the hurt away.

"I don't understand why that doll upset me so much," Dulcie said slowly. "I used to buy ugly, dirty old dolls at flea markets and make them into sculptures. Remember? I had dozens of them. Fifty or more."

I'd forgotten those dolls until now. Dulcie had taken them apart and put them back together, creating monsters like

Frankenstein—a leg from one, a head from another, mismatched arms. Some were bald, others eyeless. She often replaced their bodies with boxes filled with strange objects—hard little tinfoil hearts, pebbles, shells, beads, tiny scissors from charm bracelets, sheets of paper with cryptic words written on them, bits of broken china, pennies, knives, nails. Many of them had holes in their heads with springs, feathers, twigs, or dead flowers poking out of them. The scariest had no heads at all. As a finishing touch, she often spray-painted them with a thin coat of green paint, giving them the appearance of things exhumed from graves or the depths of the sea.

"I didn't like them," I admitted. "They scared me."

"They weren't pretty," Dulcie said with a small smile. "But, believe it or not, they sold pretty well."

The smile faded. Dulcie twisted a strand of hair around her finger and pulled it tight. "After Emma was born, I stopped making them," she said. "I painted and drew more, sculpted less. I thought I'd outgrown my dark stage. But now . . ." She shrugged her thin shoulders. "You've seen what I'm doing. Dark. Very dark."

"The people who bought your dolls might like those paintings," I said a little doubtfully.

"Maybe." Dulcie sounded unconvinced. With a sigh, she got up and went to the door. "I'd better check on Emma. Why don't you open a can of soup for supper? Chicken with rice, maybe. We could use something warm and comforting."

She got to her feet, and I watched her walk away. The spring in her step was gone, and her shoulders drooped. She looked more like Mom than ever.

While I fixed the soup, I watched the rain fall, veiling the lake, blurring the line between water and sky. Images ran through my head—the cottage, the lake, the canoe, Teresa, the doll, my dream. And Sissy—frowning, angry, full of hatred. They were all connected, I was sure of it.

16

The next morning, Emma woke up complaining of a headache. Her face was flushed, and she was coughing. Dulcie touched Emma's forehead and hurried to the bathroom for the thermometer.

Emma's temperature was high enough for Dulcie to call a doctor. "She'll see us at eleven," Dulcie told me. "Do you want to come along?"

I peered out at the rain, still pouring down. The cottage was cozy and dry, and I had no desire to go anywhere. I held up *To Kill a Mockingbird*. "I absolutely have to finish this before school starts."

After Dulcie and Emma left, I made myself comfortable on the sofa and opened my book. I was relieved to see I'd finished at least two thirds of it.

I hadn't read more than a dozen pages when I heard a knock at the door. I looked up and saw it was Sissy. Before I had a chance to tell her to go away, she walked into the house as if she owned it.

I closed my book with an angry snap. "Who invited you in?"

"Me, myself, and I."

"Well, me, myself, and I *disinvite* you." I hoped to sound even more sarcastic than she did.

Perching on the old wicker armchair across from me, Sissy

made it clear she wasn't leaving. "Look what I found floating in the lake." She pulled Edith from under her wet sweatshirt and thrust her at me.

I drew back with distaste. "Get that thing away from me."

Sissy's lips curled up in a foxy grin. "I saw Dulcie yank Edith's arm off and throw her off the cliff. Why do you think she got so riled up?"

"Dulcie didn't want Emma playing with a dirty, disgusting doll." I kept my face as blank as I could so Sissy wouldn't know I'd wondered the same thing.

"You know what? Edith looked like a dead body floating in the water." Sissy waved the doll in my face. "And you know what else? I bet Teresa looked just like Edith after Dulcie pushed her into the lake."

I tightened my grip on my book to keep myself from throwing it at her. "Get out of here!"

Sissy leaned over me, close enough for her damp, stringy hair to brush my cheek, close enough for me to smell its stale, doggy odor. "I know you hate me, but I'm not going anywhere till I feel like it."

"You ought to wash your hair," I said. "It stinks."

"You don't smell so good yourself." Clutching Edith, Sissy made a face and dashed out the door into the rain. "Catch me if you can, Ali Ali Alligator!"

As before, she ran into the woods and took the trail along the cliff top. Once again, I followed her. I had to find out where she lived and who she was. If her mother knew how much trouble her daughter caused, she'd keep her at home, make her stay away from Gull Cottage. With no Sissy to spoil things, Emma, Dulcie, and I might actually have fun again.

At first, I had no trouble keeping Sissy in sight. The red sweat-shirt flashed around bends in the trail and in and out of rocks and boulders. I ran behind her, keeping a decent distance between us. Just as I was beginning to think I'd be successful, she turned away from the lake and disappeared into that dark grove of pines where I'd lost her before.

Determined to find her, I walked slowly, listening for footsteps and looking for the red sweatshirt. Maybe it was the gloom of the day or the slow, sad murmur of the wind in the trees, but the grove seemed to grow darker and colder. Overhead, a crow cawed, and farther away another answered. I stopped, suddenly afraid.

That's when I realized where I was. The mossy rocks I'd noticed before were tombstones. Most were so old they blended into the trees and bushes, their inscriptions worn and covered with lichen. Some were newer, their names and dates still legible.

Scared almost witless, I ran toward the road. In my panic, I tripped on small headstones and tumbled to the ground more than once. Brambles caught my hair and scratched my arms, and pine branches whipped my face, but nothing slowed me down. I ran with all my strength.

Then I glimpsed what I'd been looking for—the red sweat-shirt.

With a shout, I burst out of a grove of trees. "I see you, Sissy!"

But Sissy wasn't there. Like an offering, the red sweatshirt dangled from the hand of a stone angel.

Heart pounding, I looked around, sure she was hiding nearby, laughing at me. "Sissy?" I called, my voice unnaturally loud in the silent cemetery.

No one answered.

"Where are you?" I called again.

Still no answer. Not even a giggle.

"Stupid brat!" I yelled. "You can't scare me with your dumb tricks."

This time, crows answered, shattering the quiet with raucous cries.

Angry now, I walked right up to the angel. Sissy wasn't going to frighten me. Or make me look like an idiot. I'd show her.

But as I grabbed the sweatshirt, I noticed the words carved at the angel's feet.

In Memory of Our Beloved Daughter and Sister
Teresa Abbott
March 11, 1967 to July 19, 1977

May her soul rise from the deep and be at peace

Teresa, Teresa. The name ran round and round in my head like the words of a song you don't want to hear. *Teresa, Teresa*, the wind whispered while the raindrops beat out the rhythm.

The angel's blank eyes gazed at me, its hand reaching out as if to seize mine. I edged away, but the angel continued to stare at me, its marble face expressionless, stained from years of rain and snow.

Unable to bear those eyes, I ran toward the road, dodging headstones and trees. Somewhere behind me, I thought I heard Sissy laugh, but I didn't dare look back.

It wasn't until Ms. Trent opened her door that I realized I was still clutching the sweatshirt. I threw it down and flung myself, sobbing, into the woman's arms.

"Ali!" she said. "What's wrong?"

"I was in the graveyard up the road," I stammered. "I saw an angel there, a memorial for Teresa Abbott."

Ms. Trent nodded, but she was clearly puzzled. "The family erected it years ago."

"That sweatshirt was hanging from the angel's hand." I pointed at the wet, dirty heap on the floor. "Sissy left it there."

Ms. Trent stooped to pick up the sweatshirt. "I'm not sure what this is all about," she said, "but you're soaked, Ali—as usual." She laughed and shook her head. "You know the drill. Put on the robe and give me your wet clothes. I'll stick them in the dryer, along with the sweatshirt. When you're warm and dry, we'll talk."

A few minutes later, I was once again wrapped snugly in Ms. Trent's fluffy bathrobe. Chauncy sprawled on the floor near me, sighing contentedly from time to time. The warmth inside the cottage had steamed up the windows, but deep inside I was cold and shivery.

Ms. Trent handed me a cup of tea and sat down in her rocker. "Promise to visit me on a nice sunny day next time," she said with a smile.

A log in the stove shifted and fell. I watched Ms. Trent prod it into place with a poker. Firelight danced across her face, showing a fine network of wrinkles.

"What's wrong, Ali?" She looked at me kindly.

"What did Teresa look like?" I asked in such a low voice that Ms. Trent asked me to repeat the question. "Teresa Abbott—what did she look like?"

She thought a moment, as if trying to remember. "An ordinary kid, kind of plain," she said at last. "Skinny, small for her age. Sharp featured. Didn't smile often."

"Did she have blond hair?"

"Yes. Yes, she did. In the summer, it turned almost white." She smiled. "That was the only thing about Teresa I envied—her hair. When I was a teenager, I wanted to be a blond."

I huddled deeper into the soft sofa. "Was Teresa's sister, Linda, ever Miss Webster's Cove?"

"Yes, but—"

I interrupted. "Did she wear a tiara and ride in a motorboat parade and throw roses in the lake?"

"Did Dulcie tell you that?" Ms. Trent asked. "I didn't think she remembered anything."

"No, not her. Somebody else." I fidgeted with the bathrobe's sash, twirling it this way and that. What I was thinking couldn't be true—at least I hoped not. "Was Linda beautiful, and did she have lots of boyfriends?"

"Linda Abbott was the prettiest girl in high school. All the boys were in love with her." Ms. Trent took a sip of tea. "Has Jeanine been telling you about Linda?"

I shook my head. There was one more question. And it was the scariest one of all. Hoping she'd say no, I asked, "Did Linda ever call Teresa . . . 'Sissy'?"

Ms. Trent put her teacup down slowly. "Yes," she said slowly, as if remembering something long forgotten. "That was Linda's nickname for Teresa when she was little—Sissy."

I pulled the bathrobe tighter, but I couldn't stop shivering. Cold seeped in through every seam. My feet were frozen, and so were my hands. "Do you believe in ghosts?"

Ms. Trent looked at me, hands clasped, face serious, and slowly shook her head. "I know what you're thinking, Ali, but Sissy's a common nickname. That girl might be a troublemaker, but she's *not* Teresa."

"She looks like Teresa," I replied. "She acts like Teresa. She won't tell me her last name or where she lives. If I try to follow her, she disappears."

When I began to cry, Ms. Trent moved to the couch and put her arm around me. "I know you're upset, but you're letting your imagination run away with you. Sissy is Sissy—a real girl. She's not Teresa's ghost. It's impossible."

I wanted to snuggle into her side like a little kid, I wanted to believe her, I wanted to be comforted by her soft, reasonable voice. But no matter what excuses Ms. Trent made up, I knew what I knew.

"What about the sweatshirt?" I asked. "Sissy put it in the angel's hand because she wants me to know who she is."

"She left the sweatshirt there to scare you," Ms. Trent said, still calm, still reasonable. "You know—for a prank, a joke. It's exactly the sort of thing a girl like Sissy would do."

"That's what I thought at first, but . . ." I drew away from her side. "What if Mom and Dulcie were in the canoe with Sissy? What if they did something to her? What if she wants revenge?" My fears tumbled into words as I spoke.

Ms. Trent peered into my eyes. "What happened to Teresa was very sad. But this is the real world, Ali. You exist, I exist, millions of people exist. Ghosts do not exist—there's no room for them."

"You're wrong," I said, weeping. "You're wrong."

Ms. Trent tried to hug me again, but I shrugged her arm away. If she really wanted to comfort me, she'd believe me, she'd help me, she'd tell me what to do.

With a sigh, she got to her feet. "Your clothes must be dry. Why don't you get dressed, and I'll drive you home. My old Volvo seems to be working. At least for now."

Silently, I took my jeans and T-shirt, still warm from the dryer, and headed for the bathroom to change. Just as I closed the door, I heard the phone ring. Ms. Trent picked it up.

"Yes, Ali's here. I just told her I'd—"

Dulcie. What did she want? I yanked on my clothes and ran to Ms. Trent's side.

Ms. Trent handed me to the phone. "It's your aunt."

"Where is Emma?" Dulcie shouted into my ear.

"Isn't she with you?" I gripped the receiver, frightened by the panic in her voice.

"No! We came home, you weren't here, I gave Emma an antibiotic and put her to bed." Dulcie's words fell over each other and tangled themselves into a knot. "I just went to check on her. The window's open, and she's gone. Where would she go all by herself? It's raining, she has a fever, she should be in bed."

"I don't know where she is. I've been here —"

"If you'd been home, where you belong, she wouldn't be gone," Dulcie broke in. "Don't you ever think of anyone but yourself?"

"But, Dulcie, I—"

She slammed the receiver down with a bang that hurt my ear. "She's with Sissy!" I yelled into the phone, but of course she couldn't hear me.

Ms. Trent caught my arm as I ran toward the door. "Where are you going?"

"To find Emma!" I pulled free and dashed out into the rain.

"But the sweatshirt," she called after me. "Don't you want it?" Without answering, I darted across the road. If Emma was really with Sissy—and I was sure she was—she was in danger, and I had to save her.

↤⁓17⁓↦

Heart pounding, I raced back through the cemetery. Even though I didn't look at the angel, I sensed its blank eyes following me, its hand pointing the way to the lake and the cliff top.

Once I reached the path, I slowed down. The rain had changed to a heavy mist, and I could see only about three feet ahead. I didn't want to miss my way and fall off the rocks.

"Emma," I called. "Emma!"

There was no answer. Drops of water fell from the pines, gradually soaking my clothes. Now and then, I heard a gull cry, its voice sad and lonely. I was alone in a gray nothingness, no colors, no shapes.

At last, I heard Emma's high, piping voice. "Let's go back. I'm cold."

"Scaredy cat," Sissy taunted. "*Edith's* not afraid of the canoe. Why are you?"

I slid down a narrow path to the lake, scattering pebbles. The two of them looked up. Emma was surprised to see me, but Sissy grinned as if she'd been expecting me. Even if I'd wanted to, I couldn't have returned her smile. Now that I knew what she was, I didn't even want to look at her. She seemed as real and solid as ever, but I was scared she'd shed her skin the way I shed my clothes and stand before us in her true form—bones, nothing but bones, topped with a grinning skull and a tuft of hair, dressed in the rags of her bathing suit.

"Did you find the sweatshirt?" Sissy asked, mocking me with a sly grin. "I didn't want it anymore."

She stood knee-deep in the lake. Her faded bathing suit almost matched the fog, giving her an appropriately ghostly look. Beside her, an old canoe rode low in the water. Edith lay on the middle seat, her dirty face turned up to the foggy sky.

"Where did you get the canoe?" I asked.

Sissy shrugged, and the bones beneath her skin shifted. "It's just an old wreck of a thing. No one wants it. Not anymore."

Turning to Emma, she said, "Come on. Get in."

I grabbed my cousin's shoulder. "She's not going anywhere with you!"

Sissy laughed. "Want to bet?" Turning back to Emma, she held out the doll. "If you come with me, you can hold Edith."

Emma pulled free of my hands. Before I could stop her, she clambered into the canoe and sat on the middle seat, cradling Edith. "See? I'm not a scaredy cat baby like Ali."

Sissy jumped in and picked up the paddle. "There's room for you, too, Ali."

I splashed into the cold water and grabbed the side of the canoe. "Get out, Emma, and come home. You're sick, you've got a fever. Your mother doesn't know where you are. She's worried to death."

"Worried to death?" Sissy laughed. "What does Dulcie—or you—know about death?" Her eyes dared me to ask what *she* knew about death.

For Emma's sake, I kept my mouth shut. It would be better if my cousin never learned what her so-called friend really was. "Please." I grabbed her arm and tugged. The canoe rocked back and forth, and Emma clung to the sides.

"Stop, Ali," she cried. "You'll turn it over!"

Sissy dipped the paddle in the water. "Come or don't come," she said to me, "but I'm taking Emma for a ride."

Full of dread, I climbed into the canoe and took a seat in the front. With Emma sitting between us, Sissy paddled away from shore. In a moment, the mist surrounded us. Rocks and trees vanished as if they no longer existed. I could barely see Sissy and Emma, and I heard nothing but the gurgle and splash of the paddle moving through the water. It was like the dream I'd had of the three girls—only now it was real, and I was one of them.

Emma looked around uneasily. "Where are we going?" she said. "I can't see anything."

Sissy kept paddling.

"Take me home," Emma begged. "I don't like the canoe anymore. I don't like the fog. I want Mommy."

"Sorry, Em, but I don't know which way home is. Do you?" Sissy didn't pretend to be sorry or even worried. If anything, she seemed pleased with herself.

Emma began to cry. "Don't take me where the bones are. I don't want to see them."

"Bones, bones, bones," Sissy chanted. "Teresa wants you and Ali to visit her, stay with her awhile, keep her company."

"No," Emma cried.

I reached toward my cousin, but my arm wasn't quite long enough to touch her. I didn't dare move closer, for fear of upsetting the canoe.

"It's okay, Emma," I said. "She's just teasing you. We're almost home already." I hoped I was right, but I couldn't see the shore, a tree, the dock, or anything else.

Emma hugged the doll. "Me and Edith are scared."

Sissy laughed. "Give me Edith. She won't be scared if *I* hold her."

Emma clutched the horrid thing to her chest. "If I give her to you, will you take us home?"

"Maybe."

Emma turned to me. "Should I?"

"You'd better." Sissy answered before I had a chance to say a word.

Emma thrust the doll at Sissy. "Now take me home," she begged. "I'll do anything you say, just take me home."

Sissy sat still, the paddle in her hands, the doll beside her. "How bad do you want Edith?"

"Stop teasing her," I said. "Just take us home."

Sissy ignored me. "What if I throw Edith in the lake? Do you want her enough to jump in and get her?" She dangled the doll over the water. "Should I drop her?"

"No!" Emma cried. "No, Sissy, don't. Give her to me!"

I lunged past Emma at Sissy just as the doll flew out of her hands and splashed into the lake.

"Look what you made me do," Sissy yelled.

"I didn't make you do anything. You threw that doll—I saw you!"

While the two of us shouted at each other, Emma leaned out of the canoe, desperately reaching for the doll. Before I could stop her, she toppled into the lake. I saw her hair spread like seaweed on the surface—and then vanish. At the same moment, the canoe rocked wildly back and forth and tipped over.

As I plunged down into the cold dark water, I searched frantically for Emma. Through the murk, I glimpsed a swirl of hair, a pale face, an outstretched hand. Kicking hard, I swam toward her and grabbed her arm. The two of us sank together, weighed down by our wet clothes. Emma struggled like a fish trying to escape a net, but I held her tight.

I won't let you drown, I promised, *I'll save you. I'll save both of us.*

Using every bit of strength, I swam up toward the dim light of the gray sky. We came to the surface gasping for air. Emma clung to me, coughing and choking, too weak to struggle.

I swam to the overturned canoe and tried to get a good grip on it.

"Hold on," I told Emma.

"I can't," she wept. "I can't. It's too slippery."

"You have to!"

Just on the edge of the fog, Sissy circled us, drifting in and out of sight like a shark coming in for the kill. Slowly, she swam nearer, shoving the doll ahead of her.

I put my arms on either side of Emma to keep myself between her and Sissy. "Stay away from us!" I yelled.

Sissy pushed the doll closer. "It's nice in the water, Em. If you come swimming with me, I'll give you Edith—all yours forever. No takebacks."

Emma looked at me, and I shook my head. "You can't swim."

"Don't worry. I'll hold you up." Sissy swam close enough to grab Emma's hand. The doll floated nearby, her stained face barely visible in the dark water. "If you want to be my friend," she said, "you have to do what *I* say. Not what Ali says. Not what Dulcie says."

"Go away." Emma tugged her hand free of Sissy's grip. "I'm scared of you."

Shivering with cold and fear, I watched Sissy. Framed by long wet hair, her face was sharp and bony, her skin white, her eyes shadowy. The hands holding the doll were bony. If only she'd vanish into the water and sink to the bottom, where she belonged. If only Emma and I were safe in the cottage, drawing or reading by the fire, warming ourselves with hot chocolate. If only, if only, if only. . . .

"Why are you here?" I whispered. "What do you want from us?"

Sissy swam even closer. Once more, I moved between her and Emma. I could hear my cousin's intake of breath. Her skin was cold.

"I want you to make Dulcie and Claire tell the truth," Sissy said. "They should be punished for what they did. It's not fair. They're grown up, and I'm—" She broke off and glared at me. "It's all their fault. Make them tell. Or they'll be sorry."

I stared at her, perplexed. "What can they tell? They weren't in the canoe with you."

"How can you be so dumb?" Sissy gave me a look of pure hatred. "Dulcie and Claire lied! They're *still* lying."

Emma looked from me to Sissy and back again. "What did Mommy lie about?"

"I was there," Sissy went on. "And so were they. I remember— and so do they!"

"Where were they?" Emma cried, her voice shrill with confusion and fear. "Tell me, Sissy, tell me!"

Sissy looked at me, not Emma. "Tell Dulcie what happened today." Each word dropped from her mouth, as hard as stone. "Don't leave anything out. Not the doll, not the canoe, not me. Then ask her what happened to Teresa."

"My mother and my aunt would never hurt anyone."

"No?" Sissy mocked me with her grin. "Oh, before I forget— make sure Dulcie knows the canoe belonged to your grandfather. He called it 'The Spirit of the Lake.' Good name, don't you think?"

Turning her back, Sissy swam away into the fog, taking the doll with her.

"Come back!" Emma cried after her. "You'll drown."

"You can't drown twice," Sissy called, her voice muffled by the water.

"Sissy," Emma called again. "Sissy!"

No one answered. No one came swimming out of the fog.

Emma clutched my arm. "Is Sissy really Sissy? Or is she somebody else?"

I hesitated, unsure how much she'd figured out. Finally, I said, "Deep down inside, I think you know who Sissy is."

Emma nodded slowly. "'You can't drown twice,'" she said, echoing Sissy's words.

I drew her closer to me, holding her tight. The water was cold, and our arms ached. I only hoped that someone would find us before we lost our grip on the canoe.

~18~

Just as daylight began to fade, a wind sprang up and blew the fog away, shred by shred. Not far off, I saw a motorboat headed in our direction.

"Help," I shouted, desperate to be seen. "Help, help!"

Emma yelled, too.

A man on the boat turned and looked in our direction. "There's two kids over there," he yelled to another man. "Hanging on to a canoe."

The boat turned and made its way toward Emma and me. In a few moments, strong hands pulled us out of the water and into the boat.

"Is your name Alison O'Dwyer?" the man asked.

"Yes, sir. And this is my cousin, Emma Madison. We—"

"It's the missing girls!" he shouted to his friend. "The ones we heard about on the radio. Call the harbor police. Let 'em know they're okay."

He wrapped us in blankets and poured hot tea from a thermos. Emma and I took the cups gratefully, warming our hands as we drank. I thought I'd never stop shivering.

"What the devil were you doing way out here?" he asked. "If the fog hadn't lifted when it did, we'd have passed right by and never seen you."

Emma burrowed into my side like a newborn kitten seeking warmth, leaving me to make up a credible story.

"We saw the canoe on the shore," I began, "and we thought it would be fun to try it out. But we didn't really know how to paddle, and we got lost in the fog. It was a stupid thing to do."

"It sure was," the man agreed. "The whole town's been looking for you two."

I squeezed Emma's hand, but neither of us said a word. We just huddled together under the scratchy wool blankets and watched as Webster's Cove came closer and closer.

At least half the town was waiting for us on the dock. As soon as the men tied the boat up, Dulcie ran to us. Her hair was a wild mass of uncombed curls, and she'd been crying. Sweeping up Emma, blanket and all, she held her tight. "Emma, Emma," she sobbed. "Thank God, you're safe."

I stood there, all alone. After what I'd been through, I needed comforting, too, but I had a sinking feeling I wouldn't get it from Dulcie. At any moment, I expected her to blame me for everything.

Suddenly, Ms. Trent was at my side, hugging me. "Ali, why didn't you wait for me? If anything had happened to you . . ." She hugged me again, even tighter.

Dulcie looked at me over Emma's head, as if she'd just remembered I was there. "*You* have some explaining to do," she said.

A policeman took her aside and began asking questions that I couldn't quite hear. Dulcie beckoned to me, and Ms. Trent squeezed my hand as if wishing me good luck. As my one friend disappeared into the crowd, Dulcie bundled Emma and me into the car.

"The police think you two should be checked at the emergency room," Dulcie said. Without looking at me, she secured Emma in her child safety seat and drove to the hospital.

A nurse led Emma and me to an examining room, where we stripped off our wet clothes and put on paper gowns about ten sizes too big for me and twenty sizes too big for Emma. Both of us were still shaking with cold.

A doctor examined us. She pronounced me fine, except for a touch of hypothermia, which would have been worse if we'd been in the water much longer. She said Emma was still running a fever, and might have strep throat as well as mild hypothermia.

"Continue with Emma's medicine," she told Dulcie. "Bundle them both up nice and warm, give them hot soup, hot tea, and plenty of love. They've had a terrible experience."

An hour or so later, I faced Dulcie across the kitchen table. By then, Emma was in bed, sound asleep.

Clutching her coffee mug in both hands, she seemed more unhappy than angry. In a way, that was worse. "Tell me why you took Emma out in that canoe," she said. "Without even a life jacket."

I fidgeted with my place mat as if it were vital to keep its edge parallel to the edge of the table. "Promise you won't be mad."

"Why shouldn't I be mad?"

I moved the place mat a bit to the right and then back to the left. "After you called Ms. Trent," I said in a low voice, "I left her house and went to look for Emma. I found her by the lake with Sissy. Sissy wanted to take her for a ride in an old canoe."

Watching Dulcie closely, I added, "It was called 'The Spirit of the Lake.' Sissy said it used to be Grandfather's canoe."

"Yes . . . that's what my father named it." Dulcie held the mug tightly, her whole body tense. "But it can't be the same canoe. He got rid of it after we stopped coming here."

"Sissy had that doll with her—the one you threw in the lake. She said if Emma got in the canoe, she could hold it. I tried to stop Emma, but she wouldn't listen to me. Finally, I got in, too." I shifted the place mat a fraction of an inch. "I didn't know what else to do."

Dulcie sat with her head in her hands. I couldn't see her face. "Go on," she said.

"Sissy paddled way out into the fog. We couldn't see the shore—we could hardly see each other. She started teasing Emma with the doll. And then she threw it in the water and the canoe turned over and . . ."

Dulcie got up and left the kitchen. She didn't look at me. She didn't say anything. She just walked out.

I stayed at the table, turning the place mat round and round aimlessly. Even though Dulcie had loaned me her warmest fleece bathrobe, I was still cold. Once I glanced at the window, fearing Sissy might be watching me, but the glass panes reflected the kitchen, hiding the darkness outside—as well as anything lurking there.

Finally, Dulcie came back. She sat down and shoved a photograph toward me. It was the same one I'd found at home, only it wasn't torn. There was Mom with a sad face, there was Dulcie beside her with a big grin, and there was the third girl, the one torn out of Mom's copy. Her face was almost hidden in the shadows, but her light hair caught the sunlight. Smirking with satisfaction, Sissy held the doll Edith, brand-new, her hair perfect.

Dulcie touched the photo with the tip of her finger. "That's Teresa Abbott, the girl who drowned in the lake."

To Dulcie, the girl was Teresa, but to Emma and me, she was Sissy. Even though I'd already figured it out, I shuddered.

Dulcie seized my hands and stared into my eyes. "Is Teresa . . . the girl you call Sissy?"

"Yes," I whispered.

"It can't be," Dulcie whispered. "It can't. I don't believe in ghosts, I don't *want* to believe in ghosts, but . . ." For a moment, she sat there speechless. "But there's no other explanation. Is there?"

I shook my head. Outside in the darkness, the wind rose, and something tapped the windowpane. I turned to look, expecting to see Sissy's face pressed against the glass, her thin fingers knocking to come in. But nothing was there.

Dulcie picked up her cup to drink, but her hands shook so badly she put it down without taking a sip. "It was the worst thing I ever did. I've tried to forget about it, pretend it never happened." Her voice dropped so low I could barely hear what she said. "But I can't forget her. And neither can your mother."

"Sissy doesn't want you to forget," I said.

Dulcie bent her head over the photo. "The doll," she said. "Edith. Mother gave it to Claire on her eighth birthday."

"But why is Sissy holding it?" I asked.

"Teresa loved to tease Claire with that doll. She'd snatch it way from her and make her beg to get it back. The more your mother cried, the more Teresa tormented her."

I stared at her, shocked. "You were the oldest. Why did you let Sissy pick on Mom like that?"

Dulcie studied the three girls in the photograph. "It's not a nice thing to say, but I used to be jealous of your mother," she said. "She was always sweet and nice, and I wasn't. Most people liked her better than me."

I wanted to sympathize with my aunt, but it hurt to learn that she let Sissy torment my mother. As an only child, I had all sorts of notions about sisters and how they took up for each other— blood being thicker than water and all that.

"So when Teresa teased Claire," Dulcie went on, "I'd go along with her. I guess I wanted her to like me more than Claire. Not a good excuse, but I'm afraid that's how it was." She looked past me, at the darkness outside. "Your mother was right. I should never have come back here."

I clung to the edge of my chair with both hands. "What happened the day Sissy drowned?"

Dulcie picked up the photo, put it down, turned it over to hide the three faces. "It was a few days after Claire's birthday," she began. "Mom and Dad had gone shopping in Webster's Cove. Teresa came over and started teasing Claire. She grabbed Edith and ran down the steps to the lake. I dashed after her, laughing. Claire followed me, crying for the doll."

She paused to take a sip of coffee, made a face, and put the mug down. "Cold."

"What happened next?" I asked.

"Teresa got in Dad's canoe," Dulcie said. "It was against the rules to go anywhere in that canoe without one of our parents, but I jumped in after her."

Dulcie shook her head. "But not Claire. Even then she was scared of water. She stood on the dock, threatening to tell. Teresa said if Claire didn't come with us, she'd take Edith home and keep her."

The wind had picked up, and it moaned in the pines the way it had in the cemetery. It seemed as if all the sadness in the world had been sucked up into that sound.

"Claire finally got in the canoe," Dulcie went on, "and Teresa pushed off. We hadn't gotten very far when the fog rolled in. We couldn't see the shore. It was like being lost in a cloud. Kind of magical and scary at the same time."

She started pacing around the kitchen. "Teresa tossed Edith to me. I threw her to Teresa. Claire lunged back and forth, rocking the canoe, trying to catch her doll. A game of keep-away—that's how it started. Kids play it all the time. But it wasn't a game to Claire. She begged me to give her the doll. She kept saying, 'You're my sister, Dulcie, you're my sister!'"

Dulcie stopped pacing and poured herself more coffee, hot this time. "Suddenly, I got sick of the whole thing. Sick of Teresa. Sick of Claire. Sick of the stupid doll. When Teresa tossed it to me, I threw it in the lake. I grabbed the paddle from Teresa and started to turn around. I figured that was the end of it: *Nobody* would have the doll."

She went to the window and peered out into the windy night. "But things didn't go the way I planned. Claire sat there crying, like she always did, but Teresa was stubborn. She wanted that doll so badly she jumped into the lake after it. The canoe tipped over then, and Claire and I went in, too. I got Claire to the canoe, and we hung on to the sides. But Teresa swam after the doll. I yelled at her to come back. She ignored me. And then she was gone. Just like that. In the water with us one minute, lost in the fog the next. Claire and I shouted till we were hoarse, but Teresa didn't answer."

I watched my aunt go from one window to the next as if she were still looking for Teresa. "The canoe floated to shore, where the rocks are. We left it there and ran all the way home. I told Claire it was a trick. Teresa had fooled us somehow. She'd be waiting for us on the porch. I think I believed it myself." Dulcie glanced at me. "But she wasn't there."

She picked up a sponge and wiped away a spot on the counter.

"Claire started crying again. So did I. Teresa was dead—we knew she was. And it was my fault. I'd thrown the doll in the lake. I thought I'd be charged with murder, arrested, sent to jail. I was just a child—what did I know about the law, or what could happen to me?" Her voice rose. She was breathing hard, talking fast, as if the police might arrive at any moment, sirens howling, lights flashing.

"I made Claire promise not to tell anyone we'd gone out in the canoe. We'd been in the house all day. We hadn't seen Teresa."

Dulcie sat down across from me. "When our parents came home, we were sitting right here at the kitchen table, drawing pictures, doing our best to act like nothing was wrong. A few minutes later, the phone rang. It was Mrs. Abbott. Mom turned to us and asked if we'd seen Teresa. We lied and said no. After that, we couldn't stop lying. We lied to the Abbotts, to the police, to everyone. Even ourselves. It was horrible. Horrible. I didn't mean for Teresa to die, I didn't—it was an accident."

Dulcie covered her face with her hands and began to cry. "I'd give anything to go back in time and undo what I did."

I sat there, a silent lump of misery, too shocked to say anything. My mother and my aunt had lied. *Lied.* And all these years, they'd gone on lying. And Sissy had lain alone in the lake, waiting for them to come back. Waiting for them to tell the truth.

Finally, Dulcie reached for the tissue box. Her face was pale, her eyes red rimmed and puffy.

"What are you going to do?" I asked.

"Go back to New York." She blew her nose. "We'll leave tomorrow."

"But what about Sissy?"

"Sissy?" Dulcie stared at me as if I'd lost my mind.

"Teresa, I mean." It was hard to call Sissy anything but Sissy. "I told you what she said. You have to tell the truth—or you'll be sorry."

Dulcie jumped up and went to the window again. The glass streamed with rain. "Who can I tell? Mr. and Mrs. Abbott are dead. I don't know where her sister, Linda, is."

I followed my aunt and rested my head against her shoulder. "How about the police?"

"They wouldn't be interested after all these years." Dulcie peered into the rainy night. "Besides, it was an accident. I didn't know Teresa would jump out of the canoe. I didn't know she'd drown." Her voice wavered and grew stronger. "I was scared. For God's sake, I was only ten years old!"

Tippety-tap, tippety-tap. The branch whipped back and forth in the wind, rapping against the glass again.

Suddenly, Dulcie closed the curtains and moved away from the window. "I can't talk about this," she said. "I'm going to bed."

I watched her walk toward Emma's room. I stayed where I was, my back to the window. A few moments later, Dulcie carried Emma down the hall to her bedroom. Emma was sound asleep, limp and relaxed in her mother's arms. Dulcie didn't look at me or say anything. In the silence, I heard the door close behind them.

Reluctantly, I climbed the stairs to my room. Never had I felt so sad or so totally and completely alone. Why hadn't Dulcie invited me to sleep with her and Emma? Didn't she think I needed company, too?

At the top of the steps, a cold draft rushed out to meet me, circling my ankles, chilling me from the knees down. My window was wide open, and the rain had blown inside, soaking the floor and the magazines on top of my bookcase. I rushed to the casement and struggled with the crank, fighting the wind to close it.

As I reached for the light, a cold hand grabbed my wrist. "Don't bother," Sissy whispered. "I'm used to the dark." In her other hand, she clutched Edith the doll.

More startled than scared, I tried to pull away from her, but she held me tightly. The doll fell to the floor as we struggled. "What do you want?" I whispered.

"Did you tell Dulcie what happened today?"

"Yes." I peered at Sissy's thin, pointed face. "And she told me what happened to you."

Sissy kept her icy grip on my wrist. "So she remembers after all. Is she going to confess what she did?"

"It was an accident, Sissy," I said slowly. "Dulcie didn't mean for you to drown. She didn't push you in the lake—you jumped."

Sissy tightened her hold on my wrist and scowled. "She knew I'd go after the doll. She hated me—just like you do. She planned the whole thing. She wanted me to drown."

I heard the anger in her voice, and I saw the anguish in her eyes. "Dulcie didn't want you to die," I said. "She didn't hate you. And neither do I."

Sissy let go of me and rescued Edith from a puddle of rainwater on the floor. "You used to hate me," she muttered, hugging the doll to her skinny chest. "Now you just feel sorry for me. You don't really like me. Nobody does."

I rubbed my wrist to take the chill of Sissy's hands away. She stood by the window, holding the doll tightly, her face filled with misery.

"You're cold." I took a spare blanket from the closet and wrapped it around her. Then I dried her hair with a T-shirt, rubbing her scalp hard to warm her. It was strange—she felt solid but somehow insubstantial, boneless, as if she could melt away at any moment.

"Will you comb my hair?" she asked.

I sat her down on the edge of the bed and worked a comb through her tangles. No one had done anything about her hair for a long time. But even though I was sure I must be hurting her, she sat still and didn't complain.

When her hair was smooth, she ran her fingers through it. Allowing herself a small smile, she said, "Prove you don't hate me. Let me sleep in your bed tonight. I'm so tired of the dark and the cold."

I got into bed and reluctantly let Sissy curl up beside me. It was like lying next to a snow girl made on the coldest night of winter.

"Are you scared," she whispered, "to share your bed with me?"

"You're just a little girl," I said.

"Not an ordinary one."

"No, not ordinary. Not ordinary at all."

Sissy sat halfway up. "Do you know what I am?"

"Yes, I know."

"Did you suspect all along?"

"No. You seemed like a real girl, not a—"

"Shh." She pressed her cold hand against my mouth. "Don't say it. I hate that word."

"I didn't guess till I saw the sweatshirt in the angel's hand," I said. "And read your name on the stone."

She leaned over me, and I smelled the lake on her breath. Not exactly fresh, a bit musty, a little earthy. "Make Dulcie tell—not just you, but everybody. I've been waiting a long time for her to come back."

With that, she lay down again, a small hump under the covers, not quite as cold as she'd been before.

Too tense to sleep, I lay beside her, staring into the darkness. Dulcie *had* to tell the truth. Not just for Sissy's sake but for her own. And Mom's, too. Otherwise, none of them would ever be at peace.

19

In the morning, Sissy was gone. And so was the wind and the rain. The sky was a brilliant blue, and the air smelled like honeysuckle and roses. I lay still for a moment, wishing the world was as ordinary as it seemed. Sun shining, birds singing, no dark shadows, no secrets, no lies.

Downstairs, Emma was chattering away to her mother as if nothing had happened yesterday. If only that were true.

I pulled on shorts and a T-shirt and headed for the kitchen. Dulcie looked up from the stove. "Emma's feeling much better today," she said, trying hard to sound cheerful. "Her fever's gone, and she wants pancakes."

I sat down and stared at the plate Dulcie set in front of me. I wasn't hungry, but I didn't want to hurt my aunt's feelings. She wasn't often inspired to cook a real breakfast.

"Last night," I started to say but stopped myself. Why bring up Sissy? Dulcie's smile might change to a frown. Emma's laughter might change to tears.

"Last night," I told Dulcie, "I dreamed you fixed pancakes for breakfast, and you made so many it took us till Christmas to eat them all."

Emma laughed so hard, maple syrup dribbled out of her mouth and ran down her chin. That made Dulcie and me laugh.

After we'd eaten, Emma got out her drawing tablet and busied herself making a picture with black, purple, and blue crayons. All scribbles, very dark.

Dulcie drew me aside, signaling that Emma mustn't hear. "I've made an appointment to see a lawyer in Webster's Cove today. My parents knew him. I'll talk to him about Teresa's death."

"Do you want me to come with you?"

"Not to the lawyer's. I thought you and Emma might enjoy browsing in shops, getting ice cream, strolling along the board-walk." Dulcie glanced at Emma, who was still bent over her picture, totally absorbed. "She needs a day out. And so do you."

"Hey, Em," I called. "Better get dressed. We're going to town."

Emma laid her crayons down and ran to her room. While she was gone, Dulcie and I took a quick look at her picture. Dark and scribbly as it was, we could both make out a boat with two girls in it. A third girl was in the water, along with Edith the doll.

Cars crowded Webster's Cove's narrow streets, and vacationers thronged the boardwalk and the beach. Like me, they'd been here long enough to value sunshine, blue water, and warm air. It had rained yesterday and the day before, and most likely it would rain again tomorrow and the day after.

Dulcie left us at Smoochie's, telling Emma she had a few errands to run. "I'll meet you here at noon, and we'll have lunch somewhere."

Erin was busy scooping ice cream for three teenagers. When she'd finished, she smiled at Emma and me. "Long time no see. Where have you two been?"

"Playing at our beach," Emma said.

"With that girl Sissy?" Erin asked.

Emma toyed with the candy and gum display beside the cash register. "Sissy's gone, I think."

"Hey, Em," I said. "They have tutti-frutti today. It's yummy."

Erin held up a little white paper cup, the kind you use to rinse your mouth at the dentist's. "How about a sample?"

Emma took the cup, stuck her tongue into the ice cream, thought a moment, and handed it back. "Can I have chocolate instead? That's my most favorite kind of all."

While Erin packed two scoops of chocolate into a cone, Emma stood in the doorway and watched people stroll past. A display of faded Smoochie's T-shirts swayed in the breeze over her head. Such an ordinary day, such ordinary people. I wondered if any of them had ever seen a ghost. Would they believe me if I told them about Sissy?

Erin handed me Emma's cone. "What kind do you want?"

"Tutti-frutti, of course." With images of Sissy crowding my head, I felt like an actress playing the part of a normal girl.

Erin bent over the ice cream and struggled to fill the scoop. "It's always hard as a rock in the morning. By afternoon, it'll be like soup."

"Is that mine?" Emma reached for the chocolate cone. I gave it to her, and she wandered back to the door.

Erin went on scooping, her head down. "My mother told me she visited your aunt, but she said she wasn't very friendly. Your aunt got all bent out of shape when Mom mentioned Teresa Abbott."

"Dulcie didn't mean to be rude," I said. "She just doesn't like to talk about Teresa."

Erin straightened up and wiped her hands on her apron. "So she *does* remember. Mom thought she'd repressed the whole thing. Either that or she was lying." She handed me my cone. "It must have been awful for her and your mom."

"It was." I paid Erin for the cones and followed Emma outside. Like Dulcie, I had no desire to discuss Teresa Abbott with anyone. She was our secret, a dark little shadow at the edge of the real world.

Emma and I sat on the boardwalk and ate our ice cream, slurping it down before it melted. Some teenagers were playing volleyball on the sand. We watched them shout and laugh and jump around, cheering each other on. Their voices blended with the cries of gulls and the *wish, wash* of the lake's little waves.

Down by the water's edge, a man threw a Frisbee out over the lake. His dog, a big black Lab with a red kerchief tied around his neck, splashed into the water after it. He ran out of the lake with the Frisbee in his mouth and shook so much water from his coat that a woman complained to his owner.

I wished Emma and I were down by the water playing with the dog, happy, having fun, like girls on a vacation.

Suddenly, Emma turned her chocolate-smeared face to me. "Did Mommy really push Sissy in the water?"

"No. She got mad and threw the doll into the lake, and Sissy went after it. It was foggy, like yesterday, and Dulcie and Mom couldn't find her. The canoe drifted, and they washed up on the rocks. They went home and lied to everyone because they were scared it was their fault that Sissy drowned."

"Poor Sissy." Emma edged closer to me. "Mommy and Aunt Claire shouldn't have lied."

"I think they know that now."

Side by side, we gazed at the lake, blue and calm under a cloudless sky. Children Emma's age darted in and out of the water, shrieking and splashing each other. The teenagers laughed and shouted, and the volleyball flew back and forth across the net. The dog fetched the Frisbee again and again, never tiring of the game. It seemed everyone was happy but us.

"Do you want to wade in the water?" I asked Emma. "Or build castles in the sand?"

She shook her head, and we stayed where we were.

By the time Dulcie joined us, I'd braided Emma's hair into two short plaits and tied them with a piece of string. They were a little crooked, but Emma liked them. She tossed her head back and forth to show them to her mother.

"Very cute." Dulcie eyed Emma's T-shirt, face, and hands. "It looks like you really enjoyed your ice cream. Chocolate, huh?"

Emma smiled and took her mother's hand. We walked along the boardwalk to a little restaurant with a deck built out over the lake and seated ourselves at a table shaded by a green umbrella. Dulcie and I ordered lobster rolls and iced tea, but Emma asked for chocolate milk and a hamburger. Just plain, she said, no lettuce, no tomato, no pickle. But with French fries and lots of ketchup.

The waitress—a college girl, I guessed—smiled at Emma. "I love a kid who knows exactly what she wants."

While we waited for our food, Dulcie gave Emma a few slices of bread from a basket on the table. "Why don't you go feed the gulls?"

Emma ran to the railing and began tossing bits of bread into the air. In seconds, she was surrounded by dozens of hungry gulls, screaming for their share.

Dulcie turned to me. "I told Mr. Goldsmith the whole story," she began, "leaving out Sissy, of course. He said it's pointless to go to the police now. The case was closed years ago. Accidental drowning." She took a sip of water. "He told me Claire and I weren't—aren't—responsible for Teresa's death. Even if we'd told the truth the day it happened, it wouldn't have changed anything."

"What does he think you should do?"

"Forget about it." She gave me a bitter smile. "If only it were that easy."

I thought of Sissy begging me to make Dulcie tell the truth, to take some of the blame for what happened. "But you can't just forget about it, you have to tell—"

Dulcie laid her hand on mine. "I know, Ali. Believe me, I know." She turned her head to watch Emma hurl the last of the bread to the gulls. "I'm going to talk to someone at *The Sentinel* after lunch. It's the kind of story newspapers love." Her hand tightened on mine. "Will your mother be upset?"

"I think she'll be okay with it," I said, hoping I was right.

"Here you are." The waitress set our food on the table, and Emma came running.

"Did you see me feeding the gulls?" she asked the girl.

"I sure did. You must have fed the entire population."

"They're big," Emma said, "and they have sharp beaks and mean yellow eyes, but I wasn't scared."

"I bet nothing scares you." The waitress stood with her empty tray pressed to her chest, smiling down at Emma.

"Sometimes nothing is the scariest thing of all," Emma said in a low voice, but the waitress had already turned her attention to a family at another table. No one heard her but me.

After we'd eaten, Dulcie told us she had one more thing to do before we went home. "How about you and Ali waiting for me at the arcade?" she asked Emma. "You can ride the carousel, the

Ferris wheel, the bumper cars—anything but the Tilt-A-Whirl. You'll throw up for sure on that one."

Emma clapped her hands with pleasure, too excited to notice that Dulcie had eaten less than half of her lobster roll. She'd barely touched her French fries. And she hadn't even bothered to taste the coffee she'd ordered instead of dessert. I watched her walk away, head down, shoulders slumped. If I hadn't known she was doing the right thing, I would have run after her and stopped her.

In a hurry to get to the carousel at the end of the boardwalk, Emma ran ahead, towing me along behind her. Soon she was perched on a fancy white horse wearing a garland of carved flowers, and I was beside her on a black horse. We went up and down and round and round, accompanied by old-fashioned organ music. I smelled popcorn and cotton candy and suntan oil.

Emma seemed as happy as the other children. She laughed and waved to everyone, and they waved back. It amazed me that her mood could change so quickly. Here I was, worrying about Dulcie, brooding about Sissy, wanting my mother, and there Emma was, the princess of the carousel.

By the time Dulcie came back, we'd ridden the carousel five times, the Ferris wheel once, and the bumper cars twice. We'd also eaten cotton candy and shared a box of popcorn. We were ready to go home.

At the car, Dulcie fumbled with the buckle on Emma's safety belt. "Sit still," she said, her voice sharp. "How do you expect me to do this with you wiggling like that?"

Emma frowned. "I'm not wiggling."

"There." Dulcie snapped the buckle, slammed the back door, and got into the front seat beside me.

With a jerk, she pulled away from the curb and headed into the afternoon traffic. "I hate tourists," she muttered. "Why do they have to come here and ruin everything? Crowds, trash everywhere. It's a disgrace."

Her change of mood told me things hadn't gone well at *The Sentinel*.

Not long after we got home, Emma fell sound asleep on the couch, worn out from all the excitement. Afternoon sunlight washed the walls with pale yellow, and a calm stillness filled the house.

I joined Dulcie on the deck. "They're running the story next week," she said. "A photographer's coming on Sunday to shoot some pictures. They want to talk to the police as well, and some of the other people who remember Teresa and her family."

Getting to her feet, she walked to the railing and stared at the lake. "The way they acted, you'd think I just confessed to murder. I should have gone back to New York and never said a thing about this. Or never come here at all. What was I thinking anyway?"

"Are you going to call Mom?" I asked. "And tell her?"

Dulcie looked over her shoulder at me. "Do you think I should?"

"She might want to come."

"Yes, I guess she might." Dulcie went to the door.

I followed her inside. "Can I talk to her, too?"

"Of course." Dulcie picked up the receiver and dialed our number. I heard Mom answer. In a low voice, Dulcie told her what she'd done. "I thought you'd want to be here. If we get this out in the open, maybe we can put it behind us."

From where I stood, next to Dulcie, I heard Mom crying into

the phone. "Yes," she sobbed. "Yes, I'll come. Pete and I can drive up Saturday."

"Thanks, Claire. . . . Ali wants to talk to you." Dulcie handed me the receiver.

"Are you okay?" Mom asked. The worry in her voice surged through the line.

"Yes, I'm fine."

"Dulcie shouldn't have told you."

"She had to tell the truth," I said.

In the silence before Mom spoke, I heard a familiar whisper. "Tell her about me. Let her know I'm still here. Just like she thought."

Sissy stood a few feet away where the shadows were darkest, holding the doll and frowning. "If you don't tell her, I will." With that, she vanished without a sound, unseen and unheard by anyone but me.

"Did you say something?" Mom asked.

"No," I stammered. "It's just Emma, playing with her paper dolls."

"I thought I heard . . ." For a moment or two, Mom breathed slowly into the phone as if she were trying to calm herself. At last she said, "Do you hate Dulcie and me for leaving Teresa to drown?"

The question took me by surprise. "Of course not, Mom. You tried to find her, you—"

She broke in. "Maybe if we'd tried harder, we could have saved her. If we'd told someone right away. If we'd—" She started crying. "I go over it again and again. I can't stop thinking about Teresa, about leaving her there—it's haunted me my whole life."

"It wasn't your fault. You were just a little kid, you didn't throw the doll, you——"

Dulcie had crossed the room and now snatched the phone from my hand. "Stop it, Claire," she said to my mother. "What happened, happened. Nothing can change that. You'll just have to deal with it."

I reached for the phone, but Dulcie shook her head. "Go see what Emma's doing. I'll say goodbye to your mother for you."

I retreated to the living room and tried to listen to Dulcie's end of the conversation. It sounded as if she was bullying Mom, talking tough, acting the part of big sister. Silently, I egged Mom on. *Stand up for yourself, stop crying, tell her you're an adult, too.* By the time Dulcie hung up, I was beginning to wonder if I'd ever look up to my aunt the way I used to.

Fearing she'd know I'd been eavesdropping, I sat down quickly on the sofa next to Emma. She woke up just as Dulcie entered the room, clutching a cup of coffee——her fifth, sixth? It was hard to keep count. Her blood must've been pure caffeine.

She stood by the window, looking out at the lake, ignoring both of us. Her back was tense, rigid almost. "Is your mother still seeing a shrink?" she asked.

"She's depressed," I said. "She tries not to be, but——"

Dulcie spun around and faced me. "Don't tell me about depression. She needs something to do besides moon over her flowers. She used to write poetry, she used to draw. Now she just sits around feeling sorry for herself."

"It wouldn't kill you to be nicer to her." Fed up with Dulcie, I left the house. Ignoring Emma's call to wait for her, I ran down the steps to the lake. I needed some time alone. No Emma, no Dulcie, no Sissy——*especially* no Sissy. If I saw her, I'd run.

I walked all the way back to Webster's Cove and treated

myself to ice cream. But I was still in a bad mood when I returned. Worse in a way, because I was now tired and hot.

Somehow I got through dinner without making a scene and managed to read to Emma before bedtime. Dulcie had nothing much to say—which was fine with me. An apology was all I wanted to hear from her, but I had a feeling that was not going to happen. While I read to Emma, my aunt sat in one of the old armchairs, drinking yet another cup of coffee. She'd pulled her hair up into an untidy topknot, and her hands and arms were streaked with the same black paint that spattered her jeans and T-shirt.

Sitting around feeling sorry for yourself. Isn't that what you accused Mom of doing? I thought.

"Bedtime." Dulcie roused herself to pick up Emma.

"I want to hear another chapter!"

"I'm tired, and so are you, and so is Ali. It's time we all went to bed."

Without another word, not even "Good night," Dulcie carried Emma off to bed. I guessed that meant she was just as mad with me as I was with her.

When I went up to my room, I found Sissy perched on my bed, holding Edith on her lap. I wasn't surprised to see her. It was obvious she wasn't done with us.

"Did Dulcie tell the truth at last?" she asked.

"She talked to her lawyer. He said she hadn't committed a crime. And then he told her she should forget the whole thing."

Sissy sneered. "She's been doing a pretty good job of that all along."

I bristled. "Dulcie's never forgotten a single detail of that day. Neither has Mom. In fact, Mom feels worse than Dulcie. In a way, it's ruined her whole life."

"How about me? Don't you think they ruined *my* life?" Sissy asked plaintively. "Believe me, I feel a whole lot worse than either of them!"

"I'm sorry," I said. "It was stupid of me to say that."

"Yes, it was," Sissy agreed, clearly pleased I'd apologized.

"After she saw her lawyer," I went on, "Dulcie talked to a reporter at *The Sentinel*. A photographer's coming here to take pictures, and they're going to interview lots of people, including Dulcie and my mother."

Sissy smiled a real smile for once. "That's just exactly what I wanted. Everybody in Webster's Cove will know the truth at last."

She watched me get ready for bed, and then crawled in beside me. Shivering, I moved toward the wall, giving her as much room as I could.

"Just a few more nights," she whispered, "and then you'll never see me again."

Once I would've been happy to hear that, but tonight I felt an unexpected twinge of sadness. Odd as it sounds, I was getting used to having Sissy around. Now that I knew so much more about her, it was easier to put up with her sadness and anger.

~20~

In the morning, Sissy was gone, but her pillow was damp and cold.

Dulcie met me at the foot of the steps. She'd tidied her hair, washed off the paint, and changed her clothes, but she was still tense and edgy. Behind her, I could see Emma sitting at the kitchen table, coloring a picture.

I looked at my aunt warily, braced for another outburst.

Glancing at Emma, she spoke in a low voice, "I'm sorry for my behavior yesterday. I was upset. And Claire just fell apart. I needed her to be strong, so I could be strong." She reached out to hug me, and I felt myself begin to relax.

"I never should have criticized your mother," Dulcie said. "She can't help being depressed. I know she's trying to get better. Please forgive me, Ali. I love you both, your mother and you. We're all the family we have."

I returned her hug. "It's okay, I understand." *That is, I think I do.*

Dulcie let me go and gazed at me thoughtfully. "Did you tell your mother about Teresa?"

"You mean, Sissy? No," I said. "But even if we don't say a word, Sissy will figure out a way to let her know."

"You really saw her?" Dulcie whispered. "It wasn't a kid playing a trick?"

"It was her," I said. "Teresa . . . Sissy . . . whatever you want to call her. She's been hanging around all summer."

Dulcie shook her head. "I'm sorry, Ali, but that's hard to believe, especially on a sunny day like this."

A little later, I heard a car. Although it was way too early to be Mom and Dad, I ran to the door.

Ms. Trent got out of her faded blue Volvo and waved to me. "I was driving past, and I thought I'd drop in. Is your aunt here?"

I beckoned her to follow me inside. "Ms. Trent's come to see you," I told Dulcie.

She looked up from the newspaper and made an effort to smile. "I just made a fresh pot of coffee. Would you like a cup?"

"I never turn one down." Ms. Trent followed Dulcie to the kitchen. I heard her say something in a low voice.

Dulcie turned to me. "Weren't you going to make paper dolls for Emma?"

"Yes, yes, you promised!" Emma grabbed my hand and towed me out to the deck. She'd left paper, crayons, and scissors scattered across the picnic table. "Make one like you and one like me and one like—" She stopped. "No, just make two. You and me. Best friends."

Emma watched me draw, her face so close I could feel her warm breath on my hand. While she chattered on about the clothes she wanted for her doll, I strained to hear Dulcie and Ms. Trent's conversation. I picked up a word here, a word there, enough to know they were talking about Teresa. Or Sissy. Whichever she preferred to be called.

Emma jumped up suddenly. "There's a cat. It's after a bird!"

A big black and white cat was creeping across the grass, belly to the ground, eyes on a sparrow that was pecking at seeds spilled from the bird feeder.

When Emma ran across the lawn to stop it, I moved closer to the kitchen window, hoping to hear better.

"Nothing's a secret in Webster's Cove," Ms. Trent was saying. "Ed Jones, the reporter you talked to, has a wife with a big mouth. She called Jeanine Donaldson and told her the whole story. Jeanine didn't waste a second spreading the news. By the time she told me, the whole town knew, including Teresa's sister, who lives a few miles away in Lakeport—which was news to me."

"Ali, come help me!" I turned to see Emma holding the small brown bird in her hands. "It's still alive."

While the cat watched from the bushes, I ran to Emma's side. The sparrow flapped its wings feebly. Its yellow beak opened and closed slowly. While I watched, its eyes lost their luster, and it stopped moving.

"Can we save it?" Emma asked.

I took the sparrow from her as gently as I could. "The poor little thing," I whispered. "It's dead."

Emma began to cry. "I hate cats. I hate them!"

The old stray lurked under the bush, twitching its tail. It was clear it felt no remorse. Given the opportunity, the cat would have snatched the bird and run off with it.

Emma bent down to pick up a stone. Before she could throw it, I grabbed her arm. "No," I said. "Cats can't help killing things. It's their nature."

Emma dropped the stone and touched the bird's body sadly. "Can we bury it?"

I went inside to find a large spoon to dig a grave, and Emma followed me, still crying for the bird. "Why do things have to die?" she cried, burrowing into her mother's arms. "It's not fair."

I showed the dead sparrow to Dulcie and Ms. Trent. "A cat killed it. We're going to bury it."

"Do birds have ghosts?" Emma asked Dulcie.

Over Emma's head, Dulcie and Ms. Trent glanced at each other. Ms. Trent shook her head, and Dulcie said, "Of course not, darling. There's no—"

Emma straightened up and looked Dulcie in the eye. "Don't say there's no such thing. Ghosts are real. You know it, and I know it, and Ali knows it." She hesitated a second. "And *Sissy* knows it."

Emma stood there gazing at her mother, daring her to argue.

"We came in to get a spoon," I told Dulcie, "so we can dig a grave for the bird."

While Dulcie selected an appropriate spoon, I ran to my room for a tissue box I'd thrown in the trash that morning. We wrapped the bird in an old handkerchief and laid it in the box. Then Emma and I took turns digging a hole under a lilac bush, and gently placed the box in the ground.

While we said a few words over the bird, I felt my neck prickle, as if someone was watching us. Uneasily, I glanced over my shoulder. Almost hidden in the shade of a tall oak, Sissy peered at me. When she realized I'd seen her, she ducked out of sight.

I returned my attention to the pile of earth heaped beside the small grave and spooned some onto the box. Emma followed my example. With Dulcie and Ms. Trent helping, we filled the hole and tamped it down firmly to keep the cat from digging up its victim.

Before we returned to the house, I looked at the oak tree. Sissy was gone.

Dulcie filled two coffee mugs for herself and Ms. Trent and poured lemonade for Emma and me. While my aunt and Ms. Trent sat at the table, they chatted quietly about quilting and painting. Ms. Trent said a small gallery had just opened on the main road. Dulcie asked about an arts and crafts shop she'd noticed on a side street. They both deplored the crowded roads and beach. It was comforting to hear them talk about ordinary things.

After Ms. Trent left, I sat on the deck, watching for Dad's car. It was almost five thirty. The sky had clouded over, promising rain once more, and daylight was already fading. Inside, Dulcie was preparing a special seafood dinner, and Emma was playing with the paper dolls I'd made.

Dulcie came to the window and looked at me. "It's about to rain," she called. "Aren't you cold?"

I shook my head. "It's nice out here."

Dulcie shrugged. "Suit yourself."

As she turned away, I heard a car coming toward the house. I jumped up and ran to meet my parents as if we'd been apart for years instead of weeks. I hugged Dad tight and then threw my arms around Mom. She cried, wetting my face with tears, and turned to Dulcie.

"I never thought I'd see this place again." Mom looked around, her face worried. "It's just as I remembered. Nothing's changed."

"Except us," Dulcie threw her arms around Mom. "It's good to see you, Claire."

As she hugged Dad, I glanced at the oak tree. Sissy watched from the shadows, her pale face expressionless.

Emma saw her, too. I grabbed her arm to stop her from running to meet her, but I needn't have bothered. Sissy was already gone.

"Why did she run away?" Emma whispered. "Is she still mad?"

"It's got nothing to do with you and me," I told her. "Sissy wants to see our mothers. But she doesn't want them to see her."

Taking her hand, I led my cousin into the house. For once, she didn't argue.

While the adults chatted, Emma and I set the table for dinner. No one mentioned Teresa Abbott—not then and not during dinner. Emma and I talked about swimming and drawing and Webster's Cove. We complained about the rain and the fog and the mosquitoes, and my parents complained about the heat and humidity at home.

Mom told me the kid next door had broken his ankle skateboarding. My friend Julie got a hideous permanent and was threatening to shave her head. Mrs. Burgess had named her new baby girl Meadow, of all things. We laughed and talked and enjoyed the flounder-and-scallops extravaganza that Dulcie had invented.

After we'd cleared the table and washed the dishes, Dad built a fire. Dulcie produced marshmallows for Emma and me to toast. It had begun to rain while we were eating, and it was coming down harder now. The wind had risen, too. Thunder boomed, and lightning flashed. Emma and I abandoned the marshmallows and curled up with our parents.

"I hate storms," Mom said.

"I love them—the wilder and fiercer, the better!" Dulcie jumped to her feet and ran to a window to watch the lightning. I wondered if she were putting on an act for Mom, striking a pose, trying to convince us she was fearless. She didn't fool me. I knew her too well now, maybe even better than Mom did.

"Come away from the window," Mom pleaded. "Lightning might strike you."

Dulcie laughed. "Don't be silly, Claire. The chances of that are a billion to one."

Emma ran to her mother and tugged at her hand. "Sit on the couch with me, Mommy."

Suddenly, Dulcie gasped and backed away from the window.

"What did you see?" Emma pressed her face to the glass. "Is it Sissy?"

Dulcie ran her hands through her hair, tugging it back from her face. "Come away, Emma. No one's there."

"Sissy," Emma persisted. "Sissy's out there." She pressed her face against the glass and peered into the rain.

Mom looked up from her magazine, her face anxious. "Was someone at the window?"

"Of course not," Dad said quickly. "Who'd be out in a storm like this?"

I could have said, *Someone who doesn't mind being wet.* But I didn't.

"Who was it?" Mom asked Dulcie. "Don't lie. Tell me, tell me now!"

Alarmed by her rising voice, Dad moved closer to her. "No one was there, Claire."

Mom ignored him. Her attention was fixed on her sister and the window behind her. "It was her, wasn't it?"

"Calm down, Claire," Dad begged. "Breathe slowly, deeply. Relax. You'll give yourself a headache if you get upset."

Dulcie stayed by the window, holding Emma tightly. "Do you really want to know?" she asked Mom. Her voice was calm, but her face was flushed, her eyes bright as if she had a fever.

Dad looked from Dulcie to Mom and back to Dulcie. "What kind of game are you playing now?"

"No game." Dulcie smoothed Emma's hair. "I grew out of games a long time ago."

Emma squirmed free of her mother and ran to Mom. "Don't worry. Sissy won't hurt you. She just wants to see what you look like now."

Mom shuddered and drew back. "Sissy?"

"Teresa," Dulcie said. "She's been calling herself Sissy. The girls have seen her, played with her." She hesitated a moment. "They even went out in the canoe with her."

Mom looked at me, pale and wide-eyed, like someone waking from a nightmare and finding it's not a dream after all. "You *saw* Teresa? You got in a *canoe* with her?" Shaking with anger, she turned to her sister. "Oh, Dulcie, Dulcie, how could you let them do it? I knew you wouldn't watch them. I knew it!"

"If you'd been here instead of moping in Maryland, afraid of everything—"

Emma spoke up loudly enough to get her mother's attention. "Sissy showed us how Mommy threw Edith in the water." To demonstrate, she made a throwing motion. "She wanted me to get Edith, but she fell in, too. I thought she was going to drown all over again. And then the canoe got upset and I was afraid me and Ali would drown."

Mom gasped and leaned against Dad's side. For a second, I thought she was going to faint. "See what you've done?" she asked Dulcie. "You've brought it all back. Why couldn't you have let things be?"

"So you could have headaches all your life?" Dulcie asked bitterly.

I squeezed onto the sofa beside Mom and clasped her hands in mine. "Don't you see? Dulcie *had* to come here. She had to tell the truth so Sissy—Teresa—"

"Don't say her name." Mom started crying. "I can't bear to hear it."

"Sissy won't hurt you, Aunt Claire." Emma climbed into Mom's lap and wrapped her arms around her. "She just wants you and Mommy to tell what really happened."

Dulcie gently pulled Emma away from Mom. "That's enough, sweetie," she said softly. "It's time for bed."

Emma started to protest, but the look on her mother's face silenced her. Meekly, she let Dulcie carry her out of the room.

Dad looked at Mom as if he feared she was hallucinating. "What are you so upset about, Claire? You told me Teresa drowned years ago. How can she be here now?"

Mom didn't answer. She was watching the window as if she expected to see Sissy's face.

Turning to me, Dad said, "Can you please tell me what's going on?"

Before I could answer, Mom pressed her fingers to her temples and said, "I can't stay here a minute longer, Pete. Please take Ali and me to Webster's Cove. Find a motel, a bed-and-breakfast, whatever. I'll sleep in the car if I have to—any place but this cottage."

Dad stared at her, shocked. "We can't walk out on your sister. What will she think?"

"My head aches so badly, I don't care what anyone thinks, least of all Dulcie," Mom said. "I'll lose my mind if I don't get out of here."

"I don't understand," Dad said. "What *is* it about this cottage? You'd think it was haunted or something—"

"It *is* haunted," I said. "Weren't you listening to what we said?"

"That's crazy, absolutely crazy," Dad said. "I thought you had more sense, Ali." Giving me an annoyed look, he went to the door and peered into the darkness as if he expected to see a little girl outside—a real little girl who'd laugh and admit she'd played a trick on us. Of course, he saw no one.

Shaking his head, he sat down beside Mom again. "It's a hoax," he said. "Someone with a grudge is behind the whole thing. Maybe Teresa has relatives who blame Dulcie and you for what happened. They could have a daughter who looks like Teresa." Dad sounded as pleased as if he had solved a tricky math problem. "They got her to pretend to be Teresa's ghost."

I looked at my father and almost pitied him—reasonable Dad, the man who depended on logic and common sense. There was no room in his world for the supernatural. No matter how much proof I gave him, he'd never believe me.

"Please," Mom said. "Let's leave, right now, before—"

"Before what?" Dulcie watched us from the shadowy hall. "Before Teresa drags us into the lake and drowns us? Is that what you're scared of?"

Mom got to her feet and faced Dulcie, her fists clenched as if she wanted to punch her sister. "I won't stay here another second!"

Dad put his arm around her. "Claire," he said softly, "it's after ten. We'd never find a room at this hour. And, as much as I love you, I'm not going to sleep in the car."

"Pete's right," Dulcie said. "There aren't many motels, and you can bet they're all filled by now. Why don't I make up the sofa bed?"

Dad yawned. "One night, Claire. We'll go home tomorrow."

Mom turned to Dad, suddenly tearful. "I want to leave, but

I'm so tired, I ache all over." Her eyes strayed to the window and the darkness pressing against it.

"How about a glass of warm milk with honey?" Dad asked. "That always helps you relax."

"Can we keep the light on all night?" Mom asked.

Dulcie laughed. "You sound just like Emma."

I braced myself for another quarrel, but before Mom could object, Dulcie added, "I might keep my light on, too."

After I kissed Mom and Dad good night, I gave Dulcie an extra-big hug for admitting she was scared. Maybe there was hope for her and Mom after all.

I climbed the stairs wearily, hoping to fall into bed and sleep till noon, but I should have known better. As usual, Sissy was waiting for me.

⚡21⚡

I saw you bury that bird today," Sissy said. "It had a nice funeral. You sang a song and said the right words. All that fuss for a bird."

"Emma saw a cat kill it. She wanted to—"

"A bird shouldn't get better treatment than a person," Sissy said. "Or am I wrong about that?"

"I know what you're thinking," I said, "but you have a memorial in the cemetery. There must have been a funeral and flowers and the right words and lots of people crying."

"But I'm not buried there, am I?" She held Edith a little tighter. "So none of it counts."

"But nobody knows where you are. Ms. Trent told me people searched the lake, the police sent down divers, they did all they could to find you, but—"

"They didn't try hard enough," Sissy interrupted. "Or I'd be buried in the cemetery instead of—" She broke off with a shudder and went to the window. "Do you think I like being out there?"

I joined her at the window and peered at the lake, barely visible in the rain and darkness. "If you tell me where you are, the police could get you."

"I tried to show you," Sissy said, "but you were scared to come and look. Remember?"

"I thought you were going to push me off the cliff."

Sissy laughed. "I just wanted to show you where I am. Deep down in the cold dark water, under three big rocks. All alone except for Edith . . . and the fish."

"That's where you are?" My voice dropped to a whisper, and my skin prickled with goose bumps. It was almost as if I'd just realized I was actually talking to a girl who'd been dead longer than I'd been alive.

"Why would I lie about it?" Sissy shoved her angry face close to mine. "I'm sick of being there. I want to be buried in the grave-yard where the angel is. Is that too much to ask?"

I drew away from the stale smell of the lake that clung to her. "Of course it's not too much," I stammered. "You *should* be there, it's where you belong."

"If the truth is told and I'm buried properly, if the right words are said over me and people bring flowers and someone cries, then I won't trouble anyone again."

Although it scared me to touch her, I put my arm around her shoulders. She felt solid but cold through and through, and I wished I could warm her somehow.

"Kathie Trent's gotten so old," Sissy said sadly. "Dulcie and Claire, too. I guess Linda must look different. But not me. I'm just the same. I'll never grow up. Or get old."

The sorrow in her voice hurt me. If only I could make it up to her, give her the life she should have had. But there was no way to undo what had happened that day on the lake. Thirty years ago, Sissy had lost her life, her future, and everything that might have been hers.

"Do you think I would've been as pretty as Linda?" Sissy asked. "Would I have gotten married like her, would I have had kids?"

It was hard to answer without crying. "I bet you would have been even prettier than Linda," I told her. "And you would've gotten married and had kids, and all that stuff."

Sissy pulled away, suddenly angry. "Don't you dare feel sorry for me! Just make sure all the things I said should happen *do* happen."

Leaving her words hanging in the air, she vanished, and I was alone at the window. The rain fell softly, the wind blew in the pines, the lake murmured—gloomy sounds, all of them. Sissy was right. What happened to her wasn't fair. It was sad and awful and it hurt my heart.

The next morning, I tiptoed through the living room. Dad snored on the sofa bed, and Mom slept beside him, curled close. Dulcie was in the kitchen, drinking coffee and staring at nothing.

I poured myself a glass of orange juice and sat down across from her. "Telling what happened isn't enough," I whispered. "She wants a proper burial."

Dulcie stared at me over the rim of her mug. "How can we do that? Her body was never found."

"She told me where it is."

Dulcie closed her eyes for a moment. Taking a deep breath, she said, "How will you explain that to the police? A ghost told you? I can imagine their reaction."

"I'll say I had a dream, I'm psychic, I'm—"

"Will this nightmare never end?" Dulcie lowered her head.

I leaned across the table to make my aunt look at me. "Sissy *must* be buried. The right words must be spoken. There must be flowers and somebody crying. She saw us do that for the bird. Doesn't she deserve the same thing?"

"Are you talking about Teresa?" Mom stood in the doorway behind me, her hair tangled from sleep.

Dulcie sighed. "Apparently, Teresa told Ali where her body is. She's demanding a proper burial."

I twisted around in my chair to face Mom. "She just wants peace, Mom. Is that too much to ask?"

"I dreamt about Teresa last night." Mom stood beside me and stroked my hair back from my face, her touch soft and tender, her voice calm. "She begged me to help her pass from this world to the next."

Dulcie jumped up and began pacing around the kitchen. If she'd been a tiger, her tail would have lashed furiously. "She came to me, too," she muttered. "With the same request. Usually, I don't put stock in that sort of nonsense—dreams, ghosts, things left undone, but . . ." She shrugged, and her shoulder blades shifted under her thin T-shirt. "Well, no matter. l agree that Teresa needs to be laid to rest, but how do we explain knowing where her body is? People will think we've known all along."

Dulcie's voice rose as she spoke. "Someone will say I shoved Teresa out of the canoe and left her to drown. Next thing you know, I'll be hauled off to jail."

"I was there, too," Mom said. "What we did was stupid, wrong, horrible, but you didn't push Teresa into the lake. You didn't mean for her to drown."

Dulcie sat back down and rested her head in her hands.

"Do you want more coffee?" I asked.

She surprised me by shaking her head. "All I want is to go to sleep and wake up and find out I dreamt the whole thing. It's what I've wished for all my life—it was a dream, it didn't really happen. But I just go on dreaming. I never wake up."

"I'll tell the reporter Teresa told me where her body is," I said. "I'll say I saw her ghost."

"Maybe——" Dulcie began, but she was interrupted by the arrival of a beat-up red sedan. A short man draped with cameras opened the car door and headed toward the cottage. He wore his gray hair in a scraggly ponytail, his jeans drooped below his belly, and his black T-shirt had an old rock star's picture on it. Mick Jagger, I thought. Or was it one of the Beatles—John, maybe?

"The photographer," Dulcie muttered. "He's early."

Mom ran to wake Dad, Dulcie hurried to greet the photographer, and Emma slid into a chair across the table from me. "Did you see Sissy last night?" she asked me.

"She came to my room."

"She came to my room, too." Emma paused and picked at a scab on her knee. In a low voice, she said, "She told me where her bones are."

"She told me the same thing."

Emma went on picking at the scab. Sunlight slanted through the window behind her and backlit her hair. "She wants to be buried. Like the bird."

"I know." Outside I saw the photographer taking pictures of the cottage. He posed Dulcie, tall and thin in a pair of paint-spattered denim overalls, head tilted, hair curling out of its top-knot. She didn't smile. Her face was serious, contemplative, as if she were acting the part of the repentant adult.

Emma raised her head and looked at me. "If Sissy gets buried, will we ever see her again?"

I reached across the table and patted her hand. "Sissy's here because she wasn't buried. When everything's done properly and people know what happened, she'll be at rest."

"That's what I think, too." Emma sighed and returned her attention to the scab. "I'll miss her, though. Will you?"

"Think of it this way," I said slowly. "Sissy doesn't belong here anymore. Wherever she goes next, she'll be better off. Happier."

"How do you know?" Emma looked at me mournfully. "Maybe she'll just be gone."

Dulcie saved me from trying to answer an impossible question by coming through the kitchen door with the photographer in tow.

"This is Dan Nelson," she said, "from *The Sentinel*. He's come to take a few pictures of you two, as well as some of Claire and me."

Emma looked at him. "I wish you could take a picture of Sissy. She'd like to be in the newspaper."

Mr. Nelson smiled at Emma. "I'm sure I can fit another child into my shots. Is she a friend of yours?"

"Yes," Emma said. "Me and Ali both know her."

Behind Emma's back, Dulcie shook her head at Mr. Nelson, trying to tell him to drop the subject.

"I don't think you can take pictures of ghosts," Emma said.

Ignoring Dulcie, Mr. Nelson squatted down beside Emma and looked her in the eye. "Are you telling me your friend is a ghost?"

He said it in a joking, aren't-you-a-funny-little-thing sort of way, but Emma didn't notice. "Sissy has to be buried in the graveyard, all proper with a funeral and flowers and people crying. Somebody has to get her bones. Ali and me can show you where they are."

"That's enough, sweetie." Dulcie reached for Emma's hand, glanced at me, and then turned to Mr. Nelson. "My niece had a dream about Teresa. She told Ali where her body is."

The photographer looked from Emma to me and then to

Dulcie, his whole face a question mark. "What are you talking about? Nobody knows where Teresa Abbott's body is."

"I believe in psychic powers," Dulcie lied. "If Ali says she knows where the body is, it will be there."

"We didn't just dream Sissy," Emma said. "We *saw* her. We talked to her, we played with her all summer. She was just as real as you!"

Mr. Nelson reacted the way Dad had. "You couldn't have seen her." He glanced at me. "And neither could you."

He had the look of a man who'd seen through many a hoax— UFO's, apparitions, mysterious lights—something that went with a news photographer's job, I supposed.

Mom came to the kitchen door, dressed neatly as usual, the perfect contrast to Dulcie. "You don't believe in ghosts?" she asked Mr. Nelson.

"Of course not."

Dad followed Mom into the kitchen. "I'm afraid you and I are outnumbered," he told Mr. Nelson. "Reason and common sense will not be found in this cottage."

Mr. Nelson made the mistake of laughing. "Maybe it's a female thing."

Dulcie turned on him fiercely. "Gender has nothing to do with this. It's not a hoax, either. Instead of laughing it off, maybe you should give the girls a chance to prove they're right."

"You *have* to believe us," Emma put in. "We promised Sissy."

"Please," Mom added, "let the girls show you the place. Send a diver down. It can't hurt to look."

"Think of it this way," Dad said, still joking. "If the kids are right, you'll have a great story, probably the biggest you'll ever stumble on in Webster's Cove."

Mr. Nelson rubbed his jaw. I could almost hear his thoughts:

*national news, Pulitzer Prize, TV talk shows, a best-selling book
... on the other hand, I could make a fool of myself, become the
butt of jokes, a laughing stock, never live it down. . . .*

"You've got a point," he told Dad. Pulling a cell phone out of a
pocket, he said, "I'll call the police."

A moment later, he said "Hello, Neil? This is Dan Nelson from
The Sentinel. I'm at Gull Cottage doing a recap about the girl
who drowned back in the late seventies."

A slight pause.

"Yes, Teresa Abbott," he went on. "The kids here say they
know where her body is."

Another pause, a little longer this time.

"I'm not sure how they know, but I think it's worth following
up. Maybe you could send a diver."

A pause again.

Mr. Nelson spoke a little louder. "What have you got to lose?"

When he hung up, his face was somewhere between pleased
and worried. "They're sending a diver. He should be here in a
half-hour or so."

Next he called the paper and asked for Ed Jones, the reporter
who'd interviewed Dulcie. "Got something here you might be
interested in," he said.

I could hear Ed Jones's voice but not what he was saying.

"I'll tell you this much," Mr. Nelson went on. "It involves the
Abbott girl's remains—and a hint of the supernatural."

"I'll be right there," Mr. Jones shouted into the phone.

"The supernatural is Ed's thing," Mr. Nelson grinned at Dad
as if to suggest they were linked by common sense and logic. "I
keep telling him he should get a job with one of the rags—*The
National Enquirer*, maybe."

While we waited for the police and Mr. Jones to show up, Mr.

Nelson photographed us in a number of poses, both inside and outside. He even included a few shots of Dad looking skeptical.

When Dulcie showed him the photo of herself, Mom, and Teresa, he borrowed it to make a copy.

Mom grimaced at the sight of it. "You should have destroyed that, Dulcie. Or at least removed Teresa."

Dulcie shrugged. "History's history. You can't change it by destroying a snapshot."

Turning away, she busied herself making a fresh pot of coffee. "There ought to be a pound cake in the pantry," she told me. "Why don't you get that out and fix some blueberries to go with it? I picked a quart yesterday."

By the time the policeman arrived, followed closely by Mr. Jones, we'd all fortified ourselves with cake and blueberries, coffee for the adults, and lemonade for Emma and me.

When she saw the officer at the back door, Dulcie grabbed Mom's hand. For a moment, they looked like little girls clinging to each other, scared and anxious. Neither spoke. They just stood there, holding hands, waiting for what would happen next.

Before the policeman had a chance to introduce himself, a black sedan braked to a sharp stop, and a woman I'd never seen jumped out.

"It's Linda," Mom whispered. Dulcie held her hand tighter.

Sissy's sister came into the kitchen like a blast of wind. Her curves had rounded out, but her hair was still blond, and she wore plenty of lipstick. "You never fooled me," she cried. "I knew all along you were in that canoe with Sissy."

Mom began to apologize, but Dulcie broke in before she finished. "It was an accident," she said. "We never meant to harm Sissy. We were just kids, we—"

"Sissy was just a kid, too!" Linda looked at me. "Younger than her! Why didn't you tell the truth? Do you know how much grief you've caused us? Rich summer people coming here, acting like you're above the law. Well, you should be arrested. You should pay for what you did to my sister!"

The policeman took Linda's arm and gave it a gentle squeeze. "Now, now, Linda, that's enough. I told you not to come out here. I'm not planning to make any arrests. Or press charges. I just want to get some things straight."

Somehow, he managed to calm Linda down. Then he turned to Mom and Dulcie and introduced himself. "I'm Captain Wahl," he said. "I understand you have some new information about Teresa Abbott's remains. The diver's coming by boat, but I thought we could have a little chat before he starts looking."

I wanted to hear what Mom and Dulcie and Linda had to say, but Captain Wahl told Dad to take Emma and me outside. "I'll talk to the girls later."

A motorboat was already tied up at the dock. A man in a wetsuit stood with his back to us, gazing out at the lake. It was one of those rare sunny days, and the water had never looked bluer.

Emma clung to Dad's hand. "Is he going to find Sissy?"

Dad squeezed her hand, his face skeptical. "Maybe."

I grabbed Dad's other hand and held it tight, glad for its familiar shape and warmth. "Yes," I told Emma. "He is."

A few minutes later, Captain Wahl joined us. The others trailed behind, Mom and Dulcie close together, Linda a few steps back, clearly separating herself from them. The reporter and photographer brought up the rear, heads together, exchanging opinions.

Captain Wahl took Emma and me aside. "Tell me again how you know where the body is."

"It's just bones now," Emma whispered.

"Yes, right." Captain Wahl nodded and wrote something in a little notebook. "But how do you know where the bones are?"

"Sissy told us."

"Sissy's Teresa's ghost," I added. "Emma and I have seen her lots of times. Honest we have. Last night she told us both where her . . . where she is." I couldn't bring myself to refer to Sissy's bones or her skeleton.

"A ghost." He nodded and made a few more notes. I knew he didn't believe us, but he played along as if he did. "Will you show me where you think the bones are?"

Emma and I set out along the path. Captain Wahl called down to the diver to follow in his boat. With Linda on our heels and the others close behind her, we made our way to the high point Sissy had taken me to. More fearless than I, Emma walked to the edge and pointed down.

"See those three big rocks? That's where the bones are."

Captain Wahl peered down at the calm water. "You're sure, honey?"

"Sissy told me. And she told Ali, too."

I nodded. "This is the place."

Captain Wahl signaled, and the diver anchored his boat and slipped into the water. He was gone a long time.

"Did he drown?" Emma asked.

"He has an oxygen tank," I told her. "So he can breathe under water."

At last the diver came to the surface. "I don't know how the girls knew," he called up to the captain, "but the bones are there."

Linda began to cry. "If only Mom and Dad were still alive, if only they knew she's been found."

Dulcie and Mom cried, too, but Dad stood there like a man in shock. The photographer looked stunned as well. His and Dad's concept of the world had suffered a serious blow. In contrast, the reporter grinned broadly.

Captain Wahl was the only one to speak. "Incredible," he said.

Emma took my hand and pointed. "Look," she whispered.

In the shadows under the pines, Sissy gave a thumbs-up and vanished before anyone else saw her.

Dad reached out for Emma and me. "Let's go back to the cottage."

ᴄ⑨22ᴇᴏ

The rest of the day dragged slowly past. Emma spent most of it sleeping, exhausted, I guess, by all that had happened. The policeman left, still puzzled. With a few more nasty comments, Linda departed. The photographer and Dad sat on the deck trying to find other explanations for the discovery of Teresa Abbott's remains. The reporter sat near them, still grinning, and typing away on his laptop. In the end, all three were left with the possibility that Emma and I had truly seen a ghost.

Live Action News showed up in the afternoon, along with most of the population of Webster's Cove. Tourists tramped through the yard and followed the trail to the cliff top, snapping pictures of everything with their little cameras. We were interviewed all over again by the TV reporter and videotaped by their photographers.

The media people insisted on waking Emma so they could talk to both of the girls who saw the ghost. Tired and cranky, Emma clung to Dulcie and cried. I overheard the reporter say in a hushed tone, "Four-year-old Emma, clearly traumatized by her encounter with the supernatural, sobs in her mother's arms."

Fed up, I sneaked away into the woods. Safe from reporters and tourists, I sat down and leaned against a tree trunk. "They all know now, Sissy," I said to myself. "Everyone in the state of Maine and probably the rest of the country, too."

Sissy stepped out from behind the tree, cradling Edith in the crook of her arm, her silvery hair bright against the gloomy woods. With a sigh, she sank onto the mossy ground beside me, closed her eyes, and rested her head against the tree.

"Are you okay?" I asked.

Sissy yawned. "Just tired," she murmured. "Really, really tired. All those people running around, asking questions, taking pictures. Even when they can't see you, being famous is hard on a person."

"I couldn't take it anymore, either," I confessed. "That's why I'm hiding in the woods."

"Do you think they'll bury me soon?"

"The day after tomorrow, I heard." Uncomfortable with her question, I toyed with a twig, bending it this way and that, avoiding her eyes. It bothered me to talk about her burial with her sitting beside me, as real as ever.

"That's good." Her sigh was as soft as a breeze in the treetops. "I'm not sure how much longer I can stay."

"Where are you going?" I asked, forgetting for a moment she wasn't an ordinary girl about to leave on a trip.

Sissy grinned. "That's for me to know—and you to find out."

My discomfort returned, and I twisted the twig again. When it broke with a loud snap, I tossed the pieces away.

Sissy held up her arm. "Look, you can almost see through it."

I turned my head. "Don't."

Sissy came closer. "Why? Does it scare you?"

When I slid away from her, she laughed out loud. "Better watch out. I might take you with me."

"Stop it. That's not funny."

Still laughing, she seized my arm. "Don't you like me even a little bit?"

Chilled by the touch of her hand, I pulled away and jumped to my feet, ready to run.

"No," Sissy cried. "Don't go, Ali. I was just teasing."

I hesitated, rubbing my arm to warm the spot she'd grabbed. "How do I know you're not lying?"

With narrowed eyes, Sissy stared at me. "If I wanted to kill you, I'd have drowned you and Emma both when I had the chance. Just sit with me awhile. I'll be gone soon."

Cautiously, I sat down a few feet away from her, scared to get too close.

"All I really wanted was a friend." She poked at the moss with a stick, scratching lines in it. "When Dulcie came along, I thought she was going to be my friend, but then she had to go and throw Edith in the lake and ruin everything. I wish she hadn't done that."

"She wishes she hadn't done it, too."

Sissy nodded wearily. "But she did. And look at all the trouble she caused."

"She didn't think you'd jump in the water."

Sissy gouged the moss savagely, tearing up bits of it and revealing the dark soil it grew from. "Okay, okay, it was a dumb thing to do. Don't you think I know that now?"

"I've done plenty of dumb things," I said. "Everybody has. It's just that—" I broke off and watched a ladybug settle on a leaf beside me.

"It's just that most people don't end up like me," Sissy finished my sentence.

I sighed and nudged the ladybug gently into the air. *Fly away home.*

"The water was deep and dark and cold," Sissy said, "and I

kept sinking down. I tried and tried, but I couldn't swim up to the top."

Suddenly, she reached out and touched my cheek. "You're crying."

"I know."

Sissy watched the tears run down my cheeks. "If things had been different," she said, "if I was like you instead of—well, what I am—do you think we would be friends?"

Once I would have said no without even thinking, but things had changed between Sissy and me. "Yes, I think so."

"Me, too." Sissy smiled and leaned back against the tree. Her eyelids fluttered shut, and she seemed to sleep.

I didn't know whether she wanted me to leave or stay, so I sat beside her and waited for her to wake up. While we'd been talking, the sky had begun clouding over. A gust of wind turned the leaves white-side-up, a sure sign of rain Dad always said.

When Sissy opened her eyes, I got to my feet. "I should go home before it starts raining."

Sissy stayed where she was, her back against the tree, her legs stretched out in front of her. "Bye, Ali."

"Will I see you again?"

"Maybe." She smiled at me, one of her rare real smiles.

I waved and left her there. I didn't look back.

By the time I reached the cottage, rain was coming down hard, and the last of the sightseers were driving away, leaving the driveway rutted and filled with puddles.

A couple of days later, the people in Webster's Cove held a funeral for Sissy, just as I'd told her they would. In the graveyard, over a hundred people huddled under umbrellas and listened to a minister read a tribute to a child long lost but now found. He led a prayer. We cried and threw flowers on the small coffin as it was lowered into the grave at the angel's feet.

Afterward, in the warmth of Gull Cottage, Mom and Dad discussed their plans to drive home the next day.

"Do you want to come with us?" Mom asked me.

Dulcie patted my hand. "I'll understand if you leave," she said. "I've been a witch."

Emma threw her arms around me. "Please stay," she whispered.

I hugged Emma hard. "Okay, okay, I'll stay."

Mom opened her mouth to protest, but Dad shook his head. "Summer's more than half over. Ali will be home before we know it."

So it was settled. My parents went home, and I remained at the lake. Dulcie returned to her studio and her work. She decided the paintings weren't as bad as she'd thought. One night at dinner, she told us she was going to call her show "Deep and Dark and Dangerous, a Study of Water's Changing Moods."

On sunny days, Emma and I swam and built sandcastles. We went to Smoochie's, and I talked Emma into trying something besides chocolate. On rainy days we drew and read and made clay figures. I finished *To Kill a Mockingbird* and began *A Separate Peace.* The summer had taken a turn to the ordinary.

But not quite. Just before Dulcie planned to return to New York, Emma and I decided to visit the graveyard. On the way, we each gathered a handful of wildflowers. Sissy would like them, Emma said.

Despite the sunlight, the graveyard was in shadows. A splash or two of light dappled the stone angel and the new grave at its feet.

Emma seized my hand. "Look," she whispered.

Missing one arm, hair matted and dirty, skin stained, Edith lay on the earth that was heaped over Sissy. Emma ran to the grave, but I hesitated, not sure how to interpret the doll's presence. Had Sissy left her there for Emma? Or did she want Edith to stay where she was?

Something stirred in the shadows behind the angel. In the dim light, I saw Sissy. For the first time she looked like what she was, nearly transparent, too thin to cast a shadow, her voice a whisper. "The doll's for you, Emma. To keep."

Emma reached out as if to embrace Sissy, but her arms closed on nothing. Sissy was gone. Gone for good.

Tearfully, Emma laid her flowers on the grave and picked up the doll. "Sissy wants me to have Edith."

I laid my flowers beside Emma's. Silently, the two of us stood together, thinking our own thoughts of Sissy.

After a long moment, I turned to Emma. "Let's go home," I said softly.

Hand in hand, we left Sissy resting peacefully under the angel's protective hand.

Wait Till Helen Comes

A Ghost Story for Norm

———— ✤ ————

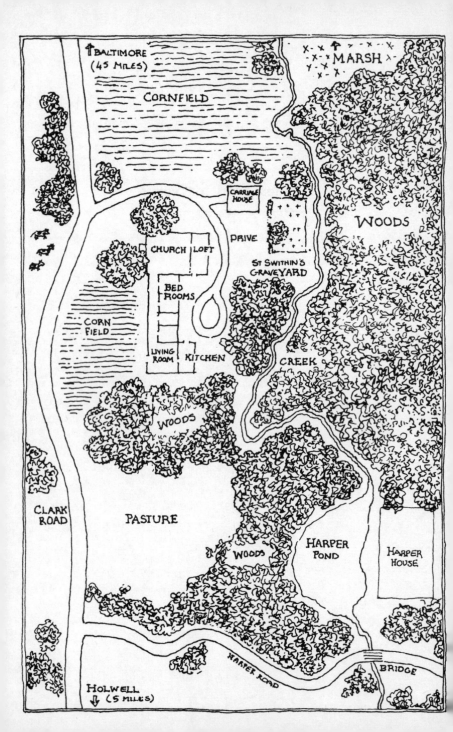

1

―――――✦―――――

"YOU'VE BOUGHT a church?" Michael and I looked up from the pile of homework covering most of the kitchen table. I was in the middle of writing a poem for Mr. Pelowski's English class, and Michael was working his way happily through twenty math questions.

Mom filled a kettle with water and put it on the stove. Her cheeks were pink from the March wind, and so was the tip of her nose. "You and Molly will love it," she promised. "It's exactly the sort of place Dave and I have been looking for all winter. There's a carriage house for him to use as a pottery workshop and space in the choir loft for me to set up a studio. It's perfect."

"But how can we live in a church?" Michael persisted, refusing to be won over by her enthusiasm.

"Oh, it's not really a church anymore," Mom said. "Some people from Philadelphia bought it last year and built an addition on the side for living quarters. They were going to set up an antique store in the actual church, but, after doing all that work, they decided they didn't like living in the country after all."

"It's out in the country?" I frowned at the little cat I was doodling in the margin of my notebook paper.

Mom smiled and gazed past me, out our kitchen window and into Mrs. Overton's window directly across the alley. I had a feeling she was seeing herself standing in front of an easel, working on one of her huge oil paintings, far from what she called the "soul-killing life of the city." She has a maddening habit of drifting away into her private dream world just when you need her most.

"Where *is* the church?" I asked loudly.

"Where is it?" Mom poured boiling water into her cup and added honey. "It's in Holwell, Maryland, not far from the mountains. It's beautiful. Just beautiful. The perfect place for painting and potting."

"But what about Molly and me? What are we supposed to do while you and Dave paint and make pottery?" Michael asked.

"You promised I could be in the enrichment program this summer," I said, thinking about the creative writing class I was planning to take. "Will I still be able to?"

"Yes, and what about Science Club?" Michael asked. "I'm already signed up for it. Mr. Phillips is going to take us to the Aquarium and the Science Center and even to the Smithsonian in Washington."

Mom sighed and shook her head. "I'm afraid you two will have to make other plans for summer. We'll be moving in June, and I can't possibly drive all the way back to Baltimore every day."

"But I've been looking forward to Science Club all year!" Michael's voice rose, and I could tell he was trying hard not to cry.

"You'll have plenty of woods to explore," Mom said calmly. "Just think of all the wildlife you can observe and the insects you can add to your collection. Why, the day Dave and I were there, we saw a raccoon, a possum, a woodchuck, and dozens of squirrels." Mom leaned across the table, smiling, hoping to convince Michael that he was going to love living in a church way out in the country, miles away from Mr. Phillips and Science Club.

But Michael wasn't easy to convince. Slumping down in his chair, he mumbled, "I'd rather stay in Baltimore, even if I never see anything but cockroaches, pigeons, and rats."

"Oh, for heaven's sake, Michael!" Mom looked exasperated. "You're ten years old. Act like it!"

As Michael opened his mouth to defend himself, Heather appeared in the kitchen doorway, responding, no doubt, to her built-in radar for detecting trouble. Her pale gray eyes roved from Mom to Michael, then to me, and back again to Mom. From the expression on her face, I imagined she was hoping to witness bloodshed, screams, a ghastly scene of domestic violence.

"Why, Heather, I was wondering where you were!" Mom turned to her, infusing her voice with enthusiasm again. "Guess what? Your daddy and I have found a new place for us to live, way out in the country. Won't that be fun?" She gave Heather a dazzling Romper-Room smile and reached out to embrace her.

With the skill of a cat, Heather sidestepped Mom's arms and peered out the kitchen window. "Daddy's home," she announced without looking at us.

"Oh, no, I forgot to put the casserole in the oven!" Mom ran to the refrigerator and pulled out a concoction of eggplant, cheese, tomatoes, and bulgur and shoved it into the oven just as

Dave opened the back door, bringing a blast of cold March air into the room with him.

After giving Mom a hug and a kiss, he swooped Heather up into his arms. "How's my girl?" he boomed.

Heather twined her arms possessively around his neck and smiled coyly. "They were fighting," she said, darting a look at Michael and me.

Dave glanced at Mom, and she smiled and shook her head. "We were just discussing our big move to the country, that's all. Nobody was *fighting*, Heather." Mom turned on the cold water and began rinsing lettuce leaves for a salad.

"I don't like it when they fight." Heather tightened her grip on Dave's neck.

"Come on, Michael." I stood up and started gathering my books and papers together. "Let's finish our homework downstairs."

"Dinner will be ready in about half an hour," Mom called after us as we started down the basement steps.

As soon as we were safely out of everybody's hearing range, I turned to Michael. "What are we going to do?"

He flopped down on the old couch in front of the television. "Nothing. It's too late, Molly. They've bought the church and we're moving there. Period."

Grabbing a pillow, he tossed it across the room, narrowly missing one of Mom's paintings, a huge close-up of a sunflower. "Why did she have to marry him? We were perfectly happy before he and Heather came along."

I slumped beside him, nodding my head in agreement. "They've ruined everything." Glancing at the stairs to make sure Heather hadn't sneaked down to spy on us, I said, "If only Heather was a normal kid. She acts more like a two-year-old than a seven-year-old. And she's mean; she tattles and lies and does everything she can to get us in trouble with Dave. Why do they always take her side — even Mom?"

Michael made a face. "You know what Dave says." Making his voice deep and serious, he said, "Heather is an unusually imaginative and sensitive child. And she has suffered a great loss. You and Molly must be patient with her."

I groaned. "How long can we feel sorry for her and be nice to her? I know it must have been horrible to see her mother die in a fire and be too little to help, but she was only three years old. She should've gotten over it by now, Michael."

He nodded. "If Dave would take her to a shrink, I bet she would get better. My friend Martin's little brother goes to some guy out in Towson, and it's helped him a lot. He plays with dolls and draws pictures and makes things out of clay."

I sighed. "You know perfectly well what Dave thinks of shrinks, Michael. I heard him tell Mom that all they do is mess up your head."

Michael got up and flipped the TV to "Speed Racer." With one eye on the screen, he set about doing the rest of his math while I sat there doodling more cats instead of finishing my poem.

After a few minutes, I nudged Michael. "Do you remember that movie we saw on TV about the little girl who did horrible things to her enemies?"

"*The Bad Seed?*"

"Yes, that was it. Well, sometimes I think Heather's like that girl, Rhoda. Suppose she burned her mother up on purpose the way Rhoda burned up the janitor?"

Michael peered at me over the top of his glasses. "You're crazy, Molly. No three-year-old kid could do anything like that." He was speaking to me as if he were a scientist explaining something to a child instead of a ten-year-old boy addressing his twelve-year-old sister.

Realizing how ridiculous I sounded, I laughed and said, "Just kidding," but I really wasn't. There was something about Heather that made me truly uncomfortable. No matter how hard I tried, I couldn't even like her, let alone love her as Mom kept urging me to. It was hard to feel pity or anything but dislike for her.

It wasn't as if I hadn't tried. When Heather had first moved in, I'd done everything I could think of to be a good big sister, but she'd made it clear that she wanted nothing to do with me. If I tried to comb her hair, she pulled away, crying to Mom that I was hurting her. If I offered to read to her, she'd yawn after the first sentence or two and say the story was boring and dumb. Once I made the mistake of letting her play with my old Barbie dolls, the ones I was saving for my children; she cut their hair off playing beauty parlor and ripped their best outfits. She even tore up a family of paper dolls I made for her, taking great pleasure in beheading them right in front of me. Then she dropped them disdainfully in the trash can and walked out of the room.

To make it even worse, she told lies about Michael and me, making it sound as if we tormented her whenever we were alone with her. Dave believed her most of the time, and sometimes Mom did too. In the six months that Mom and Dave had been married, things had gotten very tense in our home, and, as far as I could see, Heather was responsible for most of the bad feelings. And now we were moving to a little church in the country where there would be no escape from her all summer. Was it any wonder that I was depressed?

I glanced at Michael, still hard at work on his math. My own poem was now almost obscured by the cats I'd drawn all over the notebook paper. I stared at it sadly, no longer in the mood to continue writing about unicorns, rainbows, and castles in the clouds. Tearing it out of my notebook, I crumpled it into a ball and tossed it at Speed Racer as he zipped past in his little car. Then I began writing a poem about real life. Something depressing dealing with loneliness and unhappiness and the misery of being misunderstood and unloved.

2

---·---

ON THE FIRST DAY of summer vacation, Dave
and a bunch of his friends loaded everything we
owned into a U-Haul truck and headed toward
our new home in Holwell, Maryland. Dave drove
the truck with Heather sitting beside him, looking very pleased with herself, and Mom, Michael, and I followed in our old van. Behind us
was another van in even worse shape than ours,
filled with Dave's friends.

After we turned off the Beltway, the roads
narrowed and wound up and down hills, curved
past farms, tunneled through forests. As we
bounced along over ruts and bumps, Mom
pointed out the scenic spots. "See that old barn
over there?" she'd exclaim, pointing to a building on the verge of collapse. "Isn't that a perfect
subject for a painting?"

When Michael and I mumbled something

about Andrew Wyeth having already painted a hundred barns just like it, she'd spot something else — a twisted old tree, a line hung with flapping clothes, a flock of geese strutting across a yard — and get excited all over again. "You two are just going to love living here," she said more than once, never losing hope that we'd eventually agree with her.

After a couple of hours of driving, Mom turned to us and said, "Here we are!" Swinging off the road behind the U-Haul, she pointed at the little white church. "Isn't it beautiful?"

It *was* pretty. No matter how much I preferred our row house, I had to admit that Mom and Dave had picked a lovely place. Quiet and peaceful, the small building sat by the side of the road, shaded by two huge maple trees. Although it had no steeple, the tall, pointed windows and red double doors left no doubt that it was indeed a church. On one side was an addition, built to harmonize with the original building, and on the other was the carriage house Dave planned to use as his pottery workshop.

Behind it rose a forest in deep green leaf, and, on either side, fields of corn basked in the morning sun. Across the road, a herd of cows gazed at us, their big brown eyes taking in everything.

"Look, it's the welcome wagon." Michael nudged me and pointed at the cows.

"Where are the other houses?" I looked around, hoping I'd missed seeing them.

"There's a farmhouse about a mile down the road," Mom said.

"But I thought we were moving to Holwell." I frowned at Mom.

"That's our post office address," she said, looking at herself in the rearview mirror and smoothing her hair. I could tell she was a little uncomfortable at having misled me deliberately or accidentally into thinking we would at least have neighbors and the prospect of making new friends. "The town itself is only a couple of miles away," she added apologetically.

"You said there was a library," Michael said, leaning across me, his voice full of anger. "I thought you meant it was just a few blocks away or something."

"You can ride your bikes into Holwell. It's not far." Mom opened her door and prepared to get out. "I told you we were moving to the country."

Before we could say anything else, Dave's friends pulled into the driveway behind us and screeched to a stop in a cloud of white dust. At the same time, Dave and Heather got out of the U-Haul and walked toward us. I couldn't help noticing that Dave looked a little tense and Heather was dragging on his hand, trying to keep him from joining Mom. Our first day in Holwell wasn't beginning very well.

"Come on, Jean," Dave said to Mom. "Let's get this show on the road."

"I'll carry my stuff in," Michael said, jumping out of the van. I knew he was worried that somebody would drop his insect collection or misplace his books.

"How about you taking care of Heather?" Dave tugged her toward me, despite her efforts to dig her heels into the dust. As usual, she was frowning through the tangles of hair almost hiding her face.

"What should I do?" I turned to Mom, hoping she'd suggest I help her with something important, but she sided with Dave as usual.

"You could take her for a walk," Mom said, patting my shoulder. "There's a nice, little path down through the woods." She pointed off to the right of the church. "It leads to a creek. You could wade or something."

"Don't go too far, though," Dave added, prying his fingers away from Heather's clutch.

Knowing I had no choice, I tried to take Heather's other hand, but she snatched it away, scowling at me as if I'd tried to pinch her.

"Go with Molly, now." Dave succeeded in freeing himself. "Daddy has a lot of work to do, honey. You and Molly can have a real nice time."

"I don't want to go with her," Heather whined, her voice rising in pitch. "I want to stay with you, Daddy. I don't like it here."

"You heard me, Heather. Don't make Daddy cross with you."

"Come on, Heather." I started walking toward the path, and, after some more pleading from Dave, she finally followed me. Silently we entered the cool shade of the trees. Above our heads, the leaves rustled softly and the sunlight splattered down through the branches, gleaming here and there at the whim of the wind. A butterfly as big as my hand fluttered across the path, and I was glad that Michael wasn't there. If he'd seen it, he'd have gotten his net and added it to his collection.

"Look, Heather." I pointed at the butterfly as it rested for a moment on a leaf. "Isn't it pretty?"

She glanced at it. "It's nothing but a caterpillar with wings," she muttered.

After that, I didn't try talking to her until we found the creek. The water was shallow, maybe two or three inches deep, and it was racing along over a bed of stones between low banks. It was perfect for wading. Sitting down, I took off my running shoes and socks.

"Want to come with me?" I asked her as I stepped out into the clear water.

She shook her head and continued following

the path along the creek. Shrugging my shoulders, I splashed along beside her, enjoying the feel of the cold water as it rose higher, creeping up to my knees as the creek narrowed and the banks grew steeper.

After wading for about five minutes, I came around a curve and was confronted with a rusty, barbed-wire fence from which hung a No Trespassing sign. On the other side, a herd of cattle looked up from the water and lowed. For a minute, I thought they were going to charge at me, fence or no fence, and I scrambled up the bank to Heather's side.

"They're just *cows*," she said, as if she knew I was thinking that they might be bulls. "They won't hurt you."

"I know," I said, trying to sound a lot more convincing than I felt. "Do you want to go back to the church?"

She gave me one of her disdainful looks. "Well, we can't go any farther, can we?" She looked pointedly at the fence and the cows watching us from the other side.

Still carrying my shoes, I followed Heather back down the path. Instead of turning off through the woods, taking the route we'd originally chosen, we walked farther along the creek. It was a pleasant path, cool and shady, and I was too busy watching a couple of dragonflies darting back and forth across the water to pay much attention to what Heather was doing. When she stopped suddenly just ahead of me, I bumped right into her.

"What's the matter?" I asked.

She looked at me over her shoulder. "Look." She pointed at a crooked fence almost hidden by weeds and bushes. "What's that?"

Despite the warmth of the afternoon, I felt goose bumps prick up all over me. "It's a graveyard," I whispered.

It wasn't very big, and the grass had grown almost as tall as the tombstones, but here and there a stone angel lifted its marble wings toward the sky, and a cross or two tilted out of the weeds. It was without a doubt the spookiest place I'd ever seen, and I wanted to run back to the church, but Heather stared at it, fascinated.

"Are you afraid?" she asked, her thumb hovering near her mouth.

"Of course not," I lied, reluctant to expose any weaknesses to Heather. Edging back down the path toward the church, I said, "Let's go see what Mom and Dave are doing. They're probably wondering where we are."

"It would be shorter to cut through the graveyard," Heather said, her pale eyes probing mine.

"It's probably private property," I said. "You could get in trouble for trespassing."

But Heather only smiled and slipped through a gap in the fence. "Come on, Molly," she said, daring me to follow her.

While I watched, she ran through the weeds, paying no attention to the tombstones. "It's bad luck to step on a grave," I called after her.

Pausing by a stone cherub, she caressed his cheek and then whirled about, performing a weird little dance as she wove in and out of the tombstones. "Molly is afraid," she chanted, "Molly is afraid."

"You're crazy!" I shouted at her. Then I turned my back on the graveyard and ran through the woods, ducking branches that reached for my hair and stumbling over roots. By the time I got to the church, I was out of breath and my heart was pounding so hard I thought my ribs would split. Catching sight of Mom disappearing through a side door, I followed her inside and caught up with her in the hall. I grabbed her arm and almost made her drop the box she was carrying.

"Molly, what's wrong?" She put the box down and stared at me. "Where is Heather? Has something happened?"

I shook my head, still gasping for breath. "There's a graveyard behind the church," I panted. "A graveyard!"

"Of course there is. It's part of the property."

"It's ours? We own a *graveyard*?"

"No, not exactly." Mom frowned at me. "For heaven's sake, Molly, have you run in here and scared me half to death just because of a graveyard?"

"You never said anything about it. You never told me we were going to have a bunch of dead people buried in our backyard." I started crying then, and Mom put her arm around me.

"Dead people in our yard?" Michael ran out of a room down the hall. "What's she talking about, Mom?"

"You found the graveyard." Dave appeared behind Michael, grinning as if I had done something marvelously clever.

"Why didn't you tell us?" I pulled away from Mom, wiping my eyes on my shirt tail. I didn't want Dave to know what a baby I was.

"I didn't think it was worth mentioning." Dave winked at Mom. "Just think what quiet neighbors they'll be. No wild parties, no loud music, no dropping in to borrow a cup of sugar or the lawn mower. Why, I bet they won't even speak to us." He gave Mom a hug and a kiss, and they both laughed while I stood there feeling foolish.

"Are the graves old?" Michael tried to push between Mom and me in his haste to go see them.

"Hey, hold it," Dave said, stopping him. "You're not finished getting your room in order, and Molly hasn't even started. You two get to work. You can see the graveyard later."

"That's not fair!" Michael said. "Molly's been playing with Heather ever since we got here, and I've been working. Can't I go outside for just a minute?"

"Where is Heather?" Dave asked as if he'd just realized she wasn't with me.

"The last time I saw her she was dancing around the graveyard," I said. "For all I know, she's still there." Without looking at him or Mom, I followed Michael down the hall to the room I had to share with Heather. As I shut the door behind me, I heard Heather come into the house.

"Molly ran away from me," she whined, her shrill voice carrying right through the closed door.

Heaving a great sigh, I prepared myself for a lecture from Dave and set about unpacking my books and arranging them on the shelves next to my bed. It was a nice room, I thought, bigger and airier than my old room in Baltimore, and, if I hadn't had to share it with Heather, I would have really enjoyed living in it.

From the window between our beds, I could see the mountains, but when I moved closer to

see the whole view, I realized that the graveyard
was only a short distance away, partially hidden
from the house by a tall boxwood hedge. Shivering, I drew back from the window. How was
I going to sleep at night, knowing how close
it was?

3

THAT EVENING, after Dave's friends left, we had our first dinner in the church. Mom and Dave did most of the talking; they didn't make much of an effort to involve us in the plans they were making for their art projects. While they chattered about craft fairs and galleries, Heather picked at her food as if she expected to find crushed glass or rat poison hidden in it, and Michael described the huge centipede he'd caught in his bedroom, ignoring my pleas for him to talk about something less disgusting. How can a person enjoy eating spaghetti when her brother is babbling about a hideous, million-legged creature over four inches long?

As we were finishing our dessert, Mom suggested going for a walk before it got dark. Naturally, Michael suggested a tour of the graveyard, and everyone but me agreed. As they got ready to leave, I considered staying home and washing the dishes, but then I decided it might be worse to be all alone in the house. Reluctantly I followed them out the back door and down the brick path to the graveyard.

The sun was hovering on the mountaintops, and a tall oak tree at one end of the graveyard sent a long shadow over the grass toward us. As we entered the gate, a flock of crows rose from the oak and flew away, cawing loudly, as if we were trespassers. When I took Mom's hand, Heather smiled mockingly at me from her perch on Dave's shoulders.

"Molly's scared of the graveyard," she whispered in his ear, "but I'm not."

To prove how brave she was, she slipped down and ran ahead of us. Scrambling up on a tombstone, she spread her arms. "Look at me, Daddy," she called, "I'm an angel."

"Hey, get down from there." Dave grabbed her. "These are too old for you to climb on, honey. They could topple right over."

"I was just playing." Heather tugged at his beard, trying to braid it around her fingers. "At least I'm not a scaredy-cat."

While Dave was occupied with Heather, Mom turned to me and put her arm around my shoulders. "See how peaceful it is, Molly? There's nothing frightening about an old graveyard." She hugged me close.

I didn't say anything, nor did I try to pull away. Instead I snuggled closer, feeling safe as long I could feel her warm body next to mine.

"What's the matter, Molly?" Dave smiled at me over Heather's dark head. "Do you expect to see a ghost?"

Embarrassed, I forced myself to laugh. "Of course not. I'm just cold, that's all." And it was true. The sun had slipped down behind the mountains, taking the warmth of the day with it. A little breeze brought the chill of night with it as it tossed the heads of the Queen Anne's lace blooming all around us.

"Look," Michael called to us from the other side of the graveyard. "A whole family named Berry is buried here." He waved his arm at a cluster of tombstones guarded by a solemn marble angel. "This must be the Berry Patch!"

Everybody laughed at his joke but me. It didn't seem right to call out the names of dead people, especially if you were laughing. Uneasily, I followed Mom toward the angel, but I wanted very badly to go back to the church.

"Listen to this," Michael said. " 'Ada Berry, Beloved Wife of Edward Berry. April 3, 1811– November 28, 1899. Not Dead, Only Resting from Life's Weary Toil.' And here's her daughter, see? 'Susannah Berry, June 10, 1832–December 30, 1835. A Little Lamb in the Hands of the Lord.' And over here —''

"Oh, stop, Michael, stop." Mom pulled him away from the tombstone of another Berry child. "That's too sad. Don't read any more."

"I thought this was such a peaceful place," I murmured.

"Well, it is." Mom's voice wavered, though, and she looked past me at the sky where the first stars were beginning to glow.

"But don't you want to know how they died?" Michael asked. "Little kids like these probably died from smallpox or diphtheria or even measles. And this one right here, Adam Berry, died in 1863, and he was twenty-one. He was probably killed in the Civil War. A Yankee soldier, think of that."

"It's getting dark," I said, pointing out the obvious. "Why don't we go back to the church?"

"Yes," Mom agreed. "The mosquitoes have found me."

"Where has Heather run off to?" Dave scanned the graveyard, growing so dark now that everything was gray and indistinct.

"There she is." Michael pointed to the far end of the graveyard where the oak tree stood. In the shadows, we could barely see Heather poking around in the weeds.

"Come on, Heather," Dave called. "You've got all day tomorrow to explore this place. None of these folks is going anywhere."

He and Mom chuckled, and he put his arm around her waist and whispered something in her ear that made her giggle. Glancing at Heather, I saw her stop and stare at Dave and Mom. Even in the darkness I could see the look of hatred that flashed across her pale face at the sight of him embracing Mom. Then, realizing that I was looking at her, she made her face blank and walked slowly toward us, trailing her fingers across the tombstones and humming softly.

By the time we reached the church, the trees were dark masses against the sky, flickering with fireflies, and above us the sky was studded with stars and a crescent moon barely clearing the oak tree.

"Look at that." Mom paused on the back steps, her head tilted back. "I'd forgotten how many more stars you can see when you get away from the city."

"There's the Milky Way and the Big Dipper," Michael said, "and the Little Dipper too."

"And the North Star." Dave pointed at something that only he could see. "If you're interested, Michael, I've got some astronomy books we can look at."

While Mom and I washed the dinner dishes,

Dave got out a book and sat down at the kitchen table to explain one of the star charts to Michael. Finding herself with nothing to do, Heather climbed into Dave's lap and did all she could to make it impossible for him to talk to Michael.

"I'm sleepy, Daddy," she whispered. "I want you to put me to bed."

"Is your room all ready?" Dave asked.

"Yes, but I don't want to sleep there." She peeked at me, then tugged at Dave's beard.

"Why not, honey?" he asked, gently freeing his beard.

"Because of her." Heather looked at me again and snuggled closer to Dave. "I don't want to sleep with her."

Mom and Dave looked at each other and sighed as if they'd been expecting something of this sort. "Molly's your sister now, Heather," Dave said patiently. "Sisters always share."

Heather stuck out her lip and managed to squeeze a few tears out of her big, sad eyes. "She's mean to me."

"Oh, Heather," Mom said softly. "Molly's not mean to you."

When Mom tried to touch Heather's shoulder, she jerked away as if Mom had intended to hurt her. "You leave me alone!" Heather cried. "You're mean too, and I hate you both. Him too!"

She glared at Michael, then turned to Dave. "I don't want to live here with them. I want my own mother back!"

There was a little silence in the kitchen which made all the night noises — the crickets and the frogs, the wind in the leaves — seem louder.

"Now, now, honey." Dave stood up with Heather in his arms. "Daddy will tuck you in and tell you a little princess story. Wouldn't you like that?"

Heather buried her face in his neck, but as he carried her out the door, she looked at me and stuck out her tongue.

"Just ignore her, Molly," Mom said softly. "It's been a long day, and we're all tired."

"You always make excuses for her, no matter what she says or does." I flopped down in a chair beside Michael. "She's spoiled rotten."

"Oh, Molly, can't you be more understanding?" Mom looked at me sadly. "She's such an unhappy little girl."

"That doesn't give her the right to make us miserable too. The only thing that would make her happy is for you and Dave to split up. Can't you see that's what she wants?"

Mom shook her head. "That's a terrible thing to say, Molly. I'm ashamed of you."

"Molly's right," Michael said. "Heather hates

us. She's never going to be happy living here."

"If we give her enough love, she'll change," Mom said. "I know she will."

Michael and I looked at each other and shook our heads. Why couldn't Mom face facts?

"You two could try a little harder," Mom added in a crosser voice. "You've never really given her a chance. Always running away from her, teasing her, making her cry."

"Mom, that's not fair!" I jumped to my feet, ready to run to my room. "I've tried and tried and tried! But she twists everything I do all around and lies and then you believe her, not me!"

Mom turned her back and leaned on the sink. "Just try harder, Molly. Please?" She kept her face hidden as she spoke, and I realized that she was crying.

Running to her side, I put my arms around her and hugged her tightly, pressing my face into the little hollow beneath her collarbone. "Okay, Mom," I whispered, trying hard not to cry myself, "I'll try some more."

Mom hugged me fiercely. "I'm sorry, Molly. I know you've tried. I'm just so discouraged. I thought by now Heather would be happier with us, but sometimes I'm afraid you and Michael are right. She doesn't want my love." She wiped her tears away with the back of her hand and sighed. "I don't know what to do. I love Dave so much. And you all too. But Heather, I just don't know."

She made herself a cup of peppermint tea and carried it out on the back porch. Knowing she wanted to be alone, I sat down beside Michael. While he studied the star chart, I thought about Mom. I hated to see her so unhappy, but I had no idea what I could do to help her feel better. Heather sat in the middle of everything, making all of us miserable, and, as far as I could see, enjoying every minute of it.

4

————— ✦ —————

WHILE MOM was still out on the porch, Dave came into the kitchen. Ruffling his hair with one hand, he sighed. "Well, Heather's asleep," he said, "so you two can get along to bed now yourselves. Don't wake her up, Molly. I've just about run out of little princess stories."

As Michael and I started to leave the room, Dave asked where Mom was.

"On the porch having a cup of tea," I said, as I followed Michael down the hall. Behind me, I heard the screen door open and shut and then Dave's voice murmuring something to Mom.

Pausing in his doorway, Michael said, "Want to come in and talk for a while, Molly?"

"Sure. I'm not in any hurry to go in there and take the chance of waking her up."

Michael's room already looked like home. His

framed insect displays were hanging on the wall over his bed; his aquarium was set up near the window, and his scientific apparatus — microscope, magnifying glass, butterfly net, and chemistry set — was in place on the long desk Dave had made for him. Books filled his shelves, mostly plant, bird, rock, and animal nature guides with a few Encyclopedia Browns, Hardy Boys, and Alfred Hitchcocks for variety.

Picking up one of his fossils, I examined the print of a tiny skeleton embedded in its surface. "Doesn't the graveyard bother you at all?" I asked.

"I think it's great," he said. "I'm going to make it into an archeological project. I'll study all the graves, and then figure out what the people died of."

"You don't mean you're going to dig them up?" I stared at him, horrified.

"Of course not. That's against the law. What do you think I am? A body snatcher?" Michael grinned and polished his glasses on his tee shirt. "Not that it wouldn't interest me. In fact, I wish I could. They dig up Indian burial grounds and primitive Iron Age people, and they learn a lot from the things buried with them."

"That's awful." I thought of all the movies I'd seen on TV involving the opening of pyramids and the curses of mummies. "I'd be scared to disturb somebody's bones." I shuddered just thinking about how horrible it would be to discover a skeleton.

"You really are scared of the graveyard, aren't you?" Michael sounded curious.

"There's something about it, Michael." I gazed past his curly head at the window's dark rectangle, thinking of the tombstones behind the hedge, the tall weeds silvery in the starlight. It seemed to me that they waited there in the night for something, and I folded my arms tightly across my chest and tried to convince myself that I was being silly.

"Do you believe in ghosts?" Michael leaned toward me. All he needed was a pipe in his mouth to make him the perfect scientist.

I shrugged. "I don't know." As usual, his rational approach was embarrassing me. I felt silly answering his questions. Pretending to yawn, I edged toward the door. "I think I'll go to bed, Michael."

He nodded. "If you hear any funny noises or see a face at the window, just yell for me," he said as I started down the hall to Heather's and my room.

I glared at him, sure now that I wouldn't be able to sleep for fear of what might be creeping toward the church from the graveyard.

"Just kidding, Molly," he whispered as I paused, my hand on my doorknob. "The only weird thing you'll see tonight is Heather."

Ignoring him, I tiptoed into the room. Except for the moonlight shining dimly through the window, it was dark, and I moved cautiously, not wanting to trip over anything and risk waking Heather. Pulling my pajamas out from under my pillow, I undressed and got into bed. I was anxious to fall asleep as quickly as possible so I wouldn't lie there thinking about horror movies and scary stories.

But you know how it is. The more you want to sleep the more you stay awake, hearing every strange sound and translating it into footsteps in the hall, bony hands at the window, the moans of ghosts in the shrubbery. When I heard a sort of whimper, I stiffened in terror and prepared myself for the appearance of a hideous creature. Forcing myself at last to open my eyes, I saw nothing but Heather, her pale face almost hidden by her dark curls tumbling over the pillow. As I watched, she moaned again and tossed restlessly, mumbling something that sounded like "Mommy, Mommy."

Turning my back, I grabbed my cassette player and put the earphones on. Soon all I heard was the voice of Julie Harris reading one of Emily

Dickinson's poems, a good inspiration for the poetry I planned to write this summer.

I woke up to the sound of a mower droning away outside. The sun was shining, and Heather's bed was empty. Glancing at my watch, I saw that it was nine o'clock. Hoping that Michael hadn't already disappeared in quest of new insects to add to his collection, I dressed and ran down the hall to the kitchen.

I found Heather and Mom sitting at the table, finishing their breakfast. Dave was already in the carriage house setting up his pottery workshop, and Mom said Michael was in the graveyard talking to Mr. Simmons.

"Who's Mr. Simmons?" I asked, pouring milk on my cereal.

"He's the graveyard's caretaker. He comes once a month or so to mow the grass and tidy the place up." Mom sipped her coffee. "He's a nice old chap, about seventy or eighty years old, but he carries himself like a soldier."

Remembering the height of the weeds, I had a feeling that Mr. Simmons had been on a vacation or something. "Maybe it won't look so gloomy after he finishes," I said.

Mom smiled and turned to Heather. "What would you like to do today, sweetie?" she asked.

Shoving her half-full bowl of cereal across the table, Heather got up and headed toward the back door.

"Where are you going?" Mom called after her.

The only answer she got was the sound of the screen door banging shut behind Heather.

"Oh, well, I guess she'll be all right outside." Mom went to the window over the sink and watched Heather amble across the lawn toward the hedge and the sound of the mower. "Poor Mr. Simmons. I guess she wants to see what he's up to."

She crossed the room and paused beside me. "I've got a lot to do, Molly. As soon as you finish eating, please go out and keep an eye on Heather. I don't want her wandering off."

"Can't I stay in and help you?"

She patted my shoulder. "The nicest thing you can do for me is to look after Heather."

Before I could say anything more, she left the room. Glumly I ate the rest of my cereal and went outside in search of Heather and Michael. By the time I got to the graveyard, Mr. Simmons had finished mowing. He was clipping and trimming the weeds around the tombstones, and Michael was raking the cut grass into a pile next to the wheelbarrow. Heather was sitting on a fallen tombstone trying clumsily to make a daisy chain. When she saw me hesitating at the gate, she said, "Molly's afraid to come in here. She thinks something's going to get her."

Mr. Simmons looked up and smiled at me. "Well, good morning, Molly. Won't you join us?"

Taking a deep breath, I walked toward him, careful, as usual, not to step on anybody's grave. Now that the grass was cut, it was easier to see where it was safe to walk. In fact, the whole place looked at lot less scary than it had before.

"Mr. Simmons says this is a real old graveyard," Michael told me. "The church was built way back in 1825, so some of the graves are 160 years old. Isn't that something? The Civil War hadn't even happened then. But nobody's been buried here since 1950. Isn't that right?" Michael turned to Mr. Simmons.

The old man nodded his head. "They filled the graveyard up, that's what they did. Old Mrs. Perkins was the last one to get in." He pointed at a pink stone with a shiny front. "Right there she is. My first-grade teacher." He grinned and shook his head. "She's not handing out any more report cards now, is she?"

Michael laughed, but I felt sad just thinking about Mrs. Perkins. "Caroline," it said on the stone. "Dear, Departed Wife of John Albert Perkins. She will long be missed."

"And right over here," Mr. Simmons went on,

"is where my mother and father are sleeping."
He rested his old hands on two stones. "I brought
flowers for them and my baby sister, too."

I looked at the mason jars full of wild flowers
decorating the three graves. "They look very
pretty," I said, wondering if he felt sad. "It must
be awful when a baby dies," I added, staring at
the tiny headstone marking his sister's grave.

"They didn't have the medicine then, you
know," he said. "Measles, chicken pox, whoop-
ing cough, scarlet fever, that's what killed the
children."

As Michael nodded, glad that Mr. Simmons
was backing up his own theories, Heather joined
us. "Fire too," she said. "Lots of people died in
fires, didn't they?"

Mr. Simmons looked a little surprised. "They
did indeed," he said.

"My mother died in a fire." Heather dropped
a dandelion on the baby's grave and walked away.

Mr. Simmons watched her for a moment, then
turned to us. "I thought she was your sister," he
said.

"No, her father married our mother." Michael
nudged the dandelion away from the baby's grave
with his bare toe. "She's our stepsister."

"Her mother died in a fire?" Mr. Simmons
asked.

"When Heather was three. They were all alone

in the house, and Heather almost died too. She was unconscious when the rescue squad found her," I told him.

"Poor little thing," he said sympathetically. Turning away, he returned to his work, clipping carefully around each stone and whistling. The sweet smell of cut grass drying in the hot sun filled the air, mingling with the aroma of Mr. Simmons' pipe. A mockingbird perched on a tombstone and sang; butterflies flashed about, and for a while I forgot my fears and helped Michael scoop the grass cuttings into the wheelbarrow.

"You haven't mowed under the tree," I heard Heather say suddenly. She was frowning at Mr. Simmons' back as he knelt at the base of the Berrys' marble angel.

He squinted up at her. "Not enough grass under that old tree to bother with," he said pleasantly.

"There's weeds though."

"I just tend to the tombstones." Mr. Simmons returned his attention to the grass, but Heather didn't take the hint.

"But there's a grave there," she said, her lip jutting out. "I saw it."

Mr. Simmons straightened up and stared at her. "Couldn't be. Too many roots to bury somebody there."

"The tombstone is lying down in the weeds," Heather insisted. "Come with me. I'll show you." She started walking toward the dense shade under the oak tree, and Mr. Simmons shrugged and followed her.

Michael turned to me. "Aren't you coming with us, Molly?"

I started to go with them, but I felt my goose bumps coming back. The cheerfulness of the day was gone, as surely as if a cloud had covered the sun. Something was wrong; I could sense it if no one else could. Staying where I was, next to the relative safety of Mrs. Perkins' shiny new tombstone, I watched the three of them step into the oak tree's shadow. Heather pointed at something in the grass, and Mr. Simmons bent down to get a better look.

"Looks like you're right," I heard him say to Heather.

"Come here, Molly!" Michael called. "This is really interesting."

As Heather smiled at me over her shoulder, daring me as she had before, I forced myself to join them. Mr. Simmons was struggling to right a small, weather-stained stone. "Well, I'll be," he said. "I've been tending these graves for twenty-some years, and I never knew this one was here. Never even looked for it."

With the stone erect, he scraped away the dirt

and moss to reveal the inscription. " 'H.E.H,' "
he read out loud, tracing the letters with his fingers. " 'March 7, 1879–August 8, 1886. May she
rest in peace.' " He shook his head and set to
work pulling out the weeds growing around the
base of the stone. "Strange, isn't it?"

"Why is it strange?" Michael asked.

"Well, she was just a child. Seven years old.
Where's the rest of the family?"

"What do you mean?" Michael squatted beside him, staring at the gravestone.

"Well, look around, son. Families get buried
together," he said.

"That's right. Like the Berry Patch." Michael
nodded astutely.

Mr. Simmons looked puzzled for a moment,
but then he chuckled. "Yes, yes, the Berry Family. All together they are with their very own
angel to watch over them." He relit his pipe and
stood up, gazing about the graveyard.

"The stones usually say 'Beloved Daughter of'
or something like that," he mused, "but here's
this child, all by herself. No name. Just the initials. No other grave close by. It just doesn't seem
right somehow."

"It's my initials," Heather said suddenly, re-
moving her thumb from her mouth and touching the stone lightly. "Heather Elizabeth
Hill."

"My age too," she added as we all stared at her.

"Well, now, that is a coincidence," Mr. Simmons said. Lopping away the last of the weeds, he took Heather's hand and led her out into the sunlight. "I wouldn't play here," he said to her. "Even with the weeds gone, it's a good place for snakes. Poison ivy, too, from the looks of it." He gestured at the shiny green leaves flourishing in the shade and twisting up the oak's trunk.

"I'm not afraid of snakes," Heather said. "Or poison ivy either. I never get it."

Mr. Simmons frowned down at her. "You listen to what I tell you, young lady. That's the kind of shade a copperhead loves. One of them bites you, you'll know it."

Heather gave the old man a scornful look and pulled away from him. "I'll play wherever I want to. You're not my boss." Then she stalked off, head high, black curls lifting in the breeze.

"Uppity little creature," Mr. Simmons said. "How about giving me a hand with the wheelbarrow?" he asked Michael.

As the two of them trundled off toward the compost heap, I walked back to the house. Although Heather was nowhere in sight, I could hear Dave's voice in the carriage house, and I supposed she'd gone in there to tell him how mean Mr. Simmons was.

Finding a shady spot on the back steps, I sat down and gazed across the yard at the oak tree standing guard over H.E.H.'s lonely grave. Why hadn't the child's name been carved on the tombstone? Why was it all alone? I shivered again, despite the heat, and wondered how I would feel if the initials had been mine instead of Heather's.

5

———— ✢ ————

AFTER LUNCH, Mom sent Heather and me to our room to finish unpacking. "I want every box emptied and all your things put where they belong," she insisted as Heather started to whine in protest. "If you're having trouble finding places for everything," Mom added, "ask Molly to help you. That's what big sisters are for."

Without saying another word, Heather began unpacking, stuffing clothes into her bureau and books and toys onto the shelves on her side of the room. Ignoring the mess she was making, I concentrated on arranging my books and papers as neatly as possible. At least my side would look nice.

After a while, Heather lay down on her bed and shut her eyes. Thinking she'd gone to sleep, I finished putting my clothes into my bureau and lay down on my bed to read. I was so absorbed in *Watership Down* that I jumped when Heather suddenly spoke to me.

"What do you think that child's name is?" She was still lying down, gazing up at the ceiling where the leaves of the maple cast ever-shifting patterns. "Do you think it could be Heather Elizabeth Hill?"

"Of course not. That's *your* name."

"Suppose the initials were M.A.C?" Heather whispered.

"Those are my initials." I frowned at her.

"Would you be scared?"

I shrugged. "Not especially. Why? Are you scared?"

She sat up and shook her head. "No. I think it's interesting, that's all." She smiled at me. "But you would be scared, Molly. I know you'd be. You're afraid right now, and they aren't even your initials."

"Don't be silly." I opened my book again. "If you're finished asking questions, I'd like to get back to my reading."

"That's a dumb story," Heather said, getting up and staring out the window. "I hate rabbits. Who cares what happens to them?"

Ignoring her, I concentrated hard on Fiver's desperate attempts to warn the rabbits that danger was coming. This was the second time I'd read the book, and Fiver was my favorite character. I knew I would enjoy the story more this time, knowing that he was going to be all right.

Heather didn't say anything more. When I glanced at her to see what she was doing, she was still standing at the window gazing out at the graveyard as silently as a marble angel contemplating eternity.

As the days passed, the five of us got caught up in our own routines. From morning until night, Dave worked at the pottery wheel in the carriage house, throwing bowls, plates, mugs, pitchers, and jugs, mixing glazes, and tending his kiln, trying to get ready for a big August Craft Show. Although he didn't seem to mind our coming in and out, watching him work, he wasn't particularly interested in what we were doing. As long as we turned up for meals and bedtime, he didn't worry about us.

Mom was just as bad. She was terribly excited about having a real studio after so many years of setting up her easel in the corner of the kitchen or the bedroom, wherever she could find some unwanted space. She was working on a large painting of a barn. The colors were soft and muted, and all the edges were hazy as if the morning sun hadn't quite broken through the fog. You could almost smell the damp boards when you looked at it.

But Mom didn't like to be watched while she was painting; it ruined her concentration and made her self-conscious. So she'd always tell me to go outside and play. I guess she felt that we were all safe out here in the country. The things she worried about in Baltimore — drug dealers, child molesters, speeding cars — didn't exist in Holwell. The only thing she ever asked me to do was to keep an eye on Heather. She thought both Michael and I, being older, should take care of her.

Of course, that was the one thing neither of us did. Every morning, as soon as Dave disappeared into the carriage house and Mom went to her loft, Michael grabbed his butterfly net and kill jar and ran to the woods in pursuit of insects to add to his collection. Although I could have gone with him (and sometimes did), I usually took a book and my journal and wandered off somewhere to read or write.

And Heather? For a long time I had no idea where she went or how she spent her time. She might start out on the couch next to me, coloring or reading or watching television. Then, without my actually noticing, she'd disappear. She reminded me of a cat I used to own; one minute he'd be curled up next to me, and the next minute he'd be gone without making a sound.

One hot afternoon, I went outside looking for something to do. The air was hot and heavy with humidity, and I decided to walk down by the creek, maybe wade or something, just to cool off. Leaving my book on the bank, I splashed through the water without realizing how close I was getting to the graveyard. When I looked up and saw the tombstones above me, I hesitated, thinking I'd turn back in the direction of the cows.

Then I heard a voice. Was it Heather's? The breeze swirled the leaves, the creek chattered over stones, birds sang, insects chirped and buzzed, making it impossible to be sure who was speaking. Uneasily, I climbed the bank and tiptoed down the path beside the graveyard.

I found Heather sitting in the shade staring at the small tombstone under the oak tree. On the grave, she had placed a peanut butter jar filled with black-eyed Susans and Queen Anne's lace. As I watched, scarcely daring to breathe, she said something in a voice too low for me to hear, her hands flashing in the shadows as she gestured nervously.

Then she sat back, her mouth half-open, her eyes half-closed, nodding her head as if she were in a trance. All around me the leaves rustled, and I shivered, sure that the noise they made was hiding words from me that were audible to Heather. Convinced that she was in danger, I leaned toward her, peering through a tangle of honeysuckle, wondering what I should do.

"Oh, Helen," Heather said suddenly, her voice louder. "Will you really be my friend? I'll do anything you say — I promise I will — if you'll be my friend."

Again she was silent, her head tilted to one side, a smile twitching the corners of her mouth. The breeze blew again, making a dry sound, a whispering, and Heather nodded. "I'll wait for you, Helen. When you come, I'll be the best friend you ever had, cross my heart."

As she leaned forward to rearrange the flowers, I gripped the fence and called to her. "What are you doing, Heather? Who are you talking to?"

She leaped to her feet, her face pale and angry. "Molly!" she screamed, "Go away! Go away!"

"Not until you tell me what you're doing!" I shivered as the breeze gusted through the honeysuckle, filling the air with sweetness. Something hung in the space between us. For a moment, I felt it watching me. Then it was gone, and all around me the insects struck up a chorus of cheerful summer sounds.

"I don't have to tell you anything." Heather's

narrow face was almost expressionless, mask-like, as if it hid secrets, terrible secrets.

"You were talking to someone. I *heard* you. You called her Helen."

Without looking at me, Heather took a flower from the jar. Pulling a petal off, she dropped it and watched it flutter down to the grave. "You didn't *see* anybody. Or even hear anybody, did you?" She glanced at me, her tangled hair almost hiding her eyes.

"There was something," I insisted. "I know there was."

Heather shook her head and continued pulling the petals off, one by one. She watched them as they drifted with the breeze down to the earth. "Don't spy on me anymore, Molly," she said softly. "I don't like to be spied on."

"You better come out from under that tree," I yelled. "You heard what Mr. Simmons said about snakes and poison ivy."

"I'll stay here as long as I want." Heather finished stripping the flower of its petals and bent to pick up another one. "If you want me, you'll have to come here and get me," she said.

A ray of sunlight lanced down through the oak's leaves and touched the jar of flowers, and from somewhere in the branches overhead a crow cawed. Folding my arms tightly across my chest, I backed away from the graveyard. "Get bitten by a snake," I said as I began walking back toward the church. "See if I care!"

The only answer was the rustling of leaves and a faint sound of laughter. Without looking back, I quickened my pace, anxious to get away from Heather and whatever else might be lingering under that tree.

Although I tried to tell Mom that I thought that the graveyard was haunted, she was too busy fixing dinner to listen to me. "Honestly, Molly," she said, "Reading all that poetry is making you morbid. Now get busy and put ice in the glasses so I can pour the tea."

"But, Mom, if you'd been there —" I started to say, but she looked so exasperated, I stopped in mid-sentence. What was the use?

After dinner, I found Michael out on the front porch watching the stars come out. "See that one, right there?" He pointed at a bright star hanging just above the mountains across the valley. "That's a planet. Venus. You can see it in the morning, too."

I nodded and sat down beside him, trying to think of a good way to introduce the subject of ghosts. "Do you believe in things you can't prove?" I asked him.

He looked at me as if he were a little puzzled. "Like what?"

"Oh, I don't know. Ghosts and stuff like that."
I hugged my knees against my chest and turned
my back to the graveyard.

Michael laughed. "What's the matter? Are you
still scared you'll see something looking in your
window at night?"

"Don't laugh, Michael." I glared at him. "I'm
not just kidding around." Glancing over my
shoulder to make sure Heather wasn't standing
behind us eavesdropping, I told him about her
strange behavior in the graveyard.

"So?" Michael swatted a mosquito on his arm.
"You know how she is, always living in some
weird little world of her own. She probably has
an imaginary friend, and you embarrassed her."

"You didn't see her, Michael. It wasn't just
her imagination. There was something there; I
could sense it." I took a deep breath. "It scared
me, Michael."

"Oh, Molly," Michael laughed, "next you'll
be telling me you actually saw a ghost."

"I told you not to laugh!" I yelled. "It's not
funny!"

"No, it's not funny. It's not funny at all."
Michael and I spun around. Heather was
standing just inside the screen door, her face
pressing against it. "There's nothing funny about
Helen," she added softly.

"Mom should get you a collar with bells on

it," Michael said, "like cats wear to warn birds. Then maybe you couldn't sneak up and spy on people."

"Molly spies on me," Heather hissed. "She spied on me and Helen today!"

"See?" I turned to Michael.

Before he could say anything, Heather looked at us, a frown creasing her face. "Molly's right. You better not laugh, Michael. Helen doesn't like either one of you, and when she comes, you'll be sorry for everything you ever did to me."

Without waiting for an answer, Heather turned away and disappeared into the shadows in the hall.

"There," I whispered, clutching Michael's arm. "Do you see what I mean?"

Michael pulled away from me. "Don't let that little brat scare you with make-believe, Molly. You're acting like a real dope."

"I am not!" Tears stung my eyes, and I ran into the house, almost colliding with Mom as she came out of the kitchen.

"I was just looking for you and Michael," she said cheerfully. "Would you like some ice cream? Heather and Dave and I were just about to sit down and try the ice-cream maker we got last week. How about it?"

Behind her, in the lighted kitchen, I could see Dave setting up the machine while Heather watched. He turned to her and said something, and she laughed and gave him a strawberry to sample.

"Now, Dave," Mom said, "I saw that! Don't eat them all, or we won't have enough for the ice cream."

"Daddy can have all he wants!" Heather stuck out her lip and scowled at Mom.

As Dave turned to Heather, I edged past Mom. "No, thanks," I said. "I'm not in the mood for ice cream."

"But, honey . . ." Mom started, reaching out to stop me.

I kept on going. "She ruins everything," I said to Mom before going in my room and shutting the door. I hoped Heather would stay in the kitchen until I was asleep.

6

———— ✤ ————

THAT NIGHT, Heather had her first bad dream. She woke me up screaming, "Help, help, it's on fire! Put it out, Mommy, put it out!"

I jumped out of bed, switched on the light, and ran to her. She was sitting up in bed, her eyes squeezed shut, clutching her blanket. Tears ran down her cheeks, and she was trembling.

"Save me, save me!" she cried.

"Heather!" I grabbed her shoulders and shook her. "You're having a bad dream. Wake up!"

Michael stumbled into the room. "What's going on? What's wrong with her?"

Twisting and turning, Heather squirmed away from me and started running down the hall, still screaming about the fire. Dave caught her and picked her up. "It's all right, honey, it's all right," he murmured, rocking her as if she were a baby.

Suddenly she collapsed against him, perfectly relaxed. Her mouth found her thumb; her long eyelashes fluttered against her cheeks; her legs dangled like a rag doll's. Gently Dave carried her back into our room and lowered her into bed.

"There now," he whispered. Smoothing her hair back from her forehead, he kissed her.

Heather's eyes opened for a second, and she smiled at her father before sinking back into sleep.

Turning to me, Dave whispered, "What happened?"

"She was screaming about the fire. I tried to wake her up, but I couldn't. Then she jumped out of bed and ran out into the hall." I took Mom's hand and slid closer to her. Was he going to blame me somehow?

Dave shook his head and ran his hands through his hair, making it stand up in spikes. "She hasn't had those nightmares for so long; I thought she'd gotten over them." Looking at me again, he asked, "Did anything upset her today?"

"Well, she was in the graveyard," I said uneasily. "She was talking to someone. She thinks there's a girl there, Helen." It sounded so ridiculous when I talked about it that I was embarrassed. I already knew what Michael and Mom thought about ghosts; I was sure Dave would have the same reaction.

Just as I thought, Dave smiled. "Heather's very imaginative." He said it as if I'd criticized her. "And very sensitive. You and Michael haven't been asking her questions about the fire, have you?"

"Of course not!" I stared at him, shocked. Surely he knew that Michael and I had promised not to talk to Heather about the fire. Did he think we would go back on our word?

"I thought something might have stirred up her memories." He tugged on his beard, gazing at me as if he weren't sure I could be trusted to tell the truth.

"It's what happened in the graveyard," I said. "There's something bad under the oak tree; I know there is! You should make her stay away from it. Even Mr. Simmons told her not to go near it because of snakes and poison ivy."

"Snakes and poison ivy are one thing," Dave said slowly, "but don't you ever start scaring her with stories about 'bad' things in the graveyard."

"Molly thinks the graveyard's haunted," my loyal brother said. "She's sure some ghost is after Heather."

Mom and Dave both turned on me then. "That's the most ridiculous thing I've ever heard, Molly," Mom said, and Dave agreed.

"No more talk about ghosts," he said.

"Especially not around Heather. I don't want you scaring her. No wonder she had a nightmare."

"But I didn't tell *her*, she told *me!*" I pulled away from Mom, feeling betrayed first by Michael and then by her. "And, besides, you didn't see her, you didn't hear her!"

Michael laughed. "Molly didn't scare Heather," he said. "Heather scared Molly."

Dave sighed and put his arm around Mom's shoulders. "Well, no sense standing here all night arguing about it," he said. "Just don't inflict your own fears on Heather, Molly. You've been fretting about that graveyard ever since we moved in here. It doesn't bother anybody else, so forget it, okay?" He reached out and gave my head a pat.

As I started to go back into my room, he added, "I see Heather's visits to the graveyard as a way of coming to terms with her mother's death. It's probably good for her. As long as nobody scares her." He looked at me again, leaving no doubt about whom he meant.

Closing my door, I tiptoed back to bed. Before I lay down, I peeked at Heather. The moonlight shone on her face, and I was sure her eyes were open a tiny slit. "I bet you lay here and listened to every word we said," I whispered, but she didn't answer. Turning my back to her and the window, I switched on my tape player and fell asleep listening to *West Side Story*.

The next morning, after Dave had disappeared into the carriage house, Mom into her loft, and Michael into the woods, I sat at the breakfast table with Heather, watching her poke at the cereal in her bowl.

"What are you going to do today?" I asked her.

"Nothing." She carried her bowl to the garbage can and dumped most of her cereal.

"I bet you're going to the graveyard again."

She looked at me over her shoulder, tangles of hair almost hiding her face. "Maybe I am and maybe I'm not. It's none of your business, is it?"

"There isn't really a ghost, is there? You were making it all up."

"You heard what Daddy said last night. No more talk about ghosts or trying to scare me. I'm going to tell him you're still doing it." With her hand on the screen door, she added, "You better not follow me or spy on me either. You'll be sorry if you do. Helen doesn't like people who bother me."

Before I could say anything, she was gone, leaving the screen door to bang shut behind her. Running to the window over the sink, I watched her saunter across the yard and disappear through the graveyard gate. Just once, she looked back and scowled at me.

Since it was my day to wash the breakfast dishes, I filled the sink with hot, soapy water and watched the bowls and mugs and glasses slowly fill and sink beneath the bubbles. While I washed them, I wondered what I should do about Heather and the ghost. If there were a ghost. In the morning sunlight, it seemed almost likely that I had imagined the presence of something inhuman under the oak tree. Maybe Mom was right about the poetry I'd been reading. Especially the Poe.

After I finished the dishes, I made my bed, trying to ignore the tangle of sheets, blankets, and clothes on Heather's bed. Then I picked up *Watership Down* and went outside to read.

Stretching out in the shade of one of the maples, I opened my book, but the warmth of summer made it hard to concentrate. In the droning of bees, in the rustling of leaves, in the swaying of wild flowers, I imagined I heard Helen's voice whispering to Heather, calling her, promising her things. Closing my book, I left it under the tree and crossed the lawn to the graveyard. I crept along the outside of the hedge, paused when I reached the oak tree, and peered through the leaves at the little stone, expecting to see Heather sitting there. All I saw was the peanut butter jar, filled with fresh flowers.

Pushing through the hedge, I forced myself to approach the tombstone. "H.E.H," I read. "March 7, 1879–August 8, 1886." She had been dead for a hundred years, so much longer than she'd been alive. What was left of her now? A tangle of bones? Maybe nothing but dust. I shivered, cold in the shade of the oak, hugging myself to get warm.

Thinking about the snakes, I backed away from the grave, feeling the warm sunlight strike my back as I moved out of the shade of the oak. With bees droning in the Queen Anne's lace and a butterfly flitting around my head, it was strange to think of death, especially the death of a little girl, younger even than I was. Could she really still be here, haunting this grave? If she did exist, what did she want? A breeze sighed through the leaves of the oak. It was the loneliest sound I'd ever heard, as lonely as a ghost who had been lying alone in the dark for a hundred years.

Overwhelmed with a terrible feeling of sadness and despair, I turned and ran out of the graveyard, feeling my heart pound. I wanted to go to Mom, but I knew she would laugh at me, or worse, get cross. Knowing it was useless to turn to Dave, I decided to look for Michael. I guessed he was somewhere in the woods and followed the path along the creek, hoping I might find him trying to catch crawfish where the water slowed near the fence.

At the end of the path, though, all I saw were the cows, standing knee-deep in the creek and staring stupidly at me. As I looked around, wondering where Michael might have gone, I noticed a path on the other side of the creek, angling off into the trees. It looked like the sort of thing Michael would enjoy exploring, so I pulled off my sandals, waded across, and followed the path into the woods.

After walking for about ten minutes, I found myself beside the creek again. Ahead of me, the woods thinned out, and I saw a large pond. Hurrying toward it, I looked around for Michael, sure he'd be here, but there was no sign of him.

On the rising ground above the pond were the ruins of an old stone house. Although the wall was two stories high on the side facing the water, the rest of the house was a crumbling heap of rock and charred wood. Long ago it must have burned, I thought. But before that, it must have been beautiful, standing there on the hill looking out across the valley to the mountains.

While I was gazing at the house, trying to imagine it whole, I saw a flash of color, the red of a tee shirt instantly visible. Thinking it was Michael, I started to call him, then stopped myself. Heather had been wearing a red tee shirt when she ran out of the kitchen this morning. What was she doing here, so far away from home?

Running across the clearing between the house and the pond, I crept through the underbrush surrounding the ruins, trying hard to make no noise. As I reached the corner of the house, I heard Heather's voice and dropped silently to my knees. Crawling through a thicket of polk berries and honeysuckle, I spotted Heather sitting on what once must have been a terrace.

"It's lovely here, Helen," she said, turning toward a space in the air, a sort of shimmering emptiness that reminded me of heat waves thrown out by a camp fire on a hot day. I was sure that Heather could see someone or something, that she could hear a voice speaking in the breeze.

Shivering, I felt the hairs on my neck and arms rise. At any moment I expected to see what Heather saw, and I was sure that Michael would not laugh if he were here. Even Mom and Dave would have to believe me. Heather was not sitting on that stone bench alone talking to an imaginary friend. Something was with her, and I was sure it was no friend.

Very slowly and cautiously, I backed away into my tunnel through the underbrush. All of a sudden, the house seemed threatening, more frightening than the graveyard itself. Its ruined walls towered over me, smoke-scorched and smelling still of charred wood and ash. Something terrible had happened here — I knew it had — and I wanted to get away, to save myself from whatever waited here in its ruins.

Breaking free of the bushes and trees I ran toward the pond, not caring now whether Heather saw me or not. Once I reached the safety of the woods, I slowed down and finally collapsed on a fallen tree, gasping for breath.

While I sat there, trying to breathe normally, I heard someone coming down the path. Looking up, I saw Heather walking toward me. At the sight of me, she stopped, obviously startled.

"What are you doing here?" Her hands balled into fists, she stood in the middle of the path, sunlight and shadow mottling her face and clothes with random patches of darkness and light. "You followed me again!"

Standing up to give myself the advantage of height, I shook my head. "I was looking for Michael," I said, "and I saw you on the terrace, talking to someone."

Heather tilted her head to one side, her jaw protruding at a stubborn angle. "So?"

"Heather, this isn't a good place." Frightened, I reached out to take her arm, but she sidestepped me.

"Don't try to tell me what to do, Molly!" Heather's gray eyes stared into mine. "This is Helen's house; she invited me here, and I'll come whenever I want to! You're the one who better stay away."

"Listen to me, Heather, please. Helen isn't your friend. She, she — I don't know what she is, but she's dangerous. Stay away from her!" I seized the little girl's arms and shook her. "Don't come here anymore!"

As quickly as a cat, Heather wriggled away from me. "Since when did you ever care what I do? Helen's a better friend than you've been. She understands me, she likes me!" Heather's thin chest rose and fell rapidly as she backed off, her eyes huge and frightened in her pale face. "Don't you dare try to take her away from me!"

A shift in the breeze lifted the leaves over our heads, and a ray of sunlight struck Heather, glinting on a silver locket I'd never seen before. Aware of my eyes, Heather closed a small hand over the locket.

"What's that?" I moved toward her, but she turned and ran away from me, back toward the church.

"She gave it to me," Heather cried over her shoulder. "It's mine and you can't see it!"

I stood still for a moment and watched her vanish around a curve in the path, her thin white legs flashing through the weeds. Fearfully I glanced back at the ruins of the house on the hill. For a moment I thought I saw a face at one of the windows, but I wasn't sure. The honeysuckle and ivy draping the walls were fluttering in the breeze, and what I saw could have been a shadow or a patch of sunlight.

Without looking at the house again, I ran down the path after Heather.

7

WHEN I GOT BACK to the church, I found Mom in the kitchen making sandwiches for herself and Heather.

"You're just in time for lunch, Molly," Mom said, but Heather merely glanced at me before returning her attention to the peanut butter she was smearing on a slice of bread.

"I'm not very hungry." I leaned against the counter, not knowing whether I should stay or leave. Just being around Heather was beginning to make me nervous. "Where's Michael?" I asked Mom.

"I suppose he's out in the woods somewhere." Mom held a bowl of tuna salad toward me. "Sure you don't want some?"

I shook my head. "Maybe later."

Without looking at Mom or me, Heather took her sandwich and opened the screen door.

"Where are you going, Heather?" Mom asked.

"I'm eating with Daddy," she said, letting the door bang shut behind her.

Silently Mom and I watched her walk across the yard and disappear into the carriage house.

"Where were you all morning?" Mom asked me. "Were you with Heather?"

Opening the refrigerator, I made a pretence of looking for the ice tea. When I found it, I poured myself a glass and offered some to Mom, still trying to think of an answer that wouldn't get me into trouble.

"We were out in the woods," I said finally, hoping she would assume that we were together. "There's an old house way down the creek, just ruins really, and a pond. Heather loves going there, but I think it's kind of dangerous."

"What do you mean, Molly?" Mom looked puzzled. "I didn't know there were any old houses nearby."

"Well, it's there. And the pond might be very deep. Not only that, but the walls of the house look like they might fall down any minute. It's not a good place for a kid to play, Mom, and I think you or Dave should tell Heather not to go there."

Mom sipped her tea. "It doesn't sound very safe," she said, "but I'd love to see it. I might want to sketch it."

"But will you tell Heather she can't go there?"

"Of course." Mom gave me a long look. "You know, though, Molly, that Dave and I count on you and Michael to take care of Heather. It's up to you to make sure she doesn't run wild in the woods all day."

"I try to watch her, but she sneaks away from me the minute my back is turned. And Michael never even tries. He just packs up his binoculars and his other junk and disappears into the woods."

Mom carried her dishes to the sink and began rinsing them. "Molly, you are old enough to be responsible. We moved here so Dave and I would have time to work without worrying about you all." Putting her plate and glass on the counter to drain, she wiped her hands on the seat of her shorts and smiled at me. "Go on, now, and find something to do. I've got to get back to my painting."

"But I don't have anything to do!" I wailed.

"Go find Michael. He manages to keep himself very happy." With that, Mom was out the back door, across the drive, and into the church.

After spending a long, hot afternoon reading *Watership Down* and trying not to think about

Helen or the ruins of her house, I was glad to see Michael stroll out of the woods just before dinner. Marking my place with a blade of grass, I ran to meet him.

"Look at the walking-stick I caught!" Michael brandished a jar in front of my face, but all I could see in it was a dead stick. "Isn't he great?"

All of a sudden I realized that the stick had legs and eyes. Backing away, I yelled, "Don't let that thing loose in the house!"

"It won't hurt you." Michael smiled at the creature in the jar. "They're real hard to see, but this old guy moved just when I was looking at him. He's a great example of natural camouflage."

"Good for him." Walking beside the great naturalist, but not too close, I told him about the old house. "Heather says Helen used to live there, Michael. And she has this chain around her neck with a locket on it. She says Helen gave it to her. You should have heard Heather talking to her — I don't think she's making it up; I think Helen really is there. I swear I almost saw her!"

All the things I hadn't been able to tell Mom came tumbling out while Michael listened, his face blank. Finally he interrupted me.

"Molly, cut it out," he said. "You should hear yourself! You're letting that kid make a fool of you."

"I am not!" I glared at him, furious. "You weren't there; you didn't see Heather or hear her! You didn't see her in the graveyard either."

Michael held up his jar and peered at the walking-stick. "Show me the house," he said.

"It's too late now. Dinner's almost ready, and by the time we finish, it will be dark."

"Tomorrow morning then. First thing." He grinned at me through the jar. "I've always wanted to explore a haunted house. Just think, a treasure could be buried in the cellar or something."

"I'm not going inside, and I don't think you should either. The walls are about to fall down."

"You are a scaredy-cat, you know that?" Michael waved the jar at me, and I jumped away. "Bugs, graveyards, old houses — you're scared of everything."

Before I could come back with a good retort, Mom stepped out on the back porch. "Dinner's ready, you two," she called.

As usual, Mom and Dave did most of the talking, but as we were finishing our dessert, Dave turned to Heather and said, "I hear that you and Molly discovered an old house in the woods."

Heather shot me a nasty look and nodded her head. "I found it, not Molly," she mumbled, her mouth full of cake.

"Well, it sounds like a dangerous place to play.

How about you girls staying a little closer to the church?"

Heather shrugged her shoulders. "It's not dangerous. It's pretty." She gave her father one of her rare smiles. "You know how Molly is. She thinks everything is dangerous."

Dave laughed and Mom smiled. "She has a point there," he said to Mom.

"Well, it looks like it's going to fall down," I said, "and the pond is deep."

"So?" Heather stared at me. "I know how to swim. Nothing's going to happen to me there."

"Maybe we'll all take a walk and see it one day," Mom said, smiling at Heather and me. "In the meantime, though, why don't you play here?"

Heather hid her face behind her glass of milk, and I noticed a little bulge under her tee shirt. "How about the locket?" I asked her. "Did you tell your father about that?"

"What locket, honey?" Dave leaned across the table toward her, but Heather shrank away from him, her hand covering the bump the locket made under her shirt.

"It's just this old thing." She pulled the chain out of her shirt and held up a tarnished heart. "I found it in the weeds by the pond."

Michael looked at me, his eyebrows raised. I knew what he was thinking — poor old Molly, taken in again.

"Well, isn't that nice?" Dave smiled at Heather. "I bet Jean could polish it up so it would look like new."

Mom reached for the locket, but Heather dropped it back down inside her shirt. "I like it just the way it is," she said.

"Does it open?" Mom asked. "People used to keep pictures or locks of hair in those."

Heather shook her head. "It's bent, so it won't open anymore."

"Can I have another piece of cake?" Michael asked, and dinner went on, without any more comments about the house or the locket.

When I woke up the next morning, the first thing I saw were gray clouds and dripping leaves. It had rained hard during the night, and it looked like more showers were on the way. As I pulled on my jeans and a long-sleeved shirt, I told myself that I wouldn't have to take Michael to the house after all. Even he wouldn't want to go walking through wet grass and muddy fields.

But I was wrong. He was waiting for me at the kitchen table, the remains of his breakfast in front of him, his windbreaker on the back of the chair. "I thought you were going to sleep all day," he said accusingly.

"It's going to rain, Michael. You don't still want to go, do you?"

"The weather forecast says there's only a thirty percent chance of showers," he said. "You aren't scared of getting wet, too?"

I scowled at him as I poured milk on my cereal. "Where's Heather?"

"Beats me." He grinned at me. "Maybe she's gone on ahead to tell Helen we're coming."

"Very funny." I ate my cereal in silence while he read the comics. After washing the dishes, I pulled on my windbreaker and followed him outside. "We take the path down to the cow pasture, cross the creek, and go through the woods," I told him.

In silence, we waded through the water, higher now because of the rain. The cows watched us mournfully from the other side of the fence. One of them made a little snorting sound and ran clumsily up the hill away from us, and the others followed more slowly, mooing in chorus.

"They sound like they're auditioning for parts in some Great Dairyland TV Special," Michael said, as we entered the woods, still wet and smelling of rain.

Although I didn't say it, I was sorry to leave the cows behind. The woods seemed unfriendly this morning; lost in gloom, they brooded like giants on the verge of waking from bad dreams. The only sounds were the cawing of crows somewhere ahead of us, the gurgle of the creek behind us, and the swishing noise our feet made brushing against the damp weeds bordering the path.

When we reached the edge of the woods, we paused and I pointed toward the house. Against sky of ragged clouds, the ruins looked grim and desolate. Behind the house, the trees swayed in the wind, and at its feet the pond lay, its water dark gray, its surface wrinkled.

"Well, Molly," Michael said solemnly, "I don't see any face at the window. I guess Helen isn't home today. She must be staying underground where it's all dry and snug." He laughed, and I punched his arm.

"Shut up," I hissed at him. To me, the windows were full of hidden eyes watching us. The murmuring of the wind in the woods, the sighing sound it made in the weeds, seemed to speak to me, warning me to leave. I shivered. "Come on, Michael, let's go back. It's going to rain any minute." I edged away from him, back toward the path and the haven of the woods.

But Michael ignored me. Without waiting to see if I would follow, he began climbing the hill toward the house.

"You'd better not go inside!" I called after him.

Glancing back at me over his shoulder, he said,

"Why not? Nobody's here. I don't even see a No Trespassing sign."

A gust of wind lifted the trailing vines on the house and sent them billowing toward us like outstretched arms. "Michael, come back!" I shouted, as the first drops of rain came pelting down out of the sky.

"There's still some roof on this side," he yelled. "Come on, Molly, we can stay dry."

As he disappeared through one of the windows, I ran after him, too scared to go home by myself. "Where are you?" I asked as I neared the house.

"Here." His face appeared in a window almost covered with honeysuckle. "You'll be dry in here."

My legs were shaking so hard, I could hardly manage to climb into the house. It was dark and cold; the floor beneath our feet creaked, and everything smelled of mold and decay and smoke. Huddling close to Michael, I glanced around fearfully, expecting to see something hideous in every shadow. But all I saw were spiderwebs and heaps of rusty beer cans and bottles, charred wood from bonfires, graffiti on the walls, discarded newspapers, and other assorted trash.

"See?" Michael said. "There's nothing here to be scared of. Looks like teenagers from Holwell come out here, and maybe bums. But no ghosts, Molly."

My teeth were chattering, but I nodded, pretending to believe him.

"This must have been a terrific house," Michael went on. "I bet the walls are more than two feet thick, all solid rock. The house was two or three stories high with a fireplace in every room. See?"

I looked up. We were standing in front of one fireplace and above our heads, jutting out of the wall, was another fireplace. Above that was what was left of the roof. Through the holes, rain fell, and I could see patches of gray sky.

"As soon as it stops raining, I'm going home," I told Michael. "You can stay here as long as you like."

Michael shrugged and began exploring the room. "I guess it burned down," he said, poking at a charred timber lying on the floor. "It must have been an incredible fire. Probably lit up the whole sky."

Without answering him, I went back to the window and looked out, hoping the rain had stopped. Down below me, I saw the pond. And something else.

"Michael!" I called to him, "Come here!"

"Why?" He had gone into the next room.

"It's Heather! She's down there by the pond!"

Michael joined me by the window, and we both stared at her, too surprised to move. She was standing by the water, her back to us, her hair swirling in the wind, absolutely soaked.

"What's she doing?" I whispered.

"I don't know, but she'll catch pneumonia if she stays there much longer." Michael pushed me aside and climbed out the window. "Heather," he yelled. "Get away from that water!"

She turned toward him, her mouth open in surprise, one hand clasping the locket. "Go away!" she shouted as he ran toward her.

I watched him grab her and try to drag her toward the house. She was doing her best to get away from him, twisting and turning, crying and screaming, begging him to leave her alone.

"Molly, help me!" Michael yelled, and I scrambled through the window, slipping and sliding as I ran down the hillside. Grabbing hold of Heather, I helped Michael drag her up the hill and into the house.

"What are you doing here?" she cried, still struggling to escape.

"Looking for you!" I shouted. "You know you aren't supposed to be here! Mom and Dave told you last night to stay closer to the church!"

"I'll go where I want to go!" Heather slumped suddenly, her eyes filled with tears, and she began to cry. "You're hurting my arms," she sobbed. "Let me go."

"Do you promise not to run away from us?" Michael scowled at her.

"Yes," Heather mumbled. "She's gone now anyway."

We let go of her, and she slumped on the floor between us, weeping, her face hidden in her hands. "You always make her go away," she wept, "but you'll be sorry. You'll be so sorry."

"See what I mean?" I turned to Michael. Surely he would believe me now.

"There's nobody here and there never was," Michael said scornfully. "You might be able to fool Molly with ghost stories, but you can't fool me. I know a lie when I hear one."

"Just wait till she comes!" Heather turned a look of pure hatred on Michael. "She'll get you first!"

But Michael just laughed. "What's taking her so long! Why can't she get me right now?"

"The time's not right," Heather said, gazing past us both. She stared out the window at the wind-lashed vines and dark clouds.

Michael laughed again. "Oh, I'm so scared," he said in a fake quaver.

"You should be." Heather stood up then and backed away from us, just as a stone tumbled from the wall above us and crashed at Michael's feet.

"There!" Heather shrieked as Michael and I stared at the stone. "She doesn't want you here. She wants me, just me!"

"Come on, Michael!" I tugged at his arm, trying to get him to leave the house. "Let's get out of here! I told you it wasn't safe."

"It was just the wind, that's all." Michael frowned at Heather. "But Molly's right. We shouldn't stay here in a storm. We're going home, and you're coming with us."

He grabbed one arm and I grabbed the other, and between the two of us we managed to drag Heather out of the house, down the hill, and into the woods. By the time we got to the creek, she was walking sullenly, like a prisoner on her way to a beheading.

When we had almost reached the church, Michael seized the chain around Heather's neck and looked at the locket before she could snatch it back.

"Those are your initials," he said. "You didn't find this anywhere. You had it all along, didn't you?"

"H.E.H," Heather said, a little smile passing over her face. "My initials, but not my name. You want to know whose name they stand for?"

Michael sighed, but I said, "Tell us, Heather. I want to know."

"Helen Elizabeth Harper," she whispered. "My friend and your enemy." Breaking away from us, she ran toward the church, leaving us to follow, soaked to the skin and, in my case at least, too scared to chase after her.

8

"HOW DO YOU explain it, Michael?" I asked him later. We were sitting at the kitchen table, drinking mugs of hot chocolate, still trying to get warm. Although I'd made a cup for Heather, she'd taken hers out to the carriage house.

"It's just a fantasy, Molly. Lots of kids have imaginary friends. Don't you remember Mr. Maypo?"

"How could I forget? Every time you did something bad, you blamed it on Mr. Maypo. Mom and I were both glad when he left for Timbuctoo." I took another sip of hot chocolate. "But this is different, Michael. You were only three when you had Mr. Maypo. Heather's seven. It's just not normal."

"Well, she's not normal. You know that, and

I know that, but Mom and Dave just won't admit it." Michael looked into his mug. "Ugh. Skin. I hate it when my hot chocolate gets skin on it!"

While he skimmed the surface of his hot chocolate with a spoon, I sipped mine thoughtfully. "But Michael," I said slowly, "suppose she's not making it up. Suppose Helen is real."

"Oh, Molly, honestly." Michael looked disgusted. "Ghosts do not exist. The kid is lying, and you're encouraging her. Can't you see? She's littler than we are, and she wants to make us think she's got some supernatural friend who'll beat us up or something if we're mean to her. It's so obvious; any idiot should be able to figure it out."

"Thanks a lot!" I felt my face turn red. "I'm not an idiot. If anybody is, you are!" I jumped up and went to the sink to rinse my cup.

"Hey, I'm sorry," Michael mumbled. "I'm just tired of hearing all this ghost talk."

"Maybe I have some kind of sixth sense that you don't have," I said. "Did you ever think of that?" I frowned at him, not ready to forgive him for calling me an idiot.

He shrugged. "Suppose we ride our bikes into Holwell and go to the library? I bet they have a book or something that would tell us all about that old house. Once you see that nobody named

Helen Elizabeth Harper ever lived there, maybe you'll realize what a liar Heather is."

"Do you want to go right now?" I squinted at the sky, trying to decide if it was going to rain any more today.

"Sure. I think we've had our thirty percent shower, don't you?"

We got our bikes out from under the porch and rode down Clark Road toward town. It was a long way, and I was glad the rain had cooled things off. On a hot day, I would never have made it up some of the hills between our house and Holwell.

We found the library on a quiet street near the park and locked our bikes. Inside it was small and friendly, more like a living room in somebody's house than a library. Except for all the books, of course. There were hundreds of them, jammed into shelves lining the walls and forming alcoves near the windows.

"Can I help you find something?" a woman asked as I began riffling through the card catalogue.

"I hope so." Michael smiled up at her. "My sister and I just moved into an old church out on Clark Road and when we were out in the woods today, we found the ruins of an old house. It looked like it burned down a long time ago.

We just wondered if you had any information about it."

"Oh, yes." The librarian smiled. "I know what house you mean."

She led us to a row of file cabinets at the back of the room. "We have several files on historical homes in and around Holwell," she said, flicking through the folders in one of the drawers. "Is this the house?"

She laid a newspaper clipping down on the table where we could see it. "It burned down about a hundred years ago. A terrible fire," she murmured, pointing to a blurred photograph of the house by the pond.

"One of our local historians wrote this article several years ago." Setting the clipping aside before I had a chance to read it, she produced an old photograph. "Here is the house before it burned," she said. "Lovely isn't it?"

I nodded. In the picture I saw a big stone house, standing on a hill with a lawn sweeping down to a pond. On the terrace sat three people: a man, a woman, and a girl. The man and woman sat close together, their hands clasped, but the girl sat apart, her face turned away. I stared at it, wishing the people were bigger and easier to see.

"That's Mr. and Mrs. Miller," the librarian said, pointing to the man and woman.

Michael nudged me, and I smiled, relieved that

their name was Miller, not Harper. But the librarian wasn't quite finished. "And this," she went on, her finger lingering on the girl, "is Mrs. Miller's daughter, Helen."

"Helen?" I stared into the woman's face, my heart thumping.

She nodded and turned the picture over. Someone had written in a spidery, old-fashioned hand, "Mabel, Robert, and Mabel's girl, Helen. Taken in June, 1886, at Harper House."

"Harper House?" It was Michael's turn to ask questions now. I was sure I couldn't have said a word if my life depended on it. "Are you certain that's what it's called?"

"Why, of course. It's written right here." The librarian looked at the writing again, as if she were double-checking. "You see, the house was built a few generations earlier by Harold Harper. It stayed in the family till Mabel's first husband, Joseph Harper — that would be Helen's father — died. When Mabel remarried, her name changed to Miller, but folks kept on calling it Harper House. Unfortunately, Mr. and Mrs. Miller didn't live there long before it burned down."

"Were they caught in the fire?" Michael leaned across the table toward the librarian, his eyes big behind his glasses. In the silence following his question, I could hear a fly buzzing against the window behind me.

"Yes, the whole family was killed." The librarian pushed the old newspaper clipping across the table toward us. "You can read Miss Hawkins' article. It's a very complete account, right down to the ghost stories people tell about the house."

I backed away from the clipping, thinking that I had heard all I wanted to, but Michael bent over it eagerly. "Listen to this, Molly," he said, his voice rising in excitement. "Mr. and Mrs. Miller's bodies were never found. They must be buried somewhere under the wreckage. No wonder people think the place is haunted!"

I stared at him, feeling the hairs on the back of my neck quiver. "What about Helen?" I whispered. "What happened to her?"

"Oh," the librarian said, answering for Michael. "She apparently escaped from the house and ran into the pond. It was dark, and I suppose she was confused or frightened. At any rate, she drowned. According to the newspaper account, her body was buried in Saint Swithin's graveyard."

"Where's that?" Michael asked.

"Why, it's just where you live." The librarian smiled at him. "Surely you've noticed the little burial ground behind the church."

As Michael nodded and told her about the

tombstone under the oak tree, I watched the fly struggle to find a way out of the library. I wanted to find an escape too, but every word I'd heard confirmed my fear that Heather had somehow allied herself with a ghost. What I wasn't sure of was the danger — was Helen as wicked as Heather made her out to be, or was she merely a lost child looking for someone to love her?

Edging a little closer to the librarian, I said, "What kind of ghost stories do people tell about Harper House?"

"It's all in the clipping," she said a bit impatiently, flicking her fingernail at the article which Michael was still reading. "But, if I remember correctly, people claim the child's ghost haunts the graveyard and the pond."

A frown crossed her face. "They actually believe the poor girl is responsible for some of the drownings in the pond, but you know how people are. They're always looking for some sort of supernatural cause for the simplest things."

"People have drowned in the pond?" I thought of Heather standing at the water's edge in the pouring rain.

The librarian nodded. "It's a pretty place, and it's tempting on a hot day. Children don't need ghosts to lure them into a nice, cool pond." She smiled at me and added, "A child drowned last summer in the municipal pool, but nobody blamed *that* on a ghost."

"In other words," Michael said, "you don't believe the stories." From his tone of voice, I could tell he was looking for an ally.

She smiled and shook her head. "I've picnicked by Harper Pond many times, and I never saw a thing but birds and butterflies." As she began gathering up the papers on the table, she paused and gazed at the picture of the Millers and Helen sitting on the porch, innocent of the terrible event that would soon destroy them. "Nevertheless, it was certainly a tragedy, wasn't it?"

As soon as Michael and I were outside, I turned to him. "Well, what do you have to say now?"

He shoved his glasses into place on his nose and frowned. "Heather must have talked to somebody, Molly. The last time Mr. Simmons came to mow the graveyard — he must have told her about Harper House."

"But, Michael, he didn't even know Helen's grave was there. He couldn't have told her what those initials stood for."

Michael shook his head and began to pedal his bike down the street toward home. "She's made it all up somehow," he yelled back at me. "I know it's not a ghost, Molly. It's just not possible."

"Wait for me, Michael," I shouted, pumping hard. "Don't go so fast!"

He slowed down and let me catch up, but I could tell he didn't want to talk about Harper House or Helen. The little wheels in his brain were spinning round and round, trying frantically to come up with a rational solution. I had a feeling that he was just as scared as I was, maybe even more scared because science didn't have an explanation for something like Helen.

All of a sudden, Michael slowed to a stop beside a road sign almost hidden by the honeysuckle climbing over it. "Look, Molly, this is Harper House Road." He pointed at a narrow dirt road curving up out of sight over a hill. "Let's see where it goes."

Before I could tell him that I'd had enough of Harper House for one day, if not for the rest of my life, he took off in a cloud of dust. Not wanting to ride home alone, I followed him, hoping the hill wouldn't be too steep for me. By the time I had huffed and puffed my way to the top, Michael was vanishing around a sharp curve at the bottom. Putting on my brakes, I flew after him, my hair blowing straight back from my face, sure I was going to shoot over my handlebars and split my head open. By a miracle, I managed to skid safely to a stop on a narrow stone bridge just behind Michael.

Mr. Simmons was so startled by our sudden appearance that he almost dropped his fishing pole. "Well, well," he said, "where did you two come from? Straight down out of the sky?"

"That house," Michael said, pointing to the ruins just visible through the trees. "Did you tell Heather about it?"

"Heather?" Mr. Simmons fiddled with his pipe for a moment, then puffed a fragrant cloud of smoke into the air. "You mean your little sister, the one who found the gravestone?"

Michael and I nodded, but Mr. Simmons shook his head. "I haven't seen her since then. And why would I tell her about Harper House? It ought to be torn down, if you ask me. It's a haven for all sorts of goings-on — a disgrace to the town of Holwell. No place for a child to play, that's for sure."

I looked at Michael, but his eyes shifted away from mine. From the frown on his face, I knew he was struggling to invent a new theory to explain Heather's knowing so much about Helen. Turning to Mr. Simmons, I asked him if he knew Harper House was haunted.

"Who told you that?" he asked.

"The lady at the library," Michael answered.

"She showed us some old newspaper articles." Using his scornful scientist voice, he told Mr. Simmons what the librarian had said.

"Miss Williams told you all that?" Mr. Simmons laughed and shook his head. "She ought to have more sense. A grown woman scaring kids with ghost stories."

Michael frowned at Mr. Simmons. "She didn't scare me! I don't believe in that kind of stuff." Jerking his head toward me, he added, "*She's* the one who's scared to death of Helen. I don't know which one's worse, her or Heather."

"You're just fooling yourself, Michael!" Gripping the handlebars of my bike, I leaned toward him, angry that he'd made me look foolish in front of Mr. Simmons. "Helen is every bit as real as you are, and you know it!"

Mr. Simmons looked from me to Michael and then back at me. Pausing to fiddle with his pipe, he said, "Ghost or no ghost, you kids stay away from Harper House. The walls are about to cave in, and at least three children have drowned in the pond. The water's not fit for swimming; it's murky and full of weeds."

"The librarian told us that some people think Helen's ghost lures children into the pond." I gazed past Mr. Simmons at the water's surface shimmering through the leaves. It looked very peaceful in the afternoon sunlight.

"Well, now, I don't know about that," Mr. Simmons said, "but I do know a girl drowned three years ago. She was one of these lonely little creatures. No friends, nobody who seemed to care much about her — you know the kind. Well, she disappeared one day, and this is where they finally found her." He gestured through the trees at the glittering water.

"Ten feet under," he added, "and all tangled up in weeds. I hope I never see anything that sad again."

I looked at Michael and shivered, but he was staring at the ground, his forehead wrinkled.

"Well, now, I didn't mean to upset you," Mr. Simmons said a little too loudly. "I just thought you should know the pond's no place to play." Pulling a watch out of his pocket, he mumbled, "My goodness, it's after five already. Time I got myself home."

He tossed his rod and reel into the back of his pickup truck and turned to Michael. "Do you like to fish, boy?"

Michael shrugged. "I don't know how."

"Well, I'll tell you what. Next time I come over to mow the graveyard, I'll bring along an extra rod and teach you how. Would you like that?"

Michael grinned and said he'd love it. Mr.

Simmons got into his truck, threw it into gear, and bounced away in a cloud of dust.

"See? He doesn't believe in those old stories either," Michael said.

Without answering, I got on my bike and started pedaling slowly back up the hill. No matter what Michael or Mr. Simmons thought, I believed in Helen, and I was afraid she had some sort of hold on Heather. They were linked, I thought, in so many ways: by their initials, by their loneliness, by their mothers' deaths.

Like the girl Mr. Simmons had just told us about, Heather was one of those lonely little creatures, friendless and unhappy, and I was frightened. Not for myself — but for Heather.

9

———— * ————

AS MICHAEL AND I rode our bikes down the driveway, we saw Mom standing on the back porch, her hands on her hips. "Where have you been?" she said as we braked to a stop.

"At the library," I said, wheeling my bike to its place under the porch.

"And then we saw Mr. Simmons." Michael was too excited to notice that Mom was not smiling. "Guess what? He's going to take me fishing the next time he comes to cut the grass."

"But you were supposed to be here watching Heather." Mom folded her arms tightly across her chest and frowned at me. "Didn't we talk about that just the other day?"

"She was out in the carriage house with Dave when we left," I said. "You were painting, and I know you don't like being disturbed, so Michael and I just decided to go. I thought it would be all right."

As Michael started to say something in my defense, he was interrupted by Dave. He stepped out on the porch to join Mom, and Heather was right behind him, peering around his legs, her pale eyes on Michael and me.

"Do you two have any idea what a scare you gave us?" Dave asked, his voice rising. "We couldn't find any of you! We called and called. Finally I found Heather way down on the other side of the creek near that ruin you told your mother about. She said you took her there and then ran off and left her."

I stared at him. "We didn't take her anywhere!"

But he went right on talking. "Why do you treat her so badly? You've made her life miserable ever since we moved out here." He was yelling now, and his face was red. "Heather's just a little girl, a very sensitive little girl! Why can't you treat her decently? What's wrong with you two?"

As Dave continued to accuse us of tormenting Heather, the poor little victim peeked at us, smiling slyly. She was enjoying every minute of his tirade.

"Dave, please." Mom laid her hand on his arm, trying to calm him down. "Don't talk to Molly and Michael that way. There must be some misunderstanding."

Dave turned from us to Mom. "That's right, Jean! Take their side as usual!" Brushing Mom's hand away, he led Heather down the steps, past Michael and me, and strode across the driveway toward the van.

"Where are you going?" Mom called after him, her voice quavering. "Dinner's ready, Dave." She started to follow him, but stopped, halfway down the steps.

"You all eat it. I'm taking my daughter out for dinner. She needs to get away for a while." Without looking at us, Dave slammed the van door and gunned the motor. As he roared down the driveway, I saw Heather smile at us.

"I hate him!" I looked at Mom, but she had already turned away from me. I followed her up the steps. "We didn't take Heather into the woods, Mom. She lied!"

Mom paused at the doorway and wiped her eyes with the back of her hand. "But you could have stayed here or taken her to the library with you," she said. "None of this would have happened if you had done what I asked you to."

Michael grabbed my arm and stopped me from following Mom into the kitchen. "Drop it," he whispered. "She's really upset, and you'll just make things worse." His face wore its worried expression, making him look more like a little old man than usual.

Pulling away from him, I crossed the kitchen to the stove. Mom was stirring the stew she'd cooked. "I'm sorry," I said softly.

"It's all right." She watched the stew bubble and poked it with the spoon.

"Are we going to eat?" Michael asked.

"Go ahead, help yourselves." Mom handed me the spoon.

"How about you?" I asked as she walked to the door.

"I'm not hungry." Pushing the door open, she stepped outside.

"Where are you going?" Michael ran out on the porch behind her.

"For a walk." Her voice was sharp. "You eat your dinner. I'll be back soon."

Silently I filled two plates with stew, while Michael poured our milk. After we'd eaten a few mouthfuls, Michael said, "She was crying."

"I know." We looked at each other. "It's all Heather's fault. Did you see the way she was grinning when Dave was yelling at us?"

Michael nodded. "It's just what she wants — to cause enough trouble to ruin things for Mom and Dave."

"Why can't Dave see what she's doing? He's blind to everything she does." I pushed my plate away, half my stew uneaten. The kitchen was getting dark, and I felt sad looking at the three empty plates stacked on the counter. "Do you think we should go find Mom?"

Michael polished off the last of his stew by wiping his plate with a piece of bread. Then he gulped down his milk and brushed away the white mustache it left on his upper lip. "I guess so."

Turning on the kitchen light to make the room look cheerier, I hesitated in the doorway. The sky was gray and the trees were dark shapes, glittering with lightning bugs. A breeze shushed through the grass, rustling the leaves and bringing with it the scent of honeysuckle. The night seemed very still and private, and I wasn't sure I really wanted to leave the safety of the kitchen.

"Molly, are you going to stand there all night?" Michael stared at me from the driveway; the kitchen light shone on his glasses, giving him an owlish look.

"I'm coming." Folding my arms across my chest, I followed him across the yard. The grass was cold and wet, and I could feel it soaking through my running shoes. Glancing back at the lit windows, I felt homesick for Baltimore.

"Michael," I said, getting him to stop for a minute. "It was never this bad before we came here. Heather was pretty awful, but not like she is now. And we got along with Dave all right. He and Mom never had fights then."

"I know. I was thinking that too."

"It's living out here." I looked past him, at the oak tree's dark, shaggy shape dominating the sky, towering over everything else. It was Helen's influence, I thought. Whether Heather had dreamed her up or not, she had made things worse. Day by day, our lives seemed to grow unhappier, as if she had the ability somehow to reach out from the grave and touch us all with her misery.

"Maybe we should do what Mom said." I turned to Michael, studying his face in the moonlight. "Maybe we should really try to be nice to Heather."

"Are you kidding?"

"I'm worried about her, Michael. You heard what Dave said. She went back to the pond, back to Harper House. I know you don't believe she really sees a ghost, but that's not the point. Whatever makes her go there is dangerous." I paused, knowing Michael thought I was foolish. "Even Mr. Simmons thinks it's a bad place to play. He doesn't believe in ghosts — he just knows kids have drowned there."

Michael sighed. "Okay, Molly. *You* play with her; *you* try to be nice to her. See how far it gets you." Shrugging my hand from his arm, he started walking toward the graveyard. "I'm not having anything to do with that kid," he called back to me.

"Michael, is that you?" Mom came toward us.

"We were worried about you," Michael said. "It's dark."

She put her arms out and drew the two of us close to her. Then we walked back to the church, Mom in the middle, Michael and I holding her hands.

"I'm sorry I got so upset," she said, pausing at the bottom of the porch steps. The kitchen light slanted out the door, and shone on her face and hair, hiding her eyes in shadow. "I'm so worried about us, Heather, everything."

"I'm sorry too, Mom. Michael and I just can't get along with her. Or Dave. We do try, honest we do."

"I know, Molly." Mom gave me a hug. "She's such an unhappy little girl. I feel so sorry for her, but I don't know how to reach her, how to make her happy. Sometimes I think it might have been better for all of us if she had continued living with her grandmother."

She sat down on the steps, hugging her knees against her chest as if she were cold. "I tried to talk to Dave about her before you all came home, but he said I wasn't trying. He said I didn't love her enough." Mom looked at us, her eyes filling with tears again. "She isn't easy to love," she said sadly.

"Here they come," Michael said as the van's headlights swept across us.

We watched Heather and Dave get out of the van. Heather was eating an ice cream cone as she walked toward us, licking it very slowly to make it last as long as possible. Without saying a word, she climbed the steps, giving us a wide berth. I tried to force myself to reach out, to speak to her, but I couldn't. Silently I watched her vanish into the kitchen as Dave lumbered up the steps behind her.

"I'll put her to bed," he said, without stopping to look at us.

Mom stood up and followed him into the house, leaving Michael and me on the steps. For a while, neither of us said a word. We just sat there, listening to the crickets chirping under the porch.

"Well," Michael said finally, "we might as well go to bed. The little monster is probably asleep now."

"Until she wakes us all up with another nightmare." Shivering in the cool night air, I stood up and started to follow Michael into the house. A rustling in the leaves made me glance over my shoulder. "Michael!" I grasped his arm and pulled him back. "Look!" I pointed toward the graveyard.

"What?" He stared past my pointing finger.

"Didn't you see it?" I clung to him, trembling. "There was a light. It's gone now, but I saw it. Down at the end, under the oak tree. A sort of glimmer."

Michael shook his head. "It must have been a lightning bug. Honestly, Molly, there isn't a ghost lurking among the tombstones."

"I *saw* it. A bluish glow. It wasn't a lightning bug!"

"Let's go in." Prying my fingers from his arm, Michael opened the screen door, and I hurried after him into the brightly lit kitchen, shutting not only the screen door but the wooden door as well.

"You still haven't come up with an explanation for Heather's knowing so much about Harper House," I reminded him.

He frowned and looked around the kitchen as if he expected to see an explanation written on the walls. "It could be ESP," he said thoughtfully. "I didn't use to believe in all that paranormal stuff, but there is scientific evidence that a few people have some sort of extrasensory perception. I suppose it could explain Heather's knowing so much about Helen."

"You mean she has some sixth sense?"

He nodded. "It's better than believing she communicates with a ghost."

I shook my head. "You haven't seen as much as I have."

"Oh, Molly." Michael started walking down the hall toward his room. "Give it up, will you?"

He went into his room and closed the door, and I tiptoed into my room. Heather seemed to be asleep, so I got into bed as quietly as I could and pulled my Walkman out from under my pillow. Before I had a chance to turn it on, I heard Mom's voice through the bedroom wall.

"I don't see how you can continue to take her word against theirs," she was saying. "You know perfectly well she makes up all sorts of things just to cause trouble!"

"That's not true, Jean." Dave's voice rose. "Can't you see what they're trying to do?"

"No, I can't. I know my own children, and they have no reason to make you and me unhappy. They were delighted when we got married. It's Heather who wants to come between us, not Molly and Michael!" Mom's voice rose too.

As the argument grew louder, I wanted to bury my head under my pillow, but a movement from Heather's bed drew my attention to her. She was sitting up, listening to every word and smiling.

"You!" I yelled at her. "This is all your doing, isn't it? You love every quarrel they have!"

"Your mother is a witch," Heather said, "and she makes my daddy unhappy. I wish she were dead, and you and Michael, too!"

"My mother has done everything she can to make you happy," I shouted, "and all you do is throw it back in her face. You're a little monster!"

"My daddy doesn't think so. He loves me. He loves me more than he loves her, and if I want him to, he'll take me away from here and all of you." She glared across the room at me, her face fierce in the moonlight.

"You're a liar!"

"You better watch what you say to me!" Heather was sitting straight up, her hair falling in tangled curls across her forehead. "I can make you sorry, Molly. You and Michael and your mother!"

The door opened and Michael entered the room. "What's going on in here?"

Heather leapt to her feet, standing in the middle of the bed, her fists clenched. "Wait till Helen comes!" she screamed.

Dave rushed into the room just then, and Heather collapsed in a heap on her bed, weeping hysterically. Dave rushed to her side and lifted her into his arms. "What is it, Heather? What's wrong?"

"Daddy, Daddy," she wept, clinging to him.

"What have you done to her now?" Dave turned on Michael and me as Mom appeared behind him, her face pale, her hair flying.

"Nothing!" Michael shouted.

"She was listening to you all fighting," I told Mom, "and gloating! You should have heard her."

"Daddy, Daddy," Heather sobbed. "Make them leave me alone."

"There, there, Heather. Daddy's here. It's all right." He rocked her back and forth in his arms, soothing her as if she were a baby.

"Michael," Mom said softly, "go back to your room. We'll talk about this in the morning."

Michael started to object, saw the expression on Mom's face, and sidled past Dave and Heather. "We didn't do anything," he whispered to Mom.

She nodded and gave him a hug. "Just try to get some sleep, honey."

As soon as he was gone, Mom turned to me. "I'm sorry you heard us quarreling," she said. "I'll tuck you in."

When Mom bent over me, I reached up to hug her. "She hates us," I whispered. "All of us. She scares me, Mom." Tears welled up in my eyes, and Mom sat down beside me.

"Don't let her upset you, Molly," she whispered back. "She's a very disturbed little girl. I know it's hard for you. It's hard for me too, but try to understand that she's just as unhappy as you are, probably more so."

"Come on, Jean," Dave said softly. "Heather's asleep now."

Before he left the room, though, Dave turned back and looked at me. "I don't want any more of this, Molly. I mean it." Then he was gone.

Before closing my eyes, I looked at Heather. Her back was turned toward me, and I could hear the sound of deep, regular breathing. It was hard for me to believe that she could drop off to sleep so quickly after causing so much trouble, but for the five minutes that I watched her, I saw no sign that she was faking. Satisfied that she was truly asleep, I rolled away from her, closed my eyes, and tried to let my Walkman relax me.

Just as I was hovering on the edge of a nice dream about our old neighborhood, I heard Heather's bed creak and the unmistakable sound of a bare foot on the floor. Without opening my eyes, I sensed her standing by me, watching me. Then she went to the window and shoved the screen up.

I lay still, afraid that she would hear the sound of my heart beating in the silence. But after a few seconds, she climbed quietly out the window and dropped to the ground below.

I waited a couple of minutes, then got up and

peered out the window. In the moonlight, I saw her making her way across the lawn toward the graveyard. At the far end, through the hedge, a bluish glow illuminated the leaves of the oak tree. As I watched, Heather disappeared through the gate.

Shivering with fear, I climbed out the window and ran through the grass, already cold and wet with dew. Keeping in the shadow of the hedge, I crept past the gate, staying outside the grave-yard, until I reached the black shade of the oak tree. Dropping to my knees, I peered through the hedge at Helen's grave.

Dimly lit by the blue glow I'd seen from the house, Heather held out a jar of wild flowers as if she were making an offering. The silver locket gleamed on her chest, and her eyes glittered.

"Helen," she whispered, "Helen. Are you here?"

Too frightened to breathe, I saw the glimmer of blue light shape itself into the figure of a girl no bigger than Heather. She wore a white dress, and her hair, as dark as Heather's, tumbled in waves down her back. Her features were indis-tinct, her eyes in shadow, but I knew who she was.

"I'm here," the girl said. Her voice was low and cold.

Heather smiled. "How beautiful you are," she

whispered as Helen took the flowers and bent her face to smell their fragrance.

They regarded each other silently for a few moments. Then Heather spoke once more. "They have been cruel to me again," she said. "I've told them you're coming, but I don't think they believe me. Do something soon, Helen. Make them sorry." Heather leaned toward the dim figure, imploring her.

"Soon." Helen's voice was like the winter wind blowing through a field of weeds, dry and cruel. "Very soon."

"And then we'll be together all the time? You'll never leave me? You'll always love me?" Heather gazed at Helen, desperation in her voice and gestures.

"For all eternity," Helen sighed. "You and I, Heather. We'll never be alone again. I promise you." One pale hand, almost transparent, glimmered near the locket, making it shine with borrowed radiance.

"How about Daddy? He'll be with us, won't he?" Heather took a tiny step backward, away from the hand touching the locket.

Helen didn't answer. Her image wavered like a reflection on the water when a breeze ruffles the surface. Then she was gone, and the graveyard seemed to plunge into darkness. Heather cried out, reaching toward the air where Helen's shape had vanished.

"Helen, Helen, don't leave me!" she cried and fell to her knees, knocking over the jar of wild flowers in front of the tombstone. As she began to gather them up, sobbing for Helen to return, I backed away from the hedge toward the safety of the house.

Running across the grass in the moonlight, I was afraid to look back for fear of seeing Helen in pursuit. As soon as I reached the window, I scrambled through, heedless of the noise I was making, and flung myself into bed.

I don't know how long I lay there, shivering with fright, waiting for Heather to come back. When I heard her at the window, I shut my eyes tight, praying that she was alone.

"Just wait, Molly," Heather whispered in my ear in a voice almost as chilling as Helen's. "Just wait till Helen comes. You'll be sorry then for all the things you've done to me."

10

IF I SLEPT any more that night, I don't remember it. As soon as the gray light of dawn glimmered at the window, I slipped out of bed and tiptoed down the hall to Michael's room.

"Go away," he mumbled when I shook his shoulder. "It's too early to get up."

"It's important, Michael!"

"Nothing's that important." He tried to pull the blankets over his head. "It's not even five-thirty, Molly. Are you crazy?"

"Michael, please get up. Please. I saw Helen, I *saw* her!" My voice quivered and my heart beat faster as I remembered what I'd seen in the graveyard. "She was horrible, more horrible even than I imagined."

Michael squinted at me. "Are you having a nightmare or something?"

"Will you listen to me, Michael?" I grabbed his shoulders and shook him again. "Heather climbed out the window last night, and I followed her to the graveyard. Helen was there — I saw her. And I heard her. She didn't have eyes, Michael, just dark holes, and her skin was bluish white like a dead person's. She said she was coming, she'd do what Heather wants; then she vanished." I clung to him, afraid that at any moment Helen would appear, seeking some sort of horrible vengeance. "What are we going to do?"

Michael stared at me. He was wide awake, but I could tell that he didn't believe me. "Come on, Molly," he said, pulling away from me to sit up. "You must have had a nightmare. Maybe because of that picture Mrs. Williams showed us. And then the fight with Dave, and Heather making that big scene. Nobody went to the graveyard last night. Not Heather, not you. You dreamed it." He spoke slowly and calmly as if he were trying to convince himself as well as me.

I looked away, fiddling with my hair, wishing it had been a dream. I shook my head. "No, Michael, I didn't dream it."

"You say Heather climbed out the window. How did she get back in?" He groped for his glasses and settled them on his nose.

"The same way." I stood up as he got out of

bed and pulled a sweatshirt on over his pajamas.

"I'll prove you dreamed it," he said confidently. "Come on."

Grabbing his bathrobe, I followed him down the hall and out the kitchen door. The morning mist swirled across the lawn like dry-ice fog in a Dracula movie, hiding the hedge as well as the graveyard. Somewhere a crow cawed, and I shivered as I felt the wet grass under my bare feet. "Where are we going?" I whispered, fearing he meant to lead me to Helen's grave.

Shushing me, Michael went toward my bedroom window. "She could have climbed out," he said, "but she's too short to get back in that way."

"How about this?" I pointed to an old wooden box lying on its side under the window. "She probably stood on it, and it fell over when she got inside."

Michael righted the box under the window. "I guess she *could* have," he said doubtfully.

"You're spying on me again!"

My scalp prickled at the sound of Heather's voice. She was standing inside, her face pressed against the window screen.

"You better leave me alone!" Heather's voice rose shrilly. "I know what you want to do — you want to make Helen go away, but she won't, not unless I tell her to. And I never will!"

I looked at Michael, but he was scowling at Heather. "You can't scare *me*," he said scornfully.

"She's going to get you!" Heather's voice dropped to a hiss. "Just wait and see. It won't be long now."

"Heather?" Dave came into the room. "What's going on? Where's Molly?"

"Out there," Heather said. "Spying on me." Her voice quavered. "Her and Michael. They won't leave me alone." She was crying now, and I could hear Dave trying to comfort her.

Climbing up on the box, Michael peered into the room. "She's lying!"

Dave came to the window. "How long is this going to go on? Can't you see what you're doing to her? What kind of a little monster are you anyway?"

Michael glared at him. "Why don't you open your eyes and see what she's really like?" he yelled.

"Michael!" Mom took Dave's place at the window. "You and Molly get in here this minute!"

"We didn't do anything to her," Michael said without moving from the box.

"I said, come inside!" Mom frowned at us. "What are you doing out there in your pajamas at six o'clock in the morning? Wasn't last night enough? Do we have to start out today with the same business?"

Hearing the desperation in her voice, I plucked at Michael's sleeve. "Do what she says," I mumbled.

Shaking his head at the unfairness of it all, Michael jumped down from the box and the two of us walked slowly around the house to the back door. My pajamas were wet with dew from the knees down, and my feet were numb with cold. "Do you believe me now?" I asked Michael as we hesitated on the porch, afraid to go inside and face everybody's anger.

"Not about the ghost," Michael said without looking at me. "But I think she did go outside last night."

"And I followed her and I saw Helen." I tried to make him meet my eyes, but he edged away from me and opened the screen door.

"You imagined that part," he insisted. "You heard Heather giving her spiel, pretending to talk to Helen, and you thought you actually saw her. You didn't see Helen, though, Molly. You didn't! She doesn't exist!"

He walked ahead of me down the hall and went into his room, closing the door behind him. Taking the hint, I went reluctantly to my room. Dave and Heather were gone, but Mom was sitting on my bed waiting for me.

"Get dressed," she said, as if the very effort of speaking exhausted her. "You'll catch your death in those wet pajamas." She stood up wearily. "I want to talk to you and Michael later. I'll be in the kitchen."

What Mom had to say wasn't very different from what she'd said the night before. "I thought you were going to cooperate," she said finally. "I hoped you were going to try to be nicer, but what do I wake up to? Heather crying because you and Michael are spying on her. Dave upset and angry. And you two outside in your pajamas. I just don't see how you could do it, not after the talk we had before you went to bed!"

"You don't understand, Mom!" I threw myself at her, trying to climb into her lap. "There's something awful here, and it's making everything worse. It's not Michael and me. It's not even just Heather. It's something out there —" I gestured out the door toward the graveyard. "Under the oak tree, a grave."

"What are you talking about?" Mom grasped my shoulders and held me away from her, staring into my eyes.

"It's Helen," I screamed. "It's Helen!" Then I began crying too hard to talk.

"She thinks Heather has called up a ghost or something," I heard Michael tell Mom, using his mature, scientific voice. "Heather talks about a girl named Helen all the time, but Helen's just something she's dreamed up. You know, to scare us with — not me, actually. Just Molly."

"Oh, Molly, Molly." Mom rocked me, trying to make me stop crying. "Not that ghost business again. If I'd known having a graveyard on our property was going to upset you so much, I'd never have moved us out here."

"It's not my imagination," I gulped. "I saw Helen."

Mom sighed. "Dave says you have a terrible fear of death," she said, "and it's manifesting itself in your belief in ghosts."

"Why don't you ask Heather about it?" I pulled away from Mom, angry that she would turn to Dave for an explanation of my behavior and then actually believe him.

"Ask me what?" Heather and Dave appeared in the kitchen doorway.

"Tell them about Helen." I jumped off Mom's lap and confronted Heather angrily.

Shrinking back against Dave, the little girl looked up at me, her eyes wide and clear. "Who?"

"Helen, your great friend. Tell them what she's going to do when she comes!" I glared at her, furious. "Tell them how you meet her in the graveyard and in the ruins of the Harper House!"

"Daddy, Daddy, what's she talking about?"

Heather turned away from me and pressed her face against Dave's side, her arms encircling his waist. "Make her leave me alone. She's scaring me!"

"That's enough, Molly." Dave gave Heather a hug. "It's all right, honey." He and Mom looked at each other as if they were unsure what to make of me. "Are you ready to leave, Jean?" he asked.

"Leave?" I turned to Mom. "Where are you going?"

"Oh, we thought we'd take Heather with us when we go shopping. Dave needs to go to the clay supplier, and I'm low on some of my paints." Mom toyed with her coffee cup as if she were ashamed to meet Michael's and my stare. "We'll be back sometime this afternoon."

"But what about us?" I asked. "Why can't we go?"

"We thought it would be better to separate you two and Heather," Dave said. "You're old enough to take care of yourselves."

As I started to protest, Michael interrupted. "That sounds like a good idea. Come on, Molly." He picked up his empty cereal bowl and glass and carried them to the sink. "Have a nice time," he said to Mom. "With her."

He left the room without looking at anybody, obviously expecting me to follow him. I hesitated for a moment, thinking Mom might change her mind and stay home with us, but she stood up and slung her purse over her shoulder.

"You and Michael behave yourselves," she said. "We should be home around three." Giving me a quick hug and kiss, she whispered, "And please, Molly, no more talk about ghosts." She looked at me as if she were worried about my sanity. "I know you're a very imaginative girl, but don't get carried away."

I stood in the doorway watching them get into the van. As Dave pulled away, Heather peered out of the back window. When she saw me, she stuck out her tongue.

"Molly?" Michael came up behind me, carrying his collecting gear. "Want to go down to the swamp with me?"

Normally I would have said no, but I didn't want to stay in the house by myself. Not today. Not with Helen so close. So I helped him pack lunches, and we set off for the swamp, following the creek away from Harper House.

Although I couldn't help worrying about snakes, Michael assured me we were safe, and slowly I began to relax and enjoy myself. I actually helped him catch a couple of salamanders. He had brought along a plastic bowl which he lined with moss. Adding a little water and a rock, he put the salamanders into their new home and fed them a few insects.

"Are you hungry?" he asked me.

"Sure." We sat down on a fallen tree and ate our sandwiches. A bullfrog boomed every now and then from somewhere in the swamp, and I watched a snapping turtle hoist himself out of the water to bask in the sunlight. Overhead a bluejay screamed and a crow answered.

"Do you really think I imagined seeing Helen?" I asked Michael, unable even here to forget what had happened in the graveyard.

"You must have." Michael took a big bite of his sandwich and chewed it noisily.

"Then why do you think she seemed so real?" I watched the turtle flop back into the water. "She was just as real as you are."

"Maybe — and, believe me, I hate to say it — Dave is right about your being scared of dying."

"But aren't you scared? Isn't *everybody?*"

Michael poked a stick into the water and watched the long-legged skater bugs skitter away from it. "It's like nuclear war, Molly. If I think about it, I get really scared, so I don't let myself. There's no sense in worrying about things you can't change."

I envied the way my little brother could dismiss scary thoughts. "What do you think happens when people die, though? Do you think part of you lives forever?" I watched him stir the water with his stick, frowning down at our reflections. "Or do you think it's just like going to sleep and never waking up?" I persisted.

"I don't know." Michael turned to me. "I told you I don't like to think about things like that."

"Then you are scared. Just like me."

"Maybe. But I don't go around claiming I saw a ghost."

"No." I gazed out across the water. "But suppose you did see one, Michael. If Helen is real, it means something. Think what it would be like to be alone for all eternity." I shivered and drew my knees up to my chest. Hugging them, I realized how unhappy Helen must be. How afraid. How alone.

"If she's alone," I mused more to myself than to Michael, "she must want a friend, someone to keep her company. Those children, the ones Mr. Simmons told us about, suppose Helen lured them into the pond so they'd stay with her forever?"

Michael took off his glasses and rubbed them on his tee shirt. "You're really getting morbid, Molly."

"Suppose Helen wants Heather to be with her too?" I remembered the struggle she had put up when we dragged her away from the pond.

"Heather could be the one who's in danger, Michael, not us."

Michael sighed in exasperation. "If I hear much more about Helen, I'm going to get as crazy as you and Heather are!" Rising to his feet, he picked up the bowl of salamanders. "You're really a lot of fun," he added when I started to cry. I just couldn't help it.

"Where are you going?" I called as he walked off into the woods.

"Back to the church," he said without looking at me.

11

---✦---

AS SOON as I came out of the woods behind the church, I knew something was wrong. The air shimmered with heat, and it was very still. No breeze ruffled the leaves of the maples; no bird sang; no car sped down Clark Road. The clouds in the sky seemed to hover overhead, silent witnesses waiting and watching as I followed Michael toward the back door.

"Wait," I called to him. "Wait for me, Michael!" I ran across the grass and caught up with him at the steps. "Don't go in there!" I grabbed his arm, almost making him drop the bowl of salamanders.

"What's the matter with you?" Michael yanked his arm free and stared at me, almost as if he were afraid of me. "Are you going off the deep end or something?"

"There's something wrong." I stared at the back door, my heart pounding wildly and my knees shaking. "There's something in the house!"

"Molly, stop it." Michael's eyes widened behind his glasses, but he didn't move toward the door.

Before he could say more, we heard a crash from somewhere inside. Then another. As the noise increased, we clung to each other, too frightened to move.

"Let's get out of here!" Michael cried after a resounding thud from inside seemed to shake the entire house.

Running after him, I glanced back once, just in time to see a pale figure emerge from the back door. It hesitated on the steps for a moment, looking after us, then vanished.

"Did you see her?" I clutched at Michael's shirt, making him stop for a moment.

"Who?" He looked back at the house from the edge of the woods.

"Helen," I cried. "Helen! She was in the house, I saw her on the back porch."

He shook his head. "You must have seen heat waves or something," he whispered. "Whoever's in our house isn't any ghost. It's probably a motorcycle gang or something. What are we going to do, Molly?" He edged backward into the woods, putting a screen of trees and bushes between us and the church. "I wish Mom would come back."

Sinking down next to him on a log, I shivered. "I know what I saw, Michael. She was standing on the porch looking at us, and laughing. Why won't you believe me?"

"Because this is the twentieth century, and I don't believe in ghosts!" His voice shook and he moved farther away from me.

"What about poltergeists? I've even read stuff in the newspaper about them. They throw furniture and destroy stuff, and scientists don't have any explanation for them."

"Yes, but you never see them. They cause a lot of destruction, but they don't manifest themselves the way you claim Helen does." He stood up and began walking away from me.

"Where are you going?" I leapt up and crashed through the bushes behind him.

"I think we should wait up the road for Mom and Dave. The worst thing you can do is come home while the burglars are in your house. That's how people get killed."

"She's gone now," I told him. "I saw her leave."

Ignoring me, Michael pushed through the woods, still carrying the salamanders. "It's almost three o'clock," he said. "They should be coming along any minute."

We plunged through trailing vines of honey-suckle and stumbled out into the sunlight by the side of the road. Without saying a word to each other, we sat down in the shade and watched for the van.

After a half hour or so, I heard the sound of a motor. Jumping to my feet, I saw the van bouncing toward us: Dave at the wheel, Heather beside him, and Mom sitting in the back. He braked quickly when he saw Michael and me, kicking up a cloud of white dust.

"What is it? Is something wrong?" Mom struggled to open the side door as Michael and I jostled each other, anxious to get inside.

"Somebody broke into the house!" Michael gasped. "We heard them when we came home from the swamp."

"Are you sure?" Dave craned around from the front seat, frowning as if he thought Michael was lying.

"Of course I'm sure!" Michael leaned toward Dave, his face flushed. "They were making a lot of noise. I think they've wrecked the house."

Mom put her arm around me, holding me close, her face buried in my hair. "Thank goodness you didn't go inside," she murmured.

Dave put the van into gear and drove toward the church. "If they're still inside, I'll keep on driving into Holwell and call the police," he said.

"Don't worry, they're gone," I said, glancing at Heather as I spoke. She was looking out the window, her face turned away from Dave, smiling past her reflection at the green trees.

Sure enough, when we pulled into the driveway we saw no sign of anyone. The little church sat silent and deserted in the shade of the maples.

"It looks all right to me," Dave said. "This better not be your idea of a joke, Michael."

Michael stiffened beside me, a scowl on his face, but he didn't say anything. Silently he followed Dave up the steps and into the kitchen, with the rest of us close behind.

"It's freezing cold in here," Mom said, folding her arms across her chest and shivering.

Again I glanced at Heather, who had pushed her way to Dave's side. Catching my eye, she smiled. "I told you so, Molly," she whispered, never letting go of Dave's hand.

Dave led us down the hall. Everything seemed to be in order until we reached Michael's room. When Dave opened the door, we stepped back as cold air rushed out to meet us. Hesitating on the threshold, we stared at the room in horror. Everything that Michael cherished lay in a heap of rubble in the middle of the floor. His books, his specimen cases, his fossils and rocks, his microscope, his aquarium — all were smashed and broken, ruined. His bureau lay on its side — its drawers emptied, its mirror shattered. Not even his bed had been spared. The blankets and sheets had been hurled across the room, and the mattress leaned against a wall, his clock radio in fragments beside it.

"Oh, Michael!" Mom put her arms around him and let him cry great, gasping sobs that shook his whole body.

"My insects, my butterflies, everything's ruined," he wailed. "Everything."

Dave rested a hand awkwardly on Michael's shoulder. "The police will get to the bottom of this. Whoever is responsible will pay, believe me he will."

Then he turned to me. "We'd better take a look at your and Heather's room," he said.

But Heather was there ahead of us, sitting on her bed, still smiling. Her side of the room was untouched, but mine was destroyed. My books, my diaries and journals, my teddy bears had been ripped to bits. Like Michael's, my bed had been torn apart, my clothes scattered about, my china and glass unicorns shattered.

"They must have heard you and Michael," Dave said. "You scared them off, I guess, before they wrecked the entire house."

But I wasn't listening. Instead I was staring at a scrawled message on the wall over my bed. Written faintly in an old-fashioned hand, it said, "I have come. H.E.H."

"What did I tell you?" Heather whispered. Without my noticing, she had crept to my side. One cold hand touched my arm as she smiled up at me, her back to Dave.

Pulling away from her, I ran to Mom who was standing in the doorway, one arm around Michael. "It's all her fault," I cried. "She made this happen!"

"What are you talking about?" Mom drew me to her side.

"Good God," Dave said, exasperation darkening his voice. "Heather tries to comfort you, and you turn around and try to blame it on her." He lifted Heather, and she buried her face in his beard, sobbing.

"Molly, I can't believe you said that." Mom sounded shocked. "I know you're upset, but Heather couldn't possibly have had anything to do with this."

"Look!" I pointed at the wall. "See that?" But, even as I spoke, I saw Helen's message fade away like letters written in the sand as the tide rises. What had been words, letters were now meaningless cracks and scuffs on the wall.

"Darling," Mom drew me closer, caressing my back. "It's all right, Molly. We'll get it all put back together somehow."

Frightened, I collapsed against Mom, letting her stroke my back, my hair, crying as if I would never stop.

"We should check the rest of the house," Dave said after a while. "And our studios. Then I'll call the police."

Silently we followed him through the house. His and Mom's room, the living room, the kitchen, the bathrooms — nothing had been touched. Relieved, he walked down the driveway toward the carriage house, towing Heather behind him like a pull toy. A glance inside told him nothing had been disturbed. His bowls and mugs, his vases and platters sat on their shelves, either glazed or waiting to be glazed. The kiln and the pottery wheel stood silently in their places. Overhead in the rafters, a barn swallow twittered and flew back and forth, worried that we would disturb its nest.

Satisfied, Dave led us across the yard to the side door of the church. Once again we recoiled from the cold air, and I clasped Mom's hand, knowing what we would find.

Mom's big canvases had been slashed and thrown to the floor. Her easel was smashed, and her oil paints were smeared all over the walls. For a moment, I was sure I saw Helen's initials scrawled there, but, as before, they vanished too quickly for me to point them out.

Mom fell against Dave, too upset to speak. He put his arms around her and stroked her hair as if she were a child, letting her tears soak his shirt.

Heather hovered near her father, obviously displeased by the attention he was giving Mom.

"Don't cry, Jean, don't cry," Dave whispered. "If I can't fix the easel, I'll get you another one."

"But we can't afford it," Mom sobbed. "We were counting on the sale of my paintings to get through the winter. Now they're ruined. How will we pay the mortgage? How will we heat the house?"

"Don't worry, Jean. I can teach a few classes. And we've got insurance. I know it won't replace your paintings, but it will help." As Heather tugged at his trouser leg, he turned to her. "Not now, Heather!"

She recoiled from the anger in his voice. "You love her more than me," she whimpered.

Dave either ignored her or failed to hear. He started toward the house, his arm around Mom's shoulders. "We'll call the police," he said.

As Heather hung back, frowning at Mom and Dave, Michael turned to her. "Poor little

Heather," he said. "Left out in the cold by Daddy."

She stared up at him. "Do you believe in Helen now?" she hissed. "I told you she'd make you sorry! The next time it will be much, much worse. You just wait!"

"You little creep!" Michael grabbed her and shook her. "You know perfectly well you're lying about Helen. What makes me mad is the way you enjoy seeing us unhappy! You just love it, don't you?"

"I hate you all." Heather tried to pull away from him. "Now let me go! Let me go! Daddy! Daddy!"

Dave turned back just in time to see Heather and Michael struggling. Running toward us, he pulled Heather away from Michael. While she clung to him sobbing, he caught Michael by the neck of his tee shirt. "Don't you ever do anything like that again!" he yelled. "Aren't things bad enough without your picking on a kid half your size?"

As Dave strode back toward the house, carrying Heather, Michael and I sat down on the church steps. "I despise him," Michael muttered. "I despise them both."

"Me too." Although I didn't say it aloud, I knew I hated Helen most of all. Fearfully, I glanced toward the graveyard. For a second, I saw a glimmer of white in the shade of the oak, just a flash through the hedge. You're there, aren't you? I thought. Watching all of this, enjoying it even more than Heather.

A few minutes later, I saw the back door open. Heather ran down the steps and across the yard. Pausing at the graveyard gate, she looked at me, smiling. Then she pushed the gate open and vanished behind the hedge.

As I leaned toward Michael to tell him where Heather had gone, I was interrupted by the arrival of a police car. It pulled up by the steps, and a fat man in a light blue shirt and dark pants got out and went inside. From where Michael and I sat, we could hear his radio squawking.

Around twenty minutes later, he came outside with Mom and Dave. "It's a shame, a real shame," he was saying as he walked toward the church. "Never had anything like this happen around here before. Most folks don't even bother to lock their doors when they go out. Must have been some kids from Adelphia or somewhere. Baltimore maybe. Just passing through, doing drugs, looking for fun, who knows?"

Nodding to Michael and me, he followed Mom and Dad into the church and up the stairs to the loft. We could hear them walking around, talking. As they emerged from the church, the policeman stopped and wiped his forehead with a big handkerchief. His face was red and shiny from the heat.

"Are these the two that interrupted the vandals?" He peered down at Michael and me.

Mom introduced us, and Officer Greene asked us a few questions, but we couldn't tell him anything that would help him. As he put his notebook into his pocket, he thanked us. "You sure you didn't see anybody?" he asked.

"My sister claims she saw a ghost," Michael said, taking me completely by surprise.

"A ghost?" Officer Greene stared at me.

"Oh, Molly!" Mom touched my shoulder. "No more of that!"

Officer Greene turned to her. "Well, ma'am, she wouldn't be the first person to see a ghost at Saint Swithin's. I know grown men who don't like to drive past the graveyard at night." He chuckled. " 'Course I don't believe in ghosts myself. Never saw one and never hope to see one. But then they tell me only certain folk can see them. So who's to say?"

The officer patted my head and said that he was sorry about my room. "I hope we get it all straightened out, but I know that you'll never be able to replace some of those things."

Turning back to Mom, he added, "I'd sure hate for you folks to think anybody from Holwell made this mess. There's not a living soul in these parts who would do something like this."

As Officer Greene walked back to his car, still talking to Mom and Dave, I turned to Michael. "You were trying to make me look stupid again, weren't you?" I accused, but he didn't answer. He stood beside me, his shoulders hunched like an old man's, frowning at the ground.

"Why did you tell that policeman about Helen? He thought I was nuts!" I glared at Michael, feeling that he'd betrayed me.

Without looking at me, Michael shrugged, shoved his hands into his pockets and walked off toward the house. I watched him stop on the porch and pick up his bowl of salamanders before he vanished inside.

I sighed and sat down on the church steps. Michael was thinking about his specimens, I supposed: his butterflies, their wings carefully spread and pinned to the board, each one neatly identified; his grasshoppers and beetles and dragonflies, their fragile, dried shells and delicate wings neatly mounted under glass. It had taken him a couple of years to build his collection; he'd won a blue ribbon at the science fair last winter for the butterflies. No wonder he didn't feel like talking to me.

While I sat there, I saw Heather come out of the graveyard, a smile on her face. I turned away, not wanting to look at her. It scared me that she could summon up something as horrible as Helen and then stand there, safe beside her father, laughing at us. It made her seem as inhuman as Helen.

12

---✦---

"MOLLY," MOM CALLED from the kitchen door. "Come here, honey."

Reluctantly I walked toward the house. I wasn't ready to see Heather or Dave, but I couldn't sit outside by myself forever. "What do you want?" I asked Mom.

"Let's see what we can do with your room, okay? Dave is helping Michael, and I thought I'd help you."

Unhappily I followed her down the hall, past Michael's door. Glancing in, I saw him sifting through heaps of rubbish while Dave held a black plastic garbage bag, already bulging with things broken beyond repair.

"Where's Heather?" I asked Mom as we stared about the room, wondering where to start.

"Watching television, I guess. I thought it

would be best if she stayed out of this. Having her around always increases the tension."

Silently the two of us worked, and after a couple of hours we carried the last garbage bag out. My side of the room was now stripped bare of everything I owned. It looked as impersonal as a motel room; all the things that I had collected were gone. In fact, it seemed to me that my whole personality was gone, destroyed by Helen.

"I'm going to start dinner now, Molly." Mom gave me a hug and kiss, and left me sitting on my bed trying not to cry.

A sound in the hall made me look up. Heather was standing in the doorway, staring at me. Behind her, the hall was dark and full of shadows, and I felt a tiny pinch of fear, imagining that Helen watched me over Heather's shoulder.

"What do you want?" I asked uneasily.

She took her time answering. Twisting a long, black strand of hair around her finger, she walked slowly toward me, her eyes never leaving mine. Stopping a few inches away, her face too close to mine for comfort, she whispered, "Are you going to tell who did it?"

"Who would believe me?" I shrank back against the wall, wanting to put some distance between us.

An awful little smile twitched the corners of Heather's mouth. "You believe it, though, don't you? You saw her; you saw what she wrote on your wall."

"Is she really your friend?" I stared into Heather's huge gray eyes, sure for a moment that I saw fear in them.

"We're just alike," Heather said, her voice quavering a tiny bit. "She understands me, and I understand her. She's my true sister, forever and ever."

The intensity in her face made cold chills run up and down my arms. Even the hair on the back of my neck prickled. "No, Heather," I whispered. "She's not your sister. She's evil and wicked and horrible, and you better stay away from her!" I was sitting up straight now, and my voice was rising. I grasped her thin arms, my fears for myself forgotten. "Don't go near her!"

Heather twisted away, her face pale and anxious. "Shut up, Molly, shut up!" she cried. "Helen is my friend, the only one I've ever had! Don't you dare take her away from me!"

As Heather ran out of the room, she hurled one last threat at me. "I'll tell her to come again," she cried. "And this time, she'll do something worse!"

A few minutes later, Mom called me to dinner. While we ate, I watched Heather pick at her food, eating practically nothing. Every now and then, she lifted her eyes to mine. She neither smiled nor frowned, but gazed at me till I looked away, scarcely able to eat my own chicken.

Later that evening, after the dishes were washed and put away, we all settled down in the living room. While Michael and I watched a National Geographic Special about polar bears, Mom read a novel, and Dave played checkers with Heather. After a couple of games, she climbed into his lap and fell asleep, her thumb in her mouth. With her eyes closed, she looked small and helpless, almost sweet.

As I watched Dave carry her off to bed, I promised myself that I would protect her somehow. No matter how much trouble Heather had caused, I couldn't let Helen lead her into Harper Pond. From now on, I'd try to keep an eye on her day and night.

Suddenly uneasy, I glanced at the window and the darkness it framed. A gust of wind tossed the bushes, and their branches scraped across the screen. For a moment, I thought I saw a pale face peering into the living room, silently observing us. I gasped, and the face vanished into the night as quickly as the moon slips behind a wind-blown cloud.

"What's the matter?" Michael turned to me, a piece of popcorn poised halfway to his open mouth.

"Nothing." I moved away from him, ashamed to tell him what I thought I'd seen, and snuggled next to Mom. With my head on her shoulder, I felt safe, especially when she slid her arm around me and gave me a hug.

The sound of Mr. Simmons' mower woke me in the morning. Heather's bed was empty, so I dressed quickly, anxious to keep the promise I'd made last night. She mustn't go off alone, I thought. She mustn't go to the graveyard or to Harper Pond. She mustn't go near Helen.

The kitchen was deserted, so I ate a quick breakfast and ran across the drive to the church. Mom and Dave were hard at work in the loft, trying to salvage at least some of Mom's canvases, and Heather was pouting by the window, drawing pictures in an old sketchbook. It was very hot and stuffy, and no one seemed particularly happy to see me.

"Do you want me to help?" I asked uncertainly.

"No, no," Mom said hastily. "Just take Heather outside. It's much too warm for her to stay cooped up in here."

"I'm not going anywhere with her." Heather scowled at me. "I'm staying right here with my daddy."

"But, honey," Dave said patiently. "There's nothing for you to do here. Wouldn't you rather go somewhere with Molly? You could wade in the creek or go see the cows." Dave's voice had taken on a tone of honeyed pleading. He was begging Heather to be normal, to do what ordinary little girls enjoy.

She merely stuck her lip out farther. "I like it here," she whined. "Don't you want me to be here? Don't you love me, Daddy?"

"Oh, sweetie, of course I love you." Dave left the heap of wood he had been trying to reassemble as an easel and hugged Heather. "I just thought you'd have more fun playing."

"Not with her." Heather gave me a dark look from under a cloud of black tangles. "You know how mean she is."

"Go on outside, Molly," Mom said. "Maybe you can find Michael. He said something about going down to the swamp to catch insects for a new collection."

As I left the church, I saw Mr. Simmons pushing a wheelbarrow full of grass clippings toward the compost heap. "Good morning, Molly," he called. "Is it hot enough for you?"

I nodded. It wasn't even ten o'clock and I was perspiring. "Have you seen Michael?"

He shook his head. "I brought the fishing stuff

with me, hoping he might be around, but your mother told me he left the house early to catch bugs. Quite the young naturalist, isn't he?"

Coming to a halt beside me, Mr. Simmons set the wheelbarrow down. "Do you know anything about this?" He held up a peanut butter jar full of fresh daisies. "I found them under the oak tree by that little tombstone. Third time I've seen them there."

"Heather does it," I said slowly. "She puts them there every day."

"I thought I told you kids to stay away from that end of the graveyard. Didn't I warn you about the snakes and the poison ivy?" Dumping the daisies into the wheelbarrow, Mr. Simmons paused to light his pipe. "I hear you folks had a lot of trouble here yesterday. Were robbed or something. Bob Greene says he never saw anything like it."

I stared at the flowers lying limply on top of the grass clippings. "It was horrible," I said softly. "But I don't think they'll ever catch the one who did it."

"Why not?" Mr. Simmons puffed on his pipe, waiting for me to answer.

"Well," I said, glancing toward the graveyard. "Remember the day we saw you at Harper House, and we talked about ghosts?" I searched his face, expecting him to laugh. When he didn't, I went on. "I think this graveyard is haunted too."

"I've heard folks say that. My own sister was scared to death of it, wouldn't go near it after dark. But she was always fearful, afraid of her own shadow."

I smiled; Mr. Simmons' sister sounded like me. "The policeman said people don't like to drive by here late at night." I picked up one of the daisies and twisted its green stalk around my finger.

"And what do you think, Molly?" Mr. Simmons regarded me through a cloud of sweet-smelling pipe smoke. "Have you seen anything?"

I looked down at the daisy and began to strip its petals away, one by one. She's real, she's not real, I thought as I watched the petals drift to the ground. Raising my eyes to his, I said, "I've seen Helen. And so has Heather." I paused, waiting for him to laugh, to tell me I was crazy. When he didn't say anything, I went on.

"Heather says Helen is her friend. She told Michael and me that Helen would come and make us sorry for being mean to her. It was Helen who wrecked our things yesterday. She came, just like Heather said she would." My voice was shaking now, and I had to stop. Tossing the last petal to the ground, I realized that I had ended with "She's real."

For a few seconds Mr. Simmons and I were silent. All around us, birds sang and insects chirped their summer songs, but no breeze blew. The leaves of the trees hung limply, and the sun was hot on my head and shoulders.

Finally, Mr. Simmons cleared his throat. "Why would Heather tell you something so awful?" he asked me.

"Because she hates us," I said dully, feeling ashamed, as if it were my fault somehow. "She hates Mom for taking Dave away from her, and she hates Michael and me for being Mom's children. Didn't the policeman tell you that only our stuff was destroyed? Nothing that belonged to Heather or Dave was touched."

"This is a very strange story, Molly," Mr. Simmons said. "And if I hadn't heard something like it before, I'd think you made it all up. But my own sister was convinced that our cousin Rose was led to her death in Harper Pond by the very spirit you've described to me. I didn't believe it at the time, but my sister went to her grave convinced that Rose was possessed by Helen Harper."

I stared at him, my heart thumping. "Do you think Heather is in danger?" I asked.

He fidgeted with his pipe. "Oh, it all sounds

so crazy," he said. "Especially standing here in the sunlight."

"But I've seen her," I said. "I've seen Helen."

He picked up the handles of the wheelbarrow and began pushing it toward the compost heap. "All I can say is, keep Heather away from this graveyard. Don't let her near Harper House or the pond."

For a moment I stood still, watching Mr. Simmons walk away. Then I shoved open the graveyard gate and ran toward the oak tree. Overhead, a breeze sprang up, chasing sunlight and shadows across Helen's small stone. Instinctively, I stretched my hands toward the grave and whispered, "Leave Heather alone, leave her alone."

Nothing happened. A crow flew out of the branches over my head, cawing harshly; the breeze made a dry, whispery sound in the leaves, and then all was still.

I stared at the earth mounded over Helen's grave. Beneath it was her coffin. In her coffin were her bones. I imagined her skeleton lying on its back, her skull staring up into darkness, held fast by the earth, cradled in the oak tree's roots, trapped forever.

I looked at my own arms, still outstretched, and saw the veins running blue under my skin, the bones beneath them. My skeleton. My bones. Someday they would be all that was left of me.

They would lie all alone in the dark and the cold while the years spun past, years I would never see.

I wouldn't feel the sun on my back anymore; I wouldn't hear the wind rustling the leaves; I wouldn't smell the sweet scent of honeysuckle; I wouldn't see the green grass growing over me. I wouldn't think about what I would do tomorrow. I wouldn't write any poems or read any books. All my memories would die with me, all my thoughts and ideas.

I backed away from Helen's grave. It was horrible to die, horrible. Just to think of myself ending, being gone from the earth forever, terrified me. As a shadow slanted across the tombstone, I wondered if it might not be better to live on as a ghost; at least some part of Helen remained.

Turning my back on the oak tree, I ran out of the graveyard, anxious to get away from the bones buried under my feet, but knowing I couldn't get away from the bones under my skin. No matter how fast I ran, they would always be there, always, even when I would no longer be alive to feel them.

13

---✦---

TO CALM MYSELF DOWN, I took a long walk beside the creek. Although I went all the way back to the swamp, I saw no sign of Michael. Gnats and mosquitoes buzzed in clouds around my head, biting me everywhere, even through my tee shirt. I turned around and headed home, thinking Michael must have been driven away from the swamp too.

It was well after two when I walked into the kitchen to fix myself a sandwich. A note on the table told me that Mom and Dave had gone to Baltimore to shop for a new easel and replenish Mom's art supplies. They expected to be gone most of the day. "Heather is in the living room watching TV," Mom had written. "She's promised to stay in the house till you or Michael come home."

I could hear a cartoon blasting away, but when I went to ask Heather if she wanted a sandwich, I saw Bugs Bunny popping out of a magician's hat without an audience. I checked our bedroom, thinking she might be taking a nap, but she wasn't there either. Or anywhere else in the house. So much for keeping her promise, I thought as I pushed open the screen door and called her.

Instead of Heather, I saw Michael coming across the grass toward the house. He was carrying a large mayonnaise jar, and, when he saw me, he brandished it. "Look at the praying mantis I caught," he yelled. "Isn't he beautiful?"

As he thrust the jar at me, I cringed. "Get that thing away from me!"

"This is one of man's best friends." Michael gazed at me reproachfully. "He eats harmful insects. In fact, I'm going to catch some beetles for him right now. Do you want to watch him eat them?"

"Yuck." I backed away from the creature in the jar. "That's the most disgusting invitation I've ever had."

Michael shrugged. "Your loss, Molly."

"Wait a minute," I called after him. "Mom and Dave have gone to Baltimore, and I can't find Heather. Have you seen her?"

He shook his head and smiled at the praying

mantis. "Maybe this little guy thought she was a bug and ate her."

"Very funny." Angrily I watched him run off, clutching his jar, leaving me to find Heather by myself.

Although I didn't want to go back to the graveyard, I thought I might find her there. Reluctantly, I shoved the gate open and walked as far as the Berrys' marble angel. From the shelter of his outstretched wings, I saw a new jar of daisies on Helen's grave. Of Heather herself, I saw no sign.

There was, of course, only one other place to look. Harper House. Running toward the compost heap, I called Michael, thinking I could persuade him to go with me, but he had already disappeared.

As I followed the path across the field, I noticed that the horizon was ringed with clouds. They were thunderheads growing taller and darker, looming over the trees like a fleet of pirate ships. Despite the heat, I began to run. I was sure a storm was coming, and I wanted to find Heather before the thunder and lightning started.

When I reached Harper Pond, I was gasping, out of breath from running. I paused at the bottom of the hill, trying to catch my breath and ease the ache in my ribs. Above me, the ruins seemed empty, desolate. The sky showed blue behind the empty windows, and the vines billowed in a gust of wind. Uncertain of the wisdom of calling her name out loud, I scanned the walls, searching for signs of Heather: a flash of color, a sudden movement, the sound of a voice. Seeing nothing, I began climbing the hill, wishing that Michael were with me.

As I approached the house, a towering cloud drifted in front of the sun and cast everything into shadow. At the same time, a gust of wind flipped the leaves, revealing their white undersides. I knew the rain wasn't far off, and I forced myself to run toward the shelter of the bushes crowding against the ruined walls.

Burrowing through the undergrowth like a rabbit, I found myself wondering what I was doing. Heather hated me; she'd made that clear hundreds of times. And I certainly didn't love her. Or even like her. So why was I here, scrambling around in the bushes, getting scratched by thorns, scared to death of confronting a ghost? Why didn't I go home and leave Heather to Helen? After all, it was Helen she wanted, not me.

Thunder rumbled in the distance; the sky continued to darken, and the wind blew harder. Crouching in the brambles, I peered at the racing clouds, but before I could run for home, a sound from inside the house stopped me. At first

I thought it was only the wind funneling through the cracks in the walls, but the eeriness of it raised goose bumps on my arms and legs. Raising my head cautiously, I peered through the leaves screening a window just above me.

I saw Heather first. She was standing a few feet away from me, her profile turned to the window. "But I thought Daddy would be with us too," she was saying.

Scarcely daring to breathe, I peered into the shadows and saw Helen. Wearing a stained and ragged white dress, she seemed less transparent than she had in the graveyard. Her dark, lusterless hair cascaded down her back, contrasting harshly with her pale, skull-like face. Her feet were bare, and she cast no shadow. When she moved closer to Heather, she made no sound. Nothing bent or rustled when she stepped on it, and her eyes were terrible — dark and glittering and fixed upon Heather. She reminded me of a cat about to spring upon a sparrow. Merciless, without compassion or sympathy, thinking only of its own hunger.

"We don't need your father," Helen murmured. "We don't need anyone."

As she spoke, the air in the house seemed to waft toward me — cold and smelling of damp earth and stagnant water. I shivered, suddenly aware of the sound of my heart pounding loudly with fear. I couldn't abandon Heather, not now. I had to save her from Helen — whether she wanted to be saved or not, whether I wanted to save her or not.

Through my shield of leaves, I watched Helen stretch an almost fleshless hand toward Heather, a smile on her lips, death in her eyes. "Come," she said softly. "Leave this world where you are so unhappy, where no one loves you as you want to be loved. We'll go together, you and I."

Heather slowly put her hand in Helen's. "You're so cold, Helen," she whispered. "Why are you so cold?"

"Because I am alone, because nobody loves me." Helen clung to both of Heather's hands as ivy clings to oak, sending its roots beneath the bark, sucking out the tree's life. "Promise you'll never leave me; promise you'll always love me best," she whispered fiercely.

"But what about Daddy?" Heather's eyes filled with tears. "I can't love you more than I love him. I can't!"

"He betrayed you, just as my mother betrayed me. He found someone he loves more than he loves you — *their* mother!"

The hatred in Helen's voice chilled me. I wanted to leap up and run away from Harper House to escape her, but I forced myself to stay where I was, too frightened to speak or move.

"No!" Heather wailed. "No! He loves me best; I know he does!"

"Then give me my locket," Helen hissed. "I'll find someone else to give it to, someone who will love me." She held out her hand, reaching for the silver chain. "Someone who won't betray me."

Heather's fist closed over the little heart. "I want to be with you," she said, "but I want to be with Daddy, too."

"He doesn't understand you as well as I do, does he?" Helen's voice grew sweeter. "If he knew what I know, he wouldn't love you, would he?"

Heather whimpered and covered her face with her hands. Her body shook with sobs. "But I'm afraid to go in the water, Helen. I'm afraid."

"There's nothing to fear." Helen took Heather's hand. "If you don't come now, I'll go away and you'll never see me again. Never. Then what friend will you have? Michael? Molly? You know they'll never be your friends. They don't care about you. They hate you as much as you hate them."

Heather nodded her head, still sobbing, her face hidden by her hair.

"But I know all about you, Heather. Don't I? And *I* love you." Helen led Heather slowly toward the door, as if she were guiding a blind person. "It's time to go, Heather. The mermaids in the crystal palace are waiting to welcome us, to make us one of them. We'll ride on enchanted seahorses in a kingdom where the rain never falls and the rose never dies. Unicorns, elves, dragons — you'll see all the creatures I've told you about. We'll be so happy there, two princesses in our glass tower."

As I watched Helen and Heather vanish into the gloom, I yearned to enter Helen's world too. Mermaids and unicorns, crystal palaces — how I longed to see them. Eager to hear more, I pushed my way out of the bushes, heedless of the brambles scratching my legs and tangling in my hair. "Wait," I sobbed, "wait for me! Don't leave me here!"

A crash of thunder brought me to my senses. As startled as someone awakening from a beautiful dream, I cringed from the lightning that forked across the sky. As the rain began falling, I caught sight of Helen and Heather walking hand in hand toward the pond.

"Heather," I cried, but the rain fell harder, forming a silver curtain between me and the pond, hiding Heather and Helen from me.

Running down the hill, slipping and sliding on the wet grass, I reached the pond in time to see Helen leading Heather into the water. The wind blew harder, and the thunder rumbled continuously, muffling my cries.

"No, Heather, no!" I shouted as Helen led her farther from shore. Kicking off my shoes, I splashed toward them. The water was cold, and the lightning terrified me, but I plunged in deeper, trying to keep Heather in sight. It was like chasing someone into a waterfall.

When I was almost in reach of her, I tripped on a tangle of roots and splashed facedown in the pond. Sputtering and gasping, I struggled to free my feet, then looked for Heather. She was nowhere in sight. All around me, the rain poured down, and the water rose and fell in tiny waves, hiding both Heather and Helen.

Terrified, I swam toward the place I had last seen her, then dove beneath the surface, groping for an arm, a leg. Twice I came up for breath, then plunged again into the murk. Finally my fingers tangled in something I thought was an underwater weed, then recognized as Heather's hair. Grasping the long strands, I yanked her upward, struggling to get her head above water.

Holding her up, I peered through the rain, searching for the shore. I got no help from Heather. She lay still: her eyes closed, her lips blue, her hair floating around her head in dark strings.

As I got my bearings and started swimming, towing Heather, I heard a weeping sound. It wasn't the wind in the trees; it wasn't the lapping of the water — it was Helen. In front of me, behind me, to the right, to the left, sobbing and moaning, clutching at Heather with icy fingers, she begged me to give her back.

"She's mine, she's mine," Helen wept. "Don't take her from me!"

I felt a terrible chill as her fingers seized my ankles. "Give her back to me, or I'll take you both to the bottom of the pond!" she cried.

"Get away!" I kicked her viciously. "Leave us alone!"

"Give her to me!" Helen was in front of me now, so close I could see right into her horrible eyes. "You must! She has my locket and she's mine! Mine!"

"No!" My feet found the bottom, and I fumbled for the chain twisted around Heather's neck. Snapping it with my fingers, I hurled the silver heart as far as I could. As it disappeared into the rain, I cried, "There, take your locket! But not Heather — you can't have her!"

Helen moaned and turned from us to pursue the locket. Without her to slow me down, I was soon dragging Heather out of the pond. Laying her down on the ground, I crouched beside her.

She was so still, so pale. "Don't be dead, Heather," I whispered. "Please don't be dead."

Covering her mouth with mine, I tried to remember what we had learned in school about mouth-to-mouth resuscitation. Breathe, I thought, breathe! Finally she gasped and choked, opened her eyes, and stared at me. For a moment, she didn't seem to recognize me; then her eyes filled with shock. "Molly," she whispered, "Molly, what are you doing here? Where is Helen?" She twisted her head frantically from side to side, trying to locate Helen.

"She's gone," I said, glancing fearfully over my shoulder. The rain hid the pond, hid Helen — forever, I hoped.

"No," Heather cried. "No, she can't be gone. She promised to take me with her! Helen," she called out, "Helen!"

"She's gone!" I whispered, trying to hush her. "Gone!"

Heather struggled against me, trying to get up. "Let me go, Molly! I want to be with Helen, not you. Let me go!"

The rain poured down my face, blinding me, but I held on to Heather's skinny little body. Dragging her to her feet, I began climbing the hill toward the house. I had to get Heather out of the rain; I had to warm her somehow, dry her off. The church was too far away, but if I got her into Harper House we would have at least a little shelter.

"Helen, Helen," Heather shrieked. "Don't leave me." Again she tried to break away, struggling so fiercely that I could feel the bones in her arms twisting in my grip. "Let me go with my friend, my only friend," she wept piteously, suddenly collapsing against me.

"She's not your friend!" I yelled. "She tried to kill you!"

"No! No! She just wanted to take me with her. She loves me; she loves me best of all! She doesn't hate me like you do!"

"I don't hate you!" I gripped her arms tightly, my face inches from hers. "I wouldn't have pulled you out of the pond if I hated you. I'd have let you drown!"

Heather continued to sob. "If you knew me, really knew me, you'd hate me. Even Daddy would hate me if he knew everything about me." Heather looked behind her at the pond. "But she doesn't hate me. She knows everything, and she understands. We're just alike, she and I, just alike." Heather's tears mingled with the rain on her face.

"Heather," a cry came from somewhere in the rain, blown to us in the wind, a chilling and terrible cry. "Heather, where are you?"

Despite my grip, Heather broke free and ran toward the pond. "I'm coming, Helen, I'm coming!" she cried as I ran after her.

Catching up with her at the water's edge, I tackled her and threw her flat on her face in the weeds. She fought me, her wet clothes and skin making it hard to hold on to her, but she finally gave up and lay still, weeping, her body shaking with sobs.

"I can't find her," she cried. Her hand went to her throat; her fingers fumbled for the locket. "Where is it?" she cried. "What did you do with it?"

"I gave it back to her!" I peered into the rain, thinking I saw Helen's pale form hovering under a nearby willow tree. "She can't take you if you're not wearing it, can she?"

"How could you do it?" Heather wept. "How could you? My only friend, my only friend."

Struggling to my feet, I half carried, half dragged Heather toward Harper House. To my relief, she seemed to have lost her strength, her will to fight me. Faintly, I could hear Helen crying, but Heather seemed oblivious to everything. As limp as a doll, she allowed me to haul her into the ruins.

Soaked to the skin, shivering with cold, we both needed dry clothes and warmth, but the best I could do was the room Michael and I had found the last time we'd been here. At least the little bit of roof over our heads would protect us from the rain.

"This way, Heather." I guided her through the door, stepping carefully on the floorboards. "Maybe we can find matches here, light a fire or something."

My teeth were chattering so hard I could barely speak, but Heather wasn't listening anyway. Listlessly, she stared straight ahead, walking by my side like a zombie or the victim of a terrible disaster.

Halfway across the floor, I heard a splintering sound. The boards under our feet gave way and the two of us plunged downward, still holding on to each other as we fell, too frightened even to cry out.

14

TANGLED TOGETHER, Heather and I landed
on a dirt floor. For a few seconds, neither of us
moved nor spoke, too shocked to understand
what had happened. Finally I opened my eyes
and looked up. Above my head was the hole we
had fallen through, its edges ragged. A gray light
shone down through it, but all around us was
darkness smelling of mold and damp earth and
age. Shivering, I turned to Heather. "Are you all
right?"

"Helen put us here," Heather whispered. "She
hates me now because of you and what you did."
She crouched beside me, trembling with fear and
cold.

Uneasily I gazed upward at the hole, expecting to see Helen peering down at us, laughing.
Nothing was there.

"Why didn't you let me go with her?" Heather

sobbed. "It sounded so beautiful. Rainbows every day, unicorns eating roses, mermaids singing — nothing ugly or hateful." Heather began sobbing again, and I put my arm around her, trying to comfort her.

She immediately stiffened and pulled away from me. "Don't touch me," she wept. "Get away from me; I don't want you near me!"

"I didn't know you were so unhappy," I said, thinking how well she'd hidden her misery behind hateful looks and nasty acts. I pulled her back against me, shocked at how small and bony she was. "Like me or not," I said, holding her tightly, "we have to stay close to each other for warmth. People can die of this kind of cold."

"I don't care if I do die," Heather sobbed. "In fact, I hope I do. Then I could be with Helen again and go to her kingdom and be happy."

"But remember, Heather, she told you your father wouldn't be there. You might hate Michael and me and even Mom, but you don't hate him. You love him."

"But what she said is true. If he knew how bad I am, he wouldn't love me anymore."

"Why do you think you're so bad, Heather?" I peered at her small white face, yearning to read the thoughts hidden behind the mask she wore. "What did you do?"

"I can't tell; I can't tell ever. Only Helen

understands." She struggled again to break away from me, but when I tightened my grip, she gave up and slumped against my side, her face hidden.

"It has something to do with the fire, doesn't it?" I stared at the dark, wet tangles of hair snaking over her shoulders. "You and Helen. Both of your mothers died in a fire."

"Don't talk about the fire!" Heather's head came up and her eyes met mine, searching, pleading.

"You started the fire." I sucked in my breath, realizing that I must have suspected it all along. "And so did she — that's it, isn't it?"

"No, no, Molly, don't say it, don't say it!" Heather put a cold hand over my mouth, trying to silence me. But it was too late. We clung to each other in the dark.

"I didn't mean to," Heather sobbed. "I was only little; I didn't know about the stove! I thought I could hide; I thought the fire would go away, but it got bigger and bigger, and Mommy was looking for me, calling me, and I didn't answer because I thought she was going to spank me. Then I didn't hear her anymore and there was smoke everywhere. A fireman came and he picked me up and carried me away, but Mommy wasn't anywhere. She wasn't anywhere, and it was all my fault, Molly!"

Heather clung to me, weeping. "Don't tell Daddy, Molly; please don't tell Daddy. Don't tell him it was me who made Mommy die. He'll hate me; he'll hate me!"

"Oh, Heather, Heather." Cradling her in my arms, I rocked her as if she were a baby. My own tears splashed down on her dark head. "It wasn't your fault, Heather. You were only three years old. Your father would never hate you, never. You didn't mean it to happen."

But she didn't say anything. She kept crying as if she would never stop. As I hugged her, I wished that I had been kinder, more understanding, instead of resenting her so much. But how could I have known she was guarding such an awful secret?

After she cried herself to sleep, I sat still and wondered what we were going to do. It was dark now. The thunder and lightning had faded away like a retreating army, leaving behind a rear guard of rain. Our clothes were beginning to dry, but we were still damp and cold. I could feel Heather shivering in her sleep.

Overhead the ruins creaked and groaned as the wind prowled through the rooms and crept through holes in the walls. Uneasily, I remembered the stones falling from the walls during Michael's and my last visit. Heather had been so sure that Helen was responsible for what happened then — and now. Had Helen really cast us down into this place, trapped us here for some awful purpose?

Heather stirred and moaned in her sleep, and I held her tighter, determined to comfort her. "It's all right, Heather," I whispered.

"I want Daddy." She opened her eyes and looked up at me. "Why hasn't he come to get us?"

"Maybe he and Mom are still in Baltimore."

"But it's dark, Molly." Heather frowned at me. "He loves Jean more than me. He doesn't care what happens to me anymore."

"You know that's not true."

"She took him away from me." Heather's voice was small and cold. She sat up and wiggled out of my embrace.

Not wanting her to slip back into that way of thinking, I shook my head. "Look, Heather, don't you think Michael and I feel the same way sometimes? We were perfectly happy living with Mom after our father left. We didn't want to share her with Dave and you, but she loves him and he loves her. They love us too. Maybe we just have to learn to be a family. All of us. You and Michael and me and Mom and Dave."

She shook her head, unconvinced. "Daddy and I were a family. Just the two of us. And Grandmother."

"Well, Michael and Mom and me were a family, too. But now we're a bigger family."

"But not better." She stuck out her lip, pouting.

"But we'll get better. Starting with you and me, Heather." I reached out and grasped her hand. "I'll be your sister, Heather, if you'll be my sister."

She regarded me soberly, examining my face for signs of deception. "And you won't tell Daddy about the fire?"

"No, I won't tell him." I paused, squeezing her hand tighter. "But I think you should."

"Oh, no, Molly." Heather jerked her hand away. "No, don't make me do that. I can't, I can't."

"But if you tell him, you'll know he loves you." I stood up, following her as she backed away from me.

"No, no," she moaned. "No."

"Come back here, Heather." I reached for her and missed as she slipped away from me, still crying. "I'm not going to make you do anything you don't want to do. All I'm saying is —" But I didn't get a chance to finish my sentence. As I lunged toward her, eager to explain, I stumbled and nearly fell.

"What's this?" I picked up a round object from a heap of rubble. When I realized what sort of eyes I was staring into, I recoiled in horror and hurled the thing into the darkness. I heard it clatter against something unseen and pulled Heather close to me, feeling her body tremble against mine.

"What was it, Molly?" she whispered.

"A skull," I gasped. "It was a human skull! I saw its eyes!"

Heather pressed her knuckles to her mouth and stared fearfully into the shadows where I had thrown the skull. "It's them," she cried. "It's them!"

"Who?" I clung to her, terrified, imagining that we were buried alive in a hideous family crypt, surrounded by the bones of Helen's victims.

"Helen's mother. And her stepfather. They were trapped in the house in the fire, and nobody ever found their bodies." Heather's voice was shaky too.

The two of us edged back to the middle of the tiny room. A little light still shone through the hole over our heads, making the shadows around us seem darker and more menacing. What other hideous things lurked there, waiting for us?

For a while neither of us spoke. The only sounds were the drip of the rain and the cheep-cheep-cheep of a cricket. The small, cheerful noise seemed very out of place in our grim surroundings.

"Heather," I said, breaking the silence at last. "Did Helen start the fire?"

She nodded. "But she didn't mean to. She was arguing with her stepfather and she knocked an oil lamp over. The tablecloth and the drapes caught fire, and Helen ran out of the room. The fire spread so fast; it trapped her mother and her stepfather. Helen heard her mother calling her, and then the floor caved in. She ran outside, into the pond." Heather hid her face in her hands and wept. "She's been alone ever since, Molly."

"But the other little girls, the ones who drowned in the pond." I leaned toward Heather. "What happened to them? Why aren't they with her?"

"They wouldn't stay. They always faded away and left her. She doesn't know where they went. To their parents maybe. They didn't love her enough to stay." Heather leaned against me, sobbing. "And now I've left her too, and she's still alone."

I stroked her hair and tried to comfort her, wishing Mom were here. Surely she and Dave had returned from Baltimore and noticed that we were missing. Why hadn't they come to rescue us?

"I'm so cold," Heather whimpered. "So cold."

The temperature seemed to be plummeting,

and the air smelled more strongly of decay and stagnation. A glimmer of light drew my attention to the hole above us. Helen was kneeling on the floor, peering down at us. The silver chain hung from her neck, the heart slowly turning, reflecting the bluish glow of her skin.

"It was my fault," Helen cried, stretching out her hands. "My fault, Mama."

Heather looked up, then shrank against me, her bony shoulder blades jabbing against my chest. "I don't want to go with her anymore, Molly," she whispered. "Don't let her take me."

I held her tightly. "Don't worry," I whispered. "I'll protect you."

"Mama, Mama, I'm sorry," Helen wailed above us. She looked more tragic than frightening, and I ached with pity for her. She seemed unaware of Heather and me. All that existed for her was her own sorrow. Slowly she dropped down through the hole and glided past us into the shadows where I'd hurled the skull. Dropping to her knees, she whispered, "Forgive me, Mama, forgive me."

She paused. In the glow she cast, I could see two skeletons. Extending her hand, she reached out toward them. "And you too, Papa Robert. I didn't mean for you to die. Nor Mama either. Nor me, nor me."

She knelt motionless by the skeletons, her head bowed, weeping. Heather's hand closed around mine. "Poor Helen," she whispered.

As I watched, another figure appeared in the cellar. From mist it seemed to form itself into a woman wearing a long dress. Smiling, she drew Helen to her feet and embraced her, comforting her, stroking her hair, rocking her gently. For several seconds, the two figures shimmered in the darkness. Then they disappeared as quickly as images on a screen vanish when the projector is turned off. Slowly the terrible cold subsided, and I knew that Heather and I were alone and out of danger.

"It was Helen's mother," I whispered.

Heather squeezed my hand. "She forgave her, Molly; she forgave her." She looked up at me and smiled. "She knew it was an accident; she knew Helen didn't mean for them to die."

"I know." I returned the squeeze, marveling at the tiny bones in her hand.

"Helen isn't alone anymore. She isn't sad." Heather gazed at me. "Do you think my mother has forgiven me?"

"Oh, Heather, she forgave you long ago."

"And Daddy — if I tell him, do you think he'll forgive me?"

"I'm sure he will."

Heather relaxed and leaned against me, her

thumb seeking her mouth. "I wish he would come and get us," she sighed. "I want to go home."

"So do I." I toyed with her hair, twining it round my finger. It was dry now, silky soft against my skin. Tonight, I thought, when we were safely home, I would brush it for her till it shone.

15

HOURS SEEMED TO PASS while Heather slept. The rain stopped. Above my head, I could see a few stars through the holes in the roof. From somewhere in the woods an owl hooted, and the cricket continued to chirp, safe in his hiding place. Just as I was falling asleep, I heard Michael calling me.

Nudging Heather awake, I jumped to my feet. "Down here!" I yelled. "We're down here!"

I heard someone enter the room above us. "Careful," I shouted, "the floor's weak. Heather and I fell through."

A flashlight beamed down on Heather and me, and Michael yelled, "Dave, here they are!"

In a moment, Dave was lowering himself cautiously through the hole. Embracing Heather, he cried, "You're all right, thank God you're all right."

"Molly saved me," Heather said, clinging to him. "I almost drowned in the pond, and she saved me."

Dave put an arm around me and hugged me against his side, with Heather between us. "We've been so worried. What were you doing here?"

Before I could answer, I heard Michael gasp, "There's bones down there!" He was crouching above us, beaming his flashlight into the corner where the skeletons lay. In the circle of light, we saw them huddled together, still wearing the rags of their clothing.

"They've been here ever since the fire," I told Dave.

"They're Helen's parents," Heather added. "You don't have to worry, Daddy; they won't hurt you."

Dave did look a little edgy, I thought. "Let's get you home," he said to Heather. "You too, Molly." He hoisted Heather onto the floor above us, and Michael helped her to her feet. Then Dave boosted me up, and pulled himself up after me.

"Oh, Molly." Mom was kneeling in the doorway, her arms around Heather. She reached out for me and I ran to her, clinging to her as shamelessly as a baby. "I've been so scared," Mom said, hugging me tightly.

Dave picked up Heather and turned back to

Michael. "Come on," he said. "The girls need to get home and have a nice hot bath."

Michael was still peering into the darkness of the cellar, playing the beam of his flashlight on the bones. "Isn't it against the law to leave bones lying around unburied?" he asked Mom.

She moved cautiously to his side and looked over his shoulder. "They were buried," she said uncertainly, "till now."

"I'd guess that nobody knew the cellar was there," Michael mused. "Most of the ceiling fell down and blocked this room. If you all hadn't fallen through the floor, those bones would have lain there forever."

Dave nodded. He was still standing in the doorway, holding Heather. "I'll call the police when we get back to the church," he said. "They ought to be given a decent burial."

"Couldn't I keep them?" Michael asked. "I could study them, learn all about them. It would be a great science project!"

"Michael!" Mom stared at her offspring, obviously shocked.

"Well, they have bones in science class. And medical students study them. Why can't I? It's scientific."

"They have to be buried with Helen," Heather said. "Families are always buried together."

"Like the Berrys," I said, walking out of the house with Mom.

"What are you two talking about?" Dave asked.

"You know that little tombstone in the grave-yard?" I watched Michael, waiting for him to make a derogatory remark about ghosts. But he was absorbed in shining his flashlight far ahead, watching its beam fan out into a circle as he played it across the woods.

"Well," I went on, "Helen Harper is buried there. She lived in this house, and when it burned down, her parents died. Their bones are in the cellar, but they should be buried with Helen, like Heather says."

Heather and I looked at each other, firmly united. "Please, Daddy, tell the police so they'll know," she said.

"It's very important to you, isn't it?" Dave hugged Heather and she nodded.

"It's important to Helen, too," she said. "And Molly."

Dave smiled at me. "Is this some sort of an alliance?"

Slipping my arm around Mom's waist, I smiled back. "It sure is," I said.

When we got home, Heather and I each had a hot bath and steaming cups of herb tea before we went to bed. After Dave and Mom said good-night and left us alone in the dark, Heather said, "I'm sorry I told Helen to wreck your things, Molly. If I could, I'd make her come back and fix everything. Your stuff, and Michael's and Jean's, too."

"It's all right, Heather. It wasn't your fault. Helen possessed you, I think."

"But not anymore," Heather said.

"No, she's gone now."

"With her mother." Heather yawned.

"And her stepfather," I added. "They're a family now." A little whisper of a breeze puffed the curtains away from the window and set the leaves to murmuring.

"Should I tell Daddy about the fire tomorrow?" Heather asked quietly.

"I think you'll feel better if you do."

"Will he still love me?" Her voice quivered.

"I know he will. You saw Helen's mother, the way she hugged her and comforted her. She forgave her. And she hadn't stopped loving her."

Heather sighed and turned over noisily. "I'm glad you're my sister, Molly," she said, her voice slurry with sleep.

"Me, too, Heather." I meant it. For the first time, she seemed like a real, true sister instead of an enemy camping in our home, making me and everyone else miserable.

The next morning, Dave called the police and told them about the skeletons in Harper House. Although he had to do a lot of explaining, he finally succeeded in convincing Officer Greene that the bones should be buried in Saint Swithin's Churchyard, as close to Helen's as possible. When he hung up the phone, Heather ran to his side and slipped her hand in his.

"Will you go for a walk with me, Daddy?" she asked. "I need to talk to you about something."

I could hear the fear in her voice, but Dave didn't seem to notice. "Sure, honey," he said. "I've got work to do in the carriage house, but I can spare you a few minutes before I get started."

I stood at the back door and watched them walk across the yard together, her face turned up to his, his bent down toward hers. Mom stood behind me, looking over my shoulder.

"I don't know why," she said, "but Heather seems happier this morning. And last night she really surprised me. She actually let me hug her. Maybe your adventure together at Harper House was just what this family needed to pull it together."

I leaned against her, enjoying the feel of her

arms around me. "Would you still love me no matter what I did?"

"What do you mean?" Mom asked.

"Well . . ." I watched a monarch butterfly fly toward the zinnias growing in a tub near the porch. "Suppose I did something really horrible and I told you about it a long time afterward? Would you hate me?" I pulled away from her so I could see her face.

Mom smiled, but she seemed a little puzzled. "Are you about to confess to committing a heinous crime?" She made it sound as if she were joking. "*You* were the one who broke your grandmother's priceless Ming vase all those years ago!" she laughed.

"No, Mom. I'm serious." I studied her eyes, trying to read the expression in them. "Suppose I caused somebody to die. I didn't mean to; it was an accident. But I was scared to tell you. What would you do if I confessed?"

Mom brushed a strand of hair out of my eyes, her hand touching me gently. "Molly, you're not making any sense," she said slowly.

"Would you still love me? Would you forgive me?" I heard my voice rise like a child's. "That's all I want to know. Do parents love their children no matter what they do?"

Mom put her arm around me and hugged me.

"I'll always love you, Molly, always — no matter what. You should know that by now."

"But how about Dave? Would he?"

"Dave?" Mom hesitated as if she weren't sure how Dave fit into all this.

"Not me. Heather. If Heather did something awful, would he still love her?"

"Molly," Mom said, sucking her breath in hard, her eyes darkening with concern. "What are you trying to tell me?"

"The fire — Heather started it by accident, but she thinks it's her fault her mother died." The words flew out of me as if a dam had burst. "She's afraid Dave will hate her if she tells him."

"Oh, my God." Mom leaned against the door frame, her hands pressed to her mouth. "That poor little girl, that poor, poor child. To keep something like that bottled up inside all these years. No wonder she's been so closed off and untouchable."

"She was playing with the stove," I told Mom. "Somehow a fire started. She hid, and her mother died looking for her, I guess. She told me about it last night when we were trapped in the cellar. I thought she should tell Dave."

"Is that why she wanted to go for a walk?" Mom stepped out on the porch and gazed across the lawn. "I don't see them anywhere," she said.

"I gave her the right advice, didn't I?" I looked past Mom's still figure toward the graveyard, imagining Heather and Dave sitting near Helen's grave as she told him about the fire.

Mom turned back to me, embracing me fiercely. "Of course you did, Molly. Dave will understand."

Releasing me, she shook her head. "I never even suspected," she said, more to herself than to me. "She must have thought we'd all hate her if we knew."

"That's exactly what she did think."

"And the ghost — it must have been a projection of her own guilt," Mom said.

Before I could think of a good answer, I saw Heather and Dave walking toward us. He was still holding her hand, and they were smiling at each other. When she saw us, Heather pulled away and ran to me, her eyes shining with tears. As Mom hurried to Dave's side, Heather smiled at me.

"I told him everything, Molly," she whispered, "and he still loves me. He knows it was an accident." Burying her head in my stomach, she knotted her skinny arms around me and squeezed till it hurt.

A few days later, Plummer's Funeral Parlor sent a hearse to Saint Swithin's Graveyard. For the first time in almost forty years, the crows in the oak tree had a funeral to watch.

Mr. Simmons himself had supervised the digging of the graves. The minister from the new church was there, Bible in hand, and a number of people from Holwell, including a reporter for the *Journal*. It was almost a festive occasion, I thought, as I listened to the conversations around me. Most of these people knew nothing of the terrible unhappiness that the burial was bringing to an end.

At the conclusion of the service, everyone stepped forward, picked up a handful of earth and tossed it into the graves. I heard several of them comment on Heather's tears.

"What a sensitive child she must be," a stout lady observed, adjusting the angle of her large straw hat.

Her companion nodded. "You'd think she knew the poor souls personally."

"She's probably too young to be exposed to something as tragic as a funeral," the woman in the straw hat said. "I've never thought little children should be told about death. Why frighten them? Let them keep their innocence as long as they can."

The two of them walked to their car and drove off, leaving us alone, except for Mr. Simmons. "Glad to see this settled," he said, heaping the earth over the graves. "She'll rest in peace now, like them." He waved the shovel toward the Berry Patch. "She's with her own."

Heather gazed at the marble angel poised on his pedestal above the Berrys, his wings uplifted. "Daddy should make Helen one of those," she said to me. "I think she'd like to have one, don't you?"

"It would look very pretty," I said, watching Mr. Simmons pat the freshly-turned earth with his shovel.

By September, a small marble angel guarded Helen's grave, and two stones flanked hers. Her own name, not just her initials, marked her burial place, and English ivy softened the mounds of earth over her parents' graves. The cemetery had lost its gloom, and I no longer feared it.

One afternoon in early October, Michael, Heather, and I were sitting in a sunny spot not far from Helen's grave. It was a warm, sweet-smelling day, more like spring than fall. Michael was watching a huge wood beetle crawling around in its glass-jar prison, and I was reading *The Borrowers* to Heather.

"Do you want me to read the next chapter?" I was sure she wouldn't want me to leave poor Stainless facing certain capture, but when I looked at her I realized she hadn't been paying much attention to the story.

She was lying on her back, chewing on a blade of grass and staring up at the clouds drifting slowly across the incredibly blue sky. "Do you think she can see us from where she is?" she asked dreamily, her mind apparently far from Stainless' plight.

"I don't know," I said, guessing that she was thinking of Helen. It was the first time in weeks that she had mentioned her. "Wherever she is, though, she's happy," I added. "I'm sure of it."

"Me too," Heather agreed. She sat up and gazed at the angel under the oak tree. He gazed back serenely, seeming to return her smile. Suddenly she grasped my arm, her nails biting through the sleeve of my shirt. "Molly," she whispered. "Look."

She got to her feet and ran toward the angel, and I ran after her, seeing what she saw. Something shiny dangled from the angel's outstretched hand: a silver locket turning slightly in the breeze.

Before I could stop her, Heather snatched the chain from the angel's stiff fingers. As I watched, it seemed to pop open by itself in her outstretched palm. On one side was a picture of Helen. On the other was a folded piece of paper.

With trembling fingers, Heather slipped it out of the frame and spread it flat. We both read the message, written in the same hand I had once seen scrawled on my bedroom wall: "With love from Helen," it said. "Do not forget me."

Heather and I looked at each other. The sun warmed our backs as it shone down through the oak's reddening leaves. Bees buzzed in the goldenrod and a grasshopper bounded away from Michael as he approached us.

"Where did you get that old thing?" he asked, looking at the locket. "I thought you lost it last summer."

"Helen gave it back to me," Heather told him solemnly. "It's all right for me to wear it now," she added, looking at me. "Isn't it?"

I nodded, but Michael rolled his eyes skyward. "Not Helen again. I thought we'd heard the last of that ghost stuff."

"I think we have," I said. "Now."

Silently Heather fastened the chain around her neck, smiling at me as she did so. Together we walked out of the graveyard. Behind us, Michael kicked at the grass.

"I still don't believe it," I heard him yell at our backs, but it seemed to me that his voice quavered a tiny bit.

ALL
THE
LOVELY
BAD
ONES

To all the little children: —The happy ones; and sad ones;
The sober and the silent ones; the boisterous and glad ones;
The good ones—Yes, the good ones, too; and all the lovely bad ones.

—James Whitcomb Riley,
dedication to "Little Orphant Annie"

1

Grandmother met us at the Burlington airport, a big smile on her face and her arms open for a hug. With a squeal of delight, my sister rushed toward her, but I held back. Public displays of affection were okay for girls, I guessed, but not for guys. After all, I'd be thirteen soon—way too old for that kind of silly stuff.

After giving Corey a big hug, Grandmother turned to me. "Just look at you, Travis. You've shot up since Christmas. How tall are you?"

I shrugged. "About five six, maybe seven. Not all that tall. There's a guy in my class who's already six feet."

"I'm almost as tall as Travis," Corey put in, never one to be left out. "And I'm a whole year younger."

While Corey chattered about the plane ride from New York, Grandmother led us to the baggage claim. We grabbed our suitcases and headed for the parking lot. The late-afternoon air was cool and the sky was blue, a change from the heat and humidity we'd left in the city.

"Welcome to Vermont." Grandmother opened the door of a shiny red pickup truck. "Toss your luggage in the back and climb aboard."

Corey jumped in beside Grandmother, and I squeezed in by the door.

"So do you think you'll be able to stand being away

from your parents for a whole summer?" Grandmother asked.

My sister and I looked at each other and grinned. "We'll miss them a little," Corey said, "but we're used to summers away from home."

Grandmother smiled. "I'm glad you chose the inn instead of camp."

Corey and I didn't look at each for fear we'd laugh and give ourselves away. We hadn't had a choice, actually. Camp Willow Tree had made it very clear that neither Corey nor I was welcome to return. It seemed we'd failed to get into the true spirit of camp. We'd started food fights, played hooky from evening campfire, made up rude words to the camp song, overturned a canoe on purpose, and let the air out of a counselor's bike tires the day we were supposed to ride twenty miles up a mountain in the pouring rain. Was it our fault the camp staff had no sense of humor?

The truth of it was Corey and I tended to get in trouble wherever we went. Bad ones—that's what we were. Well, not really *bad*. We preferred to think of ourselves as pranksters. But like the camp staff, adults (including Mom and Dad) didn't find our antics as funny as we did.

Our parents had made us promise to behave ourselves at the inn. One bad report from Grandmother and we'd spend the rest of our vacation taking pre-algebra in summer school—a fate even worse than camp craft projects involving Popsicle sticks and feathers.

Just before the turnoff for Middlebury, we left Route 7 and took a winding road that rolled over hills, past farms and fields, red barns and sturdy farmhouses. Herds of black and white cows raised their heads to watch us go by. Beyond them, the mountains rose greenish blue against the sky.

"Here we are." Grandmother pointed to a neatly painted sign: THE INN AT FOX HILL—NEXT RIGHT. Under the words was a picture of a smiling fox. A VACANCY sign hung below.

Grandmother swung into a long, straight driveway shaded by tall trees. At its end was a three-story pink brick building. The late-afternoon sun touched everything with gold—the lawn, flower beds, and wooden rocking chairs on the front porch. Behind the inn, clouds cast their shadows on the Green Mountains.

Grandmother parked the truck, and Corey and I jumped out. I grabbed for my suitcase, but Grandmother said, "Leave your luggage for now. Henry can bring it in later. Martha's promised to have a pitcher of ice-cold lemonade, freshly squeezed, and a plateful of chocolate-chip cookies, still warm from the oven."

We followed Grandmother down a stone path bordered with dense white flowers to a brick patio shaded by a huge wisteria climbing over a trellis. Nearby, a fountain splashed into a pool, and I glimpsed flashes of red fish swimming in its depths. Flowers bloomed everywhere, and bees hummed. Birds called back and forth in the trees.

As we settled ourselves around a table, a woman strode toward us carrying a tray. Her gray hair was pulled back tightly into a knot, and her mouth seemed to have settled into a permanent frown. Without so much as a smile, she set the tray down and stepped back.

"Thank you, Martha. It looks lovely." Gesturing to Corey and me, Grandmother introduced us to the woman.

"Pleased to meet you." Still no smile, just a quick dip of the head.

"Mrs. Brewster is our cook," Grandmother told us. "People come to the inn year after year just to eat her famous blueberry pie."

Another dip of the head and Mrs. Brewster left us to enjoy the lemonade and cookies.

"Martha's a little standoffish," Grandmother admitted, "but she and her husband more or less came with the inn. And she's truly magnificent in the kitchen."

Corey jabbed my ankle with the toe of her shoe and whispered, "She looks like an old grump to me."

Grandmother leaned across the table to brush a strand of hair out of Corey's eyes. "You'll change your mind when you eat your first meal here."

Corey helped herself to a cookie. While she chewed, she looked around. "Is that a swimming pool?"

Grandmother nodded. "You can use it any time you like—as long as someone's with you. I don't have a life-guard."

She pointed past the pool to the wide grassy lawn, dotted with old-fashioned Adirondack chairs, turned to face the mountains. "If you like tennis, the court's over there. I have bicycles for the guests. The state park just down the road has a great network of biking and hiking trails."

Grandmother ate a cookie. "If it rains," she went on, "there's a library, computer, TV, DVD player, and at least a dozen old-fashioned board games. Hopefully, you'll find plenty to do."

Corey and I leaned back in our chairs and drank our lemonade, just as fresh and cold as Grandmother had promised. It looked as if it was going to be a good summer. No schedules. No organized activities. Nobody blowing whistles at us. No boring crafts. For once, we were free to do what we wanted to do. Including nothing. Nothing at all.

Corey studied the inn. "Do you have many guests?"

"There are six rooms," Grandmother said. "Four on the second floor and two on the third. We can house twelve guests, but tonight we only have two—a couple of young men."

Corey looked around. "Where are they?"

"They've gone out bicycling, but they'll be back soon for dinner."

"You must usually have more people than that," Corey said.

Grandmother sighed. "That's what I thought when I bought the place, but the inn's kind of remote. Tourists like to be closer to Burlington or Middlebury, Stowe or Woodstock." She shifted in her chair as if she were about to get up but then changed her mind.

"Actually, the inn's location is only part of the problem," she added slowly.

Corey and I sat up straighter, as if we both sensed something exciting.

For a moment, Grandmother stared at the inn, her gaze drifting from one window to the next as if she were admiring the flower boxes.

"I wouldn't bother telling you," she said at last, "but you're sure to hear the guests talking about it. Fox Hill is mentioned in *Haunted Inns of Vermont*."

Corey and I leaned closer, our eyes wide. A little shiver raced up and down my spine. A whole summer in a haunted inn—what could be more exciting than that?

"Oooh," Corey murmured. "I've always wanted to see a ghost."

"Don't be stupid," I told her. "You can't even watch a horror movie without having nightmares."

"Huh," Corey said. "Just last week I watched one of the *Scream* movies, and I didn't even close my eyes or cover my ears once!"

"Don't worry." Grandmother patted Corey's hand. "No one has seen a ghost since the Cornells sold the inn to me."

"Where do you think they went?" Corey asked.

"To North Carolina, I think," Grandmother said. "They wanted to open an inn at the beach."

"Not the Cornells," I said. "The ghosts. Where did *they* go?"

Grandmother shrugged. "In my opinion, they were never here in the first place."

"You don't believe in ghosts?" Corey looked surprised.

"Of course not." Grandmother laughed. "But sometimes I find myself wishing they'd come back. Business might improve."

"What do you mean?" I asked.

"You'd be surprised how many people come here because of that stupid book," Grandmother said. "Then they leave in a huff because they didn't see a ghost. Some even want their money back."

"Do you have the book?" I asked.

"Of course." Grandmother got up and led us into the

inn, through the kitchen, and down a hall to a large room in the front of the house. "The library," she said.

Tall windows let in long bars of afternoon light. Several pairs of soft leather armchairs flanked the windows. A matching sofa stood near the door. In front of it was a low table covered with magazines. Books crammed the shelves built into the walls.

Grandmother picked up a thick, well-read paperback and handed it to me. "Page 103," she said.

I sat down on the sofa, and Corey perched beside me. I opened the book to page 103.

The Inn at Fox Hill was built in the late 1700s. Originally a private home, it has changed hands many times. Although I checked old records, the inn's history is sketchy at best. Apparently, it served several purposes— among them, a boardinghouse, a tuberculosis sanitarium, a private school. In 1940, the place was abandoned. For fifteen years, it stood vacant. Weather, neglect, and vandals took their toll. Smothered in ivy and surrounded by weeds, the mansion was soon reduced to a shell of its former self. To passersby, it was the very image of a haunted house.

In 1955, Mr. and Mrs. Stephen Cornell, young vacationers from Boston, saw the building and recognized its potential. They spent more than ten years restoring the house and grounds. In 1967, the Inn at Fox Hill opened for business.

Soon the Cornells began receiving complaints from guests. A woman in a long white dress roamed the grounds at night, moaning so loudly she woke them up.

Others were kept awake by noisy children playing in the halls. Many reported hearing footsteps on the stairs, banging doors, barking dogs, sobs, and laughter. Lights and radios came on in the middle of the night. Water gushed from faucets. Toilets flushed continually. The power went off for no reason—and came back on again for no reason.

Rather amusingly, one woman was especially indignant about an impudent child who called her "Fatso" but who ran away before she got a good look at him. More seriously, several guests complained of theft—watches, rings, jewelry, and the like disappeared from drawers and bedside tables.

Mr. and Mrs. Cornell were as mystified as their guests. They investigated the plumbing and the wiring; they kept doors locked at night; they even hired a night watchman. Nothing helped. The incidents continued.

Soon psychics descended on Fox Hill, followed by ghost hunters with special cameras and recorders. The experts agreed: Ghosts roamed the halls of the inn.

As we all know, some people are sensitive to the presence of ghosts. Others are not. If you want to test yourself, spend a night or two at the Inn at Fox Hill. I did . . . and I was not disappointed! When I woke, the cheap ring I'd left deliberately on the bedside table was gone.

And remember, even if you don't see a ghost, you'll enjoy the Cornells' hospitality, the inn's charm, the fresh Vermont air, the gorgeous scenery, and the meals prepared by the cook in residence, the excellent Mrs. Martha Brewster, a rare marvel.

I closed the book and stared at Grandmother. "Are you sure," I began, but she cut me off with a wave of her hand.

"It's absolute nonsense." She shook her head disdainfully and returned the book to the shelf. "Five thirty," she said. "Time for dinner."

As Corey and I followed Grandmother out of the library, we glanced at each other. Without saying a word, I knew my sister was thinking exactly what I was thinking. Rappings and tappings, footsteps, doors opening and shutting—*we* could do that. And more. Bringing ghosts back to Fox Hill would be like playing haunted house all summer long.

2

The dining room was large enough for at least two dozen people, but only two other tables were occupied. The bike riders sat together by the French doors, open to a view of the mountains. Lean, sunburned guys with huge leg muscles, they didn't look as if they'd come to Vermont to see ghosts.

At another table were Mr. and Mrs. Jennings, who'd showed up just before dinner, wanting a room. They were old but not old old—probably forty or fifty. His hair was gray, and hers was an odd shade of tan (dyed, according to Corey). He wore hiking shorts, a navy T-shirt, and walking sandals over rag-wool socks. "He doesn't want people to see his ugly toes," Corey whispered.

Mrs. Jennings wore shorts and a flowered T-shirt and sandals without socks, showing her perfect red lacquered nails.

All in all, they looked pretty fit for their age, but I doubted they'd come to Vermont to bike or hike. Corey guessed they were antique collectors in search of rusty farm tools to put in their flower garden.

Then we noticed they were reading *Haunted Inns of Vermont*. Grandmother pointedly ignored their taste in literature, but Corey kicked me under the table to make sure I'd noticed.

As promised, the grim and silent Mrs. Brewster produced a great meal: spicy chicken served on rice with some vegetables I shoved aside, a basket of freshly baked rolls, and a salad.

A blonde with a freckled nose served us. She looked about sixteen, I thought. Probably in high school. She was really cute, just the kind of girlfriend I hoped to have someday.

"Tracy," Grandmother said, "these are my grandchildren, Travis and Corey. They'll be here all summer." Smiling at us, she added, "I don't know what I'd do without Tracy. She serves meals, washes dishes, and keeps the inn clean and tidy."

"You'll love it here." Tracy leaned a little closer to Corey and me. "The inn's supposed to be haunted, but so far I haven't seen a thing. Kind of disappointing, actually. I was hoping to have some scary stories to tell when I go back to school."

Grandmother shook her head. "I thought you had better sense."

"I know *you* don't believe in ghosts, Mrs. Donovan," Tracy said. "But you can't prove they don't exist."

"You can't prove they *do* exist, either," Grandmother pointed out.

"Well, why not give them the benefit of the doubt?" Corey asked. "It makes things more interesting."

"That's enough silly talk." Grandmother frowned at Corey's plate. "Eat your dinner before it gets cold."

Tracy left to refill the bike riders' water glasses, and I dug into my dinner, washing it down with gallons of iced tea and topping it off with peach cobbler à la mode. Except for the vegetables, it might have been the best meal I'd ever eaten.

Corey ate most of hers, which was amazing. Usually she picks at her food, which drives Mom and Dad insane. If she doesn't eat enough, they worry she's anorexic. If she eats too much, they worry she's bulimic. I think she just likes the attention.

After dinner, Grandmother dropped into a rocking chair on the porch and gazed at the mountains. The trees cast long shadows toward the inn. High in the sky, swallows dipped and soared, catching bugs on the fly.

The bike riders sat down nearby and spread out their maps to plan the next day's ride. "I say we go this way."

"After today," the other said, "I was hoping to take it easy tomorrow. How about this road along the river?"

"We came up here to get in shape, Tim."

As they argued about their route, the screen door opened and Mrs. Jennings stepped out, *Haunted Inns of Vermont* in her hand.

"Excuse me, Mrs. Donovan," she said, "but my husband and I read about Fox Hill in this book, and we were just wondering—"

Grandmother smiled and shook her head. "I'm sorry to disappoint you, but no one has seen a ghost here for at least three years. Maybe they took their little ectoplasmic selves down to North Carolina with the former owners."

Mrs. Jennings sighed. "According to the author, you have to be in tune with the spirit world to see ghosts. Just because no one has seen them doesn't mean they're not here."

"I'm glad *I* don't have such an ability," Grandmother said pleasantly. "The real world's scary enough for me."

Mr. Jennings joined us just in time to hear the end of

the conversation. "How about you kids?" he asked. "Do you believe in ghosts?"

Corey and I put on serious faces. "Definitely," I said.

"I've *seen* a ghost," Corey added.

"Really?" Mrs. Jennings drew in her breath, obviously ready to believe anything. "What was it like? Can you tell us about it?"

I hid a grin behind my hand. Could she tell them about it? The Jennings didn't know how much my sister loved an audience.

"Well," Corey began, "last winter, I was sleeping over at my friend Julie's house, and something woke me up in the middle of the night. This old lady was standing at the foot of the bed and staring at Julie."

Corey paused a moment to let the suspense grow, I guessed.

"When the old lady realized I was awake," she went on, "she smiled at me and put a finger to her lips. Then, real slowly, she backed away from the bed and walked out of the room, watching Julie all the while, like she was never going to see her again."

The Jenningses hung on every word. Grandmother listened, too—but in her case, she seemed to be wondering what my sister was up to.

"The next morning," Corey said, playing to the Jenningses, "I expected to see Julie's grandmother, but when I asked where she was, Julie's mother said she lived in Pennsylvania. 'Then who was that old lady in Julie's bedroom?' I asked. They all looked at me like I was crazy—even Julie. 'There's no old lady here,' her father said. 'You must have been dreaming.'"

Corey paused to swat a mosquito. "Just then the phone rang," she said, "and Julie's mother went to answer it. First she said, 'No, oh, no.' Then she asked when. And then she started crying."

She took a deep breath and dropped her voice to a whisper. We all leaned closer to hear her. "It turned out Julie's grandmother had died just about the time I saw the old lady. She'd come to say goodbye."

Mrs. Jennings grabbed her husband's hand. "Oh, I'm all over goosebumps."

"Me, too." Corey rubbed her arms as if she were cold. "I can still see that old lady smiling down at Julie."

"Incidents like that are often reported," Mr. Jennings put in. "It's a well-documented phenomenon—the last farewell."

Mrs. Jennings turned to Grandmother. "What do you think now? Surely you believe your own granddaughter."

Grandmother was staring at Corey. "I must admit I didn't know she was such a good storyteller."

Corey wasn't a *good* storyteller—she was a *brilliant* storyteller. No matter what Grandmother thought of Julie's grandmother's last farewell, the Jenningses totally believed Corey. In fact, I almost believed her myself.

While Grandmother rocked silently, the Jenningses told a few ghost stories they'd either read or heard about—last farewells, phantom limousines on deserted roads, old-fashioned ladies in brown who appeared and disappeared in dark hallways.

The bike riders stopped arguing and listened. Tim even threw in a story of mysterious blue lights that hovered over a mountain down south somewhere. His buddy,

Robert, said he didn't believe in that stuff—which earned him a nod of approval from Grandmother.

Tracy joined us and claimed her grandfather had seen his dog's ghost at the very spot on the road where he'd been killed by a car. And her sister once visited a friend's house and saw a lady in a long gray dress walk through a wall and vanish. "The house was really old," she added. "And the people who lived there had seen the ghost themselves."

Gradually, the stories faded away and we sat together silently, each of us thinking our own thoughts—about ghosts, I guessed. Some believing, some not, and some not sure. The moon was almost full, and stars studded the sky—thousands, maybe millions, more than I'd ever seen in New York.

"It's getting chilly." Mrs. Jennings got to her feet with a shiver and headed for the door with Mr. Jennings behind her.

The bike riders yawned and followed the Jenningses. "Big day ahead," Robert said. "At least seventy-five miles."

Tim groaned.

As Tracy started to leave, Grandmother asked her to tell Mr. Brewster she needed him.

A few moments later, a short, bearded man crossed the lawn toward us. For a moment, I thought an ancient garden gnome had come to life, but it turned out to be Mr. Brewster. He wore a frown as permanent as Mrs. Brewster's, made even sterner by his drooping mustache.

"These are my grandchildren, Corey and Travis," Grandmother told him. "They'll be sleeping in the two rooms on the first floor in the back. Can you help them with their luggage?"

Mr. Brewster got our suitcases from the truck and carried them inside as if they were packed with feathers instead of books and shoes and clothes that weighed a ton. Like Mrs. Brewster, he didn't say a word to anyone, just sort of grunted an acknowledgment of Grandmother's request.

"Henry's a bit taciturn," Grandmother said. "But he totes luggage up and down the steps, fixes everything that breaks, and keeps the grounds in shape. In some ways, the two of them run the place."

She laughed as if the Brewsters were lovable characters in a sitcom, but I thought it would be annoying to depend on such cranky people.

We followed her and Mr. Brewster through the kitchen and into an annex built onto the back of the inn.

"This used to be the servants' quarters," Grandmother said, "but the Cornells made it into a modern apartment for themselves."

At the end of a hallway, Mr. Brewster set our luggage down and walked away without a word.

Grandmother opened the doors to two small identical rooms. "I meant to paint the walls and hang new curtains, but somehow I never got around to it. The season started with a dozen bicyclers and then a busload of senior citizens, which was good for business but took all my time."

"It's great," I said. "A bed, a bureau, a table, a chair, and a lamp. What more do I need?"

Corey nodded. "You should see the cabin I had at

camp last summer—four bunk beds, eight girls, and an outhouse a mile away."

Grandmother smiled and excused herself. "It's been a long day. If you two don't mind, I'll go to bed and leave you to unpack."

As soon as she left, I followed Corey into her room, almost identical to mine. "Where did you come up with that granny story?"

"I saw it on a TV show about ghosts. The Jenningses really ate it up, didn't they?"

"Are you thinking what I'm thinking?"

Corey grinned. "Ghosts are about to reappear at the inn," she said. "In fact, I predict the Jenningses will have their own experience with the supernatural before they leave."

"They'll go home and tell other people," I said, "who'll come to the inn hoping to see ghosts. They won't be disappointed."

"Soon Fox Hill will be booked up every night," Corey went on. "Grandmother will have to turn people away."

"They'll camp out in the yard."

"They'll look in the windows."

"There'll be a traffic jam from here to Burlington."

"The Learning Channel will send a team of psychics and ghost hunters."

"We'll be on the evening news."

"Anderson Cooper will do a week long special on CNN."

"Someone will write a book like *The Amityville Horror*."

"It'll be a bestseller."

"They'll make a movie of it!"

"We'll star in it!"

"We'll be famous!"

By this time, we were shouting and laughing and jumping on Corey's bed.

"Travis!" Grandmother shouted from the doorway. "Corey! What on earth is all this ruckus?"

We tried to stop laughing. "We're just fooling around," I said while Corey hiccupped hysterically.

"Well, please calm down," Grandmother said. "You'll disturb the guests."

That made Corey and me laugh again. Grandmother had no idea how disturbed the guests were going to be.

"It's almost ten, and you haven't even started unpacking," she said with a frown. "At the risk of sounding like a camp counselor, I suggest you save that task for tomorrow, put on your pajamas, and go to bed."

"We're sorry," I said, making a real effort to sound sincere, but I hadn't quite gotten the laughter out of my voice.

"Don't be mad," Corey added, faking much better than I had. "We're just so excited to be here. I guess we got carried away."

Grandmother came into the room and gave us each a kiss. "I'm not mad. Just tired. Now settle down and go to sleep."

After she left, I went to my room and put on my pajamas. When I tapped on Corey's door, she said, "Come in."

Still wearing her shorts and T-shirt, she was rummaging through her suitcase, scattering clothes everywhere. At last she found what she was looking for.

She held up a white nightgown and swirled it in front of me. "At breakfast, I'll tell the Jenningses I saw a ghost in a long white dress, flitting around under the trees—like the ghost in the haunted inns book."

"How do you know they'll believe you?"

"They believed the granny story, didn't they?" Corey smoothed the gown. "People like the Jenningses are easy to fool because they *want* to see ghosts. You don't have to convince them—they already believe. All I have to do is go outside tomorrow night wearing this and they'll think they're seeing a real ghost."

"But won't they recognize you?"

Corey sighed the way she always did when she thought I was too stupid to be her brother.

"We'll ride bikes to Middlebury and buy white make-up and that black stuff teenagers use on their eyes. Maybe we can find a long filmy scarf to hide my hair. After Grandmother goes to bed tomorrow night, I'll smear my face dead white and make big dark circles under my eyes, like empty eye sockets. I'll put on my nightgown and dance around under the trees in a scary way, moaning and groaning. Maybe I'll even shriek." She frowned. "Too bad I didn't bring my Vampira costume from last Halloween. It would've been perfect, but who knew I'd need it up here?"

"So that's the plan—you impersonate a ghost and scare the Jenningses, and they go home and spread the word?"

Corey grinned. "It's a start. We can think of more stuff, like footsteps and moans and groans and crying babies."

"And howling dogs and rappings and tappings and strange blue lights."

By the time I went back to my own room and climbed into bed, I was too excited to sleep. I lay awake a long time, my mind racing with ideas. With Corey's and my help, Grandmother would be a rich woman by the end of the summer.

3

The next morning, Corey and I found the Jenningses on the patio, drinking coffee. I leaned against the trellis, slightly embarrassed, but Corey sat down between them. Without hesitating, she whispered, "Did you see it last night?"

"See what, dear?" Mrs. Jennings nibbled at her croissant, her eyes fixed on my sister.

Corey drew a deep breath and somehow managed to look pale. "The ghost."

"Ghost?" Croissant in midair, Mrs. Jennings gasped. "You saw a *ghost* last night?"

"Shh," Corey hissed. "Grandmother told me not to tell anyone. She insists I imagined it, but I swear I saw it."

"After that story you told, I knew you were sensitive to the spirit world." Mr. Jennings looked at Corey with awe.

"Tell us everything. Don't leave out a single detail." Mrs. Jennings kept her voice so low I had to move closer to hear her.

"Something woke me around three A.M.," Corey said. "That's the demons' hour, you know—halfway between midnight and dawn."

"Yes, yes." Mrs. Jennings patted Corey's hand. "Go on."

"Well, I went to my window," Corey said. "At first, I didn't see anything, but I heard sort of a low moaning sound." As she spoke, a gust of wind skittered across the table, blowing the paper napkins onto the lawn. Mrs. Jennings shivered.

"Then I saw this woman in white," Corey went on, "flitting about under the trees. For a moment, she looked toward the house, straight at me, and I ducked behind the curtain. When I got the nerve to look again, she was gone."

Mrs. Jennings leaned toward Corey. "What did she look like?"

"She was wearing a long white dress, and her face was really hideous—white as a skull with dark circles where her eyes should be." Corey shuddered. "She moaned and groaned and then shrieked, like a banshee or something."

"I heard it, too!" Mrs. Jennings whispered. "But I didn't know what it was."

"You must have been terrified," Mr. Jennings said.

"I'm still shaking." Corey held out her trembling hands as proof. "It was definitely evil. Not sweet like Julie's grandmother. Wicked."

"Oh, my goodness." Mrs. Jennings stared at my sister. "Oh, my dear, how absolutely dreadful."

The breeze danced in the flower bed, shaking the blossoms. Wind chimes clinked like someone laughing. For a moment, I thought I saw something move in the shifting shadows under the trees.

Mr. Jennings turned to me. "Did you see it, too, Travis?"

This was my sister's show, so I shook my head. "Corey ran into my room and woke me up. I've never seen her so scared. In fact, she scared *me*. She's really psychic, you know." Psycho was more like it, but why spoil things with the truth?

"Do you think the ghost walks . . . every night?" Mr. Jennings asked, voice low, practically quivering with excitement.

"Ghosts usually do the same thing over and over again," Corey said. "Like they're atoning for something they did—or didn't do—while they were alive."

Mrs. Jennings sighed with envy. "Sometimes I get feelings, sensations, a sort of shiver. But I've never actually seen anything."

"Nor have I," Mr. Jennings admitted sadly. "We've gone to many so-called haunted inns, but we've been disappointed every time."

To keep from laughing, Corey avoided looking at me. "Get up at three A.M. tomorrow and watch those trees." She pointed at a grove of oaks. Even in the morning sun, the shadows they cast seemed denser and darker than anywhere else. "*That's* where I saw the ghost," she said.

The Jenningses stared at the grove as if they hoped to catch a glimpse of the ghost in broad daylight. "We'll be watching," Mrs. Jennings promised.

Mr. Jennings set his coffee mug down with a clink and got to his feet. "In the meantime, Louise and I have sightseeing plans."

"And some shopping to do," Mrs. Jennings put in. "I want to visit the glass factory near Quechee and browse in a few antique shops on the way. There's a cheese store, too, and an artist's studio. . . ."

We watched them get into their car and drive away. Corey grinned at me. "They won't be disappointed tonight."

A couple of hours later, we parked our bikes in front of a tourist-bait shop on Middlebury's main drag and went inside. We found white and green face makeup, black stuff for Corey's eyes, dark purple lipstick, and a bunch of other junk—rubber eyeballs that glowed in the dark, plastic spiders and rubber snakes, spray-on cobwebs, a haunted-house sound-effects CD, a lantern, candles, and flashlights that cast a blue beam. In a secondhand store, Corey bought a long white filmy scarf.

By the time we'd eaten a couple of slices of pizza and washed them down with bottles of soda, we'd spent about a quarter of our entire summer's allowance. And we had a fifteen-mile ride back to Fox Hill, mostly uphill this time. Balancing our shopping bags on the handlebars, we set off for the inn.

We spent the rest of the afternoon at the pool. We'd swim for a while, then lie in the sun and plan our ghost act, then dive back into the water. We had the place to ourselves. The bike riders had pedaled off to add more muscle to their legs, the Jenningses were still touring the countryside, and Grandmother was sitting on the patio dozing over a novel. Every now and then, Mr. Brewster cruised past on a riding mower, pretty much ruining the peace and quiet. He never looked our way.

At dinner, a new guest joined us. Mr. Nelson was short and skinny. He reminded me of a really strict math teacher who gave me a C and ruined my report card in sixth grade. He sat at a table by himself, reading a science book propped open with his saltshaker—*Global Warming in Our Lifetime: Fact or Myth?* It was clear he had no wish to be sociable. Why make friends when the world is about to end?

The Jenningses talked Tracy's ear off with tales of their day of shopping, the lovely lunch they'd eaten, the bargains they'd found. Cheese! Barn-board paintings! Pure Vermont maple syrup! A rusty child's wagon for the garden back home!

While they chattered, the bike riders discussed their ride—seventy-five miles in five hours, a near miss with a logging truck, an eagle sighting, a flat tire. Tim was making a major effort to stay awake, but Robert looked ready to hop on his bike and ride another fifty miles before bedtime.

After we'd eaten, everyone congregated on the porch again. Mr. Nelson sat at the end of the row of rocking chairs and kept his nose in his book. While Tim dozed, Robert studied his map, obviously planning another grueling ride. The Jenningses darted little looks at Corey and me, probably eager to talk to us alone.

When it was too dark to see the map, Robert woke Tim up. Mr. Nelson closed his book. They said good night and went to their rooms. A few minutes later, Grandmother excused herself.

As soon as she left, the Jenningses parked themselves in rockers next to ours.

"What a perfect night for a sighting." Mr. Jennings pointed to the full moon rising above the mountains.

"Bright light, no clouds. If the ghost comes, we'll get a good look at it."

"I'm not sure I want to see her again," Corey said. "She was pretty scary."

"I plan to sleep like a log," I put in. "No ghosts for me."

"Not us," Mr. Jennings said. "We'll be wide awake."

A cool breeze swept across the porch, rocking the empty chairs as it passed. The shadows of the morning glory draping the porch trellis quivered and shifted, and the wind chimes laughed on the dark lawn.

Mrs. Jennings pulled her sweater tighter and stood up. "It's getting cold."

"We're in Vermont," Mr. Jennings said.

Giving his wife a little hug, he said good night to us, and the two of them went up to bed.

By two thirty A.M., Corey had caked her face with white makeup, hollowed out her cheeks with green eye shadow, circled her eyes with black, and coated her mouth with purple lipstick. The scarf hid her hair.

"Do I look horrible enough?" she asked.

"If you looked any worse, *I'd* be scared of you."

We sneaked out the back door and ran across the lawn. Taking care not to be seen, we darted into the inky blackness of the oak grove. Anchored to earth with its shadow, the inn was dark. Everyone was asleep—except the Jenningses. Although we couldn't see them, we knew they were peering out their window, waiting to see the ghost.

Corey stepped onto the moonlit grass. Waving her arms slowly and dramatically, she glided along, sleeves and scarf fluttering. She dipped and swayed, she moaned and groaned, and then turned to stare at the inn. Stretching both arms, she pointed her fingers, threw back her head, and screamed.

Over my head, the leaves on the trees rustled and shook, as if Corey had awakened sleeping squirrels and birds. Something twittered softly, and the bushes swayed.

With goosebumps racing across my skin, I watched Corey run toward me. "Quick!" she hissed. "We have to get back to bed before anyone comes looking for us."

As she spoke, lights went on in the inn and the carriage house, and someone shouted.

Fearing we'd be caught, I ran after Corey. At the back door, she dragged me inside and we dashed to our rooms. I jumped into bed and burrowed under the covers.

Moments later, Grandmother called, "Travis? Are you awake?"

I pushed back the blanket and sat up, blinking at her. "Wha'?" I croaked, trying to sound as if she'd waked me from deep sleep. "Hunh?"

"I heard a noise." She went to my window and peered out. "It sounded like it came from that grove of trees."

"Didn't hear it," I muttered and lay back down.

Grandmother went to my sister's door. "Corey?"

"Asleep," she murmured. "Didn't hear."

"It must have been a screech owl." Grandmother sounded as if she was trying to convince herself. "I'm sorry I woke you." The door closed, and the inn was silent again.

I curled up under the covers and tried not to laugh out loud. We'd done it—ghosts had returned to Fox Hill.

After a while, I heard Corey tiptoeing down the hall to the bathroom. She was in there a long time, but before she went back to her room, she stopped to see me.

"Boy, was that stuff hard to get off. My whole face stings." She touched her cheek and winced. "If I hadn't found some cold cream, I'd still be scrubbing."

"You were great," I told her.

She bounced on the bed and laughed. "I think I woke up *everybody* with that scream."

"People for miles around heard you," I told her. "The cows won't give milk tomorrow, the chickens won't lay eggs, and the corn will wither on the stalks."

"Black dogs will turn white overnight." Corey laughed. "Flowers will drop their petals."

"Barns will collapse," I shouted. "Chimneys will topple!"

"Shh," Corey hushed me. "You'll wake Grandmother."

I clapped my hand over my mouth and tried to stop laughing.

Corey hugged herself in delight. "I can't wait to hear what everybody says tomorrow!"

4

The next morning, Corey and I found the Jenningses waiting for us in the dining room.

"We saw it!" Mr. Jennings whispered. "We actually saw it. And *heard* it."

"It pointed at us and screamed." Mrs. Jennings pressed a hand against her heart. "It was terrifying."

Corey feigned disappointment. "Oh, no, I must have slept right through it." She glanced at me. "Did you see it?"

I shook my head, trying to look as bummed as Corey. "I guess I was really tired."

By then, the bike riders had joined us. "Are you talking about that noise last night?" Tim asked.

"What was it?" Robert wanted to know. "A cougar or something?"

Mrs. Jennings stared at him. "You didn't see it?"

Robert shook his head. "It woke us up, but by the time we got to the window, it was gone."

"If it was a cougar, we should stay off the trails," Tim said. "A few years ago, one of those big cats killed a bike rider in California."

At that moment, Mr. Brewster walked past on his way to the kitchen. "That was no cougar," he muttered.

"Are you sure?" Robert asked.

"Of course I'm sure." Mr. Brewster stopped and

scowled as if Robert had called him a liar. "I've lived in Vermont all my life, so I ought to know what a cougar sounds like."

It was the most I'd ever heard him say.

"If it wasn't a cougar, what was it?" Tim asked, his eyes widening like a kid's at a horror movie.

Mr. Brewster had already lost interest in the subject. With a shake of his head, he disappeared into the kitchen, leaving us to stare after him.

"A ghost," Mrs. Jennings said. "It was a ghost."

Robert laughed. "That's ridiculous."

Mrs. Jennings frowned at Robert. "My husband and I saw it ourselves—as plain as plain can be, by that grove of trees." Mrs. Jennings waved her hand toward the window and the oaks. "It pointed at the inn and screamed in the most hideous, inhuman way!"

Robert laughed again, but Tim just stood there, as if he wasn't sure what to think.

Mr. Jennings laid a hand on my sister's shoulder. "This young lady saw it the night before last."

Corey shuddered. "It was awful."

Before Robert could say anything sarcastic, Tim grabbed his arm. "Lay off, will you? *You* didn't see it. *They* did."

Across the room, Mr. Nelson looked up from his newspaper. "So the ghosts are back," he said. "I was hoping they'd gone for good."

Just then, Grandmother came into the dining room. Tracy was right behind her, carrying a tray heaped with breakfast goodies. "What's back?" Grandmother asked.

"The ghosts." Mr. Nelson grimaced. "Didn't you hear the screams last night?"

Tracy gasped and almost dropped the tray. "I thought it was a screech owl."

"I heard what *sounded* like a scream," Grandmother said. "I must admit it scared me, but after I went back to bed, I realized what it was."

Corey and I darted a quick glance at each other. Had Grandmother guessed we'd played a prank on the Jenningses? I held my breath and waited for her to denounce us.

"Some people a mile or so down the road breed peacocks," she went on. "One must have flown the coop—so to speak." She smiled at her own joke. "A peacock's cry sounds remarkably like a human scream."

"There," Robert said to Tim. "I *knew* there was a rational explanation."

"But what about the ghost?" Tim asked. "All three of them have seen it."

Grandmother looked at us, plainly annoyed. "You were talking about ghosts the other night, swapping stories, trying to scare each other," she said. "You expected to see a ghost, and you've convinced yourselves you did."

Mrs. Jennings frowned at Grandmother. "I didn't *imagine* that ghost. If you'd been at your window, you would've seen it, too."

"You were looking out the window at three A.M.?" Robert asked in disbelief.

"Corey saw the ghost the night before at exactly three A.M.," Mrs. Jennings said. "She told George and me to watch for it in the grove of trees."

I held my breath, hoping the phone or the doorbell

would ring—anything to distract Grandmother from questioning my sister and me.

Unfortunately, no one called and no one came to the door. Grandmother fixed Corey with a steely gaze. "You never mentioned seeing a ghost."

Unable to meet Grandmother's eyes, Corey stared at the floor. "You wouldn't have believed me," she whispered. "But I saw it and I was scared and I told Mrs. Jennings because I knew *she'd* believe me."

While we were talking, Mr. Nelson had gone back to reading his newspaper.

I sidled over to him. "Why did you say the ghosts were back? Have you seen them before?"

He put down the paper with some irritation. "I've been coming to Fox Hill every July for twenty years," he said. "I remember the purported ghosts, as well as the reporters and the psychics and the nuts who came to witness the goings-on. They swarmed upstairs and down, ranting about cold spots, setting up bizarre recording devices and infrared cameras, making nuisances of themselves. Fools, that's what they were. Idiots." He took a sip of coffee. "The inn is much better off without ghosts," he said, "and the maniacs who flocked here to see them—*they* caused the most disturbance, by far."

Across the room, Robert seated himself noisily. "Get a move on, Tim," he said in a loud you-can't-fool-me voice. "We're doing a century ride today."

Before he joined his friend, Tim smiled at Corey. "My girlfriend is psychic, too," he told her. "She sees all kinds of things, just like you do—including those blue lights I was telling you about the other night."

Grandmother watched Tim join Robert at their table. Turning to Corey, she said, "I don't know what you're up to, but I simply do not believe one word of this ghost nonsense."

To the rest of us, she said, "Breakfast is ready. Please take your seats, and Tracy will serve you."

Corey and I sat down, and Grandmother sat between us. "No more ghost talk," she said. "I won't have you scaring the guests with silly stories."

Corey kicked me under the table, and I kicked her back. She giggled.

"I'm serious," Grandmother said.

We both nodded and turned our attention to the plates Tracy set down in front of us—scrambled eggs with cheese, home-fried potatoes, and a big cranberry muffin.

That afternoon, three couples, all friends of the Jenningses, arrived and requested rooms. Mrs. Jennings had told them about the ghost sighting and they were full of questions. Grandmother became increasingly annoyed, but no matter what she said, the new guests refused to be discouraged. If the Jenningses had seen a ghost, the ghost was real. And they wanted to see it themselves.

"Aren't you glad you have more guests?" Corey asked at dinnertime.

"Not if they're coming to see ghosts," Grandmother said. "They're bound to be disappointed." Sipping her iced tea, her expression as sour as a lemon, she regarded the four couples huddled around a table by the window.

Mrs. Jennings was describing the screaming phantom

to her friends. "It pointed right at me, and cursed me. Not George. Me. It cursed *me*."

"Oh, my goodness," Mrs. Bennett, one of the new guests, gasped. "You must have been terrified."

As Mrs. Jennings shivered, Mr. Jennings said, "You should have seen its eyes. They were red, and they glowed like hellfire."

"Oh, for heaven's sake," Grandmother muttered more to herself than to Corey and me. "This is getting more ridiculous by the moment."

Without waiting for Tracy to bring coffee, she left the dining room. The others followed her outside, chatting noisily. Corey went to the library to read, and I followed Tracy into the kitchen.

"Do you think Mrs. Jennings really saw a ghost?" I asked.

She looked up from a sinkful of soapy dishes. "Maybe," she said slowly. "But I can't be sure unless I see it myself."

"Wouldn't you be scared?" I was hoping she'd say yes and faint in my arms or something, but she merely shrugged. Without even looking at me, she said, "Ghosts can't hurt you."

Mrs. Brewster laid a heavy hand on my shoulder. "Unless you want to help Tracy clean up," she said, "I suggest you find someone else to talk to."

Taking the hint, I left Tracy to her dishes and went outside. Grandmother was sitting in a lawn chair, enjoying the last of the sunset, Robert and Tim were playing a relaxed game of tennis, and Mr. Nelson had settled himself in a rocking chair, his face hidden behind the evening paper. The Jennings party was seated in a circle, taking turns reading from the haunted inns book.

No one noticed me stroll across the lawn to the haunted grove—as Mr. and Mrs. Jennings now called it. The sun had just sunk behind the mountains, and the air was growing cool and damp. A breeze rustled the leaves, and a bird called. As I stood in the shadows, looking at the inn, I had a sudden feeling I wasn't alone.

Expecting to see my sister, I glanced behind me. No one was there, but the feeling lingered. "Corey?"

I peered into the shadows gathering under the trees. For a second, I thought I saw something duck out of sight behind one of the tall oaks.

"Hey," I called. "I see you." My voice sounded loud in the quiet evening—and a little high pitched, almost as though I was scared. Which, of course, I wasn't.

No one answered. Leaves rustled, and something on the ground snapped—maybe a branch cracking under a foot, maybe an animal scurrying past unseen.

With a shiver, I left the grove and hurried back to the inn. I told myself I'd heard a squirrel or a bird. But I couldn't shake the feeling that someone had been watching me.

5

In the middle of a bad dream, I woke up to see a hideous face hanging over me in the dark.

"Wake up, Travis," it moaned. "It's time to go to the grove."

"No, no!" I pushed the thing away from me, only to hear it laugh.

"Fooled you," Corey crowed.

"Brat," I muttered, too embarrassed to come up with a clever retort.

"It's time for the ghost to walk." Corey glided toward the door.

Shoving my blankets aside, I got out of bed and tiptoed outside behind my fearless sister. As soon as I stepped into the shadows under the trees, I began to shiver, just as I had earlier. The night seemed darker here, colder, spookier. The leaves whispered, the shadows shifted and changed and formed new shapes.

I glanced at Corey, but she didn't appear to notice anything out of the ordinary. With a giggle, she danced across the grass, waving her arms dramatically, her head thrown back, her filmy nightgown fluttering. Just as she had the previous night, she stopped suddenly, turned toward the inn, and screamed loudly. The echo made it sound as if a dozen ghosts—or a hundred peacocks—were shrieking an answer.

With one more piercing scream, Corey fled into the

shadows, and the two of us raced back to the inn. Again, I sensed someone close by, not just watching me this time but following me. Someone silent and swift, darker even than the night. I wanted to look back, just to prove nothing was there, but I didn't dare.

Corey usually outran me, but a surge of adrenaline sent me speeding into the inn well ahead of her.

I dove into bed just before Grandmother poked her head into my room. "Travis?" she whispered, "are you awake?"

I lay still, eyes tightly closed, breathing deep, regular breaths.

She closed my door, and I heard her go to my sister's room. "Corey?"

No answer. I pictured Corey huddled under the covers, made up to look like a ghost from your worst nightmare, and hoped Grandmother wouldn't pull the blankets back.

Soon I heard Grandmother return to her bedroom— where she probably lay awake pondering the noisy peacocks down the road.

I snuggled deeper into bed. Between talking about the hauntings and playing the ghost game, I'd set myself up to imagine I'd been watched in the grove and followed to the inn. As Grandmother said about the Jenningses, I was obviously susceptible. Nothing was in the grove. Nothing had followed me. It was ridiculous. *I* was ridiculous.

But what was that noise in the hall? Was someone standing just outside my room, ear pressed to my door? I lay still and listened so hard my ears buzzed. Nothing. . . . No, *not* nothing. A tiny creak, a flutter in the air, a cold draft across my face, a whisper of sound almost like a giggle.

"Corey, is that you?" I sat up and peered into the darkness. I was alone in my room.

Feeling foolish, I lay back down and pulled the blanket over my head. The loudest sound was my heart pounding. I might as well have been five years old.

In the morning, the guests gathered in the dining room to talk about the screaming ghost. The newcomers were almost too excited to eat the waffles Mrs. Brewster had prepared.

After Grandmother left the room to take a phone call, Tracy came to our table. "I heard the scream last night." She smoothed her hair back behind her ears and grinned. "Tonight, I'm going to camp out in the grove—I want to see the ghost for myself. You know, up close and personal."

Corey and I glanced at each other, frozen for a second. "You'd better not," I said. "No matter what you think, that ghost is definitely dangerous."

"Don't be silly." Tracy laughed.

Mrs. Brewster stuck her head out of the kitchen and gestured to the bicyclists' table. Tracy turned and noticed Robert holding up his coffee cup. "Excuse me," she murmured to Corey and me. "I'd better get back to work before the old battle-ax fires me."

As Tracy fetched coffee for Robert, Corey and I left the inn and settled into a pair of Adirondack chairs at the shady end of the lawn. "Do you think she'll go to the grove tonight?" Corey asked.

"If she does, she won't see anything."

"What do you mean?" Corey frowned as if she suspected I was about to edge her out of the starring role in our little drama.

"We'll be inside," I said, "trying some new tricks. Footsteps. Doors opening and shutting. Sobs and moans and spooky laughter."

We got up and ambled across the lawn, talking about things we could do with flashlights and string and sound effects. Without noticing where we were going, we ended up in the grove. Even in the daylight, it was a gloomy place. The shade seemed too dark, the air too cold, too still. Moss grew thick on the damp ground and furred the tree trunks. Toadstools sprouted everywhere, some red, some yellow, some white—all poisonous, I was sure. A crow watched us mournfully from a high branch, but no birds sang.

Corey shivered and folded her arms across her chest. "Tracy's a lot braver than I am. I wouldn't sleep here by myself. Not if you paid me."

"Me, either." I glanced at her. "Last night I swear somebody was hiding here in the shadows, watching us."

Corey drew in her breath and hugged herself tighter. "I thought it was my imagination."

We were both whispering, as if someone might be listening as well as watching. When the crow cawed from its perch overhead, we both jumped and then tried to pass it off with a laugh.

"Let's go," Corey said. "This place gives me the creeps."

We left the grove and wandered through a sunny patch of weedy ground, leaping with grasshoppers and humming with bees. Wild thistles grew taller than our heads.

A narrow path led toward a dilapidated shed and the remains of a barn, its roof fallen in and its walls collapsed. Vines and brambles crawled and curled over the weathered wood, prying the boards apart.

Corey stopped suddenly and pointed at a row of small square stones barely visible among the weeds. "What are those?"

We knelt down to look closer. A two-digit number had been chiseled into each stone, but years of rain and snow made them almost illegible.

"They must mean something," I said.

"But what?"

I shook my head, puzzled.

Losing interest, Corey pushed her hair back from her face. "It's boiling hot. Let's go swimming."

She headed toward the inn, but instead of following her, I stood there, contemplating the row of stones. "Forty-one," I read, "forty-two, forty-three, forty-four." My eyes moved from stone to stone. There were twelve of them. And many more in other rows, all numbered.

"Travis," Corey yelled. "Are you coming?"

Suddenly aware of the heat and the gnats buzzing around my head, I ran to catch up with my sister.

Corey and I spent the rest of the morning in the pool, then got dressed and went to the dining room for lunch. Robert and Tim had checked out that morning to explore New Hampshire's White Mountains. Mr. Nelson was gone, too, claiming he had no desire to experience any more supernatural manifestations. The Jennings gang was still there, along with a new couple from Albany who'd already been drawn into the ghost conversation.

Just as I took a bite of my hamburger, another new-comer swept into the room. Short and plump, with a head of frizzy blond curls, she wore layers of dark gauzy clothes that seemed to float in the air around her. Her arms clanked with silver and copper bracelets. She sported a ring on each of her chubby fingers, as well as a few on her round little toes, and a small silver hoop in one nostril. Earrings dangled to her shoulders in a shower of stars. Her scarlet lipstick matched her nail polish. She'd taken care to coat her eyelids green and spike her lashes with mascara.

With much twittering, she joined the group at the Jenningses' table.

"Don't stare," Grandmother whispered.

"Who is she?" Rude or not, neither Corey nor I could take our eyes off the woman.

"Miss Eleanor Duvall," Grandmother said with a sniff. "A self-proclaimed ghost hunter."

"Really?"

Grandmother tapped Corey's wrist. "Eat your hamburger and stop looking at her. I'm sure she loves the attention."

Despite Grandmother's injunction, Corey and I watched Miss Duvall as if she'd hypnotized us.

By the time we'd finished eating, Grandmother was thoroughly annoyed with both of us. "You're from New York," she said. "You must see people like her every day."

We shook our heads. Even in the East Village, Miss Duvall would have stood out from the crowd.

"Oh, no," Grandmother muttered. "She's coming this way."

Indeed she was, followed by the Jenningses and all their friends.

"Don't talk to her about your so-called ghost sightings," Grandmother warned Corey. "Or we'll never get rid of her."

"I'm Edna Frothingham," one of the newcomers said. "And this is Miss Eleanor Duvall, the world-famous psychic and ghost hunter. I called her as soon as I heard from the Jenningses."

Miss Duvall bared a mouthful of tiny teeth in a smile aimed at Corey. "You're the little girl who sees ghosts," she proclaimed, jangling her bracelets like a musical accompaniment.

Just then the phone rang, forcing Grandmother to excuse herself. "Not a word," she hissed in Corey's ear.

But of course Corey couldn't resist a chance to take center stage. "Yes," she said modestly. "I see ghosts all the time."

"Lovely." Miss Duvall sat down in Grandmother's chair. The others gathered around the table, hanging on every word their new leader uttered.

Corey told her about the granny ghost, the ghost of the haunted grove, and the other presences she felt in the inn—the crying baby she heard late at night, the footsteps in the hall outside her door, the sobs, moans, and spooky laughter, the howling dog, and so on. There was no end to her imaginings.

Obviously enjoying herself, my sister had everyone's total attention. Even Tracy drew near, clutching a tray to her chest, her eyes wide, her mouth half open.

"You are truly gifted," Miss Duvall whispered to

Corey. To the others she said, "Often it is children who are most in touch with the spirit world. It is to be expected. After all, they are closer to the other side than we. As the great poet William Wordsworth says, 'Our birth is but a sleep and a forgetting. . . . Heaven lies about us in our infancy.'"

The Jennings gang nodded solemnly, as if they all knew Wordsworth by heart and understood exactly what Miss Duvall meant. Which was more than I could say for myself.

"When I first spoke with Corey, I knew she was special," Mrs. Jennings said, taking the role of my sister's discoverer.

Miss Duvall turned to me. "And how about you, Travis? Do you share your sister's powers?"

Taken by surprise, I said, "Sometimes I sense things. Like the grove. It's, it's—I can't explain it, but—"

"The grove, yes!" Miss Duvall rose from the table in a whirl of gauze and a tinkle of jewelry. "Take me there. I must see it!"

With some reluctance, Corey and I led the whole group of adults across the lawn and into the grove. Immediately, they all began to shiver. The woman from Albany made the sign of the cross, and her husband mumbled a prayer. Mrs. Jennings said she felt faint and took her husband's arm. Her friends gathered closely about Miss Duvall.

"Are you all right, Eleanor?" Mrs. Frothingham asked.

Eyes closed, Miss Duvall swayed as if she'd fallen into a trance. With outstretched arms, she turned in a slow circle, breathing heavily. "Come forth," she whispered. "Show yourself, spirit of darkness. I fear you not."

She stood still and waited. Nothing happened. Nothing that we could see or hear, that is. But something was there. Something that sent shivers racing up and down my spine and prickled my scalp. Corey actually reached for my hand and held it tightly, something she wouldn't do normally.

Opening her eyes at last, Miss Duvall stared at us, the dim light silvering her hair. "It is here," she whispered, "just as the child said. But it does not wish to reveal itself. Perhaps there are too many of us."

With a nervous gesture, she smoothed her clothing and took Corey's other hand. "Come," she said, "we'll return tomorrow when Chester arrives."

"Chester?" I asked.

"Chester Coakley, my associate," Miss Duvall explained. "He was delayed by a nasty piece of business in Salem but should arrive tomorrow with our equipment."

Once we left the grove, the guests began babbling away about the presence in the trees. If Corey and I hadn't felt the thing ourselves, we would've had a good laugh at their expense.

That night, Corey and I made plans for some new tricks. Well after midnight, we tiptoed out of Grandmother's apartment, through the silent kitchen, and into the hall. Scarcely breathing, we crept up the stairs. Moonlight streamed through the tall window on the landing.

"Look. There's Tracy." Corey pointed outside.

We watched the girl cross the lawn, lighting her way with a flashlight. After she vanished into the grove's shadows, we lingered for a moment, watching her light appear and disappear among the trees.

"Just like Nancy Drew," Corey whispered.

"Don't go to the grove, Nancy," I intoned in a spooky voice. "Don't open that door, don't go down those steps, stay out of the attic, watch your—"

"Shut up." Corey hustled me up the stairs.

At the top, we paused and listened. Except for a chorus of snores, all was silent. The guests' doors were closed. No lights showed. At the opposite end of the hall were the back stairs, our escape route to the kitchen.

We looked at each other, and I nodded. Corey began to sob in a high breathless voice, and I waved a tiny pocket flashlight. Its faint blue light barely lit the darkness. Under our bare feet, the floor boards squeaked and creaked. I tapped at one door, then another, and laughed a horrible laugh.

As the guests began shouting and stumbling about in their rooms, we ran silently down the stairs and hid under the kitchen table.

Upstairs, Miss Duvall screeched joyfully, "Sobs, rappings, laughter, footsteps, a blue light—a classic visitation!"

Grandmother opened the door of her apartment and stepped into the kitchen. From our hiding place, Corey and I watched her bare feet pad past.

As soon as she headed upstairs to quiet the guests, my sister and I scurried back to our rooms and jumped into bed. We'd done it again.

I would've laughed out loud if Tracy hadn't screamed somewhere outside in the dark.

By the time Corey and I reached the front door, Grandmother and the guests had gathered around Tracy.

"What's wrong?" Grandmother asked her. "What were

you doing outside at this time of night? I promised your mother I'd make sure you behaved—"

"I went to the grove," Tracy sobbed. "To see the ghost, and it, oh, Mrs. Donovan, it, it—" She collapsed into Grandmother's arms, weeping.

"We heard the ghost, too," Miss Duvall put in, her voice rising. "It was roaming the hall, sobbing and moaning."

"There was a blue light," Mrs. Bennett added.

"Blue," her husband agreed. "But very dim. Spectral."

"It pounded on our door," Mr. Jennings added. "It laughed like a maniac."

"There must be *two* ghosts!" Mrs. Jennings cried. "One outside and one inside."

"Maybe more," Mrs. Frothingham whispered.

Finally, Miss Duvall turned to Tracy, who was still crying in Grandmother's arms. "What did you see?"

"I didn't *see* anything," Tracy sobbed. "But something was there, I *felt* it, it was cold and horrible. Evil." She clung to Grandmother and cried harder.

Corey and I stared at each other. We could explain the inside ghost, but the outside ghost was beginning to frighten both of us.

Keeping one arm around Tracy, Grandmother said, "I think it's time we all went to bed and got some sleep. Tomorrow I'll ask Martha what she put in her tomato sauce—it must have been pretty potent."

If Grandmother had hoped for a laugh, she was disappointed.

"Don't blame the food," Miss Duvall said. "This inn is haunted. Just wait till Chester sets up his equipment tomorrow! Then you'll see."

With that, she flounced upstairs, her gaudy silk robe and nightgown fluttering, her bare feet seemingly too tiny to bear her weight. Even without jewelry and makeup, she was an amazing sight.

The other guests followed her, murmuring to each other about the sobs and laughter, the blue light, and the terrifying presence in the haunted grove.

Flashlight in hand, Grandmother led Tracy back to her room in the carriage house, and Corey and I went to bed. For once we didn't feel like talking about the ghosts of Fox Hill. Or even thinking about them.

6

The next day, Corey and I cornered Tracy in the kitchen. She'd been surrounded by guests all morning, and we wanted to talk to her alone.

"Tell us what happened," Corey begged.

"Every detail," I added. "Don't leave anything out."

Tracy shook her head. "Can't you see I've got dishes to wash?"

Mrs. Brewster looked up from the laundry she'd been sorting. "Go ahead. Tell them. I'd like to hear it myself."

All three of us stared at her, surprised by her interest. Without looking at us, she went on separating white napkins from blue napkins.

"I don't want to talk about it anymore," Tracy murmured.

"You've told everybody else, but I haven't heard a word." Mrs. Brewster frowned at a red sock. "How did that get in with the table linens?"

"Okay," Tracy said, gulping a little. "I wanted to see the ghost—which was totally stupid—so I went to the grove and waited for it to come. After a while, I started hearing a lot of rustling sounds, like squirrels or mice in the leaves." Without looking at us, she paused to wipe her soapy hands on her apron. "Then I thought I saw a face."

"Are you sure it wasn't one of these two playing tricks on you?" Mrs. Brewster scowled at Corey and me as if she knew exactly what we'd been doing. We both edged away from her sharp eyes.

Tracy shook her head. "Laugh if you want, but there was something in the dark watching me." Her voice dropped so low I could hardly hear her. "It wasn't Corey or Travis . . . or any other living soul."

Mrs. Brewster picked a stray blue napkin out of a pile of white tablecloths and waited for Tracy to go on. But Tracy just stood there, twisting her apron and trying not to cry.

"Is that all?" Mrs. Brewster sounded disappointed.

Tracy nodded. Tears ran down her face, and she wiped them away with her apron. "You wouldn't say 'Is that all' if you'd been there."

Mr. Brewster entered the kitchen as quietly as a ghost himself and frowned at us all, even Mrs. Brewster. "Leave the girl be," he said. "Can't you see? She don't want to talk about it."

With a sigh, Mrs. Brewster picked up an armful of tablecloths and headed for the laundry room. "Bring the napkins," she told Tracy, "and help me get the wash started."

As Tracy walked past, I grabbed her arm. "I know just what you mean," I told her. "Something's in the grove. I've felt it, too."

Corey nodded. "It's a scary place."

Although we hadn't spoken loudly, Mr. Brewster said, "If I was you, I'd stay away from there. No sense looking for trouble."

"What do you mean?" I asked.

He hesitated, hands deep in his pockets, chin stuck out.

"Trouble finds folks who look for it." Then, without another word, he left the kitchen. A moment later, we saw him walking toward the vegetable garden, pushing a wheelbarrow.

Corey made a face at his back and darted out the back door. I followed her. As we walked along the hedge separating the vegetable garden from the lawn, we heard Mr. Brewster say, "I thought you was doing the laundry."

"Tracy can do it," Mrs. Brewster said.

Peeking through the hedge, we watched her sit down on a bench. Mr. Brewster leaned on his hoe beside her, the weeding forgotten.

"Bound to be trouble now," he muttered.

"It's those grandchildren," Mrs. Brewster said. "Soon as I saw 'em, I knew they'd stir things up. Bad ones— that's what they are. I can spot 'em every time. They've got her up and about. And the little ones, too."

Mr. Brewster nodded, his face glum. "They wake up easy."

"And it's so hard to lull them back to sleep, poor dears."

"Mrs. Brewster!" Tracy called. "There's something wrong with the washer. Soap's everywhere. I can't shut it off!"

Mrs. Brewster shook her head. "Yep, things are stirred up, for sure. Next it'll be the lights and the TV and the plumbing."

"They'll keep me busy." Mr. Brewster sighed. "Not a moment's peace, that's for certain."

Mrs. Brewster got to her feet. "Better come with me," she said, "and take a look at the washing machine."

Mr. Brewster grunted to himself and laid down his hoe. "Weeds can wait, I reckon."

Corey and I crept away to the terrace behind the house and sat down at a table almost hidden by wisteria.

"What were they talking about?" I asked. "*Who* did we wake up?"

"They must be nuts or something," Corey said. "Blaming us when all we did was play a few pranks."

"It's not fair. We're not bad." A wasp settled down to explore a smear of jam on the table. I swatted it away absent-mindedly. "They act like it's our fault the washing machine broke."

The wasp landed on the table again. Corey watched it probe the jam, her forehead wrinkled as if she was memorizing its shape and color, its legs, its wings. It wasn't like my sister to be quiet so long.

At last, she looked at me, her face full of worry. "Maybe they think we woke up the ghosts. The ones that used to be here."

I stared at her. "But we faked it."

Corey shook her head. "We didn't fake what scared Tracy, and we didn't fake what scared you and me. Something's in the grove—and the Brewsters think we stirred it up." She glanced at the wasp. "Like we poked a stick in a hornets' nest, and they all flew out."

I glanced over my shoulder at the grove and felt the hair on my arms prickle. Part of me wanted to say "Don't be ridiculous," but another part of me was scared she was right.

Corey clasped her hands, twisting her fingers until her knuckles turned white, a worried frown on her face.

"What if we did, Travis?" she asked in a voice so low I had to lean close to hear her. "What if we did?"

"If we woke something up," I said, "let's hope Chester Coakley and Miss Duvall can put it back to sleep."

Corey got to her feet. "He should be here by now."

We came around the corner of the inn just in time to see a dusty black hearse pull into a parking place. KEEP THE DEAD PEACEFUL was painted on its side in large white Gothic letters, and underneath, in smaller letters was:

CHESTER COAKLEY
PSYCHIC INVESTIGATOR
THE MAN TO CALL WHEN THINGS GO BUMP

The license plate said, I C B-YOND.

The driver's door swung open, and out stepped a tall, thin man with a long gray ponytail and matching beard. He wore a Grateful Dead baseball cap, black jeans, and black boots. His faded black T-shirt said, I SEE—AND I CATCH—DEAD PEOPLE.

From the porch came a cry of delight. Clothing aflutter, Miss Duvall hurried down the steps and threw her arms around the man, almost knocking him flat on his back.

Chester Coakley had arrived.

The Jennings gang poured out of the inn and raced across the grass, calling out greetings. As Miss Duvall introduced them, they formed a respectful circle around Chester Coakley.

Catching sight of Corey and me, Miss Duvall beckoned to us. "Come and meet Chester."

Chester regarded us with the saddest eyes I'd ever seen.

His face was long and narrow, and his brow was carved with deep lines. He shook our hands and in a melancholy voice said, "Eleanor has told me all about you."

Turning to Corey, he added, "You are a sensitive, I hear."

For the first time, Corey seemed a little uneasy about her newly acquired psychic powers. With a shrug, she backed away from him.

"Don't be so modest!" Miss Duvall engulfed Corey in a smothering hug. To Chester, she said, "This little girl has witnessed several psychic manifestations. Indeed, I believe she's the catalyst for everything that's happened."

Chester nodded. "The catalyst. Of course. The one who sets everything in motion."

Miss Duvall returned her attention to Corey. "You see, dear, ghosts will not manifest unless someone sensitive to their presence is nearby. Obviously, the inn's previous owners were sensitives, like you. When they left and your very rational grandmother arrived, the ghosts became dormant. Now you're here, and they're once more on the prowl."

Corey shook her head, clearly alarmed.

"Don't be frightened," Miss Duvall said softly. "You have a great gift."

"No," Corey said. "It was a—"

I think Corey would have confessed everything if Grandmother hadn't arrived just then and interrupted her.

Barely concealing her dislike for the newcomer and his vehicle of choice, she gave him a teacher look that once must have terrified her students. "Mr. Chester Coakley, I assume?"

Chester gave a little bow and removed his baseball cap. "At your service, Mrs. Donovan."

Grandmother didn't return his smile. "I've given you a room on the second floor. Would you like to see it?"

"Sure—just give me a minute to grab my gear."

With obvious distaste, Grandmother watched Chester pull a tripod, strobe lights, and a camera bag out of the hearse. Miss Duvall took a crate of recording equipment and trudged into the inn behind Chester and Grandmother. The Jennings gang traipsed through the door after them, leaving Corey and me alone in the driveway.

"What a pair of nut cases." Hoping for a laugh, I tried to imitate Miss Duvall and Chester. "Oh, she's a catalyst, there has to be a catalyst."

Corey didn't even smile. Without a word, she turned her back on me and walked away.

"Where are you going?" I called after her.

"To my room. I want to be alone for a while."

I watched her go, hair swinging, shoulders squared, obviously upset. "Don't be stupid," I shouted. "You aren't a catalyst. They're crazy—and so are the Brewsters!"

But she kept going. Didn't look back. Didn't slow down. I could've run after her, but I knew it wouldn't do any good. When Corey got into one of her moods, you just had to wait until she got over it.

Not used to entertaining myself, I wandered around the grounds looking for something to do. I tried batting a tennis ball against the wall, but I kept missing it. I went inside and played a video game. I read a few pages of a Harry Potter book I'd already read three times. I started a crossword puzzle, but it was too hard.

Too lazy to put on my bathing suit and swim, I went back outside and walked through the garden to the place where I'd found the row of stones. I stared down at them, still puzzled.

Suddenly, a shadow fell across the weeds. Mr. Brewster stood a few feet away, blocking the sun. "What are you doing here?"

From the way he said it, you would've thought I'd climbed over a fence and trespassed on his own private land.

Instead of answering his question, I asked him one of my own. "What are these stones for? Why do they have numbers on them?"

He studied me as if I were a subspecies of the human race that should be extinct by now. "There's copperheads round here. Lots of 'em. Best stay away lest you get bit."

I looked at the mass of weeds and brambles growing over everything. Mr. Brewster had a point. It was snake territory, for sure.

I followed him back to the inn. "You didn't answer my question."

"You didn't answer mine," he said.

"But don't you wonder about those stones? Somebody went to a lot of trouble to line them up and write numbers on them."

"Whoever done it's dead and gone." Mr. Brewster stopped and scowled at me from under his bushy eyebrows. "Told you before. Leave things be that don't concern you."

With that, he walked a little faster, as though he was anxious to get rid of me. I slowed down and let the gap between us widen. Grumpy old man. Grandmother should fire both of the Brewsters. Surely she could find a good-natured hired man and a cook even better than Mrs. Brewster—people who might smile once in a while.

Although—or maybe because—Miss Duvall and Chester were looking for her, Corey stayed in her room until dinner.

I knocked on her door once, but she told me to go away. "I'm reading," she said.

"Is it a good book?" I asked.

"Yes."

"What's the title?"

"Go away."

I took her advice and left without even making a joke about a book called *Go Away*. In her present, very bad, mood, Corey wouldn't have been amused.

By dinnertime, the inn was full, and Tracy had to rush from table to table, taking orders, bringing food, and refilling water glasses.

Miss Duvall and Chester were holding forth at the Jenningses' table, describing their methods of discovering and recording ghostly presences.

Grandmother gave Chester a dark look. "Imagine a grown man driving around in a hearse, pretending to be a ghost hunter. Surely he can't earn a living doing that." She sighed. "Then again, maybe he can. Some people will believe anything."

For once, Corey had nothing to say. Still in her mood, she sipped her water and poked at the food on her plate, rearranging it instead of eating it.

"You're very pale," Grandmother said to her. "Do you feel all right?"

Corey shrugged. "I'm fine. Just not hungry."

Across the room, Chester's voice rose. "I tell you, the little girl's responsible. It's the same with poltergeists. They feed off the psychic energy of young people. Especially if the child is disturbed."

Chester had lowered his voice somewhat, but all three of us heard his last comment.

Corey looked at Grandmother, alarmed. "I'm not disturbed," she whispered.

Grandmother opened her mouth to speak, but I was too fast for her. Thinking to turn Chester's words into a joke, I said, "Of course you're disturbed, I've known that since the day Mom brought you home from the loony bin."

Grandmother stared at me, her face stern with anger. "That wasn't funny, Travis. Can't you see your sister's upset? Apologize for your insensitivity."

Before I had a chance to say anything, Corey jumped up from the table so hastily she overturned her chair. Without a word, she fled from the room.

Chester turned to us in dismay. "I'm so sorry," he said, "I didn't mean Corey's disturbed. I just—"

Grandmother rose to her feet with all the dignity of thirty years of teaching and stared the man down. "Please refrain from discussing the supernatural in Corey's presence. And mine and Travis's as well. This is our home, not a boardinghouse for ghosts."

With that, she hurried after my sister.

Tracy broke the embarrassed silence by entering the room with the dessert cart. Unaware of what had just happened, she moved among the tables, describing the evening's choices: apple pie à la mode, peach upside-down cake, crème brûlée, and "Death by Chocolate."

I guess if Tracy hadn't come along with the cart, I might have run after Grandmother and Corey, but who can turn down the world's best chocolate cake? Not me.

No sooner had I taken the first bite than Chester and Miss Duvall joined me. "Do you mind?" Chester asked as they sat down.

Of course I minded, but I was too polite to say so. Wimp that I was, I swallowed my mouthful of cake and smiled.

"Is your sister all right?" Miss Duvall asked. "Chester didn't mean to hurt her feelings. He was speaking in general of children who cause psychic manifestations, especially poltergeist activity."

"I don't suppose Corey has a history of shaking beds, broken furniture, loud noises, flying objects, rappings and tappings, and so on?" Chester asked.

"My sister is *not* disturbed." I glared at the man, sitting there in his dopey cap, wearing his dopey T-shirt. Suddenly, I hated him and his gray ponytail and his hearse. I decided to tell him the truth—maybe he'd go away and take the Jennings gang with him. If these were the kind of guests who came to the inn to see ghosts, I'd like to see the end of them.

"Corey's not psychic," I said in a voice loud enough for everyone in the dining room to hear. "If you want to know the truth, she and I—"

Before I could confess, Miss Duvall interrupted me. "I am so sorry, Travis. Chester has an unfortunate habit of asking thoughtless questions."

Here she broke off and scowled at Chester. He merely

shrugged and leaned back in his chair, grinning in such a vacant way I wondered if he was on some kind of medication.

"As for Corey's psychic powers," she went on to me, "I've been in this field long enough to recognize the real thing."

I laughed. "You're wrong. Corey and I faked everything."

Miss Duvall gave me a long, thoughtful look. "No," she said. "You and your sister may have begun this as a game, but the ghosts are awake now. Putting them back to sleep will not be easy."

A twinge of alarm raced across my scalp. "Putting them back to sleep will not be easy" echoed Mrs. Brewster's words from this morning a little too closely. Suppose everyone was right, and we actually *had* woken the ghosts of Fox Hill?

I must have kept my fear to myself, for Miss Duvall got to her feet and beckoned to Chester. "We have equipment to set up in the grove."

"You and your sister are welcome to join us," Chester said.

"Thanks," I said. But no thanks. Watching them leave the room, I told myself they were crazy. But an annoying little voice whispered, "What if they're not?"

7

The Jennings gang followed Miss Duvall and Chester, twittering about the grove and what they might see.

Mrs. Jennings paused and smiled at me. "I know you're a skeptic, Travis, but I hope you and Corey will join us tonight. Eleanor is convinced we'll have a better chance of seeing the ghost if your sister's with us."

"Don't count on it," I told her.

Mrs. Jennings sighed. "Chester was very tactless at dinner, but then I suppose that's how it is when you're a genius. The ordinary rules don't apply." With another smile and a pat on my shoulder, she hastened after the others, leaving a trail of sickeningly sweet perfume behind her.

Across the room, Tracy cleared tables. The setting sun shone through the windows and backlit her hair, making it shine like fine threads of gold.

She turned and caught me staring at her. "What do you think of Chester and Eleanor?" she asked.

"Bona fide nut cases, both of them."

With a serious face, she set her heavy tray on my table. "If you'd been in the grove last night, you wouldn't sound so smug."

More embarrassed than smug, I scraped the last bit of chocolate icing from my plate and licked it off my fork, tine by tine. "It's all fake," I said. "Corey and I wanted to make people think the inn was haunted so Grandmother would get more guests. She dressed up like a ghost and—"

Tracy shoved her face so close to mine we were almost nose to nose. Which would have been a thrill if she hadn't been so mad. *"There was something in the grove last night*—and it wasn't Corey!"

She snatched up my plate and fork, dumped them on her tray with a clatter, and huffed out of the dining room.

There I was, all by myself, surrounded by empty tables covered with dirty linen and crumpled napkins. It was obvious Tracy was never going to be my girlfriend. Not only was I tactless and offensive, but I was shorter and younger than she was.

"It was your imagination," I called after her, but the only answer I got was the *whop, whop, whop* of the kitchen door swinging back and forth.

"But what if it wasn't?" the little voice asked, a little louder this time. "What if . . . What if . . . ?"

Exasperated, I tossed my napkin on the table and went to find Corey. I wished we'd never thought of the ghost game.

As it turned out, Corey agreed with me. I finally found her sitting on the patio in the dark all by herself. At first she refused to look at me or answer any questions.

"Why are you mad at me?" I asked her. "What did I do?"

She turned to face me. "I told you I wanted to read, but you made funny noises outside my door, threw apples at my window, and thumped on my wall. You even unplugged my light and my radio and changed the time on my clock."

I stared at her. "Are you crazy? I knocked on your door once, and you told me to go away and I did. I never made funny noises or threw apples or thumped on your wall or anything."

"Then who did? Mr. Brewster?"

"Corey, I swear to you I did not do that stuff."

"Oh," she said sarcastically, "then it must have been the ghost."

We looked at each other in the moonlight, electrified by the same thought.

"No joke," I whispered.

"No." Corey folded her arms across her chest and shivered. "No joke."

Delicate shadows from the wisteria vine patterned the table and Corey's face, shifting as the breeze blew. From somewhere in the darkness, an owl hooted and another answered. Much closer, I heard something that sounded like a muffled giggle.

"Did you hear that?" I whispered.

Corey shuddered. "A mouse," she said. "A cat, a bird. Nothing to be scared of."

"Admit it," I said. "You *are* scared—and so am I."

She shook her head stubbornly. "Speak for yourself." At the same moment, we heard a whispering sound in the bushes and then the giggle—louder this time, followed by an eddy of cold air that tousled my hair and then Corey's.

My sister jumped to her feet. "Let's go inside."

The two of us ran to the inn and dashed through the

kitchen door, sure we were being chased by an invisible gang of ghosts.

Mrs. Brewster was scrubbing the sink. She frowned when the screen door slammed shut. "What's the big rush?" she asked. "A person would think something was after you."

Neither Corey nor I knew what to say. We just stood and stared at Mrs. Brewster, wishing we were safely home in New York or even at Camp Willow Tree—anywhere but here.

"I thought you two were out there with them so-called psychics." She waved a hand in the direction of the grove, where flashlights bobbed about in the dark. "They're aiming to take pictures of things that don't want their pictures taken," she muttered.

Grandmother opened the door to her apartment and poked her head into the kitchen. "Corey and Travis," she said, "it's time you were in bed."

At that moment, the power went off, and the inn became totally dark and silent—no lights, no radios, no humming refrigerator. Not a sound.

"Go get Henry," Grandmother told Mrs. Brewster. "The power's out again. I meant to get the wiring checked the last time this happened."

Grandmother had no sooner lit a candle than we heard a commotion outside—shouts, screams, the sound of people running toward us as if they feared for their lives.

Tripping over each other in their haste to get inside, the Jennings gang poured into the kitchen. Behind them, Chester was yelling, "We got an image!"

Grandmother closed her eyes and shook her head. "I

don't believe this." In a louder voice, she repeated herself. "I do *not* believe this."

Someone giggled, and Grandmother glared at me, her face stern in the candlelight. "This isn't funny, Travis!"

"I didn't laugh."

The guests milled around the kitchen, stumbling over things in the darkness. "Why are the lights off?" Mrs. Jennings cried.

"Please turn them on," Mrs. Frothingham begged. "We've had a terrible scare."

"Serves you right, you silly old scaredy cat," someone whispered, causing an outburst of giggles.

"Travis, apologize at once!" Grandmother said, shocked.

"It wasn't me!"

"I don't care who said it," Mrs. Frothingham cried. "Just turn the lights back on."

"I'm sorry, but the power's off." Grandmother lit more candles. As the kitchen brightened, something scurried into the shadows, too quickly to be seen.

"I can fix tea," Grandmother offered.

Some wanted tea. Others wanted something stronger. Two or three wanted to leave the inn at once.

The only ones in need of nothing were Eleanor Duvall and Chester Coakley. They were ecstatic. Not only had they seen something, but they'd captured its image on video.

"See?" Chester showed us a grainy image in the camera's monitor. Whatever it was wore a long dress and its hair was loose, but its face was too blurred to make out any features.

"She came like a blast of cold air," Miss Duvall said. "Silent, not a sound, but emanating malice."

"You probably saw the strobes light up," Chester put in. "She tripped the wires like I hoped and triggered the camera. It's the best paranormal experience I've ever had—and the best footage I've ever shot. Or seen, for that matter."

Mrs. Jennings clutched her teacup with shaking hands. "I'm very glad you children were not with us," she quavered. "I'll never get another good night's sleep."

Her friends nodded and cooed to each other in soft, comforting voices. Mrs. Frothingham sobbed into a wineglass. The wives were done with ghosts. No one wanted to see another one. In fact, they wished they hadn't seen the one they just saw.

The husbands laughed and talked too loud, already beginning to doubt they'd really seen a ghost.

"The image on that videotape," Mr. Bennett said. "It was probably the strobe lights. They caused a glare in the camera lens or something."

"Trick photography," Mr. Frothingham declared. "Double exposures. Easy to fake."

Mr. Jennings was the only husband to disagree. "No, it was the real thing," he insisted, gulping down a glass of something that made him cough. "I'm glad I saw it, but I don't care to see another."

Just then, every light came on, almost blinding us with their brilliance. The refrigerator began humming, and the dishwasher started—even though it hadn't been running before the power failure. Radios and TVs all over the inn came on, blasting noise at top volume.

Mr. Brewster stood at the top of the basement steps looking gloomier than usual. "I went to the fuse box," he said, "but before I so much as touched it, the power come back."

"How odd," Grandmother said.

"Nothing odd about it, ma'am." Mr. Brewster shook his head. "They been stirred up good and proper now."

Without another word, he trudged out of the kitchen, accompanied by a giggle that earned me a dirty look from Grandmother. I shook my head in protest, but she'd already turned her attention to Mrs. Brewster.

"What on earth was he talking about?" Grandmother asked.

"You'll find out soon enough." Squaring her shoulders, Mrs. Brewster strode out the door behind her husband.

Clearly bewildered, Grandmother looked at the guests. "Has everyone gone crazy?"

Chester patted her shoulder. "It's the ghosts," he said. "I told you, the girl's a catalyst."

Grandmother shrugged Chester's hand off. "I want you and your equipment out of here tomorrow morning. We've had nothing but trouble since you and that woman showed up."

Taking Corey and me by our arms, Grandmother ushered us out of the kitchen. In the doorway, she paused. "Will someone please turn off the radios and the television? Or at least turn them down?"

Snapping off her own television and radio, Grandmother frowned at me. "I expect you to apologize to Mrs. Frothingham tomorrow. You were very rude."

"But, Grandmother, I didn't—"

Silencing me with a look, she said, "If you continue to lie to me, I shall be forced to call your parents." She opened her bedroom door. "I need a good night's sleep. Please don't disturb me." With that, she walked into her room and shut the door.

I followed my sister into her room and sat beside her on the bed. "She hates us," Corey said. "We'll have to go to summer school now."

I shook my head. "She's just upset. And you can't blame her. This has been a really weird night. Especially for some-one who doesn't believe in ghosts."

Corey sighed. "I wish we knew what Mr. Brewster thinks we stirred up."

Before I could come up with an answer, the light went off and the bed began to shake. Back and forth, up and down, jolting us like a carnival ride, harder and faster. We tried to hold on to the headboard, but in seconds we were thrown to the floor with a loud, bone-jarring thud. Too stunned to move, we cowered together while invisible fingers pinched us and pulled our hair and tweaked our clothes.

"Stop it," Corey yelled at me. "You're hurting me, stop it!"

"*You* stop it," I shouted, pushing her away.

At that, the room's dark corners rang with laughter. The empty bed bounced as if a gang of kids were jumping on it. The radio blared from one end of the dial to the other, and the bedside lamp flashed on and off. The closet door opened and slammed shut, opened and slammed shut, over and over again. Things thudded and thumped all around us. A book hit me in the head. A picture fell, and the glass in the frame broke.

"Who are you?" I cried in a voice so high and shaky I hardly recognized it as mine. "What do you want?"

An outburst of laughter answered me. Somebody yelled a string of cuss words

"I told you to go to sleep!" Grandmother stepped into the room and gasped, her face pale with shock. "What on earth have you done? Have you gone crazy?"

The closet door lay on the floor, the wood splintered from the hinges. Corey's clothes were scattered everywhere, some no more than ripped rags. Bureau drawers hung open, spilling their contents. Pages torn from books lay in drifts on the floor. Feathers from pillows still floated in the air. My sister covered her face with her hands and began to cry.

Grandmother stared at us as if we were monsters. "Why did you do this? What kind of children are you?"

"Bad children," a kid's voice whispered. "Lovely bad children!"

"What did you say?" Grandmother asked me.

"Nothing," I whispered. Out of the corner of my eye, I saw the shadows in the corner move, shifting the darkness from one place to another.

"It wasn't us," Corey sobbed. "We didn't do anything."

"Of course it wasn't the children." Chester peered over Grandmother's shoulder, grinning with apparent delight at the state of our room.

Grandmother whirled to face Chester, eager to take out her anger on him. "What are you doing here? This is my apartment, not part of the inn. Please leave at once!"

"Let him speak, Mrs. Donovan." Miss Duvall floated into the room on her tiny little feet, wearing her usual layers of filmy clothes. "Chester is the only one who can get to the bottom of this."

Her words caused an outburst of giggles from the corner. The same kid's voice whispered, "Fat bottom, fat bottom, fatty, fatty, fat bottom!" The giggles grew louder. Somebody said a rude word, which provoked even louder giggling.

Grandmother looked at Corey and me, alarmed for the first time. "Stop it," she ordered. "Or I'm sending you home tomorrow."

"Don't blame Travis and Corey," Chester said. "Can't you see they're just as scared as you are?"

"Ouch!" Miss Duvall began slapping at her rear end as if she were being pinched. "Stop it, stop it right now, you imps of Satan!"

The shadows raced around the walls, laughing and taunting her with insults relating to the size of her rear end.

Ignoring Miss Duvall, Grandmother looked at Chester as if she wished she could send him to the principal's office. "I am not scared!" she said, but the tremor in her voice gave her away.

"Old granny scaredy cat!" An invisible hand tugged at grandmother's sweater. "Nyah, nyah, nyah!"

Grandmother whirled around to stare at Corey, still crying on her bed, and me, sitting beside her. It was obvious we couldn't have been responsible for the tug on her sweater.

"Who did that?" she yelled. "What sort of tricks are you playing?"

For an answer she got a series of rude noises and a loud outburst of giggles, along with more cuss words.

While this was going on, Chester was aiming his camera at the corner where most of the noise came from. "Wow! Oh, wow!"

"Amazing manifestation," Miss Duvall whispered into her microphone. "Laughter, voices, poltergeist activity. My hair is standing up . . . the air is electrifying!"

Suddenly, a cold wind shot into the room. The curtains blew out straight from the windows, and the clothing and torn pages rose from the floor and spun around like tiny tornadoes. A low moan, almost a sob, rose from the corner. The shadows twisted and turned, now long, now short, and raced around the walls as if they were being chased.

Then the lights went out, and a harsh voice cried, "Enough! Back to where you belong. You will be punished for this!"

The moaning changed to high-pitched squeaks and yelps. Invisible hands pushed me out of their way, invisible feet stepped on mine, elbows poked my sides. The moonlight streaming through the window dimmed as shadowy shapes fled into the night, followed by something bigger and darker and far more terrifying.

After a sudden silence, the lights came on again. Torn clothing and shredded paper fell back to the floor. The curtains drooped. Whatever had been among us was gone.

Chester and Miss Duvall huddled together, elated by the activities they'd witnessed, but Grandmother sank down on the bed beside Corey and closed her eyes. My sister continued to sob.

I went to the window. The grove was a patch of inky

shadows on the moonlit grass. *"Who are you?"* I whispered. *"What do you want? Why are you here?"*

Nothing answered. Nothing stirred. A blanket of darkness lay over the earth, hiding everything. Shivering, I crept closer to Grandmother.

8

M iss Duvall was the first to break the unnatural silence. "Surely, Mrs. Donovan," she said in a theatrically low voice, "you can no longer harbor even the slightest doubt that the inn is haunted."

Grandmother raised her head and stared at the psychic. "Frankly," she said, "I don't know what to think."

"How else would you explain what we have all witnessed in this room?" Miss Duvall asked.

Grandmother rose to her feet, a little unsteadily, but with her dignity intact. "If you and Mr. Coakley are somehow responsible for this, I will bring a lawsuit against you."

Miss Duvall drew herself up as tall as possible and gave Grandmother a look of utter dismay. "I assure you that neither Chester nor I—"

Grandmother swept past as if the woman was of no more importance than a toadstool. "Please go back to your rooms," she said, "and do not enter my quarters again. By checkout time tomorrow, I expect you both to be gone."

"But—" Chester began.

"Nothing you can do or say will change my mind," Grandmother said. "I want you both out of here."

Turning to Corey and me, she added, "As for you two, please go to bed at once. We'll talk about this in the morning. I am exhausted."

Still protesting, Chester and Miss Duvall followed

Grandmother out of the room. "Don't you understand what this means to paranormal research?" Chester said.

Grandmother shut the door, and we didn't hear her answer.

"Please don't leave me here by myself, Travis," Corey begged. "I'm scared to death they'll come back."

She tossed me a blanket and an extra pillow, and I tried to make myself comfortable on the floor. I didn't want to be alone any more than my sister did.

"I kind of wish Grandmother *would* send us home," Corey said. "I don't like it here anymore."

"Even camp doesn't seem so bad now," I said. "Swimming in a freezing lake at seven A.M., eating lumpy oatmeal and mystery meat and mushy lima beans, hiking ten miles uphill."

"Making potholders and clay animals, singing those dumb camp songs, striking out in softball. . . ." Corey's voice slowed and thickened and finally trailed off in a sleepy mumble.

I turned this way and that, but whether I lay on my side or my back or my stomach, I couldn't relax. Every sound frightened me—a rustle in the leaves, a sigh of wind, the tap, tap of a branch against the window, a creak in the hall outside the door.

At any moment I expected to hear giggles and feel the pinch of invisible fingers. Worse yet, what if the thing from the grove came howling through the window again?

Early in the morning, I left Corey sleeping and hobbled back to my room, as stiff as an old man from sleeping on the floor.

Pages from books littered the floor, my favorite sweatshirt was now sleeveless, my T-shirts were torn in half, shreds of my socks hung from the ceiling light. My chair lay on its back on top of my desk, which was now on my bed. The mirror over the bureau was cracked, and the bureau's drawers were on the lawn, their contents scattered on the grass.

"Wow, what a mess." Chester stood outside my window, staring into my room.

Before I knew what he was doing, he'd climbed over the sill. "Mind if I take some pictures? This should be documented."

"Help yourself," I said. "Maybe you'd like to clean it up when you're done."

Chester laughed as if I were joking and began shooting. "The socks are a nice touch," he said, aiming his camera at the ceiling light.

Corey appeared in my doorway and glared at Chester. "Why are you still here?"

"We've got until noon to check out." Chester moved to my bed and photographed the desk and the chair from several angles "This is amazing stuff! Poltergeist activity, laughter, pinching, cussing, cold spots—I'll be the envy of every paranormalist in the world!"

"What are you doing in here?"

Grandmother took Chester by surprise. Clasping his camera to his chest, he backed away. "The children invited me in," he lied. "They—"

"Well, I'm *dis*inviting you," Grandmother said. "Get out of my grandson's room!"

"Yes, ma'am. I was just leaving anyway." Chester left the way he'd come in.

Grandmother looked around. "Please explain what's going on," she said in a weary voice. "If you can, that is."

"You were in Corey's room last night," I said. "You saw what we saw, you heard what we heard. I wish we could explain it, but . . ." I shrugged, unable to think of anything else to say.

Grandmother removed the chair from the desk, set it on the floor, and, with a sigh, sat on it. Shutting her eyes, she took a deep breath. "That's right. I saw, and I heard. As a result, I lay awake for hours trying to think of an explanation. And failed. Utterly."

Rising to her feet, Grandmother said, "I suggest we have breakfast. After that, please clean up your room. When everything is back to normal, I'd like to pretend last night did not happen."

Turning my back on the wreckage, I followed Grandmother to the dining room. She could chase off the psychics, she could make me clean up my room, she could pretend last night hadn't happened—she could even send Corey and me back to New York—but the ghosts were here, and they weren't leaving.

Not until they got what they wanted . . . whatever that was.

9

After breakfast, most of the guests checked out in support of Chester and Miss Duvall. At least that's what they claimed. I had a feeling some of them had had their fill of ghosts and didn't want to spend another night at Fox Hill.

Grandmother watched them leave. "So much for ghosts bringing business to the inn," she said.

A few minutes later, the Kowalskis joined us on the porch.

"What on earth was going on last night?" Mrs. Kowalski asked. "Our TV and radio came on, as well as the lights."

"We heard a lot of commotion, too," Mr. Kowalski added. "People shouting and running up and down the steps. We came here for peace and quiet, not wild parties."

Grandmother sighed. "I apologize for the disturbance. It won't happen again. The guests who were responsible are leaving today"

"It was that strange man with the hearse, wasn't it?" Mrs. Kowalski asked.

"And his bizarre lady friend." Her husband shook his head. "Crazy as loons, the pair of them. Going on and on about ghosts. What a load of hooey."

Mrs. Kowalski ran a hand through her short gray hair.

"Those two should get some exercise and clear their minds. Yoga would help. So would an organic diet."

Rackets in hand, the Kowalskis headed for the tennis court, and Grandmother turned to Corey and me. "Time to get some exercise yourselves," she said. "Go clean your rooms."

It took us all morning to sort through the wreckage. It was clear we'd need new clothes. New books, too—the pages of our summer reading books were scattered everywhere. Corey's favorite teddy bear had been torn limb from limb and his stuffing strewn on the floor.

I left Corey weeping over the bear and went outside to retrieve my bureau drawers. While I was gathering what was left of my underwear, I saw Mr. Brewster watching me.

"Don't expect no pity from me." He spat in the grass and started to walk away.

"Wait." I hurried over and stepped in front of him. "Please tell me about the ghosts."

"Get out of my way, boy." He tried to step around me, but I blocked him, as though we were playing basketball.

"Mr. Brewster, I have to know what they want, so I can make them go away."

For the first time I heard him laugh—a sort of growl combined with a cough. "They been here afore you, and they'll be here after you."

"But what are they? *Who* are they?"

The man sighed and wiped his forehead with an old handkerchief. "It woulda been best if them Cornells had never seen this house. Never bought it. Never fixed it up." He seemed to be talking more to himself than to me. "Some places ought to go to ruin. Let the bricks fall and the grass grow over them. Let it all be forgot and the dead stay dead."

With that, he stepped around me and headed toward the inn.

I stood where I was, cold despite the sun's heat, and watched him walk away. Then I gathered up the bureau drawers and their ruined contents and carried them back to my room.

Just before noon, the service bell rang. Grandmother rose from her chair with a sigh, laid her book aside, and headed for the office. Corey and I followed her inside. Surrounded by their luggage and gear, Chester and Miss Duvall were waiting to settle their bill.

Ignoring the couple's greeting, Grandmother sat down at the computer and looked up their account. As the bill was printing, she frowned. "I would appreciate your saying nothing about last night's events," she said.

"Oh, I can't agree to that, ma'am," Chester said. "I've already e-mailed my associates with the details. And spoken to my editor at *Chronicles of the Dead*."

"This sort of story simply cannot be swept under the rug," Miss Duvall added. "The public has a right to know."

"If you mention the name of this inn in a book or a magazine article or anywhere else," Grandmother said, "you will hear from my lawyer."

"But that's censorship," Chester put in. "You can't—"

"I can—and I will." Grandmother handed him the bill.

"That will be three hundred and seventy-seven dollars and five cents, including tax."

Chester slapped his credit card down on the counter, and Grandmother ran it through the machine. "Thank you," she said and handed the card back.

"But think of the free publicity," Miss Duvall said.

"I am," Grandmother said.

With a shrug, Miss Duvall swept out of the inn behind Chester. We watched the ghost hunter get into his hearse and drive away, with the psychic close behind in her VW.

"I feel better already," Grandmother said.

At lunchtime, the nearly empty dining room was so quiet I could hear bees buzzing in the flower boxes at the windows. The Kowalskis had ordered a box lunch and were off hiking in the hills, toting binoculars, bird books, cameras, and plenty of sunscreen.

Tracy came to our table to refill our glasses. "I hear you had a lot of trouble last night." Her hand shook as she spoke, and she spilled a few drops of water.

Grandmother watched her daub at the puddle with a corner of her apron. "Oh, leave it," she said impatiently. "Water won't stain anything."

"Sorry." Tracy stepped back from the table. "I don't know what's wrong with me. I just feel so nervous all the time. Everything makes me jump." Her eyes roved the room, lingering in the corners.

"We're all a little edgy," Grandmother said. "But now that those so-called psychics are gone, I'm hoping things will return to normal. Two guests are checking in this afternoon, and another three tomorrow. They asked about bike trails and hiking paths, shopping, historic sights—that sort of thing. Not one of them mentioned an interest in ghosts."

Tracy didn't seem to be listening. "I keep seeing things out of the corner of my eye," she said in a low voice. "But when I look straight at them, they're gone."

"That's just your imagination working overtime," Grandmother said.

Twisting her apron, her face red, Tracy said, "I called my mother this morning and told her about all the weird stuff. She said maybe I should come home."

Grandmother stared at her. "Tracy, didn't you hear what I just said? We have five reservations. You can't quit. I need you."

"I didn't say I was quitting," Tracy whispered. "I just said my mother thinks I should come home."

"And what do *you* think?" Grandmother asked. "You're sixteen years old. Surely you have your own opinions."

"Yes, ma'am, of course I do." Tracy's eyes got watery, and her lower lip quivered. I wanted to leap up and defend her, perhaps throw my arms around her and protect her, but I just sat there like a nincompoop.

"Well?" Grandmother asked, her voice softening at the sight of a tear rolling down Tracy's cheek. "Will you stay and help me?"

Tracy wiped her eyes with her hands. "I'll stay," she said, ". . . as long as the ghosts don't come back."

If I hadn't felt so sorry for her, I would have reminded her of what she'd said before she did her Nancy Drew act in the grove—"I'm not afraid of anything."

"I don't expect any more manifestations," Grandmother said. "Not with that lunatic and her crazy companion out of the picture."

"Do you really think Mr. Coakley and Miss Duvall faked the whole thing?" Tracy asked.

"I don't know how they did it, but I'm sure they were responsible."

I glanced at Corey. She sat quietly, poking her salad this way and that in an effort to make it look as if she'd eaten some of it. She'd been so quiet all day I was beginning to worry about her.

"I hope you're right, Mrs. Donovan." Tracy's eyes returned to the corners of the room, as if she'd just glimpsed something moving in the shadows.

"A man who wears a ponytail and drives around in a hearse is simply not to be trusted." Grandmother ate the last of her sandwich and got to her feet. "Neither is a woman over twenty who polishes her nails black, pierces her nose and heaven knows what else, and claims to have psychic powers."

With that, she left the dining room, her faded denim skirt swinging.

Tracy sat down at our table and rested her chin on her hands. "If your grandmother didn't need me, I'd leave right now." She tried to pour herself a glass of water, but this time it slopped all over the table.

"Clumsy," someone whispered.

"What did you say?" Tracy turned to me.

"I didn't say anything."

"Clumsy, sloppy girl."

Tracy jumped up and whirled around, trying to see

who'd spoken. Her apron slid to the floor, its strings untied, and the same giggling we'd heard last night rippled around the room. Here and there, a cloth slithered off a table, forks, spoons, and knives rose into the air, and napkins whirled like eddies of leaves on a windy day. China plates and cups smashed against walls. Ketchup bottles spurted like ruptured arteries and splattered tables and carpets.

The three of us cowered together, our flesh pinched, our hair pulled, our faces slapped by invisible hands, until we screamed.

With a bellow of rage, Mrs. Brewster barreled into the room, her chest heaving. "Behave, bad ones, behave!" she screamed.

"It's not us," I yelled. "We didn't do anything!"

But it wasn't us Mrs. Brewster was looking at. Her eyes were focused on the swinging chandelier. "Stop it this minute!"

Behind her, a pitcher of water rose from a table, sailed through the air, and dumped itself on the old woman's head. The giggles changed into wild laughter. A cold draft swirled around us. Giving us a few last pinches, something swept out of the room.

Tracy ran to Mrs. Brewster and began drying her with a tablecloth. "Are you all right?"

Mrs. Brewster pushed Tracy aside and surveyed the dining room. "One of you fetch Mr. Brewster," she said. "Tell him it's worse than before."

As I ran out of the room to find Mr. Brewster, I bumped into Grandmother rushing into the room.

"No," she cried. "I don't believe this!"

"I want my mother," Tracy wailed.

Leaving them to settle things, I dashed out the back door and began searching for Mr. Brewster. I found him weeding the vegetable garden.

"Mrs. Brewster sent me to get you," I shouted. "She says it's worse than before!"

The old man dropped the hoe and came running. He didn't ask for an explanation. He knew.

"So they done all this," he said glumly, taking in the dining room. Overturned chairs, linens on the floor, puddles of water, broken china, ketchup on the walls, Tracy weeping, his wife rubbing her wet hair with a tablecloth.

Turning to Corey, Mr. Brewster added, "You and your pranks. I hope you're satisfied, miss."

Without looking at him, my sister ran out of the dining room. When I followed her, she tried to slam her door in my face, but I managed to push my way into her room.

"What's wrong with you?" I yelled. "Why won't you talk to me? Are you mad at me?"

"I'm scared," she whispered. "Just scared. That's all." She sank down on her bed and began to cry. "I want to go home."

I sat beside her and patted her shoulder. "Don't you think I'm scared, too?"

"Let's call Mom."

"No." My chest was so tight with fear I thought I was having a heart attack. "We started this, and we have to finish it."

Corey raised her head and looked at me with teary eyes. "But how do we do that?"

"They're ghosts," I said. "They must be here for a reason. Unfinished business or something."

"The Brewsters know more than they're saying," Corey muttered.

As she spoke, I glanced out the window and saw Mrs. Brewster walking slowly across the grass toward the barn. Her hair and dress were still wet from the pitcher of water. She looked tired. While I watched, she vanished behind the hedge.

"I wonder where she's going," I said.

Corey perked up. "Let's follow her."

We ran across the lawn and peeked through the hedge. Mrs. Brewster was standing in the weeds, staring down at the numbered stones. "It's too bad, that's what it is," she said softly. "You ought to be sleeping peaceful. All of you."

As she spoke, shadows stirred among the stones and whispered in the grass.

"That boy and girl are bad ones," she muttered, "full of pranks and mischief, just like you."

She cocked her head like a robin listening for a worm to turn in the earth. "No, it ain't punishment they need," she said. "No more than you needed it."

She cocked her head again, listening hard to the rustle in the weeds, and then looked up, straight at our hiding place. "Come out from there. Didn't nobody teach you manners?"

Corey and I stepped through a gap in the hedge. A cloud drifted across the sun and turned the day cold.

"Who were you talking to?" I whispered.

"Nobody." Mrs. Brewster frowned at Corey and me, her face grim.

"You were talking to *them*." Corey's voice shook. "They're here, I can feel them all around us, watching, listening."

Hoping to calm her, I took my sister's hand, but she snatched it away. "Tell us who they are," she cried. "Tell us what they want! Tell them we're sorry. Tell them—"

"'Sorry' can't change nothing," Mrs. Brewster interrupted. "It's got to run its course now."

"But can't you just tell us who they are?" I asked.

"I can't," Mrs. Brewster said, "but maybe *they* will." With that, she pushed past us and strode off toward the inn. Even her shadow looked angry.

For a moment, I thought Corey was going to run after her and keep begging for answers, but she stayed where she was, head down, staring at the numbered stones.

"Come on." I reached for her hand again. "Let's go back to the inn."

The cloud had moved past the sun, and the day was hot again, thick with humidity and buzzing, biting bugs.

Corey watched a butterfly drift from one stone to the next, pausing to fan its wings. "I never really believed in ghosts before," she said.

"Me, either."

As I spoke, a pebble hit my cheek, then another and another. Suddenly, the air was full of pebbles, striking Corey and me but too small to do more than sting. At the same moment, the giggling started. And the whispers.

Corey and I ran toward the hedge, pebbles flying after us, but before we reached it, a shadow detached itself from the deep shade and blocked our path. Corey covered her face with her hands, but I stared into the darkness so hard my eyes stung. Someone was there, but I couldn't see more than a vague shape.

"Who are you?" I whispered.

"Who are you?" it whispered back, coming a little closer.

"What do you want?"

"What do you want?"

"Stop copying me!"

"Stop copying me!" it yelled in a shaky voice just like mine. "Stop copying me, stop, stop."

Laughter erupted all around us. A hand pulled my hair so hard I saw strands floating away.

Corey cried out in pain and stumbled backward, holding her cheek, the skin red from a slap.

"You'd better be scared," someone whispered. "We're the bad ones, the lovely bad ones, the bad, bad, bad ones."

Corey and I ran, but we couldn't escape the laughter or the pinches, slaps, and yanks at our hair. It was like being chased by a swarm of stinging hornets. Only worse. When hornets sting you, you know what they are. You can see them.

Somewhere near the grove, our pursuers gave up and let us escape. But we kept running until we reached the inn and stumbled through the kitchen door.

Mrs. Brewster looked up from the chicken she was preparing and scowled. Before she could say a word, we rushed past her and headed for the library. Neither of us wanted another scolding.

10

We collapsed on a couch in the library, breathing hard and soaked with sweat, our skin dotted with red marks left by the pebbles. The afternoon sun slanted through the tall windows and lit the bookcases on the opposite wall. Dust motes floated in the columns of light. The air was quiet, undisturbed. The only sound was the drowsy hum of bees in the flower boxes.

In other words, everything felt normal. Ordinary. On the surface, at least.

Corey picked up an old *New Yorker*. She leafed through it, not even pausing to read the cartoons, then threw it aside.

As restless as my sister, I prowled around the room, studying the books on the shelves, wishing I could find something to read but knowing I was in no mood to sit quietly. Something was going to happen—I could sense it in the air like electricity before a thunderstorm.

Suddenly, a pamphlet slid off a shelf and fell to the floor at my feet. Corey gasped, but I picked it up and read the title—*The Strange History of Fox Hill, as Recorded by the Reverend William Plaistow*.

"*They* must have knocked it off the shelf," Corey whispered.

We looked around the room uneasily. The back of my neck prickled as if someone was watching me, but I heard no giggles or whispers and felt no slaps or pinches.

"They want us to read it," Corey said.

Cautiously, I opened the pamphlet. With Corey pressed close to my side, I began reading out loud.

"This treatise is dedicated to those who suffered at Fox Hill Poor Farm, especially, if I may borrow a few lines from John Greenleaf Whittier, the children:

> *The happy ones; and sad ones;*
> *The sober and the silent ones; the boisterous and glad ones;*
> *The good ones—Yes, the good ones, too;*
> *and all the lovely bad ones."*

"Poor farm?" Corey stared at me. "What's that?"

"It's where they used to send people who didn't have anywhere else to go."

"Like the workhouse in *Oliver Twist*?"

"Yes." I turned the page and went on reading.

"Built in 1778, Fox Hill Farm was originally the home of Jedediah Cooper. Unfortunately, Jedidiah's great-grandson, Charles Cooper, amassed enormous gambling debts, which made it impossible for him to pay his property taxes. After repeated warnings, the county seized the farm in 1819 and attempted to sell it at public auction. When no buyer stepped forth, the county put the property to use as a poor farm in 1821.

"Mr. Cornelius Jaggs was appointed overseer of the poor. He chose his sister, Miss Ada Jaggs, to supervise the children. These two ran Fox Hill for the next twenty years. Apparently, their harsh, perhaps even cruel, treat-

ment of the helpless people in their care eventually caused an outcry from the local populace. After a public hearing in 1841, the two were dismissed from their positions, and the poor farm was shut down.

"Cornelius Jaggs left the area at once and vanished into the fog of history. Deserted by her brother, Ada Jaggs hanged herself in a grove of trees not far from the house."

Corey and I looked outside at the grove. Even though there was no breeze, the leaves of the tallest tree stirred and its branches swayed. A bunch of crows rose into the air, cawing, and flew away as if something had disturbed them.

The page turned all by itself. A cloud drifted across the sun, and the dim light made it hard to read the faded print.

"Ada Jaggs is buried at Fox Hill, along with many poor souls who suffered and died on the farm.

"Among her dead companions are at least a dozen boys whom she singled out for her most severe punishments. Guilty of no more than normal high spirits, these boys, my lovely bad ones, had their lives cut short by a cruel and wicked woman."

The whisper I'd been expecting now ran around the walls. "Bad, bad, bad. *She* was the bad one. Bad beyond telling, bad beyond belief."

The whisper died away, but no one giggled. No one pinched or kicked or slapped. Sorrow filled the room. It pressed down on us, heavy and dark and so full of pain we could hardly breathe.

A cold hand touched my face. "Don't be afraid."

With Corey pressed against my side, I focused on the shadow standing in front of me. Slowly, a boy took shape, maybe ten or eleven years old, his face pale and freckled, his clothes ragged. He stood as straight and tall as he could and stared into my eyes.

"I'm Caleb," he said. "That's Ira, and Seth."

Two boys stepped out of the shadows. Ira was about the same age as Caleb, dark and melancholy. Seth was the littlest of the three, with a tangled head of red curls and two missing front teeth. I guessed he was about seven.

"There's more of us," Caleb said. "But we've been chosen to do the talking."

"I'm sorry we scared you," Ira said, "but—"

"I ain't sorry," Seth said. "We're the bad ones! We got to live up to our name."

Giggles ran along the shadowy walls like a stream running over pebbles, chuckling to itself. "Bad ones, bad ones, bad, bad, bad."

Speechless, Corey and I huddled together like scared sheep and stared at the boys—the ghosts, that is. The bad ones.

And they stared at us. Seth made a sudden lunge as if he meant to pinch us, and we scooted backward. The giggles got louder.

"What do you want?" Corey whispered.

"You woke Miss Ada up with your tomfoolery," Caleb said. "And she woke us up. Now you have to put us back to sleep."

"And her, too," Seth put in.

"So we can rest easy," Ira said. "Without her coming after us, over and over and over. Didn't she cause us enough grief when we were alive?"

"But—but how can we?" I stuttered and stammered, unable to say anything that made sense. "I mean, what can we do, we're just kids. We aren't—"

"I told you it wouldn't do any good to talk to them," Ira muttered to Caleb. "The living know nothing."

A whisper of mutterings swept around the room, from shadow to shadow. "Stupid, stupid, stupid," someone chanted. "Don't know nothing—either one of you."

"Pinchy, pinchy, pinchy," someone whispered, plucking at my skin.

"Ouch, that hurts!" I shouted, trying to evade the invisible fingers.

"Stop it!" Corey flailed her arms as if she was trying to hit the shadows romping around us.

"Boys, boys," Caleb called. "Leave them be. They can't help being ninnies."

The voices whispered to themselves, but they withdrew to the corners of the room and sulked there.

"Pay the shadow children no mind," Ira said. "They don't mean any harm."

"Now," Caleb said to us, "you read about Miss Ada. I reckon you know she's in the grove."

Seth giggled. "You might say that's where she hangs out."

Caleb and Ira whirled to face Seth. "Hush your foolish mouth!" Caleb yelled. "Don't make mockery of her."

"Do you want her barging in here and hurting us again?" Ira asked.

Seth's mouth turned down, and he looked at the floor. "She don't come out till dark," he whispered. "She can't hear what we say in the daytime." He raised his head and looked at the older boys. "Can she?"

"She always had a wicked sharp ear," Ira said. "No telling what she can hear and when and where."

Caleb nodded. "So it's best not to go making jokes about her way of dying."

"She blames us for it," Ira said.

"She blames *you* for what *she* did to herself?" Corey asked.

"She's the blameful sort," Caleb said. "All that she did to us was our fault."

"We made her do it," Ira said.

"If we'd been good children, she'd have fed us cookies and milk," Seth said, "and put us to bed under blankets soft as clouds and warm as cats."

"But we was bad, baaaaaad, baaaaaad," the shadow children whispered.

"And so she punished us," Ira said. "For our own good."

"Even though it pained her most horribly to hurt us," Caleb added in a voice as sweet as the sweetest lie ever told.

"She loved the stick she beat us with," Ira muttered. "And that's the truth of it."

"She beat us for *her* good," Caleb agreed. "Not ours."

"Baaaaad, baaaaad," the shadow children hissed. "*She* was baaaaad."

"Badder than us," Seth said, "badder than the devil hisself."

Grandmother appeared in the doorway. "Corey and Travis, I've been looking all over for you. It's time for dinner."

It was clear she didn't see the bad ones. Caleb shrugged and grinned. "Like most folks, your grandma only sees what we *do*. She don't see *us*."

"Watch this." Without even taking a step, Seth was standing in front of Grandmother, waving and grinning at her. "Hi, there, Granny!"

Grandmother shivered. "It feels cold all of a sudden. Is the window open?"

Caleb frowned, but Seth giggled and kicked Grandmother's shin lightly—just a tap, really.

Puzzled, Grandmother stared around the room. "I could swear someone just kicked me, but—"

In a second, Seth was at the reading table. Grabbing a couple of magazines, he tossed them at Grandmother. They zoomed past her head and fluttered to the floor behind her.

"What in the world?" As Grandmother whirled to look at the magazines, Ira grabbed Seth's right arm and Caleb grabbed his left arm. All three vanished. A draft of cold air followed them past Grandmother and out the door.

"Did you see that?" Grandmother asked. "The wind blew those magazines right off the table." Her voice shook, but she crossed the room briskly and began closing the windows. "It must be the cold front the weatherman predicted."

As she shut the last window, the dark clouds I'd noticed earlier burst, and the wind drove sheets of rain against the glass.

"Looks like we're in for a bad storm." Grandmother led the way toward the dining room, thunder crashing and lightning flashing. "I hope we don't lose the power."

While we waited for our meal, I asked Grandmother if she knew the inn had once been the county poor farm.

"Poor farm?" She looked at me in amazement. "Whatever gave you that idea?"

I laid the pamphlet on the table. "I found this in the library."

She picked it up and read the title out loud. "My goodness, I went through all the books in the library when I bought Fox Hill, but I swear I never saw this."

Mrs. Brewster chose that moment to arrive with our dinner. "Where did you get that pamphlet?" she asked.

"Travis came across it in the library." Grandmother opened the pamphlet, her face puzzled. "Oh, what a pity. Most of the pages have fallen out."

Mrs. Brewster turned her sharp old eyes on me. "You just found it on the shelf, did you?"

"Well, actually, it sort of fell on the floor, and I picked it up," I muttered.

She set my plate in front of me. "They're telling you what they want you to know," she whispered. "Better pay heed."

Grandmother looked at Mrs. Brewster. "What was that?"

"Nothing. Just telling Travis he'd better eat that chicken before it gets cold. It's best ate warm."

With that, she set the rest of the plates down and crossed the room to take the Kowalskis' order.

"Where's Tracy?" Corey asked.

"Her mother came for her this afternoon," Grandmother said. "She promised she'd come back next week to help with a busload of senior citizens arriving on Monday. They'll be here three nights—twelve people. If she doesn't show up, I'll have to put you and Travis to work waiting tables and cleaning rooms."

Grandmother took a bite of chicken and glanced out the window at the dark clouds and flashing lightning. "I just don't understand how a sensible girl like Tracy can be so silly."

I heard a creaking sound and looked up. In the center of the ceiling, Caleb perched on the chandelier. Every now and then, he twirled it around, as if it were a swing. So far, no one but me had noticed the noise.

Ira opened and shut the door to the kitchen, making it appear as if the wind was doing it. Grandmother looked annoyed. "Henry will have to do something about that door," she said.

On the other side of the dining room, Seth stole Mrs. Kowalski's napkin. She asked Mrs. Brewster for another. He took that one, too. And the one after that.

"I've brought you three napkins," Mrs. Brewster snapped. "What are you doing with them?" She sounded as if she was accusing Mrs. Kowalski of stealing them.

Mrs. Kowalski looked offended. "I put them on my lap," she said, "but they keep disappearing. It's *very* peculiar."

Mrs. Brewster glanced around the room. To my amazement, she looked right at the chandelier where Seth now perched with Caleb. She frowned and shook her head at him. He stuck out his tongue and laughed.

"Stop it right now," she said crossly.

Corey kicked me under the table. "Mrs. Brewster *sees* them," she whispered. "She sees them!"

I nodded, too flabbergasted to speak.

In the meantime, Mrs. Kowalski was scowling at Mrs. Brewster. "Stop doing what?" she asked. "I told you I'm not doing anything with the napkins! They just keep—"

Mrs. Brewster tossed a napkin on the table and headed for the kitchen, her broad back stiff.

"That woman has no right to speak to me like that," Mrs. Kowalski told her husband. "*I* don't know where the napkins went."

Twittering to themselves, the shadow children gathered around the two new guests, Miss Baynes and Miss Edwards, who had checked in that afternoon. Unaware they were being watched, the old women sipped their iced tea and talked in low voices. Their hair was beauty-shop perfect, and their clothes were without creases or wrinkles.

Suddenly, the casement windows blew open, the chandelier spun round and round, and the kitchen door banged like a series of pistol shots. Thanks to Ira, Mr. Kowalski's coffee spilled, and Seth dropped a mouse on the old ladies' table. They screamed as it darted to the edge, ran down the tablecloth, and scurried across the floor.

It all happened so fast no one knew what to do first. Grandmother leapt up to close the windows. Mrs. Brewster came rushing out of the kitchen to mop up the coffee and bring Mr. Kowalski a fresh cup.

The old ladies were acting like comic-strip women,

screeching and turning this way and that in case the mouse made another foray.

"I've never seen a mouse in the dining room," Grandmother said, all aflutter with embarrassment.

"I'll make sure you don't never see another one," Mrs. Brewster muttered with a scowl at the chandelier where Caleb, Ira, and Seth sat grinning at her. "'Tain't funny, 'tain't funny a'tall."

"The health department would fail to see any humor in a mouse infestation," Miss Baynes agreed in a voice as frosty as her hair.

While Grandmother's attention was focused on Miss Baynes and Miss Edwards, Corey and I made a quick retreat to the lounge to watch television. We had no idea what the bad ones would do next, but we didn't want Grandmother to blame us for it.

11

Wielding the TV remote, I clicked through horror movies, nature shows, sitcom reruns, and dozens of commercials until I found a dumb comedy on HBO. We'd seen it before, but it was just the thing to take our minds off the ghosts. And to delay going to bed.

Just as we were getting interested in the movie, the scene suddenly changed. One minute, a bunch of rowdy teenagers were laughing it up at a party; the next minute, a pair of horses was pulling an old farm wagon along a muddy road in the country. It was almost dark. Rain poured down. The trees were bare. Mountains loomed against the sky, their tops hidden in clouds. There wasn't a house or a barn in sight. No livestock. No people. Just woods and fields and mud.

"Did you switch channels?" Corey grabbed the remote from me and clicked the number for HBO, but the scene didn't change. She tried TMC, MTV, CNN, ABC, PBS, even HTV. The horse and wagon was on every channel.

"Something must be wrong with the satellite dish," I said. "Maybe the wind or—"

I took the remote back and turned the TV off, but the movie stayed on. The driver hunched over the reins, soaked through. Behind him, a family huddled in the open wagon, heads down, wet, cold, miserable. The camera zoomed in on a sign clumsily lettered "County Poor Farm."

"Oh, my gosh!" Corey grabbed my arm. "It's Fox Hill!"

The camera shifted to the inn's front porch. A short, plump man stood there, watching the wagon approach. His face was round, but there was nothing jolly about his expression.

Beside him was a woman. Her face was pale and hard, her eyes small and close set under straight dark brows. She wore a long black dress, buttoned to her chin. She, too, stared at the wagon.

The man pulled out a pocket watch. "It's John Avery with the Perkins family, right on schedule." His voice was nasal, harsh, and unpleasant. "Four of 'em. Man and wife, baby girl, boy."

The woman frowned. "More shiftless folks for us to feed and shelter," she said with a sniff.

"I hear the boy's ill mannered," the man said. "No respect for his betters. Ungrateful. Surly. A bad one."

The woman's thin lips twitched up at the corners. "Once he's in my care, he'll change his ways."

The man glanced at her with approval. "You have never failed to break the spirit of the most rebellious child."

The wagon pulled up beside the porch. "All right, you lot," the driver said. "Ride's over."

Hauling their rain-soaked belongings in a couple of small sacks, the Perkins family climbed out of the wagon. The woman looked weak and frail, and the baby clung to her, its tiny hands gripping its mother's shawl.

The man helped his wife to the muddy ground, but he was almost as sickly as she was.

The camera zoomed in on the boy, showing every feature clearly—freckles, chipped front tooth, shaggy blond hair.

"Caleb," I whispered. "It's Caleb."

The short, plump man peered at Mr. Perkins. "You fit to work?"

"Yes, sir, Mr. Jaggs." A deep, hard-edged cough interrupted Mr. Perkins's answer. Somehow he controlled it and went on. "I'm fit. I'd still be working my own land if—"

"No excuses," Mr. Jaggs snapped. "I've heard so many pitiful stories it's a wonder I can sleep at night."

The family stood in a crooked row, soaked by the rain, all heads down save Caleb's.

Miss Ada turned to him. "You, boy," she said. "I don't care for the look in your eye."

Caleb shrugged. "There's much in this world I myself don't care for, ma'am. This place, to name one."

"How dare you speak to me with such insolence." Miss Ada struck Caleb across the face with her open hand.

He flinched, but I swear his eyes dared her to strike him again.

Mrs. Perkins gasped and stepped forward as if to shield Caleb. "I told you to mind your tongue, son."

Mr. Jaggs signaled to a burly man lurking near the steps. "Joseph, take the boy away."

"No," Mrs. Perkins said. "He's just a child, he didn't mean to be impudent."

Joseph ignored the woman. Grabbing Caleb's arm, he dragged him away.

At the same time, Mr. Jaggs summoned an old woman from the house. Gesturing to Caleb's mother, he said, "Show Mrs. Perkins to the women's quarters, Sadie. I'll see to Mr. Perkins."

"Please," Mrs. Perkins said, "let me stay with my husband."

Miss Ada raised an eyebrow and turned to Mr. Jaggs. "Mrs. Perkins must think she's a guest at a grand hotel. Perhaps she'd like a nice soft bed and a warm fire."

The old woman tugged at Mrs. Perkins's arm. "'Tis best you do as they say," she whispered. "The men's quarters are separate from the women's. You won't see much of your husband whilst you're here."

Pressing the baby close to her heart, Mrs. Perkins allowed the old woman to lead her away.

Head hanging, Mr. Perkins trudged off behind Mr. Jaggs. Even after he was out of sight, we heard him coughing.

The camera shifted to Joseph and Caleb. The man dragged the boy into a building behind the inn—the carriage house, I thought—and took him down a steep flight of stairs into a dark basement. Opening a heavy wooden door, he thrust Caleb into a small cell.

"Mebbe the rats will teach you to keep a civil tongue in your head." With that, he slammed the door shut and locked Caleb into a room that was smaller than a closet, maybe three feet by three feet. No way to lie down unless you curled yourself into a ball. Dirt floor. No window. No light. No heat. Not even a blanket.

Caleb hurled himself against the door and beat on it with his fists. He yelled, shouted, kicked. Exhausted, he finally gave up and sank down on his haunches.

The camera moved away from Caleb, out of the cell, out of the building, farther and farther until it seemed to be high in the sky looking down on Fox Hill and the farmland rolling away to the mountains. The scene slowly dimmed, and the screen went dark.

Alone in the silent room, Corey and I stared at the TV as if we were waiting for part two to begin. When nothing happened, Corey turned to me. "How did they do that?"

She meant the bad ones, of course. I shook my head. Too much had happened too fast for me to understand any of it.

While we sat there puzzled and scared, we heard Grandmother's footsteps in the hall. "What are you two doing, sitting in the dark?" she asked. "Is the TV broken?"

I got to my feet, aching with exhaustion. "We were just going to bed."

"Good," Grandmother said. "I was coming to tell you to do just that."

Corey yawned and followed me out of the guest lounge. At her bedroom door, she paused to whisper, "I don't want to see any more about the poor farm."

Then, without another word, she closed her door and left me in the dark hall.

I'd seen enough myself, but I had a feeling there was more, and, like it or not, we were going to watch it.

12

I hadn't been asleep long when I woke up freezing cold. Seth had yanked my covers off. He perched at the foot of my bed, laughing. Caleb bounced a ball against the wall over my head, and Ira rocked back and forth in the rocking chair.

"What?" I mumbled, still half asleep.

Seth giggled. "We ain't done with you yet."

I pulled the blankets toward me, as if it was the most natural thing in the world to deal with mischievous ghosts.

"Travis is cold," Ira observed.

"Cold—I scarcely 'member what that's like," Seth said.

"Being dead has its advantages." Caleb jumped to his feet and raised an arm in a theatrical gesture. "'Fear no more the heat o' the sun,'" he proclaimed. "'Nor the furious winter's rages.'"

"'Thou thy worldly task hast done,'" Ira added. "'Home art gone, and ta'en thy wages.'"

"Shakespeare," Caleb said. "We had to memorize it in school, back before we came here."

"Little did we know then," Ira said, his face suddenly sad, "how soon we'd 'come to dust.'"

"But we ain't cold and we ain't hot and we ain't hungry," Seth reminded them. "We done been put out of our misery, boys."

Caleb yanked my covers off again. "There's still much for you to learn."

Pulling a sweatshirt over my pajamas, I followed the bad ones to the door.

My sister stood in the hall with the shadow children. "They woke me up, too," she said glumly.

The TV was already on in the lounge. On the screen, a deep snow covered the ground, and a fierce wind roared in the trees. The camera led us to a brick building, gone now. Inside, the ceilings were low, the rooms small and cold and dark. The only heat rose through floor vents from a stove on the first floor. Wrapped in a thin blanket, Caleb's mother huddled on a narrow cot. She held the baby to her breast, rocking it gently. Two women sat nearby, as if trying to share the warmth of their bodies with her.

"She's dead," one woman whispered. "Let her go, there's naught more you can do."

"Poor little baby," the other whispered. "It's a cruel world, a wicked world with no mercy."

Caleb's mother didn't answer, nor did she give up the baby.

"Please, Sarah," the first woman begged. "Lay her aside. We'll see she has a proper burial."

"The good Lord has taken her," the second said, "to spare her suffering."

At last, Caleb's mother let the women have the baby. "He should have taken me," she whispered, "not her."

"He'll take us all soon enough," the first woman said.

The scene slowly faded, and a new image appeared. The men's quarters this time, as cold and bleak as the women's. Two men stood over a bed where a dead man lay. Caleb's father. Without a word, they moved the body to a board and covered it with a cloth. Picking it up, they carried it down the stairs and to the barn. The morning was gray, and the ground was muddy. The maples had begun to bud, and a blackbird sang a few notes.

"First his little daughter, then his wife," one man said. "All he had left was the boy."

The other man coughed. "And him none too well from the looks of him."

"No worse'n the rest of us."

Mr. Jaggs appeared at the barn door, and the man who had just spoken spat into the mud. "Should be *him* we're burying."

"And her, too," the other said as Miss Ada joined Mr. Jaggs.

Again the picture faded.

Corey and I looked at Caleb. "Your whole family died here?" I asked.

"And me, as well," he said.

"All of us." Seth waved his hand at Ira and the shadow children watching us from the corners.

"And many more," Ira added.

Images appeared on the TV, silent this time. Gaunt, ragged people lined up for watery soup and hard bread. They worked outside in pouring rain and wind, in the cold of winter and the heat of summer. They shivered in dark, cold rooms. They went coatless and barefoot in the snow. They coughed and wheezed and sickened and died.

And all the while, Mr. Jaggs and Miss Ada passed their days in warmth and comfort and dined on fine food. They ordered beatings and whippings for the farm inhabitants and then slept soundly under feather quilts. They went to church in Sunday finery. They entertained guests. They complained of the detestable poor in their care and the county money wasted upon them.

"Truth to tell," Ira said, "the county's money went to them, not us. They ate beef, and we ate gruel."

A new picture appeared on the TV. Miss Ada sat at a desk, writing in an account book.

"That's the one she showed the county inspector," Caleb told us. "It was all lies."

The camera shifted to Miss Ada's bedroom. She was writing in another account book. When she finished, she put the book in a metal box and locked it.

"That's the true account book," Caleb explained, "for her and Mr. Jaggs, so they'd know how much money they'd hidden away."

"They also wrote the names of those who died and what they died of," Ira added.

"Even the ones they said ran away," Caleb said. "All the names of the dead are in that book."

As he spoke, a new picture formed on the TV screen. Miss Ada was beating Caleb's back with a cane. His shirt was off, and you could count his ribs.

"I'll teach you to steal food!" she yelled as she brought the cane down again and again.

When Caleb's back was bleeding, she thrust him aside and grabbed Ira. "Thief! Liar!" she cried as she beat him.

Last of all, she turned her attention to Seth. "With whom did you share the cheese?" she asked softly. "Tell me, and save yourself a beating."

Seth stared up at the woman, his small face clenched with hatred. "I didn't share it with nobody. I et it all myself."

Miss Ada caressed the cane with her long, slender fingers. "Those children knew the cheese was stolen from my pantry. They must be punished, too."

"I ain't telling you nothing," Seth said.

"Maybe this will change your mind." Miss Ada brought the cane down across his back with a loud *whack*. She paused and looked at him. "Well?"

"You can beat me till you bust your cane," Seth said, wincing from the blow. "I won't tell you nothing."

In horror, Corey and I watched her take the cane to Seth again. When she was through, she called Joseph. "Take these boys outside and leave them there till morning. I want the name of every child who ate that cheese. Perhaps a night in the cold will loosen their lips."

Joseph grabbed the boys as if they were no more than unwanted kittens and dragged them outside. Without a word, he turned and went back into the house. The door slammed. The bolt slid home.

The boys huddled together on the snowy ground, barefoot and coatless. The wind roared in the trees, and icicles shone in the moon's cold light. Slowly, the picture dimmed.

"In the morning, we knew something had changed," Caleb said. "We weren't cold. And we weren't hungry."

"And our backs didn't hurt none from the beating," Seth put in.

"That was almost the strangest part of all," Ira said.

"So we just lay in the snow," Caleb said, "thinking all three of us must be dreaming the same dream."

"Then the back door opened," Ira said, "and Mr. Jaggs

saw us lying on the ground. 'Get up, boys,' he hollered, 'I'm not finished with you!'"

"We rose up to face him," Caleb said, "but our bodies stayed on the ground. That puzzled us greatly."

"We grabbed each other's hands because we felt too light to stay on earth," Ira added. "I reckon that's when we figured out what had happened to us."

Caleb nodded. "The trouble was, we weren't ready to be dead."

Seth sighed. "It weren't fair."

On the screen, Mr. Jaggs strode angrily across the frozen ground toward the boys' huddled bodies. "Get up!" he yelled.

When no one moved, he nudged Seth with his boot. The boy's body rolled over. His sightless eyes stared up at Mr. Jaggs.

The man recoiled. "Dead." He stared at Ira and Seth. "All three."

Frightened, he retreated to the steps and opened the door. "Joseph," he called in a high voice. "Ada. Come quickly."

"What is it?" Miss Ada called from inside. "I've scarcely touched my breakfast."

Joseph appeared in the doorway, looked at the boys, and called to Miss Ada. "Come quickly, Miss."

Holding a dainty teacup, Miss Ada peered over her brother's shoulder. "What's the matter with them?" she asked crossly. "Why don't they get up?"

"Good Lord, Ada, can't you see?" Mr. Jaggs stared at her, his voice shaking. "They're dead."

Miss Ada choked on her tea. "Dead? How can they be dead?"

Joseph stared down at the boys. "It was cold last night, miss, below freezing."

"How do we explain their deaths?" Mr. Jaggs asked.

Miss Ada gripped her teacup, her face pale. "Why, we say what we always say when there's a mishap," she stammered. "They died of fever. Or they ran away."

"But the county inspector is visiting this afternoon," Mr. Jaggs said. "He'll see the bodies. He'll know they froze to death."

Miss Ada seemed to recover her wits. "For heaven's sake, Cornelius. We'll bury them before he arrives and report them as runaways."

"We done similar many times afore," Joseph put in.

"But not on the inspector's visiting day." Mr. Jaggs looked uneasily at the men and women's quarters. "They'll be coming out any moment. They mustn't see the bodies."

The picture dimmed, and a new one slowly formed. Wrapped in sacks, three bodies lay on the ground, screened from the house by a tall, shaggy row of bushes. Near them, Joseph struggled to dig three graves in the cold earth. Neither Mr. Jaggs nor Miss Ada was there to help. The only sound was the thunk of the pickax and the rustle of the wind in the bushes. A bunch of crows streamed past, cawing as they flew. Far away, a dog barked.

Gradually, Corey and I made out the ghostly shapes of the boys standing in the hedge's shadow. They watched Joseph and murmured among themselves.

Every now and then, the man raised his head and looked around, as if he expected to see someone. The boys were invisible to him, but he seemed to sense they were there. He dug faster, cursing to himself, perspiring despite the cold wind.

When the graves were ready, he dumped each boy into the earth and began shoveling dirt on top of their bodies. From a nearby tree, the crows cawed to each other, taking in the scene with their beady eyes.

Joseph shook his fist at the birds and swore loudly. "Get away from here!"

The crows stayed where they were, cawing and hopping from branch to branch as if they were mocking him.

Joseph flattened the earth over the graves. The sound echoed from the barn and the crows cawed louder. When he was done, he marked each grave with a small white stone. As he trudged away, his work done, the camera zoomed in on the stones: 27, 28, and 29. No name, no date—just a number. Slowly, the camera moved back and panned the scene. The stones stood in a row with many others, each marked with a number.

The nameless dead of Fox Hill County Poor Farm lay buried in the very place that had puzzled Corey and me a few days ago.

From the hedge's shadow, the boys crept toward the graves and stared down at them, their faces as sorrowful as mourners at a loved one's burial.

Once more the picture dimmed and faded to black.

13

I ra looked down at us from the top of the bookcase. "Now you know how we came to be what we are," he said.

"The lovely bad ones," Caleb added with a sad smile.

"That's us," Seth boasted.

And the shadow children echoed, "Bad ones, bad ones, lovely bad ones. Lovely, lovely, lovely!"

Caleb wedged himself between Corey and me on the sofa. "We tormented those three from the day we died till the county came snooping around, asking questions they couldn't answer."

"Joseph was the first to skedaddle," Ira said. "We'd just about run him ragged with tricks and pranks. Soon as he heard rumors there'd be an inquiry, he took off."

"Mr. Jaggs was close behind, hugging the money box to his belly." Caleb laughed. "I wish I could've seen his face when he opened it and found nothing inside but old newspapers and stones."

All three laughed. "That were one of our best pranks," Seth said.

"A true gentleman," Ira said. "He left his own sister in the lurch."

Seth sighed. "Then she went and hanged herself and ruined all our fun by becoming a ghost herself."

Ira looked uneasily toward the dark windows. "Better not say more."

"Do you think she heard?" Seth asked in a low voice.

By now, Corey and I were shivering with fear. What we'd seen on the TV screen had been bad enough, but the idea of Miss Ada outside in the dark was even worse. It was all too easy to picture her stalking toward the inn on soundless feet, her face grim, the cane in her hands.

"Can she still hurt you?" Corey whispered.

"Yes, but it's different from before," Caleb said. "In the old days, she beat us and spoke cruelly and starved us and worked us hard."

He hesitated as if he were looking for the right words. When he went on, his voice was so low we had to lean closer to hear him.

"Now all she has to do is *look* at us," he whispered. "There's a darkness in her eyes that brings back all the hurt of being alive. We feel the grief we felt then, the hunger, the thirst, the cold. Every bad thing that happened to us happens over and over. Our folks die. Our little sisters and brothers die. We die."

"And she laughs," Ira hissed in anger.

"When she comes, there's no one to help us," Seth said. "And no place to hide, except in the cold, dark ground."

Neither Corey nor I knew what to say. We just sat there, taking in the awfulness of what we'd heard. The boys watched us. The wind blew harder and the rain pattered like tiny footsteps on the driveway.

"When we go down into the earth," Caleb said at last, "we sleep the way cats do, ready to wake at the least sound."

"If it hadn't been for you," Ira muttered, "we'd be sleeping right now—and so would she."

Seth yawned. "Sometimes it's fun to wake up, but

truth to tell, it wearies me. I wish I could close my eyes and never open them to this world again."

Ira went to the window and peered out. "Watching for her is the worst part. She could be anywhere, you know."

"Not *any*where," Caleb said. "She can't leave this place any more than we can."

Suddenly, the shadow children began to move, flitting this way and that, a child's profile here, the outline of a hand there. Their whispering grew louder. "Run and hide, run and hide."

As Caleb, Seth, and Ira faded into the darkness with the others, a cold wind blew through the window.

"There is no escape for you," a voice cried. "There is no peace!"

The shadow children twisted and turned. They rushed from one corner to another, but they couldn't reach the window or the door. She was already ahead of them, blocking their way out.

Corey leapt to her feet. "Stop," she cried. "Leave them alone!"

A tall shape spun toward us, and we saw Miss Ada's white face, skin stretched tight over her skull, eyes sunk in blackness, hair tangled and coarse. The smell of earth clung to her. She wore the rags of a long dress, but her feet were bare.

"You made a mockery of me," she hissed. "You are as bad as they are. Just wait, you wicked, disrespectful children— you will be punished."

Miss Ada turned back to the shadow children. But they had drifted out the window like smoke, leaving only the echo of laughter behind.

"I'll see to you later!" she shrieked at us and vanished as suddenly as she'd appeared.

Stunned, Corey and I ran to the window, but all we saw was the dark night and the falling rain. Lightning flickered and briefly lit the lawn. The grove crouched silent and still, hiding its secrets.

Long after I went to bed, I lay awake. Miss Ada's face seemed to hang in the dark over me. Her voice rang in my ears.

"I'll see to you later, I'll see to you later, I'll see to you later, later, later, later. . . ."

It was almost light by the time I finally shut off her voice and fell asleep.

Corey hadn't slept any better than I had. We sat at the breakfast table and picked listlessly at our food. Lulled by the monotonous sound of the rain tapping on the windows, we were barely able to keep our eyes open.

Grandmother peered at us. "What's the matter with you two? You look like you didn't sleep a wink last night."

"It's the weather," I mumbled. "This kind of rain makes me feel like staying in bed all day."

Corey yawned so widely I could see her tonsils. "When is it supposed to stop?"

"Sometime this afternoon, the paper says." Grandmother sipped her coffee. "How about a trip to Burlington? We could go shopping to replace the clothes that—" She broke off, her face troubled. "The clothes that were, um, somehow ruined the night those people . . ." Her voice trailed off without finishing the sentence.

It wasn't a night Grandmother liked thinking about. There had been too much she didn't understand, couldn't explain. Too much that didn't fit into her rational view of the world.

Corey and I wasted no time getting ready to go. We needed a break from the inn—and the bad ones—for at least a few hours.

Grandmother had some errands to do on Church Street, so she turned us loose in the Marketplace. "I'll meet you back here in an hour," she said. "We'll have lunch and then shop."

Marketplace was a pedestrian area, kind of like an open-air mall, with plenty of shops, including Gap and a bunch of other big-name stores as well as little-name stores, craft places, and tourist traps. There were fountains and benches and sculptures and lots of open-air eating places deserted because of the rain.

The weather drove us in and out of stores where stuff was too expensive or we already had it or we didn't like it.

We ended up in the Dusty Jacket, a secondhand bookstore, mainly because we'd noticed a huge orange tabby sleeping in the window. Corey wanted to make sure he was real.

"Indeed, he is real." The man behind the counter had a bushy gray beard and thick gray hair. Perched on the end of his nose was a pair of old-fashioned glasses with gold rims. He wore a plaid shirt tucked into faded corduroy trousers. For some reason, I liked him right away.

"A watch cat," he added, "that's what Mog is. He guards the place at night."

Corey poked her head around a display of books to get a better look at Mog. The cat opened one eye a slit, twitched an ear in Corey's direction, and went back to sleep.

"Resting up for his nocturnal rounds," the man said.

"Does he really chase burglars away?" Corey asked.

He laughed. "Well, I've never been burgled, so I reckon he does."

"I bet it's mice he chases," Corey said. "Not burglars."

"Oh, yes, he chases a fair number of mice. Catches them, too. And then lines them up in a row on the counter for me to admire."

While Corey and the man talked, I prowled around the store. Like most used-book stores, there didn't seem to be much order. No Dewey decimal system, for example. Just piles of nice old books with yellowing pages, going soft around the edges.

"Are you looking for anything special?" the man asked.

"Local history, I guess."

"I have lots of local history," he said, "going all the way back to Ethan Allen and the Green Mountain Boys. Ethan was born here, you know. In fact, his brother started the University of Vermont."

He pulled a biography of Ethan Allen off a shelf and showed it to me. "Good read," he said. "I recommend it highly. All yours for fifty cents."

"What we'd really like to find is a history of Fox Hill," Corey said.

"Are you staying at the inn?"

"Our grandmother owns it," I told him.

"Elsie's your grandmother? Well, I'll be. She's one of my regulars, a real nice woman. Comes in sometimes just to visit Mog." He offered his hand. "My name's Jack Pumphrey."

I shook his hand. "I'm Travis Donovan, and this is my sister, Corey."

"What's going on at the inn these days?" Mr. Pumphrey asked. "There were a lot of strange stories before Elsie bought the place, but I haven't heard much lately."

Corey and I exchanged a glance, unsure what to tell Mr. Pumphrey. Taking a deep breath, I decided to ask him what I really wanted to know—*needed* to know. "Do you believe in ghosts?"

Mr. Pumphrey hesitated a moment, as if he, too, wasn't sure what to say. "I hope you won't think I'm crazy for telling you this, but I once saw a ghost myself, right here in this store. Of course, I didn't realize he was a ghost at first. He was standing by that shelf over there, looking at books. There was nothing out of the ordinary about him. But when he left, he walked out through the wall instead of the door. *That* gave me a turn."

Mr. Pumphrey laughed nervously and picked up his cat. "Scared poor Mog, too. He puffed up to twice his normal size and ran and hid. I didn't see him for the rest of the day. He's a real fraidy cat. Thunder and lightning scare him, too."

"Did the ghost ever come back?" Corey asked.

"Not that I know of, but Vera Bartholomew, who runs the antique shop around the corner, claims she's seen the same chap in her place. He's particularly fond of one old armchair. She's thinking it used to belong to him. Could be, I guess, could be."

Mog squirmed, and Mr. Pumphrey set him gently down. "Why are you two so interested in ghosts? Have they showed up at the inn again?"

"Yes, sir," I said. "They sure have."

Deep in thought, brow wrinkled, Mr. Pumphrey stroked his beard. "Ghosts have been seen there off and on for years," he said. "Boys, mostly. And a woman. Hanged herself a long time ago." He reached down to stroke Mog who was rubbing against his legs and purring. "You want your lunch, don't you, sir?"

He straightened up and grinned. "Just last week, some nut driving a hearse came in here with a hippy-dippy woman. They wanted books about Fox Hill, but I didn't have anything that suited them. They both claimed they'd seen ghosts there."

"That was Chester Coakley and Eleanor Duvall," Corey said. "They're psychics. Grandmother accused them of faking the ghosts and threw them out."

Mr. Pumphrey laughed and went on stroking Mog. "That sounds like Elsie. She has her mind closed against any possibility of the supernatural. Won't even discuss it."

"What did you tell them?"

"The truth," he said. "I've always suspected that the previous owners milked the sightings for all they were worth. Maybe even faked them to get publicity for the inn."

"Believe me," I said, "the ghosts at the inn are just as

real as the man you saw walk through the wall of this store."

He gave both of us a long, considering look. "You've actually seen them?"

"Yes, sir," I said.

"Lots of times," Corey put in. "Not just at night, either. We know their names and how they died and what the poor farm was really like."

"And you're not scared?"

"Just of Miss Ada," Corey said. "She's the woman who hanged herself."

"We've made friends with the boys," I said, boasting a little. "They call themselves the bad ones, but they're just ordinary boys."

"Ordinary boys who happen to be dead?" Mr. Pumphrey asked.

"It's not their fault they're dead," Corey said. "Miss Ada left them outside in the cold all night and they froze to death. She's still mean to them—even now when they're all dead, including her, she won't leave them alone."

Mr. Pumphrey looked at us long and hard, as if we'd said something that worried him, maybe even scared him. "Let me give you some advice," he said. "Stay away from those boys. The dead have their place. And the living have theirs. It's dangerous to cross the line that separates them from us."

For a moment, he watched the raindrops race one another down the shop's window, thinking of what to say next. "It's one thing to watch a ghost walk through a wall," he said slowly. "It's something else to ask him how he did it."

"We couldn't stay away from those boys even if we wanted to," I told Mr. Pumphrey. "They follow us everywhere."

Just then the bell over the door jangled, and a rosy-faced woman rushed inside, struggling to close her umbrella. "Has the book I ordered come in?" she asked Mr. Pumphrey.

"Excuse me, children." He turned to the woman. "I was just about to call you, Abigail. *The Murder at the Vicarage* arrived in this morning's mail. It's in good condition—a little foxing, but on the whole it's a fine first edition."

As Mr. Pumphrey handed the book to Abigail, Corey nudged me. "It's past twelve. Grandmother's going to be mad if we keep her waiting much longer."

"We have to go," I told Mr. Pumphrey. "We're supposed to meet our grandmother."

Abigail handed her credit card to Mr. Pumphrey. "Thanks so much for getting this for me. It's the only Agatha Christie first edition I don't have."

As he ran the card through his machine, Mr. Pumphrey watched us open the door. "Say hello to Elsie for me," he said. "And remember, you can't trust the dead. They go by different rules than the living."

Mog meowed as if he, too, wished to warn us. Then he hopped into the window and watched us run toward Church Street.

Huddled under her umbrella, Grandmother frowned when she saw us. "I've been waiting for fifteen minutes. Where have you been?"

"At the Dusty Jacket." I pointed down the brick walk-

• 502 •

way to the little building squeezed between the Nearly New Emporium and the Vermont Crafts Shop. "Mr. Pumphrey said to say hello for him."

Grandmother's frown turned to a smile. "Jack Pumphrey can talk the ear off a rabbit. Did you meet his cat?"

"Mog's huge," Corey said, "and so sweet and pretty. I wish I had a cat just like him."

"He's also a great mouse killer," I said.

"So I've heard." Grandmother started walking down Church Street, dodging puddles and other people's umbrellas. "What would you like to eat?"

"Pizza," Corey and I said. It was the one thing Mrs. Brewster never fixed and probably never would.

"I know just the place," Grandmother said.

The windows of Nel's Pizzeria were steamed up, giving it a cozy, welcoming look. As soon as we stepped inside, we smelled tomato sauce and cheese and baking pie crust. Crowds of college kids occupied most of the tables, but the service was quick, and we soon had a pizza the size of the moon, gooey with cheese, runny with tomato sauce, and topped with meatballs the size of a baby's fist.

"How does it compare with New York pizza?" Grandmother asked.

When Corey and I both gave thumbs up, she looked at our empty plates and laughed. "Foolish me. I thought we'd have enough left over for an after-dinner snack."

Stuffed with pizza, we headed for Wade's of Vermont, where Grandmother bought us each a pair of jeans, two pairs of shorts, three T-shirts, and extra underwear and socks.

"Let's hope nothing happens to these," she said. "I can't afford to replace them."

"Don't worry. The ghosts like us now," Corey said. "Except for Miss Ada, of course. She hates—"

Grandmother stopped right in the middle of the sidewalk and stared at Corey. Rain dripped off her umbrella and splashed into the puddles. "What are you talking about?"

Corey's face turned red with embarrassment. "Just because you don't believe in ghosts doesn't mean they aren't real."

"Not that ghost nonsense again," Grandmother said. "Sensible people simply do not subscribe to such foolishness."

"How about Mr. Pumphrey?" I asked. "Do you think he's sensible?"

"Jack's a bit eccentric, but I suppose he's fairly sensible." She looked at me closely. "Are you saying Jack Pumphrey believes in ghosts?"

"He's seen one in his shop," Corey said. "And so has the lady who runs the antique store."

"And so have *you*," I said. "You just won't admit it."

By now Grandmother was unlocking the truck. "Get in out of the rain," she said crossly. As she edged out of her parking space, she said, "Not another word about ghosts!"

Corey and I looked at each other. We'd have something to say to each other when we got home, but for now we'd keep our mouths shut.

14

After we'd put our new clothes away, Corey and I went outside for a walk. The rain had stopped, but the lawn was puddled with water. Our shoes were soon soaked, but we slogged through the mud, not paying much attention to where we were going.

"Is Mr. Pumphrey right about the boys?" Corey asked. "Are they dangerous?"

"No matter what he says, I'm not scared of them," I said. "They're just kids."

"*Dead* kids," Corey reminded me.

"Save your worries for Miss Ada. *She's* the dangerous one."

Corey gnawed on a fingernail, her face worried. "What do you think they want?"

"Maybe we should ask them."

As luck would have it, I'd no sooner spoken than I realized we'd wandered into the burial ground. Caleb, Seth, and Ira grinned down at us from an apple tree. The shadow children clustered around them, a profile here, a leg dangling there, a hand holding a limb—like one of those pictures where you have to find hidden objects.

"We been waiting on you," Seth called.

Jumping down from the tree, the bad ones led us to a row of stones.

"This here's mine," Seth said. "And there's Caleb's and

Ira's. But who's to know withouten our names writ on 'em?"

Corey looked at him solemnly. "Travis and I can write your names on these three stones."

"That's right kindly of you," Seth said, "but we want proper headstones, like you see in a church graveyard."

"And not just for us," Caleb said. "For *all* the folks lying here forgotten."

"Do you know their names?"

"Course not," Seth said. "None of us ever seen a burial."

"Joseph dug the graves at night," Ira explained. "By sunup, the job was done, and we didn't know who was put where."

"Until we became as we are now," Caleb corrected him. "We mourned all the folk they buried here after us. Said the right words for them and tried to send them over the river to the place where they belonged."

The shadows stirred. "We stayed, though," they whispered. "All us boys, all us bad ones—we stayed."

"There's just one here with a name." Seth pushed his way through a thick tangle of bushes and honeysuckle vines and pointed. "There she lies."

A cracked stone lay face-up on the ground, covered with so much moss I had to scrape it off before I could read the inscription:

MISS ADA JAGGS
3 APRIL 1789 – 17 MARCH 1841
A WICKED HEART IS ITS OWN REWARD

Corey pressed against my side. "A wicked heart," she whispered.

"It's true, ain't it?" Seth asked.

"Her heart was wicked through and through and black with hate," Ira said quietly.

"Who wrote the inscription?" I asked.

"A man from the county office ordered it done," Caleb said. "But it was our idea. We whispered it to him so sweetly he thought it was *his* idea."

Ira kicked Miss Ada's stone. "He wanted to put names on all our markers, but he couldn't find the burial records."

"That's 'cause he didn't know about her secret account book," Seth said.

"Now if you two were to find *that*," Caleb added, "everybody could have their proper stones. And maybe we could rest easy."

"Are you saying Corey and I . . . have to find Miss Ada's book?" I stared at Caleb. "Don't *you* know where it is?"

"She used to keep it under the floor in her room," Caleb said.

"But she could have hidden it somewhere else," Ira pointed out.

"After all, we wasn't watching her every second of every day, was we?" Seth asked.

"Do you remember which room was hers?" I asked Caleb.

"Number seven." He pointed at a window on the second floor, the Jenningses' old room, the one with a good view of the grove . . . and the stupid ghost imitation that had started all the trouble.

Corey looked at me. "Is anyone staying there?"

"I think it's those two old ladies, Miss Baynes and Miss Edwards," I said.

Seth giggled. "I sure riled them up with that mouse at dinner, didn't I?"

"I *thought* that was you," Corey said, laughing herself.

"They're usually gone all day," I said, in an effort to steer everyone's attention back to the room—and to the account book that might or might not be hidden there.

"Let's see if we can find it." Corey ran to the inn with me close behind. The bad ones followed us on soundless feet, blending in with the shadow children.

We paused at the front door and listened. All was silent except for the grandfather clock ticking to itself in the hall. While Corey kept watch, I sneaked into the office and lifted the spare key to room 7 from its hook.

On tiptoe, we crept up the wide stairs to the second floor and paused again to listen. The doors to the occupied rooms were closed. The other doors were open. We didn't hear Mrs. Brewster's vacuum cleaner, nor did we see any other signs that she was cleaning the rooms.

Cautiously, we approached number 7. I knocked, but there was no answer.

"Nobody's home," Seth said.

Slowly, I stuck the key in the lock and turned it gently. Feeling like a burglar, I eased the door open. Corey and I— and the bad ones—stepped inside. I locked the door behind us. The room was empty. A pink sweater hung on the back of a chair, and a pair of neatly folded tan slacks lay on the seat. Shopping bags from Simon Pearce sat in the corner. On the desk was an assortment of tin cookie cutters made by Ann Clark of Vermont. Grandmother had dozens of them, and so did our mother. Not that Mom ever baked—she collected them and displayed them on a wall in the kitchen.

But we hadn't come to look at cookie cutters. On our hands and knees, we crawled across the floor looking for loose boards. We covered every inch, but each board was nailed down tightly.

"Maybe we should pull them up," Ira suggested.

"No," I said as Seth tugged at a board. "Try the walls. Maybe there's a hole behind something."

We started with the little Currier and Ives prints and moved on to the mirrors. As Corey and I struggled to move a tall pine bureau, Seth said, "*Hsst*—the old ladies are back!"

Just as he spoke, I heard Miss Baynes say to Miss Edwards, "Shopping tires me out more than it used to. Let's have a rest before dinner."

They were in the hall, right outside the door. As one of them put a key in the lock, Corey and I slid under one of the beds. Hidden by a floor-length dust ruffle, we heard the women enter the room, accompanied by the rustle of more shopping bags.

"Woodstock was just delightful," Miss Edwards said. "So many nice stores."

"And lunch was delicious," Miss Baynes said. "If the inn at Woodstock wasn't so expensive, I'd cancel our reservations here and take a room there."

"I'm sure we wouldn't see a mouse in the dining room."

"Indeed not."

The bathroom door opened and shut behind Miss Edwards, and Miss Baynes lay down on her bed. The mattress creaked and sagged over our heads. Corey and I scarcely dared to breathe.

Suddenly, Miss Baynes sneezed and sat up with a jerk.

The bathroom door opened, and Miss Edwards said, "What's the matter?"

"Someone just tickled my nose with a feather!"

Miss Edwards laughed. "You must have been dreaming." The next second her laugh turned into a gasp. "My sweater!" she cried. "It just floated out the window!"

Both women ran to look. "There it is!" Miss Baynes said. "It's caught on the branch of a tree. See? The wind must have blown it there."

"But it's not windy," Miss Edwards said.

That's when the giggling started.

"What's that?" Miss Baynes asked.

Little ripples of laughter ran around the walls.

"It sounds as if someone is having a joke at our expense." Miss Edwards opened the closet door. "Come out, right now!"

The giggles got louder. At the same moment, a Simon Pearce shopping bag slid across the floor and bumped against Miss Edwards's legs. A few small pictures fell off the wall, and the bathroom door opened and shut three times.

As the women ran from the room, Seth joined us under the bed. Convulsed with laughter, he drummed his heels on the floor. "That was fun," he crowed.

Corey gave him an annoyed look. "They'll leave for sure now."

Following her lead, I slid out from under the bed and left the room while we had the opportunity. Seth came with us, hiccupping from laughing so much.

Behind the office's closed door, Miss Baynes and Miss Edwards were complaining to Grandmother. "It must be your grandchildren," Miss Edwards said.

"Didn't they cause enough disturbance in the dining room with their childish pranks?" Miss Baynes asked.

We didn't wait to hear Grandmother's answer. Sneaking out to the porch, we sat down in the rocking chairs farthest from the front door.

Seth joined us and rocked happily back and forth, his red curls blowing in the breeze he generated.

Corey glared at him. "We get blamed for everything you do. It's not fair!"

Seth scowled. "You think dying when you're just seven's fair?"

"Nothing's fair," I said. "You're both old enough to know that."

"Not me," Seth said. "I weren't old enough when I died to know about what's fair and what's not."

"Well, you're a lot older than seven now," Corey said.

"No, I ain't. I was seven then and I'm seven now and I'll always be seven. So there."

"What if you had to be ninety-nine forever?" Corey asked. "And you had to hobble around and you couldn't see or hear and—"

I gave her a nudge with my elbow. "Shut up, Corey. You're giving me a headache."

"I was just trying to say—"

"Well, stop trying," I said. "Seth isn't even here anymore."

She looked around, surprised. While we'd been arguing, Seth had disappeared.

A little later, Miss Edwards and Miss Baynes stalked out of the inn. Mr. Brewster followed them, hauling their little wheeled suitcases and all their shopping bags. We sat very still and hoped they wouldn't see us.

Without looking to the right or the left, they got into their Honda and slammed the doors. As soon as Mr. Brewster had wedged everything into the trunk, they took off, driving faster than the average person their age, I thought.

"All that," I said, "and we didn't even find the account book."

15

I've been thinking." Ira appeared on the porch railing,
looking glum, as usual. "Maybe she buried the book
in the grove before she hanged herself."

I imagined Corey and me digging one hole after another, fighting roots and rocks with our shovels, sweating in
the heat, bitten by gnats and mosquitoes—not a pretty
picture.

"What makes you think so?" Corey asked.

"Well, she wouldn't leave it in her room, would she?
Somebody might find it there." He pushed his dark hair
out of his eyes. "Most likely she reckoned nobody would
dig up the grove."

"Why would they?" Caleb sat down next to Ira, swinging his bare feet. "Nobody knew there *was* another book."

"But it's spooky in the grove." Corey toyed with her
fingers, twisting them this way and that, as if she wanted
to tie them into a knot.

"Spooooky," Seth whispered in her ear, "*Spooooky*."

"Go away." Corey swatted at him as if he were an
annoying fly. "You get on my nerves."

Seth pulled the barrettes out of Corey's hair and
laughed as long strands fell in her face.

Corey got up so fast the rocker swung wildly back and
forth. "Quit it!" she yelled at Seth.

Grandmother heard the noise and came to the door.

"I've been looking for you two," she said. Her voice was calm but stern, and she had a teacherly gleam in her eye that meant Trouble, with a capital T. "Come inside. I want to talk to you."

Seth giggled and made a face. "Nyah, nyah, you're in for it now!"

Ira grabbed the younger boy's arm. "Leave off."

The three faded from sight, and Corey and I followed Grandmother into the office.

"I'm very disappointed in your behavior," she began. "Because of your pranks, Miss Baynes and Miss Edwards have canceled the rest of their stay here. They—"

"We didn't do anything to them," I said.

"It was Seth," Corey added. "We told him not to, but—"

"Seth?" Grandmother stared at Corey. "Please don't tell me he's one of your ghosts."

"But he is," Corey insisted. "He's the worst one of all, he's—"

"Corey, I simply can't believe this." Grandmother turned to me. "Travis, tell me the truth. Why did you let a mouse loose in the dining room last night? And why did you booby-trap room seven? What on earth do you have against those two women?"

"Corey's not lying," I said. "It *was* Seth."

"Seth." Grandmother drummed her fingers on her desk top. "Seth."

"Yes'm?" Seth came as if in answer to his name. "What is it you want?" He drummed on the desk, too.

Grandmother jerked her hands back, but the drumming went on. She looked right through Seth at Corey and me. We held up our hands to show we weren't—couldn't be—responsible. Thanks to the shadow children, the sound had gotten much louder.

"Stop making that noise!" Grandmother raised her voice to be heard above the drumming. She was plainly frightened but trying hard not to be.

"It's not us," I said.

"It's Seth," Corey said, "and the others."

"I'm going to call your parents right now and tell them to come and get you," Grandmother shouted. "I cannot allow you to destroy the inn's reputation. Not to mention my sanity!"

As she reached for the phone, Seth picked up an eraser and threw it across the room, followed by a handful of pens and pencils. A stapler rose into the air and floated a few inches from Grandmother's nose. The printer churned out a stream of blank paper, the computer flickered on and off, and the radio suddenly changed from classical music to loud rock. Doors and windows opened and shut with loud bangs, and a swivel chair spun as it rolled around the room, banging into walls.

Grandmother just sat there, watching the office dim and brighten as the shadow children filled the air with a blizzard of spinning paperclips and thumbtacks.

"It's true," she whispered. "The inn really is haunted . . . everything I've believed is wrong." With that she put her head down on her folded arms and closed her eyes.

"Now look what you've done!" Corey yelled. "You've upset Grandmother!"

The shadow children giggled and retreated, but Seth

plopped down on the edge of Grandmother's desk. Regarding her sadly, he touched her hair.

Grandmother shuddered and looked up. "You must be Seth." Her voice was weak, but she seemed to be back in control.

"You can see me now." He looked pleased.

"Yes."

"That's 'cause you believe in me." He grinned. "Sorry I had to scare you into it, but you was a hard nut to crack."

Ira and Caleb appeared on either side of Seth. "Sorry, ma'am," Caleb said. "But we couldn't let you send Corey and Travis away."

"We need them to help us, you see," Ira added.

"Even though they're none too smart," Seth put in. "But we ain't found nobody else. Most folks just run off, like them silly old ladies."

"Or they try to trap us with machines of one sort or another," Ira said. "Cameras and the like."

"Those psychos got no business messing with us," Seth said. "If we wanted our pictures took, we'd pose."

"Psychics," Caleb corrected him. "That's what they call themselves nowadays."

Grandmother just sat there staring at the boys as if she was too stunned to say a word. Finally, she said, "What do you want my grandchildren to do?

"Just three things," Caleb told her.

"Truth to tell," Seth piped up, "they's a hard three things."

"First, they have to find Miss Ada's secret account book," Caleb went on, "the one that has the names of the dead who are buried here."

"Then they have to mark the graves with proper stones," Ira said, "the kind with names, not numbers, wrote on them."

"And last, they got to exercise Miss Ada," Seth said.

"Exorcise," Corey said.

Seth frowned. "That's what I said."

"No, you didn't," Corey said. "You—"

I gave her a little sideways kick. "Drop it."

"Yes," Seth said. "Drop it or I'll drop you."

"Stop squabbling," Grandmother said as if she were in her fourth-grade classroom. With a sigh, she leaned back in her chair. She looked very tired. "I don't understand any of this," she said.

"We'll explain it to you," I said.

Grandmother closed her eyes. "I'm listening."

Helped here and there by the bad ones, Corey and I told Grandmother everything we knew about the poor farm; Miss Ada Jaggs and her brother, Cornelius; the burial ground; the secret account book; and so on. By the time we were done, it was almost five o'clock.

Wearily, Grandmother got to her feet. "I don't know what to think," she murmured. "I just don't know."

Mrs. Brewster chose that moment to appear in the doorway. "Time for dinner," she said, and then gasped when she noticed the mess the bad ones had made. "It's them again, ain't it?"

Without hesitating, she plunged her hand into a particularly dark corner and hauled Seth out by his shirt front. "Naughty boy," she said. "Why can't you stay where you belong and stop causing trouble?"

Seth squirmed and wiggled, but he couldn't break away

from her. "Let me go, Aunt Martha!" he yelled. "I don't need you looking after me. I can take care of my own self!"

While we stared at her, Mrs. Brewster shrugged. "You might say me and Henry inherited this here boy. He's my great-great-great-grandfather's nephew. The care of him's been passed down from generation to generation. We try to protect him, like his mama wished, but he sleeps light. Don't take much to wake him up."

Without releasing the struggling Seth, she gave Corey and me a dark look. "You and your thoughtless ghost games," she muttered. "This here boy is suffering on account of you. Why didn't you leave him be?"

"Don't go blaming them," Seth said. "They didn't know no better."

"*You* know who's to blame, Mrs. Brewster," Caleb said. "But you're scared to face her."

With a final jerk, Seth pulled away from Mrs. Brewster. Shielding himself with Caleb, he stuck out his tongue. "I don't need no aunties looking after me."

Then they were gone.

"So you knew all about this, Martha?" Grandmother asked.

"Small chance you'd have believed me even if I'd told you."

"Too true." Grandmother sighed. "I used to believe the dead rested in peace. After my husband died, it was a consolation of sorts." She turned her head and looked out the window. 'Fear no more the heat o' the sun,'" she murmured, "'Nor the furious winter's rages.'"

The bad ones had quoted the same lines. Like them, like

Corey and me, Grandmother was learning there might be plenty to fear after death.

"Most do rest in peace," Mrs. Brewster said softly. "Live a good life and die a good death—that's all you got to do. Those two things." She rubbed her hands together and added, "I came to tell you dinner is served."

With that, she strode out of the office.

"'Live a good life and die a good death,'" Grandmother said. "If only it were that simple."

After we'd finished eating the best steak I'd ever sunk my teeth into, the inn's only guests stopped at our table.

"Did Miss Baynes and Miss Edwards leave early?" Mrs. Kowalski asked. "We'd planned an afternoon at Lake Bomoseen tomorrow."

"Unfortunately, they had . . . a change of plans," Grandmother said.

"It would have been nice if they'd told us." Mrs. Kowalski patted her frosted hair, showing off her perfectly polished nails. "George and I were looking forward to getting to know them better. Such dears."

Grandmother regarded the woman over the rim of her coffee cup. "They left in a hurry."

"Oh, dear." Mrs. Kowalski pressed a stray strand of hair more firmly into place. "It wasn't an emergency, was it?"

"I don't think so." Grandmother set her cup in its saucer. *Clink.*

Mrs. Kowalski lingered a moment. When it became clear that Grandmother wasn't going to tell her anything else, she said, "I guess George and I will drive to Bomoseen without them."

With her husband trailing behind, like a dog trained to heel, Mrs. Kowalski headed for the porch and the rocking chairs.

Grandmother looked at Corey and me. "I can't believe I'm saying this," she said with a sigh, "but something must be done about the ghosts. We're completely booked next week. I can't afford to lose my guests."

Mrs. Brewster appeared at Grandmother's elbow. "More coffee?"

"Yes, please," Grandmother said. "And do join us, Martha. I need all the help I can get with this ghost business."

Almost on cue, the light dimmed slightly as the shadow children filled the corners. Caleb, Ira, and Seth pulled extra chairs over and sat down, their faces hopeful.

"I wish I could have some of that there coffee." Seth sniffed so deeply his nose wrinkled. "It sure smells good."

"Coffee's not for boys," Grandmother said. "When you grow up, you can drink all you want."

"Grow up?" Seth stared at Grandmother. "When do you think I'll do that, Granny?"

Grandmother actually blushed. "I'm sorry," she said, "I wasn't thinking." She poured a cup from Mrs. Brewster's pot and held it toward him.

Seth didn't take it. "I reckon you forgot I'm dead and I can't drink nothing. Nor can I eat."

"Oh, dear." Grandmother's face turned even redder.

Seth touched her hand. "It's all right, Granny. It's plain you ain't used to dining with the likes of us."

Mrs. Brewster leaned toward Seth. "We've got important matters to discuss, so sit still and be quiet or I'll call Henry. He'll fix your wagon."

"Uncle Henry can't do nothing to me." But Seth sat back in his chair and folded his hands in his lap, the very model of a good boy.

Grandmother turned to Martha. "The boys here say they want three things done: First, Miss Ada's account book must be found. It contains the names of the people buried here. With it, we can match the numbers on the grave markers with the names of the dead."

Mrs. Brewster nodded. "She kept two books, but the one you want, the true one, was never found. Me and Henry have looked, and so have all our kin before us."

"We'll find it." Grandmother looked at Corey and me as if she expected us to solve the problem by pulling the book out of thin air.

"Secondly," she went on, "we must erect proper headstones for the graves."

"It would comfort the poor souls," Mrs. Brewster said with another nod, "to know they've not been forgot."

"And thirdly . . . " Grandmother hesitated as if she dreaded saying the last one. "Thirdly, Miss Ada must be exorcised."

Mr. Brewster spoke up from the doorway. "She won't go willingly. Not that one."

The shadow children twittered like scared baby birds, and all three bad ones folded their arms tightly across their chests and looked grim.

"She's got to go," Caleb said. "Or there'll be no peace for us—or you, either."

"What can we do?" Grandmother asked.

"*You* can't do anything," Ira said in his deepest and most serious voice. "The ones who started this must be the ones who finish it."

Corey grabbed my hand and stared at the bad ones. "Do you mean us?"

"Granny wasn't the one flitting around the grove in her nightie," Seth said. "Nor was Aunt Martha."

"If I recollect rightly," Caleb put in, "it was you, Corey—with Travis helping."

Grandmother frowned at us. "I always suspected it was you two."

"Me and Henry knew all along," Mrs. Brewster said. "They're a pair of bad ones themselves, full of sass and mischief just like Seth here."

I bit my lip to keep from grinning. There was no denying it. We *were* bad ones, always in trouble—but not wicked. Like to like, the lovely bad ones—Corey and me and Seth, Caleb, and Ira. I glanced at Corey but failed to catch her eye. She sat beside Grandmother playing with a strand of her hair, thinking her own thoughts.

"Even if this is Corey and Travis's fault," Grandmother said, "I can't allow them to endanger themselves. Good or bad or just plain mischievous, they're my grandchildren. I'm responsible for their well-being—and I love them."

"I agree with Caleb," Mr. Brewster said. "Your grandchildren got us into this mess. It's only fair they get us out of it."

"After all," Mrs. Brewster put in, "Miss Ada can't kill them or hurt them. The worst she can do is scare them."

"But how can we get rid of her?" Corey whispered.

And how do you know she can't hurt us, I wondered.

"After the first two things are done," Caleb said, "we'll come up with a way to send Miss Ada wherever she must go next."

I hoped Caleb was right, but for now I didn't want to think about facing Miss Ada. Not with darkness coming on.

16

The night passed quietly. No visits from the bad ones. No visits from Miss Ada. I slept dreamlessly and woke to a morning full of sunshine and bird song. Not that I expected it to stay that way for long. Miss Ada was sure to cause problems before the day was over.

As soon as we'd eaten breakfast, Corey and I borrowed a couple of shovels from Mr. Brewster (without telling him, because we didn't want him asking questions) and went in search of the bad ones. We found them exactly where we'd expected them to be, stretched out on tree limbs in the grove, waiting for us.

Seth dropped down from a limb at least three stories above the ground. Ira and Caleb landed on either side of him like apples falling from a tree.

"Where should we start digging?" I asked.

"That's where she hanged herself." Seth pointed to a twisted tree that cast an especially dark shadow. "And this here's the very branch." Like a monkey, he jumped up and grabbed a long limb. Swinging back and forth, he said, "She turned and she twisted and she—"

"Hush!" Ira grabbed Seth and pulled him back to earth. "What do you think you're doing?"

As he spoke, Miss Ada's tree shook, as if a gust of wind were blowing through it. Its leaves rustled, and its branches creaked. A dozen or so crows shot out of their roosting places and flew away, almost deafening us with their loud cries.

At the same moment, the shade under the tree deepened and darkened, and the temperature dropped so low I shivered. On the ground, a shadow swung back and forth, as if cast by a body hanging from a rope.

Suddenly, Miss Ada was there, twisting on her rope, her distorted face a hideous shade of purple. "You won't find it," she said with an evil smile. "It's hidden where no one dares look."

The bad ones began to sob and tremble and cry out, as if remembering beatings and hunger and cold winter winds, the deaths of loved ones, things lost and gone forever, babies' cries and mothers' prayers.

Terrified of Miss Ada's power, Corey and I dropped our shovels and grabbed the bad ones' hands. Pulling them along with us, we fled from the cold grove. Our ears rang with their cries, our eyes burned with their tears. Like them, we felt again every pain and loss we'd ever suffered.

On the sunlit lawn, we fell to earth in a heap, aching with misery and shaking with fear.

"See what you did?" Caleb yelled at Seth, who was still crying for his mother. "You woke Miss Ada with your foolish shenanigans!"

"Didn't I warn you?" Ira cried. "Didn't I tell you—"

"I'm sorry." Seth kept on weeping. "I forgot, I was just funning, I didn't mean—"

"Oh, stop your crying," Caleb said more gently. "I shouldn't have shouted at you. When she brings the old pains back, they hurt so bad I can't hardly think straight."

Seth wiped his eyes with his dirty fists. "I want my mama, I want my pa. I hate this place."

"All of us hate being here," Caleb murmured.

"We were unlucky," Ira said. "You and Caleb and me and everyone else who ever lived and died on this poor farm."

While the bad ones talked among themselves, I stole a quick look at the grove. In my mind's eye, I saw Miss Ada hanging from the tree, her feet dancing in the air, her face contorted. My stomach heaved, and I thought I was going to throw up.

But there was no sign of her now. One by one, the crows flew back and settled themselves noisily in the trees.

With a shudder, I touched Caleb's shoulder. "What did Miss Ada mean when she said the book was hidden where no one would dare to look?"

He frowned, his forehead as wrinkled as an old man's. "Maybe it's buried with her."

"That's impossible," Corey said. "Dead people can't take things with them."

"Mr. Jaggs could have put it there," Ira said.

"But he ran away," I said.

Ira nodded. "But he sneaked back after Miss Ada hanged herself."

"She was laid out in the parlor," Caleb explained, "the guest lounge you call it now. He came to see her in the dead of night."

Ira looked up from the clover chain he was making. "We were scared to go near the house with her lying there, but we saw the old codger steal away before daybreak. He had plenty of time to leave the book with her."

Pausing to knot another clover stem, he added, "As she said, who'd dare look for it there?"

"Not me!" Corey glanced across the sunny lawn at the grove and shuddered. At the same time, I shook my head.

The bad ones fixed us with their mournful stares. "You promised," Caleb reminded us.

Ira nodded, his dark eyes solemn. "It's the first thing, remember?"

"Find the names and make the proper gravestones," Seth said in case we'd forgotten.

"No one can rest in peace if you don't," Caleb added.

"Even if the book *is* there," Corey put in, "it's rotted away by now."

"Not if it's in the metal box where she always kept it," Caleb pointed out.

I shook my head again. "No way. Impossible. Forget it. I'm not doing it." Expecting Corey to follow me, I jumped up and started to walk away, but when I looked back, she was still sitting on the grass with the bad ones.

"Where are you going?" she called.

I stopped, unsure what to do. I was ashamed to admit it, but part of me (a *big* part) wanted to call Mom and Dad and tell them I was coming home. I'd hitchhike if I had to. Anything to get away from this place.

Trailed by the bad ones, Corey ran to my side. "Don't you dare walk out now, Travis. We *promised* to help them."

"But we can't dig up—"

"You big yellow belly," Seth said. "Don't you go and skedaddle."

"Listen here," Caleb put in. "She's not in her grave anyway. She's over yonder." He pointed at the grove.

"She doesn't always stay there," I reminded him.

He didn't have an answer for that.

"She's naught but rags and bones if that's what scaring you," Seth said.

Frankly, that was plenty scary.

"We have to find the book," Corey said. "We *have* to. No matter what happens."

Seth turned to me with a sneer. "Ain't you ashamed to be bested by a girl? You're nothing but a sissified nancy boy."

"Don't call him names," Ira told Seth. "You'll just make him mad. And what good will that do?"

Seth scowled at me. "Nancy boy," he muttered again. "Where's your dress? And your hair ribbons?"

"Be quiet, Seth," Caleb said.

"I'll say what I like." As he spoke, Seth put some distance between himself and Caleb.

While Caleb's attention was focused on Seth, Corey took me aside. "I'm scared, too," she whispered. "In fact, I'm terrified, but we don't have any choice—and you know it."

What could I say? She was right. Since my legs were shaking too hard to stand up, I sank down on the grass near Caleb. "Okay, okay," I croaked, "we'll do it."

Caleb sighed with relief. "Meet us at her grave tonight."

"Why not do it now," I asked, "while the sun's shining?"

"Nobody digs up graves in broad daylight," Ira said.

"It's got to be done proper," Seth added, still keeping his distance from Caleb.

"At the stroke of twelve," Caleb said. "The time it's been told in stories since way past when."

With that, the bad ones pulled one of their vanishing acts, and Corey and I found ourselves alone on the lawn.

"Midnight," I muttered. "They're making it as hard as they can."

I glanced at my watch. We had almost twelve hours to kill before we tried our luck at grave robbing.

17

Fortunately for us, Grandmother was too busy dealing with a surprise vanload of senior citizens to pay much attention to Corey and me. Mrs. Brewster had made an emergency trip to Middlebury to buy food for the unexpected guests, and Mr. Brewster was occupied schlepping suitcases and other paraphernalia.

Taking advantage of the activity, Corey and I lay low at the swimming pool all afternoon. If no one saw us, we wouldn't have to answer any questions.

When we showed up for dinner, the dining room was packed with laughing people, talking loudly and roaming from table to table taking pictures of each other. No one saw Seth poking his head into every group shot, showing off his gap-toothed grin.

Caleb and Ira contented themselves with watching from the ceiling fan. Round and round they went, their faces solemn, causing no disturbance, for once.

Mrs. Brewster lingered at our table. "The bad ones are here. Did you notice?"

"Yes." Grandmother watched Seth strike a silly pose for a lady with a video camera. "Will he show up when she looks at her pictures?"

"She'll think the camera's broke," Mrs. Brewster answered. "All her pictures will be ruined by white streaks—like light got in."

When Mrs. Brewster crossed the room to refill water glasses, Grandmother turned to us. "Have you made any progress finding the account book?"

We shook our heads and busied ourselves with the chicken Parmesan, another excellent gourmet treat from Mrs. Brewster.

"Even though I can see those boys, I still find it hard to believe my own eyes." Grandmother frowned at the perfect green bean she'd speared. "Was it a mistake to send those psychics away?"

Ira dropped down from the fan and took a seat beside her. "They were flimflammers," he said. "You were right to tell them to leave."

Seth took a seat on her other side. "No matter what they tell you, folks can't catch us with those fancy ghost-hunting machines."

"What about priests?" Grandmother asked. "Does exorcism work?"

"Rarely," Ira said. "The trouble is they usually don't take the time to get to know spirits. If you don't know what's holding us here, you can't make us leave."

Grandmother started to laugh. "I'm sorry," she told the bad ones who looked not only puzzled but hurt by her giggles. "I just can't believe I'm actually having this conversation. Sometimes I'm convinced I've lost my mind and I'm hallucinating."

The bad ones looked at each other as if they were both thinking the same thing. "Maybe you are," Ira said in that solemn way of his, ". . . hallucinating."

Grandmother smiled. "Actually, I wouldn't mind if I were temporarily insane. At least I'd have a chance of regaining my faith in a rational world where the dead stay dead and don't swing on chandeliers." While she spoke, she watched Seth perform acrobatic feats overhead.

One of the new guests pointed at the chandelier. "Look at that!"

"What's making it swing?" another asked.

As the diners sat staring, their chicken forgotten, Seth imitated the daring young man on the flying trapeze. He was, of course, invisible to them.

An elderly woman gasped and got to her feet. "It's going to fall!" she cried.

As the guests began to hurry out of the room, Caleb and Ira joined Seth and told him to stop. With Seth protesting loudly, all three vanished, and the chandelier slowly came to a stop.

Grandmother hastened after the guests. "It's all right," she assured them. "The chandelier does that sometimes. It's stopped now. Please come back and have dessert. Martha's prepared a double chocolate cake with her own special raspberry sauce. It's absolutely delicious."

Murmuring to themselves, the guests returned reluctantly to their tables. Mrs. Brewster hustled about, serving generous slices of dark chocolate cake sitting in pools of raspberry sauce.

Although the guests eyed the chandelier from time to time, the cake placated them. Soon the room filled again with voices and laughter.

Grandmother looked at the people at the other tables and sighed. "Just think," she said slowly, "once I was as ignorant as they are."

Corey and I went on eating, savoring each bite of cake

as if it might be our last. Grandmother sipped her coffee, her cake untouched.

Mrs. Brewster passed our table on her way to offer more coffee to the guests. "Isn't it to your liking?" she asked Grandmother.

"The cake?" Grandmother touched it with her fork. "Sorry, Martha. I'm sure it's delicious, but I'm not very hungry tonight."

"Nothing affects the children's appetites," Mrs. Brewster observed.

"Are you offering seconds?" I asked.

"It's all gone." With that, Mrs. Brewster bustled across the room to refill coffee cups.

"Bummer," I muttered.

"Here, split mine between you." Grandmother slid her plate toward us.

"Are you sure you don't want it?" Corey asked.

Grandmother nodded. "Take it, please. We don't want to hurt Martha's feelings."

Grandmother watched us eat and then excused herself to sit on the porch for a while. By the time we joined her, she was surrounded by the guests. One woman had read *Haunted Inns* and was full of questions.

"Have you seen any ghosts?" she asked. "Heard any strange sounds? Felt cold spots?"

Grandmother shook her head, but she didn't meet the woman's eyes.

"When that chandelier started to swing, I thought it was ghosts, for sure," the woman said with a nervous laugh.

The other guests chuckled uneasily. "That's the strangest thing I've ever seen," one said.

"You say it happens often?" another asked.

Grandmother pressed her hand against her forehead and got up. "You'll have to excuse me," she said. "I'm not feeling very well."

Leaving the guests to chatter among themselves, Corey and I followed Grandmother inside. She stopped in the kitchen and asked Mrs. Brewster to call Tracy. "These folks will be staying until next week's group arrives," she said. "I could really use some help, and I'm sure you could, too."

"I'll do my best to talk her into coming," Mrs. Brewster said. "Too bad she's such a nervous nellie." She looked at Grandmother closely. "If you don't mind my saying so, Mrs. Donovan, you don't look too good."

"I don't feel too good, either," Grandmother admitted. "When your world view changes overnight, it's bound to leave you a little shaken."

"I reckon so." Mrs. Brewster's eyes shifted to Corey and me. "See what your pranks have led to? Misery for everybody."

"That's not fair," Corey began, but Grandmother silenced her with a shake of her head.

"Hush, Corey," she said wearily. "I'm going to my room to read." She held up *Bleak House*, a thick novel by Charles Dickens. "The odious Mr. Tulkinghorn has just put poor Lady Dedlock in a terrible position, and I'm anxious about her."

Corey and I started to follow Grandmother into her apartment, but Mrs. Brewster stopped us. "Find that account book," she said, "and get this business done with. It's hard on your poor grandmother."

"It's hard on us, too," Corey said.

"Well, don't expect any sympathy from me." Finished with us, Mrs. Brewster picked up a scouring pad and attacked a blackened pot. "I sure wish Tracy was here," she muttered.

Before we left the kitchen, I glanced at the clock. Seven thirty-five. Four hours and twenty-five minutes to go until midnight.

To pass the time, Corey and I tried to play chess, but we couldn't concentrate. We set up Monopoly, Scrabble, and Clue but were unable to finish a game before our minds wandered to the burial ground. We took turns reading to each other from a collection of Edgar Allan Poe stories we'd found in the library, but considering what lay ahead, they were too scary.

At ten o'clock we sneaked into the kitchen and ate almost half a gallon of chocolate-chip ice cream. Back in my room, Corey suggested a game of hangman. Deciding that was a bad idea, we started working a crossword together. As we puzzled over a five-letter word, third letter "T," meaning "beyond the fringe," the grandfather clock chimed eleven forty-five.

"Oh, no," Corey whispered. "It's time."

As silently as our shaking legs could carry us, we sneaked through the kitchen and outside. High in the sky, the man in the moon looked down, his sad face slightly askew, and watched us run across the lawn. Dark on the silver grass, our shadows raced ahead of us.

We plunged into the bushes and battled our way through the brambles to the burial ground. The bad ones sat in their favorite tree, obviously waiting for us.

"Land sakes," Caleb muttered. "I'd forgotten how much noise the living make."

"It's those galumptious big shoes they wear." Seth swung his feet, bare as usual. "They're fit for elephants, they are."

I looked down at my thick-soled running shoes. They didn't look galumptious to me. But shoes were hardly the issue tonight.

Soundlessly, the bad ones dropped from the tree and joined us. "You're late," Ira said. "According to my reckoning, it's one minute past midnight."

"We had to find two more shovels," I said. "We left the others in the grove."

"And we almost forgot this." Corey held up a battery-operated lantern.

"Well, we'd best get busy." Caleb led us through the underbrush to Miss Ada's burial place. Corey switched on the lantern and set it on the ground. She looked surprisingly calm, but my heart was hammering so hard it shook my chest, and my hands were clammy with fear.

Cautiously, I poked at the dirt with my shovel.

"You got to work faster than that," Seth said.

"Or we'll be here for a month of Sundays."

"Won't digging wake her up?" Corey whispered.

"We *told* you she ain't here." Seth kicked at the dirt. "Don't you never listen?"

All of us looked at the grove. An owl called, but nothing stirred in the dark trees. What's to stop her from coming, I wondered.

Reluctantly, I put more muscle into my task. The ground was surprisingly soft, and my shovel bit into it easily. Corey started digging, too. Soon we'd dug down at least three feet without coming across anything. Despite the cool night air, we were both sweating.

"Here, let me try." Seth grabbed Corey's shovel and went to work. Caleb took mine, and Ira settled down on his haunches, his eyes fixed on the grove.

All around us, the shadow children romped and played. "You're it," one cried. "Catch me if you can," another called.

Suddenly, Seth dropped his shovel and jumped backward. "I hit something."

"A tree root, most likely," Caleb said in a low voice. "Or a rock."

Ira grabbed the lantern and held it over the hole. Held fast by roots, the corner of a box protruded from the earth.

"Her coffin," Ira whispered.

We drew back. There was no sound but the wind in the trees, yet we felt Miss Ada's presence out there in the dark.

"Don't make a sound," Ira whispered. "Don't say a word, just finish digging."

Seth thrust his shovel at me. "I done my part."

Caleb and I bent to our task. Cautiously, we cleaned the dirt from the coffin's top. The lantern's light illuminated a tarnished metal plate: HERE LIE THE MORTAL REMAINS OF MISS ADA JAGGS.

My knees turned to water. It was all I could do to stand there and watch Caleb push the side of his shovel under the lid.

Corey grabbed Caleb's arm to stop him from prying the lid off. "Suppose the book's not in there?"

"It has to be," he muttered.

As Caleb leaned back on the shovel's handle, Corey covered her face with her hands. "I don't want to see her," she whispered.

Neither did I, but I couldn't turn my eyes away. Hypnotized with dread, I watched Caleb lever the lid up with a hideous screeching sound of nails pulling out of wood. In the coffin's darkness, I saw a skull, tangles of hair, and rags of clothing. Cradled in the bones of Miss Ada's hands was a rusty iron box.

Caleb reached down, grabbed the box, and handed it to me. "Take this back to the inn. Write down the names and numbers of the dead, so you can make proper tombstones for us all."

Seth and Ira closed the coffin lid, picked up the shovels, and began tossing dirt back into the grave. I wanted to help, but Caleb looked at the grove fearfully and shook his head. "Get out of here," he whispered. "Before she comes."

Leaving the bad ones to refill Miss Ada's grave, Corey and I ran across the lawn. The box was heavy and smelled of damp earth. It was slippery and awkward to hold. At any moment, I expected to hear Miss Ada's voice or feel her bony hand clutch my arm, my shoulder, my shirt. The harder I ran, the slower I seemed to move.

But, at last, Corey and I were at the inn's back door, fumbling with the knob, trying to be quiet but desperate to get inside. Fortunately, Grandmother was a sound sleeper, and we managed to get back to my room without waking her. I put the box on the floor. With a twist of my wrist, I broke the rusty padlock and lifted the lid.

The account book's leather cover was damp and stained

with mold. I picked it up, hating the rotten feel of it in my hands, and opened it.

Miss Ada had recorded the names of sixty-seven people, their ages, the dates they died, and the number assigned to them. Her old-fashioned handwriting slanted neatly to the right, and each letter was perfectly formed.

I opened my notebook and picked up a pen. Slowly and carefully, I copied the sixty-seven names, their ages, death dates, and burial numbers.

By the time I was finished, it was after three A.M., and Corey had fallen asleep on my bed. Too tired to worry about Miss Ada or anything else, I lay down on the rug and fell fast asleep.

18

I n the morning, Corey and I carried the account book to the dining room. Grandmother was already seated at the table, drinking coffee and reading the morning paper. Mrs. Brewster was putting fresh flowers in little vases. The sun slanted in through the open French doors, bringing with it the sound of Mr. Brewster's riding mower and the sweet smell of cut grass.

It was hard to believe, but in this very room, Miss Ada and her brother had once eaten their fancy meals while the poor starved. The lawn Mr. Brewster mowed had been fields where men labored from dawn to dusk. People had died in what was now the carriage house.

I laid the account book in front of Grandmother. She set down her cup and stared at the soiled leather cover. "Where did you find this?"

"The bad ones told us where to look," I said, unwilling to tell her exactly where it had been hidden. "It has all the names and numbers, so we can make proper stones for the graves."

"Sixty-seven people are buried here," Corey put in.

"That many?" Grandmother opened the book and ran her finger down the list of names. "How awful."

"Miss Ada recorded the money they got from the county and how they spent it," Corey said. "Hardly any of it went to the poor people. They used it for themselves."

Grandmother looked at the accounts and shook her head. "Shameful, absolutely shameful."

Mrs. Brewster hovered at Grandmother's shoulder, scowling at the book. "The worst of it is, nothing's changed. All you have to do is look around at the rich people getting fat on the poor. Even the government ain't above it."

With a sigh, Grandmother closed the book and pushed it aside. "The county historical society will be interested in this."

Mrs. Brewster took our breakfast order. "When will you see to the headstones?" she asked Grandmother.

"The sooner the better." Grandmother turned to us. "I suggest we visit a stone mason in Barre today."

A few hours later, Grandmother led us into the office of Daniel Greene and Sons, Ltd. After a brief conversation with Mr. Greene Jr., Grandmother practically went into shock at the cost of purchasing sixty-seven gravestones.

"There's a less expensive option," Mr. Greene told us. "We could chisel all the names and numbers on one large stone at a savings of . . . "

He did some quick figuring on his calculator and came up with a price Grandmother could afford. "I'm willing to reduce my profit," he said, "because of the historical significance of what you're doing. There's many a name on this list whose descendants live here still. They deserve to know where their ancestors are buried."

Leading us outside, Mr. Greene showed us a number of precut stones and we chose a big pale pink marble slab. After more discussion, he promised the memorial would be ready as soon as possible.

Before we went back to the inn, we stopped at the historical society and asked to see Mrs. Bernice Leonard, the head archivist. She accepted Miss Ada's account book with gratitude.

"My great-great grandfather died at that farm," she said softly. "And so did his wife and some of his children. Their surname was Perkins. Are they among those in your book?"

Corey and I stared at the woman, gray haired and small, rosy faced, her hands clasping the unopened book. She had eyes as blue as Caleb's. And that dimple in her left cheek. It was as if something of Caleb lived still, his eyes and his dimple passing down and down and down from one Perkins to another.

"Abraham and Sarah Perkins." Grandmother opened the book and pointed to their names. "And their children, Matty and Caleb."

Mrs. Leonard touched the names. "I'm descended from their oldest son, Jonathon. He wasn't sent to the poor farm because he was indentured to a blacksmith." With a smile, she shook Grandmother's hand. "Thank you for bringing this to me."

"Thank Corey and Travis," Grandmother said. "They're the ones who found the book."

We left Mrs. Leonard turning the pages of the book and got into the truck, hot inside from sitting in the summer sun.

"I wish we could tell Mrs. Leonard about Caleb," Corey said.

"I don't think that would be a good idea," Grandmother said.

"Why not?"

Grandmother eased out of her parking space and headed south on Route 12. "I'd rather keep the ghosts secret," she said. "If word gets out, we'll have people like Chester Coakley banging on the door. Believe me, I don't want any more ghost hunters at the inn—no matter how many rooms they take."

That evening after dinner, the shadow children drifted through my window and filled the room with their familiar whispers and giggles. A few moments later, Corey arrived with Seth, Caleb, and Ira trailing behind her.

"Did Granny order the stones?" Seth asked me.

"Separate headstones turned out to be *really* expensive," Corey said in a low voice, looking ashamed.

"So there's going to one big pink stone with all the names and dates and numbers on it," I finished for her.

Surrounded by the shadow children, they whispered together for moment.

"That will do," Caleb said, "though we would have liked to have our own stones."

"I was hoping for a lamb," Seth said. "Or an angel."

"What of the account book?" Ira asked. "Did you put it somewhere safe?"

"We gave it to Mrs. Leonard at the county historical society," I said.

"She says she'll see it gets published, so everybody can read the truth about the poor farm."

"A fact simily," Corey added.

"*Facsimile*," I corrected her. "An exact copy of the original."

"Whatever." Corey shrugged.

"Mrs. Leonard is descended from your brother Jonathon," I told Caleb.

"And she's got your dimple," Corey added.

Caleb touched his cheek in wonder. "So Jonathon lived and got married and had a family? That's grand, that is."

"How about me?" Seth asked. "Is she kin to me, too?"

"The Brewsters are your kin," Ira reminded Seth.

Seth shrugged. "Yes, but the society lady sounds more highfalutin than my grumpy old auntie."

Corey yawned then, a big one without even covering her mouth, and rubbed her eyes.

"We didn't get much sleep last night," I reminded the bad ones.

At the same moment, the shadow children began whispering to each other. "Time to go," they whispered, "time to rest."

Caleb watched them drift along the wall toward the window and slip outside. "We'd better go, too," he said.

"Good luck with the third thing," Ira whispered.

In a snap of the fingers, the three boys were gone. A strange stillness lingered in the room, and the air felt charged the way it does before a thunderstorm.

"Wait." I ran to the window and peered out. The moon-white lawn was empty, the night silent. "Are you coming back? Will we see you again?"

There was no answer, just a stirring of leaves in the grove—and that odd silence.

Corey joined me at the window, standing so close her

shoulder touched my arm. I could feel her trembling. *"Good luck with the third thing,"* she whispered, echoing Ira's words.

"The third thing." I stared at my sister. "The account book, the tombstone, . . . and Miss Ada."

Suddenly, a breeze sprang up, and the curtains blew inward, brushing my face and my arms. They felt cold and damp, but when I tried to push them away, they clung to me, twisting around my body, trapping me.

"Give me my book," a voice hissed in my ear. "The one you stole from my grave."

19

It wasn't the curtains that trapped me. It was Miss Ada's dress. Shaking with fear, I staggered backward, trying to free myself, but the more I struggled, the tighter the dress wrapped around me.

Nearby, Corey cried out in fear. I felt her lunging, twisting, turning, but she couldn't escape, either.

Miss Ada's bony hands clutched us, numbing us with cold, weakening our arms and legs. Limp with fear, we gave up and stumbled against her. If she hadn't held us so tightly, we would have fallen to the floor at her feet. Released from the tatters of her dress, we stared into her face, little more than a skull, its eyes as dark as the grave.

"My book," she said. "Give me my book."

"We don't have it," I whispered.

Miss Ada's eyes glowed with hatred. "Wicked children, I saw you take it."

"It's—it's not here," Corey stammered.

"We gave it to the historical society," I added.

Miss Ada seemed to grow taller. Angrier. "You had no right to do that! It was my book." She shook us. "You will be punished for this."

Despite my terror, I managed to say, "You can't hurt us, you're dead, and we're . . ." My voice cracked and broke. I couldn't go on, not with her standing there, smiling a smile I wished I hadn't seen.

Keeping her grip on us, Miss Ada drew us close, closer yet, so close that all we saw was her eyes. It was as if the rest of the world had vanished. Nothing existed except Miss Ada's eyes. In their darkness, I saw every shameful thing I'd ever done—mistakes I'd made, mean things I'd done, people I'd hurt. I saw things I'd wanted but not gotten, things I'd lost. I saw my failures, my sorrows, my tears. I saw myself as Miss Ada wanted me to—a loathsome boy, despicable, unloved, pitiful and weak, stupid and selfish.

The smell of death filled my nostrils, the cold of the grave chilled me to the bone.

Beside me, Corey wept. "Stop," she sobbed. "Stop, please stop."

Miss Ada straightened up and sneered down at us. "Do you still believe the dead cannot hurt the living?"

Corey and I stared at her, speechless with misery and fear.

"Consider the years I've lain in the grave," she went on in a low voice, "learning the ways of darkness, strengthening myself, seeking vengeance."

"We're sorry," Corey whispered. "We didn't mean any harm. It was just a game, a prank. If you let us go, we'll never—"

"Hush!" Miss Ada shook Corey so hard she cried out with pain. "Your apologies and promises mean nothing to me. You mocked me, dug up my grave, stole my account book, exposed my secrets, collaborated with my enemies. You must be punished!"

With a terrifying strength, she yanked us through the open window and into the night. Unable to keep up, we stumbled behind her, arms aching, too weak to break away from her. The grove lay ahead, a black blot on the lawn.

"What are you going to do to us?" Corey whimpered.

"What does it matter?" Miss Ada pulled us into the grove. "You are worthless. You have nothing to live for."

"Nothing to live for, nothing to live for. Nothing, nothing, nothing." The word spread out around us like fog, dark and cold, obscuring everything. It was true. I was worthless. No one loved me, no one cared. If I died, no one would miss me.

"Nothing, nothing, nothing." The word was in the wind, in the grass, in the leaves, in the song the crickets sang.

I stopped struggling. *"Nothing, nothing, nothing."* I stopped fighting. *"Nothing, nothing, nothing."* I didn't care what happened to me. *"Nothing, nothing, nothing."*

Nearby Corey struggled with Miss Ada. She struck at her, she kicked. "Do something, Travis!" she yelled. "Help me!"

But I just stood there watching my sister. Couldn't she see we *deserved* to be punished?

Keeping a tight grip on Corey, Miss Ada pointed upward. "See the noose up there? It's waiting for you. Climb to that branch, boy. *My* branch. The one *I* chose. Put the noose around your worthless neck and jump."

"No, Travis," Corey cried. "Don't listen to her—don't do it!"

Miss Ada shook my sister. "Be quiet," she said. "You'll be next."

While Corey sobbed, I began to climb slowly, like someone in a dream, hand over hand, from one branch to the next. All around me leaves rustled and sighed.

"Nothing, nothing, nothing." They brushed my face softly, tenderly. The tree swayed gently, lulling me. *"Nothing,
nothing, nothing."*

The noose was just above my head. It turned slowly in
the breeze. All I needed to do was climb to the next limb
and slip it over my head. I boosted myself up carefully. I
didn't want to fall. I had to do exactly as Miss Ada said.
Follow her instructions. Atone for all the bad things I'd
done.

As I reached for the noose, I looked down. Miss Ada
stared up at me. Corey huddled at her feet. From this
height, they were no bigger than the dolls in my sister's
dollhouse.

"No," my sister cried. "Don't do it, Travis!"

I shook my head sadly. "I must," I whispered to myself.
"I must."

I reached out for the noose. The rope was hard, thick,
old. It stank of mold. I tried to lift it over my head, but
my hands shook so hard I dropped it. I watched it swing
back and forth, back and forth, now in moonlight, now in
shadow.

At the same moment, the breeze picked up and cool air
struck my face. Suddenly, the darkness in my head began
to lighten. Corey stood motionless below me, looking up,
waiting. If I obeyed Miss Ada and put the noose around
my neck, my sister would die, too.

"Do it!" Miss Ada screamed up at me. "Now!"

I shook my head, scared to defy her openly. The noose
swayed, and I inched away from it, closer to the tree's solid
trunk.

Miss Ada strode to the tree and began to climb. Her

ragged dress fluttered, and the moon splashed shadows across her bony face. "You will do as I say, boy!"

Safe on the ground, Corey watched. For her sake as well as mine, I forced myself to say, "No. I won't do it. I won't . . ."

"You will do as I say." Miss Ada stopped just below me and reached for the noose. "Take it," she said. "Accept your punishment like a man, not a whining boy."

"No," I whispered. But even as I spoke, I found myself weakening. Miss Ada was so near I could smell her earthy odor. Her hair swirled like a black cloud, blocking my view of Corey. I shut my eyes to keep from seeing her, but this close, her power over me began to grow again.

"Caleb," I whispered, "Seth, Ira—where are you?"

Just above my head, the leaves parted, and Caleb peered down at me. Ira and Seth crouched beside him. Over their heads, the shadow children made the branches sway.

"Climb up here!" Caleb whispered. "Don't let her get close."

Grabbing his hand, I scrambled higher into the tree. Miss Ada lunged for me, but even though my legs and arms shook, I managed to outclimb her.

"Come back here, you wicked boy," she cried, "and do as I say."

Nauseated, I held a branch tightly. Part of me still wanted to obey Miss Ada, but a stronger part of me wanted to save Corey. And myself.

"Caleb Perkins, is that you?" Miss Ada yelled.

Caleb poked his head out of the leaves. "Yes, ma'am, it's me, all right."

Ira and Seth peered down at Miss Ada. "We're here, too."

"Go back to the ground where you belong," Miss Ada cried. "The boy and girl are mine now. Do you hear me? Go!"

"We ain't going nowhere," Seth said.

"You have no power to punish the living," Ira put in, his eyes bigger and darker than ever.

Miss Ada reached for a higher limb and began hoisting herself closer to us. "Have you forgotten who I am," she hissed, "and what I can do?"

Caleb looked Miss Ada square in the eye. "Not a one of us has forgotten who you are or what you did to us and ours, but Ira and me have figured something out." He leaned a little closer to her. "Now that we're dead, all our suffering's over. You can't hurt us unless we let you."

"And you can't hurt Travis and Corey unless *they* let you," Ira said.

Caleb's hand held mine tightly, pulling me toward him, away from Miss Ada.

She glared up at the bad ones. "Whatever I did to you was your own fault," she said. "You defied me, you were never satisfied, never grateful. You *made* me punish you, you *made* me hurt you."

As Miss Ada ranted, the shadow children surged down from the treetop, laughing and mocking her. Limb by limb, branch by branch, they drove her down the tree.

"Old lady witch," they chanted, "lives in a ditch, counts every stitch, wants to be rich."

On the ground once more, Miss Ada shook her fist at the bad ones. "Everything I did was for your own good. You had to learn your place in the world!"

While she hurled anger and spite at them, the shadow

children dropped to the ground, barely visible in the moon-light, and circled the woman. One reached out and drew Corey into their midst. Ira, Caleb, Seth, and I scrambled down and joined them.

Holding hands, we whirled Miss Ada into a wild dance. Arms flailing, rags flying, hair tossing, she stumbled gracelessly as she reeled.

"Old lady witch," the shadow children sang, "go home to your ditch, scratch your itch, you'll never be rich!"

"Let me go," she cried. "Or—"

"Or what?" the shadow children jeered. "Your cane can't hurt none of us no more. We never eat, so you can't starve us. We don't feel the cold, so you can't freeze us."

"And you can't kill us," Seth shouted, "'cause we're already dead!"

With that, the shadow children retreated, still laughing. Corey dodged Miss Ada's outstretched hands, and the woman fell to the ground in a heap.

I put an arm around Corey and stared at the motionless bundle of rags and bones. "Is she gone now?"

Seth shook his head. Poking Miss Ada with his toe, he said, "Best get up, old lady."

Slowly, the rags stirred. Miss Ada raised her head but remained where she'd fallen. The moon cast the noose's shadow across her face. Exhaustion hung from her shoulders like a heavy weight.

The three boys stood in a row and stared at her. Behind them, the shadow children watched her silently.

"How dare you look at me like that." Miss Ada stood up slowly and faced us, unsteady on her feet but as full of pride and anger as ever. Her hair blew around her face like dead grass, and her mouth opened like a dark hole. "Go back to your resting places."

The shadow children murmured to each other, filling the air with a sound like the rustling of leaves in an autumn breeze. But none of them moved. All kept their eyes on the woman.

"Why do you defy me?" she cried.

"Tell us you're sorry," Ira said, and the shadow children's voices grew louder. *"Yes, yes, yes, say you're sorry."*

"Sorry?" Miss Ada stared at the bad ones. *"Sorry?* You should apologize to *me*, not I to you!"

"It's the only way to save yourself," Ira said calmly.

"You'd better think of saving yourself," Miss Ada said in a voice deadly with scorn. "You deserved everything I did to you—and more!"

"Are you sure you're not sorry?" Ira asked.

"Not even a little bit?" Caleb added.

"How can the likes of her be sorry?" Seth asked. "She's got no heart. Never did. Never will. She'll be howling in the grove till the world ends."

"Old lady witch," the shadow children jeered again, "dead in her ditch, dead from the itch, never to be rich."

Ira stretched out his hand and touched the woman's shoulder. She jerked away, wincing as if he'd hurt her. "Don't you dare lay your filthy hands on me!"

"Say you're sorry for all you did to us," he pleaded, "not just us children but all the folks who lived and died on this farm."

"I told you, I have nothing to be sorry for." Miss Ada's bony hands clenched and unclenched the rags of her once fine silk dress. Her dull hair fell down her back, uncombed and matted with dirt and weeds. "I had a job to do, and I did it as I saw fit."

"If you weren't sorry," Caleb asked, "then why did you kill yourself?"

Seth started to say something, but Caleb put his hand over the little boy's mouth. "Shh," he whispered.

"Sorry had nothing to do with it," Miss Ada muttered. "My brother had taken our money and deserted me. I was ruined. Why live? They would have sent me to jail or . . . or . . . to a poor farm."

Seth jerked away from Caleb and laughed in Miss Ada's face. "I would've dearly loved to see you eating the stale bread you fed us!"

Miss Ada turned away to stare across the lawn at the inn. A man stood there, as still as death itself, barely visible in the darkness. "Cornelius," she whispered, "is that you?"

The man said nothing, but he raised his hand and gestured for her to join him.

Without knowing why, I cringed in fear. There was danger here. Corey sensed it, too, and drew closer to me. I could hear her breathing fast and shallow.

But Miss Ada gave a glad cry and took a step toward the shadowy figure.

To my surprise, Ira seized her arm. "Don't go—"

Furious, Miss Ada slapped his hand away. "Out of my way, boy. My brother has come for me at last."

"No!" Ira made another futile effort to stop her. "Look again!"

Caleb touched Ira's shoulder. "Let her go where she

must go. We can't give her eyes to see what she won't see."

"Let her go to the devil hisself!" Seth clapped his hands and laughed out loud.

The shadow children giggled. "Old lady witch," they chanted, "old lady witch, dead in the ditch."

Too scared to move or speak, Corey and I watched Miss Ada make her way across the lawn to the waiting man.

"I thought you'd left me to take all the blame," she called to him.

The figure in the shadows said nothing, but he held out his arms to her. At the same time, he grew taller and more menacing. In her eagerness to join him, Miss Ada didn't notice the change until she'd almost reached him.

Stopping a few feet away, she stared up into his face. "You're not Cornelius," she whispered, "You—you are—"

He reached out to embrace her, but with a desperate cry, Miss Ada turned and ran back to the grove. "I won't go with you. I won't!"

The man followed her silently. His shadow glided before him, engulfing everything in darkness.

To my horror, Miss Ada grabbed Corey. My sister screamed and struggled to escape, but her captor held her tight.

"Let her go!" I flung myself at the woman, but she dodged aside, leaving me holding nothing but a scrap of her dress.

"Take the girl!" Miss Ada thrust Corey toward the man. "Take her brother, too. Take all of them!" Her voice rose to a shriek. "But leave me be!"

"It's you I want, Ada." The man shoved Corey aside. "Not

her," he said in a low, chilling voice. "Not him. Not the others. Just you!"

"No, no, I implore you! Haven't I suffered enough?" Miss Ada wrung her hands in prayer. "Please, have mercy, don't take me!"

"Mercy?" The man laughed with scorn. "Mercy?"

"I didn't do anything," she whispered. "It was Cornelius. *He* made me do what I did. As for them"—she pointed at the bad ones—"if they'd done what I told them, if they'd obeyed me, if they'd respected me—"

"If." The man shook his head. "Such a little word to make such a big difference."

When he reached for her, Miss Ada tried again to escape, but no matter which way she moved, the man blocked her path. She wept, she cried, she begged, but he was implacable.

"Enough!" he shouted. With one swift move, he lifted her off her feet and into his arms. She kicked, she beat him with her fists, she cried for help, but he carried her out of the grove as if she were a child. Their shadows swept across the lawn, darkened the inn for a moment, and at last vanished into a darkness blacker than the night.

In the terrible silence that followed, I put my arm around Corey's trembling shoulders, glad for her human warmth. For a minute, maybe more, we stood as still as stones, staring at the empty lawn. As much as I'd feared and hated Miss Ada, I couldn't help pitying her.

Beside me, Ira whispered, "Poor soul."

Caleb sighed. "We tried to save her, but—"

"She weren't worth saving," Seth said. "Truth to tell, I'm glad she's gone where she's gone."

The shadow children echoed Seth. "Gone, gone, gone."

"But what happened to her?" Corey asked. "Who took her? Where did she go?"

"Don't fret yourself," Caleb said quietly. "It doesn't matter where she went or who took her."

"All you got to know is she ain't coming back," Seth said with a grin. "She's been exorcised but good."

"Soon we'll be gone, too," Ira said in his melancholy way.

"But not where she went," Seth added hastily.

"All we need now is that stone," Caleb said, "with our names and dates on it. Then we'll be free of this place."

Surrounded by the shadow children, the boys huddled together in the dark grove, their faces pale and weary of waiting.

"The stone will be ready soon," I promised—but I hoped not too soon. I wanted the bad ones to stay a while, even though I knew that they, too, had to go where they had to go.

20

A week or so after Miss Ada left Fox Hill, Corey and I were sitting on the patio, drinking lemonade and reading. The bad ones had gone off somewhere the way they often did now, saying nothing, just disappearing. Ira had told us it was getting wearisome to stay visible, so we supposed they were resting somewhere—maybe in the grove, maybe at the burial ground, maybe someplace we didn't even know about.

Suddenly, the *beep, beep, beep* of a truck backing up shattered the bird song. Corey and I dropped our books and ran to the front of the inn. With Grandmother watching from the porch, a flatbed truck maneuvered through a gap in the bushes bordering the poor-farm burial ground.

Tracy opened the screen door and poked her head out. She'd been back for a couple of days, but she was still a little jumpy. "What's that truck doing here?"

"It's bringing the headstone," Corey said. "For the burial ground."

Tracy looked at us, suddenly tense. "What burial ground?"

"Behind the barn," Grandmother said. "Corey and Travis discovered it. We thought we should memorialize the people laid to rest there."

Tracy closed the door and stared at us through the screen. "Does it have something to do with the ghosts?"

"It's just an old burial ground, Tracy," Grandmother said patiently. "The ghosts are gone now. I told you it was a hoax."

She bit her lip. "I'd better go make the beds," she said.

"Don't you want to see the men put up the stone?" I asked, thinking it might scare her and I could hold her hand or something.

"No," she said, "I have work to do."

Mrs. Brewster came up behind Tracy. "After you make the beds, please start the laundry. We're low on table linens."

"Yes, ma'am." Tracy disappeared, and Mrs. Brewster came outside to join us.

Followed by Mr. Brewster, we walked across the lawn to the burial ground. Unseen by the workmen, Caleb, Ira, and Seth waved to us from their favorite tree, and the shadow children flitted here and there among the graves.

It took the men a while to get the slab of marble off the truck and into place. The bad ones watched every move they made, coming so close to the men it's a wonder they weren't stepped on.

One of the man shivered. "This place gives me the creeps," he said. "Not that I believe in ghosts, but—" He broke off with a laugh.

"Tom, you been out in the sun too long," the other man said.

In the meantime, Seth picked a handful of daisies and dropped them by the stone.

The two men watched the flowers float down to earth. Neither one looked at the other. "Windy today," Tom said.

The shadow children gathered around the men and

began tossing flowers and giggling. "Pinchy, pinchy," they whispered.

The man named Tom swatted his leg. "Mosquitoes," he muttered. "Fierce, too."

The other slapped his neck. "Worse than usual. Must be those new ones from Africa or someplace."

Corey and I covered our mouths to hide our grins.

When Grandmother got out her checkbook, the two men were already in the truck, revving the engine.

"Don't worry about that now, ma'am," Tom said. "We'll tell Mr. Greene to send the bill." And off they went, leaving a cloud of dust and the smell of gasoline behind.

"You rascals." Grandmother frowned up into the maple tree. "You scared those men off."

"It was purely an accident on my part," Seth said. "But that bunch"—he pointed at the shadow children—"they done it a-purpose."

Grandmother's frown vanished and she laughed. "Is the memorial satisfactory?"

Seth grinned. "Yes, ma'am, Granny. That's a mighty fine hunk of marble."

Grandmother looked at Caleb and Ira.

"We got what we wanted," Ira said, "all the names and dates and numbers. Everything spelled proper, too." His fingers brushed his and his family's names.

"I reckon we're at peace at last," Caleb added, with a sigh of pure contentment.

While the bad ones thanked us, the shadow children swarmed over the big stone, dappling it with patches of darkness, finding their names and the names of their friends and relatives.

"Here I am—Samuel Greene!" one called out. "And here's my ma and pa and my two little brothers, all of us dead on the same day of typhus."

"And here's me—Edward Bellows—and my ma and pa, taken by the same wicked typhus."

"It was a hard life we lived," Seth said, "but it was over way too soon."

Mr. Brewster gazed at him. "We won't know what to do when you're gone. Martha and me been watching you for more than forty year now."

"Tell your ma the Brewsters kept their word to look after you, generation to generation," Mrs. Brewster said.

"Yes, Auntie." Seth suffered the woman to hug him. "I'll tell all you done, and they'll be right pleased."

"When will you be leaving us?" Grandmother asked.

"We'll wait till dark," Caleb said.

"So the stars can guide us," Ira added.

All this time, my sister and I had just stood there, trying not to cry and failing miserably. "We'll miss you so much," Corey said.

"Why, we'll miss you, too," Caleb said. "You've been good friends to us. All of you—"

"Even Granny," Seth put in. "She weren't keen on us at the start, but she come round real good at the end."

Grandmother smiled and tried to hide her tears. "Well, it's been a strange experience for me, a person who didn't believe in ghosts and never expected to see any—let alone miss them when they left."

"Wasn't it Shakespeare who said, 'There are more things in heaven and earth, Horatio, than are dreamt of in your philosophy'?" Ira asked.

Caleb nodded. "*Hamlet,* act one. Something else we memorized in our school days before we set foot in this cursed place."

"Little did we think then that we'd soon be ghosts ourselves," Ira said in his melancholy way, "haunting the place we died, looking for justice, just like Hamlet's father."

Seth clapped him on the back. "But we got justice at last, didn't we?"

"And we got rid of Miss Ada," Caleb said.

Seth grinned. "So you needn't be gloomy no more, Ira."

Ira smiled, but the sadness in his eyes was still there.

"Now," Caleb said, "it's time to take a last look at this place, boys."

Without inviting us to join them, the bad ones vanished, and we were left to admire the new stone and its sixty-seven names.

Late that night, long after the guests had gone to bed, we sat on the porch, waiting to say goodbye to the bad ones. When they finally showed up, they blended in with the shadow children, as if they'd lost the strength to become visible.

"Thank you once more for all you did for us," Caleb said.

Ira carefully placed an old pot in Grandmother's hands. "It's the money Mr. Jaggs aimed to steal from the poor farm."

Grandmother opened the pot. "Gold coins," she whispered.

"Two hundred and twenty five-dollar pieces," Ira said.

"You're rich, Granny!" Seth crowed.

Grandmother lifted a handful of coins and let them run through her fingers, *clinkety-clink.* "I'll see this goes to a good cause," she said. "Habitat for Humanity, maybe, or Oxfam."

"Surely you'll keep it for yourself," Seth said.

Grandmother smiled at him. "That wouldn't be right, Seth. This money was stolen from the poor, and it must go back to the poor."

"Granny's right." Ira put his arm around Seth.

Seth sighed. "Maybe you could keep just one for yourself—to remember us by."

Grandmother's smile widened. "Oh, I don't think there's any danger of my forgetting you."

They gathered around us then and said their goodbyes. The shadow children clung like cobwebs to our arms and legs, whispering and giggling.

Then, the lovely bad ones drifted away across the lawn like milkweed blown by the wind. They rose slowly into the sky, as if they were climbing stairs only they could see. Higher and higher they went, shrinking until they were no more than dots of light indistinguishable from the stars.

Long after they'd disappeared, we sat quietly and stared at the sky, trying to imagine where they had gone. Was it a long journey? Would they remember us when they got there?

With a sigh, Mr. Brewster got to his feet and reached down for his wife's hand. "Come on, old girl. Tomorrow's coming soon. You got breakfast to cook, and I got chores to do."

Grandmother put her arms around Corey's and my shoulders and hugged us close to her side. "It already seems like a dream."

"But it wasn't," I said.

"It was totally real," Corey agreed.

More real than we'd ever imagined the night Corey had run across the lawn in her ghost costume. We'd sure learned a lot about ghosts since then—maybe even more than was good for us.

Suddenly, Grandmother said, "Look!"

High above the earth, a shooting star streaked across the sky.

We gazed at each other, our faces solemn. No one said it, but I knew we were all thinking the same thing. The lovely bad ones were home at last.

ABOUT THE AUTHOR

MARY DOWNING HAHN is an acknowledged master of ghost stories for young readers. Her popular favorites include *The Doll in the Garden*, *The Old Willis Place*, *The Ghost of Crutchfield Hall*, and *Wait Till Helen Comes*, which has been adapted for film. Ms. Hahn's books have received more than fifty child-voted state awards. Formerly a librarian, Ms. Hahn lives in Columbia, Maryland.